Colder than the Grave

JD Kirk is the author of the multi-million bestselling DCI Logan series, set in the Highlands of Scotland. He also does not exist. Instead, JD is the pen name of former children's author and screenwriter, Barry Hutchison, who was born and raised in Fort William. He still lives in the Highlands with his wife and children. He has no idea what the JD stands for.

Also by JD Kirk

DCI Logan Crime Thrillers

JD KIRK

COLDER THAN THE GRAVE

CANELOCRIME

First published in the United Kingdom in 2021 by Zertex Crime

This edition published in the United Kingdom in 2024 by

Canelo
Unit 9, 5th Floor
Cargo Works, 1–2 Hatfields
London SE1 9PG
United Kingdom

A CIP catalogue record for this book is available from the British Library.

Paperback ISBN 978 1 80436 826 8

Look for more great books at www.canelo.co

Printed and bound in Great Britain by Clays Ltd, Elcograf S.p.A.

I

Chapter 1

In the beginning, there was only pain.

Not a lot. Not too much. Not at first.

That would come, but not quite yet. Not right now.

Then there was the confusion. The fog. His mind grasped for the 'where' and the 'when' and the 'who' but found nothing substantial enough to hold onto.

The room reshaped itself around him like a sliding picture puzzle, arranging the walls and ceiling into somewhere new and unfamiliar. Somewhere he had never been.

Somewhere he did not want to be now.

He couldn't feel his legs. Couldn't move his toes.

A light was blinding him. He couldn't tell from where. It sent shadows scurrying across the walls, twisting them into monstrous shapes that wanted to devour him. Swallow him whole.

He could feel them tugging at his limbs and his head, pulling him down, drowning him in this stranger's bed. He fought to resist, but he was too weak. Too far gone. There was nothing he could do but surrender to them. Try to breathe. Try to survive whatever was happening, whatever this torture being inflicted upon him was.

But breathing was shallow and difficult, like his lungs were balloons half-filled with water or treacle.

Or blood.

He remembered… what? Not something, exactly, but not quite nothing, either. Not the details, but the emotions that went with them.

Anger becoming fear, becoming terror, becoming the slow, gradual acceptance that this was it. This was how it ended.

This was how he died.

And then, there was only pain. Then confusion. Then light.

Was that it, then? Was this death?

Was this Hell?

He called out, but his lungs burned and his lips cracked, and the only sound that emerged was a throaty wheeze, like the final rattle of a corpse.

He tried moving again. Raising an arm. Lifting his head. But his bones had been filled with molten metal that weighed him down and sizzled like a branding iron inside his flesh.

His eyes burned, too, the light too bright, too powerful. He tried to blink but found he couldn't. His muscles made the movement, but the relief of the darkness would not come.

He forced his head to the right—a small nudge from him, then gravity did the rest. Pain tore up his neck and into his scalp, drawing a burbled whimper from his dry, broken lips. It echoed, and he became aware of the dome of plastic over his mouth and nose. Of the swirling oxygen flooding his lungs.

There were machines beside him. Something bleeping. A thing that whirred. Neither one came into focus, no matter how hard he tried.

He could feel his legs now. He wished that he couldn't. They felt tight, like the skin had been shrunken into leather. Pain rushed through them, shooting up the nerve endings and jolting his brain.

It burned through the confusion. Just patches, here and there.

He remembered a face at a window.

A body on a floor.

An icicle of agony stabbing into his kidneys and radiating outwards until it filled every part of him, consuming him from without and within.

And then...

And *then*…

A door opened, here and now. The texture of the light changed. Behind him, though. No way he could turn in time.

'Oh, no, no, no,' a voice reprimanded. 'We can't have you awake, can we? Not yet.'

He heard a hiss. Felt a sting, then fire bloomed from the crook of an arm.

A hand rested on his head. A voice spoke in a whisper.

'We need to keep you sleeping for a long, long time.'

And as the dark rose up to claim him, for a moment, he almost remembered his name.

Chapter 2

Olivia Maximuke was in two minds about this latest version of her mother. Over the years, she had grown so used to her mum being a distant figure, too tied up in her own life and her own problems to pay much attention to her daughter—even if those problems were all entirely of her own making, and mostly the result of some exciting new addiction or other.

Recently, though, she'd sorted herself out, stopped the drug abuse, the self-harming, and the ego-boosting one-night stands that had, in reality, left her feeling even more worthless than she had the evening before.

Now, she was making up for lost time. Now, it wasn't a lack of attention that Olivia suffered from, it was an over-abundance of it. She swore, the woman was trying to suffocate her.

She had been sitting across the kitchen table watching Olivia eating her cereal for the last five minutes, her chin resting on one hand, a look of exaggerated concern creasing her face.

And creasing her face it literally was. Olivia was still getting used to seeing her without half an inch of makeup smeared inexpertly across her more important features, and she'd never seen her mum looking this old before.

And yet, she looked all the better for it.

'What?' Olivia asked when the weight of the silence became too much.

'Are you OK, honey?'

'Fine. Why?'

Her mum cocked her head to one side and smiled. It was a quizzical thing, like she didn't quite understand the question.

'You just seem… you know.'

Olivia shook her head. She didn't.

'You've just been a little… quiet. Withdrawn lately.'

'Have I? Sorry.'

Her mum reached across the table, hands grasping until they found her daughter's arm. 'We don't apologise for feelings in this house. Not ever. OK?'

Olivia nodded, then slurped some cereal off her spoon. 'OK.'

'Say it like you mean it.'

'Jesus. OK. Fine.'

'It is a boy?'

'What, no?'

'Is it a girl?'

'God, Mum! No!'

'Is it a boy and a girl? That's a thing now, isn't it? *Throuples*. That's all the rage these days. Father Conrad was telling me all about it on our run last week.'

And there it was, Father Conrad's first mention of the day. Her mum's latest addiction.

'Is that what's bothering you, sweetheart? Is it a throuple thing?'

'What the fuck are you talking about?' Olivia jerked her arm free. 'No! It's nothing like that.'

And it wasn't, much as she might wish it was. Boy trouble, girl trouble, or any variation thereof would've been infinitely preferable to the truth. She'd have gladly spoken about that, let her mum have her moment to shine.

Olivia would've ignored all the advice, of course. A former drug-addict and work-experience prostitute turned Born Again Christian wasn't really someone you wanted to take dating tips from. But she'd have listened. She'd have shared. And part of her would've loved it.

She couldn't share the truth, though. Not with her mum. Not with anyone.

She couldn't speak of what she'd done.

Of what had been left for her to find right here in this kitchen.

Or of why she was spending every moment of every day living in fear of what was to come. What was to happen.

The things she imagined he might do to her.

The knot of dread that had kept her awake for nights on end tightened in her gut. She clanked her spoon down into her half-empty bowl and pushed it away.

'I'm done,' she announced, getting up from the table.

'You haven't eaten nearly enough. You'll be hungry. Father Conrad says that breakfast is the most important meal of the day. It's in the Bible. I think. I don't know. I've not finished it yet.'

'I'm not hungry. I'll have something at lunchtime.'

'Oh, you just reminded me! I made you a packed lunch. Cheese and salami. Your favourite.' She smiled tentatively. 'It... it is still your favourite, isn't it?'

Olivia's gaze crept to the fridge and lingered there. She tried not to picture the note that had been stuck to the front.

Tried not to visualise the human hand that had been left for her on one of the shelves, and which was now weighed down at the bottom of the Caledonian Canal.

'No. I'm not keen. I'll get something at school,' she muttered, then she wheeled around, hurried out of the kitchen, and didn't once look back.

–

Tony Hicks hated days like these. *Weekdays.*

Weekdays meant work, and work meant early starts, mouthy kids, and whatever fresh disaster was just waiting in the wings to surprise him. A knackered boiler, maybe. A broken window. Some tubby-arsed first year shitting, pissing, or throwing up after P.E. class.

Or, as on one particularly memorable occasion, all three at the same time.

He wouldn't have minded too much if he was given a bit of respect. That wasn't too much to ask, was it? For the teachers not to flash him patronising smirks while peering down their noses at him. For them to take a minute to ask him how his day was going, and to actually stick around to hear the answer for once. He wasn't looking to be treated like royalty, but the odd wee word of thanks every once in a while wouldn't go amiss.

'*Thanks for keeping the place running, Tony. I don't know how you do it.*'

But no. Instead, it was all '*someone's shoved a tampon in one of the girls' toilets and flooded the place*' or '*there's a hell of a farty smell in the science corridor. Sort it out, will you?*'

He looked out through the visor of his helmet at the front gate and gave a grunt of resentment.

Fucking weekdays.

Tony swung his leg over his motorcycle, forced the helmet up off his head, then tucked it in one of the bike's saddlebags. Since he wanted it to still be there when he got back, he secured the bag with its padlock, fastened a chain through the motorcycle's back wheel, and spun the dials of the combination locking mechanism.

It was then that he spotted the car. It was parked—or possibly abandoned—at the far end of the school car park, straddling two spaces, its front end pointing in the direction of the building's front gate.

It wasn't a teacher's car. He knew all of those. There was something familiar about it, though, which told him maybe it was a parent's. Or maybe even one of the sixth years. Some of them had their own cars now. The fact that it had clearly been parked by an absolute wanker lent that theory some support.

Then again, it was barely half-seven in the morning. What sixth year was up and about at this time of day?

It was black. One of those mini-SUV things that every second bastard on the road seemed to be driving. A Peugeot, he thought, though they were all so interchangeable, the aesthetic differences so insignificantly incremental, that it was hard to be sure.

Whatever it was, it wasn't bloody staying there. Parking was enough of a nightmare as it was without some bugger straddling the white lines. And who'd be the poor Joe Soap who'd get the complaints when the last members of staff to arrive failed to find a space?

'Fucking muggins here,' Tony muttered, and he went striding across the car park in the direction of the offending vehicle.

His initial plan was to take a note of the registration, then compare that with the sign-in sheets at the front office. Anyone—teacher, visitor, or pupil—bringing a car onto the premises had to write down their number plate. Find the plate in the sign-in book, and he'd have his culprit.

He was halfway there when he realised that someone was sitting in the driver's seat. This was good, of course, as it made things much simpler. Truth be told, though, Tony was a little disappointed. He'd been quite looking forward to putting his detective skills to the test. It would've made for a far more interesting morning than broken doorknobs and leaky pipes.

'Oi!' he barked, announcing his presence as he stormed over to the SUV.

The driver was buried in shadow. If he moved, it wasn't much, and as Tony got closer, he suspected the bastard was sleeping.

'This isn't a bloody campsite!' he said, rapping his knuckles on the driver's side window. 'You can't just park here all night and…'

He noticed the handcuffs first. They secured one hand to the steering wheel, the metal digging furrows in a fleshy wrist.

There was a bag of white powder on the dashboard, burst open so its contents filled the vents and grooves in the plastic like tiny drifts of snow.

It was on his face, too, congealing blobs of pink on his chin and across his bloodied lips.

'What the fuck is…?' Tony mumbled, then he gave another cautious tap on the glass. 'Hello? Mate? You all right?'

He shifted his position, and the angle of the sunlight on the glass changed, revealing yellowing eyes that were stuck wide open, but looking at nothing. The face was a graduation of blacks and purples, like the evening sky stretching into night. The cheeks were bloated, the nose bloodied.

His other arm—the one not fastened to the steering wheel—was strapped into a sling, pinning it to his chest.

And there was a grubby grey bandage, the janitor noted, where his hand should have been.

Tony Hicks hated weekdays.

And this one had only just begun.

Chapter 3

Detective Chief Inspector Jack Logan was wakened by the insistent buzzing of his phone on the bedside table. Mistaking the alert for the morning alarm, he fumbled for it, blindly slapped at the screen in search of the 'snooze' option, then finally opened his eyes when he heard the tinny voice coming from the speaker.

'Hello? Jack?'

For one confusing moment, he wondered how Detective Superintendent Mitchell had become the voice of his alarm, then realisation made him sit upright and cradle the phone in against his ear.

'Yes. Yes. Hello. Sorry, I'm... driving,' he said.

'Good. Are you on your way in?'

He checked his watch but wasn't yet awake enough to understand what all the little dials and numbers meant.

'Aye. On my way now. What's up?'

'You're going to have to take a detour. Millburn Academy. You know it?'

Logan confirmed that he did. A little too well, as it happened.

'We've had a shout. Uniform's on the scene. Janitor found a body in the car park.'

'A kid?' Logan asked, thumbing sleep from his eyes.

'I don't know. Hopefully not, but I don't have a lot of information,' Mitchell said. 'Still, that's what you're for, isn't it?'

'Ma'am,' Logan said. It was the most noncommittal response he could think of this early in the day. 'I'll let you know what I find out.'

'Good. Oh, and Jack?'

'Ma'am?'

'Don't forget to get dressed first.'

There was a pause—a microscopic moment of smugness—then the line went dead.

Logan muttered something uncomplimentary in the phone's general direction, dropped it onto the duvet, then yawned.

He had barely closed his mouth again when another phone buzzed on the opposite side of the bed. A figure stirred beneath the sheets, groaning at the second rude awakening in as many minutes.

A hand reached out. A voice spoke with an Irish twang, muffled by the covers. 'Hello? Shona Maguire.'

She listened to the voice on the other end, while Logan swung his legs out of the bed.

'Right, I'll be there shortly,' she told the person on the other end of the line, then she pressed her thumb a little too firmly against the button that ended the call, and made some mumbled moaning noises about the unfairness of the world.

She wrestled herself around in the bed in time to see Logan almost fully dressed and doing up the buttons on his shirt.

'Morning,' he said. It came out a little too politely, like he was greeting a senior colleague. He was still getting used to this and hadn't quite settled into things. Not yet. He hoped, though, that he'd have plenty of time to get acclimatised.

He fished his car keys from his pocket and twirled them around on a finger.

'Looks like duty calls.'

—

Paff-paff. Paff-paff.

There was something rhythmic about it. Something hypnotic. Like some sort of meditation.

Paff-paff. Paff-paff.

DS Hamza Khaled sat on the end of his bed, slowly polishing a shoe. He'd been polishing it for about twenty minutes now, dipping the end of the brush into the thin container of black paste, and buffing it across the leather. Back and forth. Back and forth.

He could hear his wife and daughter downstairs. They were playing a game of some kind, judging by the thumping, the exaggerated roaring, and the squeals of delight.

Their laughter came up through the floor, but found only silence there. Silence, and the paff-paff-paff of brush on leather.

Hamza looked down at the shoe, and his own warped reflection stared back up. He had polished the material until it was like some dark and smoky glass—a Gothic mirror image of the real world, with another DS Khaled trapped on the other side.

He swiped the brush back and forth, like he could buff out his reflection and eradicate the other him. But at the end of every stroke, he was still there, brighter and clearer than ever.

How long had he even been sitting there? He wasn't sure. He recalled getting the newspaper from the recycling bin and spreading it out on the floor to protect the carpet. He remembered digging out the plastic tub that contained the wooden-handled brushes and half-empty tins of polish.

But when that was? He couldn't say.

He heard the phone ringing downstairs. The brush kept the beat like a metronome as he listened to Amira rushing to answer the call, while Kamila went thudding along the hallway after her.

Hamza couldn't hear the words his wife said, but he recognised the tone. There were only two reasons the house phone ever rang—Amira's family, or Hamza's work. Amira was using her phone voice, which meant it definitely wasn't the former.

The brush swiped back and forth. Back and forth. Back and forth. He stared ahead at the bedroom wall, and listened to the call being ended, the phone being hung up, and the creaking of the staircase as his wife made her way up to break the news.

'You left your mobile off?' Amira asked, appearing in the doorway.

Hamza blinked, like a spell had been broken, and looked back at her via the dressing table mirror. 'Hmm? Oh. Aye, might be. Was that—?'

'Yes. You've to call in. Something to do with a case, I'm guessing. Sounds urgent.'

'Right. Aye.' He gave a final few swipes with the brush, then ran a polish-stained duster over the shoe to finish off the sheen. 'I'd best be off, then.'

'Mummy, come down!' Kamila called from the hallway. 'It's Peppa Pig time!'

Amira rolled her eyes and smiled, then started to turn away. She stopped when she saw her husband's shoes. 'Interesting look you're going for.'

Hamza leaned forward on the end of the bed and looked down at the shoe on the floor beside him. It was completely unpolished, the scuffed, dull leather appearing even worse next to the diamond-like sheen of its opposite number.

'Ah.' He sighed. 'Shite.'

—

Detective Constable Tyler Neish was leaning slightly to the right. He was becoming increasingly sure of it.

Not politically—he didn't pay all that much attention to that sort of thing—but literally. Physically.

It had been about a fortnight now since he'd had his operation. It had gone well, by all accounts—if you ignored the fact that he'd lost fifty percent of his testicles in one fell swoop—and while he was being closely monitored, it had been decided that chemotherapy wasn't currently on the cards.

The removed bollock had been replaced by some sort of prosthetic one. *To even things up*, the doctor had said.

Tyler suspected they'd overdone it, though. There was the slightest tug to the right when he stood in front of the mirror, like his weight was now being distributed unevenly onto one foot more than the other.

It was problematic. He'd long harboured dreams of being an Olympic athlete—although admittedly he'd never told anyone, or done any work whatsoever in pursuit of it—and this sort of thing could really hamper his chances.

Well, that and his complete lack of sporting ability.

Still, it would've been nice to have had the option.

He was also putting on weight, he noted, squeezing an early-stage flab roll between finger and thumb. Was that a side effect of the procedure, he wondered, or the direct result of having spent two full weeks lying mostly motionless while binge-eating chocolate and crisps?

Probably some combination of the two.

He turned away from the mirror at the sound of the bathroom door opening. The act of turning to face the opposite direction now took fewer than six steps, which told him he was on the mend. A week ago, the same movement would have taken him over forty tiny shuffles, some balancing arm movements, and quite a lot of silent prayer. At this rate, he'd be back running around in no time.

Just not, sadly, on a professional sporting basis.

There was always the Paralympics, he supposed.

Sinead bustled into the room, tucking her shirt into the waistband of her trousers. She stopped when she saw him up and about, and frowned like something was wrong.

'You OK?'

'I'm grand, yeah. I mean… still missing a goolie, obviously, but otherwise fine.'

'Great! That's really good. Didn't expect you to be up and about yet,' she told him, hunting the dressing table for her car keys and wallet. 'You feeling better?'

'Feeling pretty good, actually, yeah,' Tyler said. 'All things considered.'

'Brilliant! You can make sure Harris gets off for the bus on time, will you? He's eating breakfast.' She found the missing items and pocketed them. 'And there's been a shout. Since you're feeling better, can you empty the dishwasher and stick the washing machine on?'

Tyler winced, and his hand slipped gingerly to his crotch. 'I would, but I'm not sure all that bending's such a good idea quite yet.'

Sinead smiled and planted a kiss on his cheek. 'Nice try. Empty the dishwasher and do the washing.' She headed for the door, trailing instructions in her wake. 'And it's option C for the washing machine. Not F. Because F—'

'Fucks the clothes up. Aye. That's the third time you've told me that.'

Sinead stopped in the doorway. 'Aye, well, maybe if you hadn't done it three times…'

'Why even have it as an option?' Tyler asked. 'Why put a button on there that ruins clothes? It's meant to be a washing machine, not Russian Roulette.'

Sinead chose not to confuse the issue by explaining the needs for different types of washing cycles. Instead, she just shrugged, blew him a kiss, and headed down the stairs.

'You look good, by the way,' she called back to him. The front door opened, and her voice rose up one last time. 'And no, you're not leaning to the right!'

Chapter 4

Geoff Palmer and his Scene of Crime team were already crowding the school car park when Logan pulled up in his BMW. The Uniforms on cordon duty raised the tape, and he pulled into one of the bays at the opposite end of the car park to where all the action was happening.

He switched off the engine and took a sip of the coffee he'd made before leaving the house. It had been Shona's idea to buy some takeaway-style coffee cups the last time he'd been in Asda, and while he wouldn't go so far as to say it had changed his life, it had certainly made access to caffeine more readily available.

Taking the cup with him, he got out of the car and approached the crowd of white paper suits, steeling himself for another encounter with Palmer.

It wasn't that Geoff was a complete arsehole. He *was* that, obviously, but it was the specific type of arsehole he was that caused most of the problems. It was as if some scientist somewhere had analysed every aspect of Logan's personality, then used that information to build the ultimate irritating bastard. Even setting aside his personality for a moment, everything about him, from the curve of his shoulders to the angle of his eyebrows, seemed to have been custom designed to get right on the detective's tits.

Logan could hear him as he drew closer to the tent at the far corner of the car park. His voice somehow managed to be both an echoing boom and a nasal whine, like the sound of fingernails on a blackboard amplified via a cheap loudspeaker.

It did nothing to further endear him in any way.

'Yes, well, I've been doing this a lot bloody longer than you have, so just do as you're told. All right?'

Logan waited by the inner cordon and sipped coffee through the slot in the cardboard lid of his cup. Six paper suits were doing widths of the car park, walking in a staggered line, heads down, gazes fixed on the ground just a foot or so ahead of them. They were searching for evidence, of course, but they looked for all the world like kids mortified by the behaviour of their boorish father.

Christ, the man was an absolute arsehole.

Logan had just completed the thought when the absolute arsehole in question appeared through the flaps of the tent. His pudgy face was a bullseye of anger, surrounded by the circle of his white hood, and his mood did not improve when he set eyes on the DCI.

'About time,' Palmer said. He jerked out a hand gesture, indicating the Uniforms dotted around the school grounds. 'It's been all monkeys and no bloody organ grinder around here. Half of them don't know how to set up a cordon. Mind you, since most of them look like they're still in school, that's hardly a surprise.'

'Morning, Geoff,' Logan said. He'd found that remaining composed and polite really wound the bastard up, so he smiled through the resentment bubbling away inside him. 'Sorry to hear that. I'll be sure to have a word.' He indicated the tent with his coffee cup. 'What have we got?'

Palmer scowled, practically humming with rage. He'd been looking for an argument and was furious that none had been forthcoming.

'Dead fella in a car,' he said. 'Missing a hand, by the looks of it, although obviously, we won't be able to investigate properly until a pathologist sees fit to finally—'

'All right, lads?'

Shona Maguire's sudden appearance caught them both off guard. Palmer's sneer became a smile that somehow managed to be even more unpleasant to look at.

'Ah, there she is! We were just talking about you,' he laughed, suddenly all pep and zing.

Shona completely ignored the remark and gave Logan a nod. 'Detective Chief Inspector.'

'Dr Maguire,' Logan replied. 'Good to see you again.'

'And you.'

'Keeping well?'

'Not bad, thanks,' Shona replied, and they both sipped their coffees from identical cups.

'We can let you in to look at the body in a minute,' Geoff said, forcibly reinserting himself into the conversation. 'Just checking the car exterior for prints and what have you.'

Shona nodded. 'Right.' She turned back to Logan to continue their conversation, but Palmer rushed to fill the momentary silence.

'Oh! Forgot to say, I've got a bit of exciting news.'

'You're transferring?' Logan asked, sounding a touch more hopeful than he'd intended.

'What? No! No, nothing like that.' Palmer laughed off their visible disappointment. 'Funny. But no. Remember a couple of weeks back in Glen Coe? We were saying there's no proper comedians anymore, just all that lefty woke nonsense?'

'I'm pretty sure you said that, no' me.'

'I think you agreed.'

'I think you're talking out of your arse,' Logan replied. 'But go on.'

'Yes, right. Well, I thought there's no point complaining about it, is there? Moaning doesn't get you anywhere. If you want things to be different, you've got to make them different. You've got to *be the change*, haven't you?'

'Sounds like lefty woke bollocks to me,' Shona remarked, and then she sipped her coffee to hide her laughter.

'Aye, you went "Full Bono" on us there, Geoff,' Logan agreed. 'What's the point you're going for here?'

Palmer drew himself up to his full, unimpressive height and puffed out his chest. Technically, he puffed out his stomach, but his chest came along for the ride.

'I'm doing a gig,' he declared. 'Stand-up comedy.'

Logan and Shona both stared at him, unblinking, for several seconds.

'Comedy?' Logan eventually said.

'You?' Shona added.

'Yes! Isn't it brilliant? I've fancied it for years. That business with Archie Tatties was just the kick up the backside I needed.'

'Aye, well, it's good when something positive can come out of a quadruple homicide, right enough,' Logan remarked.

'The act's called "Effing & Geoffing",' Palmer continued.

'Who's "Effing"?' Logan asked.

'Eh?'

'I assume you're the "Geoffing". Who's the "Effing"?'

Palmer stared back in silence, like a Brit abroad waiting patiently for the funny foreign gentleman to repeat whatever he'd just said, only this time in the Queen's English.

'Jesus Christ,' Logan muttered. 'You said you were "Effing & Geoffing". That's a double act, surely?'

'Oh. No. It's just me,' Palmer explained. 'It means swearing. "Effing & Geoffing". The act's a bit blue, so it lets people know what to expect.'

'I think they'll be expecting two people,' Shona said. 'It definitely sounds like a double act.'

'Well, if it's good enough for Neeps and Tatties...'

'Exactly. Because they were two people,' Logan pointed out. 'You're not. You're just one person, Geoff. Thankfully.'

Palmer snorted. 'Well, I can hardly just call myself "Geoffing", can I? That doesn't make sense.'

'You could always be just Geoff,' Shona suggested.

Palmer contemplated this. '"Just Geoff". I like that.'

Logan shook his head. 'No, she meant—'

'"Just Geoff",' Palmer said, ignoring the clarification. '"*Just Geoff*". Yeah, that works. It's stripped back. It's simple. Just me on the stage with a microphone. Me and a mic.' His eyes widened. His body stiffened with excitement. 'Oh! Geoff and Mike!'

'You're going double act again,' Shona pointed out.

'Even more so than the last one,' Logan agreed.

'Fine. "Just Geoff", then,' Palmer said, looking just a touch disappointed. 'The show's at La Tortilla Asesina,' he said, mangling the pronunciation. 'The Spanish restaurant. On Castle Street.' He aimed the next part exclusively in Shona's direction. 'You should come along. It'll be a laugh.'

'Will it, though?' Logan asked. 'I've known you for a couple of years now, Geoff, and I don't think I've ever seen you smiling, never mind cracking a joke.'

'Oh, I know jokes. I know plenty of jokes,' Palmer said, taking the comment as some sort of personal attack. Which, to be fair to him, it was.

'Go on, then,' Shona urged.

Palmer hesitated. 'Go on what?'

'Tell us a joke,' Logan said.

'What, now?'

The DCI shrugged. 'I mean, if you don't know any…'

'Of course I do! I know loads,' Palmer said. 'But what about him?' He jabbed a thumb in the direction of the tent.

'What about him?' Logan asked. 'He's hardly in a position to nick your material, is he?'

'I mean, isn't it a bit… disrespectful?'

'Depends on the joke. If it's "what do you call a dead guy in a tent?", then aye, maybe give it a miss.'

'Come on, Geoff. I could do with a good laugh,' Shona encouraged. 'Let's hear it.'

Palmer seemed to battle with himself for a moment, then relented with a twinkle of an eye and a nod of his head. 'Right.

You asked for it. Here's one—it's a bit blue, though. You have been warned!'

He coughed into his clenched fist, cleared his throat, raised an index finger like he was making some grand and important proclamation, and began.

'What did the condom say to the penis?' he asked. He smirked, fighting back the urge to laugh at his own material. 'Don't know? It said, "cover me, I'm going in!"' He grinned, but was met by a silence so absolute you could've heard a pin drop. Clearly, they hadn't got it. 'You know. *In*,' he said, clarifying. 'Like… in the vagina?'

'Jesus Christ,' Logan muttered.

'Shouldn't it be the other way around?' Shona asked.

Palmer frowned, his eyebrows dipping into view from above the elastic seam of his hood. 'What…' he muttered. 'The arse?'

'What? God! No! I meant shouldn't the penis be saying that to the condom?'

The Scene of Crime man stared blankly back at her.

'Why would a penis be covering a condom?' Shona pressed.

Logan shook his head. 'It doesn't make sense, Geoff.'

Palmer's lips moved silently as he went back over the last few seconds of conversation. His grin returned, but his eyes betrayed his panic. 'Och, you know what I meant! I just got it mixed up.'

'Don't do that tonight, for Christ's sake. They'll eat you alive,' Logan warned, revelling in every exquisite moment of Palmer's discomfort. 'But all right, all right. These things happen. Let's hear another one.'

Palmer quick-fired the next one, keen to make up for the last attempt.

'Fine. What do you call an expert fisherman? A Master Baiter!'

Shona and Logan both smiled. It wasn't for the reason Geoff thought, but he took encouragement from it anyway and pressed on.

'Which sexual position creates the ugliest kids?' He pointed to Logan. 'Ask his mum!'

Shona laughed at that. Not at the joke, of course—nobody in their right mind would laugh at the joke—but at the absurdity of the whole situation.

Heartened, Palmer took a little bow, then returned to his sales pitch, buoyed by his mirth-making success. 'See? I'm pretty good, if I do say so myself. You should come along,' he said, once again aiming the suggestion firmly and exclusively in Shona's direction.

'We should both go,' Logan suggested.

Palmer wrinkled his nose. 'Hmm. Not sure it'll be your scene.'

'With material as strong as that? How could it not be?' Logan asked. 'How do we get tickets?'

'You just turn up,' Palmer said.

'I'd like to get tickets, though. Don't want to miss out.'

'No, I mean there aren't any tickets.'

Shona nodded sagely. 'Sold out. I'm not surprised.'

'Well done, Geoff.' Logan patted the much smaller man on the shoulder. 'I guess you'll just have to tell us how it went next time we see you.'

'Shame,' Shona said. 'I was looking forward to that, too.'

Palmer's eyes narrowed a fraction. He looked at the pathologist and the detective in turn. Somewhere, buried deep at the back of his brain, a warning light finally alerted him to the fact they were taking the piss.

'Aye, well. Your loss,' he told them, then he sniffed, about-turned, and marched into the tent, already barking orders to whichever poor bugger was working away inside.

'"A Master Baiter",' Logan said. 'I mean, Jesus Christ. Where did he get that, the *Bumper Book of Shite Jokes*?'

'Is it wrong that I actually do want to go?' Shona asked.

'What, to see him dying on his arse?'

'Exactly! We could go undercover. You take your car, I'll take mine, and we'll just happen to meet up. No one will be any the wiser. It'll just be two people randomly bumping into—'

'Morning, sir,' said Sinead, joining the conversation. 'Shona.'

She watched them both take a hurried step backwards, immediately clocked the matching coffee cups, and her face lit up in a big beaming smile.

Damn it! She knew!

'Are you…? Are the two of you finally…?'

'Shh,' Logan urged, waving a hand for her to keep her voice down. 'No. We're not… we aren't…'

The smile on her face was going nowhere. He sighed and lowered his voice to a whisper.

'We're keeping it quiet.'

'Oh, right!' Sinead said. She shifted her gaze between them both. 'Why?'

Logan opened his mouth as if to respond, but no words came. Shona jumped in with an answer for him.

'We just thought, you know, for professionalism's sake? Two people working closely alongside each other getting into a relationship. It could be… problematic.'

'You do remember who you're talking to here, yeah?' Sinead asked. 'Tyler says hello, by the way.'

'Silly bugger still think he's leaning sideways?' Logan asked.

'Mostly, yeah,' Sinead confirmed, then she adopted a look that could only be described as 'heartfelt pride'. 'Look at you two!'

'Don't ever do that face again,' Logan warned with a scowl. 'It's just… we're just…'

'It's early days,' Shona said. 'And, frankly, I'm embarrassed by him. By the whole thing. Ashamed?' She considered this for a moment. 'No, maybe not ashamed. That's too far. But close. As a woman who cuts up dead bodies, exists exclusively on Pot Noodles, and is close personal friends with a thirteen-year-old, I've got a certain reputation to maintain. So we'd rather keep it quiet for the moment. Just until I decide if I'm keeping him.'

'Right! Yes! Of course,' Sinead replied, shoving down her excitement. 'You've got to keep him, though. I mean, who else is going to put up with him?'

'I know. I do feel a degree of responsibility,' Shona agreed. 'Like when you find a cat that's been hit by a car.'

'Oi!' Logan protested. 'I am standing right here, you know?'

—

Olivia trudged around the corner with her schoolbag on her shoulder, then stopped when she saw the policemen at the front gate.

She'd left early, the house having felt particularly stifling that morning. She'd taken a different route—she did that most mornings these days—and had wound her way through a network of alleyways and back paths where no cars could possibly follow, and where she had a chance of losing anyone who might be following her on foot.

She'd seen neither. The first faces she'd encountered since walking out the back door, in fact, were those of the police officers currently eyeballing her from the gate.

One of them checked his watch, frowned, then looked her up and down. 'Bit early, aren't you?' he asked. Then, before she could reply, he told her that the school was closed and that she should go home.

Her gaze crept past him to where a knot of other officers stood around like they were waiting for a show to start. Beyond them, down at the far end, a smaller group stood outside a big white tent.

She recognised Logan first, his size drawing the eye more forcefully than the two women next to him. Next, she noticed Shona Maguire, and she felt a pang of something. Sadness, maybe, or regret.

Those nights eating popcorn on Shona's couch suddenly felt like a lifetime ago. A simpler time. The Good Old Days, when the worst thing she had to worry about was her mum's drugs and alcohol consumption, and whether her dad was going to answer the letters she'd sent him in prison.

That was before *him*. Before Oleg. Before he'd forced her to ferry his drugs around. Before she'd betrayed him and left him for dead.

And before she'd found out that he wasn't.

He was out there somewhere, alive. And he was coming for her. The hand in her fridge could not have made that clearer.

If Shona was there, then that meant they'd found a body. Olivia peered at the tent, like she might be able to stare straight through the material and see what was inside.

It might be a coincidence, of course. It could be completely unrelated. The body under that tent might be a teacher, or a pupil, or just some randomer who'd suffered a heart attack while cutting across the school car park.

But she knew it wasn't any of those things. Deep down in her bones, she knew it was Borys. Poor, simple, one-handed Borys.

It was another message. And it was meant for her.

'You hear me?' the policeman asked, his tone clipped and irritable. 'School's shut. You need to go. You can't be here.'

'Who died?' she asked. 'Did someone die?'

'None of your business,' the other officer chipped in. With a flick of his wrist, he pointed back the way she'd come, like he was shooing an unwelcome dog. 'Leave. Now.'

Olivia tore her gaze from the tent, then looked at both officers in turn. She studied their faces with such a degree of scrutiny that they both shifted on the balls of their feet, suddenly uncomfortable.

Then, with a nod, she turned her back, picked a different direction to the one she'd taken to get there, and slipped away without another word.

Chapter 5

By the time Hamza arrived, Shona was inside the tent, giving the body a once-over, and Sinead had gone off to coordinate the door-to-door enquiries. Logan raised his coffee cup in greeting to the approaching DS, then his eyes were immediately drawn down to ground level.

'The hell's going on with your shoes?' he asked, when Hamza came plodding up. 'Could you no' find two of the same pair?'

'They are the same pair,' Hamza said, looking down at his feet and wiggling them. The shoe on the left shone like some onyx gemstone, while the one on the right was a dull, sheenless matt. 'I was polishing them when the phone went. I'd only done one.'

'Right. Fair enough,' Logan said. He studied the shoes again, then met Hamza's eye. 'You look like a nutter.'

'Sorry, sir,' Hamza said. 'I can go home and change them, if you want?'

There was something not quite right about the DS. More than just his footwear. There was a weariness about him, Logan thought. A lack of energy, like there was a weight on his back that was taking all his strength to hold up.

'No, it's fine,' Logan told him. 'Just sort it when you can.'

'Will do, sir,' Hamza said. He turned away from Logan, but didn't look at the tent, either. Not really. Not quite. The DS rolled his tongue around in his mouth a few times, like he was working up the willpower to ask the question. 'What've we got?'

Logan hesitated, but then moved on. If Hamza was going through some sort of personal problem, now wasn't the time or place to discuss it. Besides, it was probably just an off day. They all had them.

Although, this wasn't the first time Logan had noticed something off about Hamza in recent weeks. He'd put it down to concern about Tyler, but DC Neish was firmly on the mend now, and the Detective Sergeant still seemed preoccupied.

'Body in an SUV. Male, twenties, we reckon. Missing a hand. Palmer hasn't given us much more than that for now. Shona's in there doing her thing, then we can get a look for ourselves.'

'Right,' said Hamza, though he seemed less than thrilled by the prospect. He turned and looked at the three-storey building beside them. 'Victim connected to the school, do we think?'

'No idea,' Logan admitted. 'Waiting to see if we have an ID.'

'Has anyone run the plate on the car?'

Logan shook his head. 'Not yet, no.'

Hamza drew air in through his teeth. He still hadn't looked directly at the tent. It was as if he was looking in every direction but that one.

'We got a message out to teachers and parents not to come in or send their kids? I could go and do that, if you like?' he suggested.

'I've got Uniform on that,' Logan said. He couldn't hold his tongue any longer. 'You all right, son?'

Hamza nodded too quickly, like he'd been poised and waiting for the question. 'Fine, sir, aye.'

'You seem a bit... detached.'

DS Khaled dredged up a smile from somewhere. 'Rough night with the wee one. Didn't get much sleep.'

That was the only explanation Logan was likely to get, he suspected. He could push for more, of course, but he'd likely be wasting both their time. If Hamza didn't want to talk about it, he couldn't force him.

'Right. Well, suck it up,' he instructed. 'I want you with me in there when Shona's done, and I want you sharp. All right?'

Hamza nodded. The smile, which had been almost convincing, became paper-thin. 'Right you are, sir. Not a problem. Is DI Forde back up the road yet?' He asked, quickly changing the subject.

Logan shook his head. 'Not due back until Friday,' he said. 'Ideally, we won't have to drag him back in for this.'

He had been surprised when Detective Inspector Ben Forde had put in a request for holiday time. Getting the old bugger to take a holiday usually required either threats or bribery.

Logan had been even more surprised when Ben said he was taking a few days in Fort William—a location they had just spent the best part of a fortnight in while working on two different cases.

It would be a good opportunity to get some fresh air, Ben had said. Maybe do some walking. Logan had immediately become suspicious—fresh air wasn't exactly in short supply around Inverness, and there were plenty of scenic walking routes to choose from.

Still, the DI had seemed excited by the prospect, and if it meant not having to banish him from the office later in the year so he was forced to use up all his holiday time in one go, Logan was all for it.

'Hang on,' Hamza said, turning his attention back to the building. 'This is that school, isn't it? We were here last year.'

'Aye,' Logan confirmed. Their investigation into a vigilante killer the papers had called 'The Iceman' had brought the DCI here to this very car park.

He had come close to being run over and killed not far from the spot he was standing on. At the same time, the Ford Fiesta he'd been forced to drive for months had been utterly destroyed, so it had been a day of mixed emotions.

'You think it's connected to the new body?' Hamza asked.

'Too soon to say,' Logan told him. 'Could be a coincidence.'

'Never put you down as a big believer in those, sir.'

'No,' Logan admitted. 'I'm not.'

Fabric rustled beside them, and both men turned as Shona stepped out of the tent, kitted out in a disposable mask, gloves, and apron. She exhaled as she removed the mask, then gave Hamza a smile of acknowledgement and snapped off the rubber gloves.

'He's dead, Jim!' she announced, in her best impersonation of Doctor McCoy from *Star Trek*. She flinched, like she may have intended this remark to remain internal, then quietly cleared her throat. 'Sorry, that was inappropriate. He, um, he is dead, though. That part was accurate.'

'Right. Well, that's a start,' Logan said. 'Anything more to give us, or…?'

'Maybe. But you have to ask nicer than that.'

Logan let out an exaggerated sigh. 'Apologies, Dr Maguire. Would it be possible for you to—'

'Wait,' said Hamza, cutting the role-play short. He looked between them both, and Logan felt his heart sink. 'Are you two finally…? You know?'

Shona shot Logan a sideways look. *Diagonally* sideways, given their height difference. 'I will say this, you've taught them well,' she remarked.

'We're trying to keep it quiet,' Logan told Hamza.

'Although, I have to say, pretty unsuccessfully so far,' Shona added.

'So keep it to yourself, will you, son? Just for now.'

Hamza mimed zipping his mouth shut. 'No problem, sir,' he said. 'Your secret's safe with me.'

'What secret's that, then?' asked Geoff Palmer, shuffling over to join them. He grinned at Logan so broadly that the corners of it were lost beneath the elastic of his hood. 'That you're *gay*?' He clapped his gloved hands together, pointed at the DCI, and exclaimed, 'Zing!'

'Aye, that's right, Geoff,' Logan said.

Palmer's smile faltered. His eyebrows, which had been stuck out of sight beneath the hood, made a comeback as a confused frown.

'What?'

'I'm a practising homosexual,' Logan told him. 'You got a problem with that?'

'What?' Palmer's gaze made its way around every member of the group. 'No. I don't… I wasn't…'

'Because if you're thinking of making any funny remarks, I would think again, Geoff,' Logan warned. 'I swear to God, if a single homophobic or otherwise inappropriate statement comes out of your mouth, I will have you in front of a tribunal so fast your feet won't touch the floor.'

Palmer looked mutely back at him for several seconds, then nodded and walked away with his head down.

Then, a moment later, he walked past in the opposite direction and scurried off towards his van.

'Right then, Dr Maguire,' Logan said, turning back to Shona. 'You were saying?'

Chapter 6

Without Ben and Tyler, the Incident Room felt empty.

Sinead had spent the last half hour preparing the Big Board, while Hamza made calls, checked databases, and set up the case files.

A uniformed sergeant—Cowan, or Cowie, or something— had taken over as SO at the scene when the detectives had left just after eleven, and three different constables had come knocking in the past ten minutes to pass on his report that things were still under control.

'Here's an idea,' Logan had suggested after the third such occasion. 'Maybe only come and tell us if things *aren't* under control, eh?'

The constable had agreed that this did indeed seem like a better idea, and had promised to pass the message on to the others.

Logan had sat at his desk for a while after that, scribbling notes in his pad and letting his mind wander back over the morning's events, all the while pointedly ignoring the Post-It note on his computer monitor that said Detective Superintendent Mitchell wanted to see him. She'd call if it was important, he reasoned. Either that, or he'd hear her shouting from along the corridor.

'Right, I think we're set,' Sinead announced, stepping back to admire the board.

It had been barely five hours since the body had been discovered, but they'd got lucky with a wallet and the car reg, and had been able to build a pretty decent picture in a short space of time. The big free-standing cork board already had a wealth of information on it, all neatly lined up and arranged.

Still, without Tyler and Ben, there was a sense that they weren't quite ready to get started, like performers killing time while they waited for the rest of the cast to arrive.

But neither man was coming. Not today.

Logan and Hamza both rotated their swivel chairs to face the board, Hamza scribbling a final few notes on his pad as he turned.

Clearly, Logan wasn't the only one who'd noticed the eerie quietness of the office, as Sinead looked a little less comfortable than usual when she launched into her summary.

'OK, so, we got pretty lucky with ID, as you know. Our vic's name is Borys Wozniak. Age twenty-three. Born in Poland, but lived in Inverness since he was five. Car was registered to his flat near the Eastgate. Rented place. Lives there on his own. Neighbours haven't seen him in a few weeks, though no one was able to be any more specific.'

'Car was bought in cash two months ago from one of the Arnold Clarks on Harbour Road,' Hamza said, tapping the end of his pen against his notepad. 'Actual cash, I mean. Not with a card.'

'There's an alarm bell ringing, straight off. How much did he pay?' Logan asked.

Hamza checked his pad again, then shook his head. 'Sorry, I didn't ask.'

'You didn't ask? Why not? Could be telling.'

'Aye, I know. I must've just forgotten. Sorry,' Hamza said. 'A guess? Around ten grand, but I'll check when we're done.'

The cost of the car might turn out to be a completely useless nugget of information, of course, but they wouldn't know that until somewhere down the line. For now, the job was simply to gather everything they could. Hamza knew that, so there was no excuse.

Logan decided to let it slide. For now, anyway. 'Right,' he said. 'Well, just make sure you do.'

'Uniform's looking into next of kin,' Sinead continued. 'They think we've got a hit. His dad's not on the scene, and his mum is a bit of a… local character. Well-kent face around the nick, apparently. Lena Wozniak?'

Logan shook his head. 'Means nothing to me.'

'I'm told you'd remember her if you'd met her. I've suggested I go talk to her, since I'm told she doesn't react well to people in uniform.'

'You're not going on your own,' Logan told her. 'Hamza, go with her, will you?'

'What?' Hamza blinked. 'Aye. Yes, of course.'

Logan's look lingered on the DS for a moment, then returned to Sinead. 'What about Borys himself? Any record?'

'Minor stuff. Cautions for fighting and possession, both when he was nineteen. Seems to have kept his nose clean since.'

'Well, he rubbed somebody up the wrong way. Where does he work?'

'He doesn't. He's on Universal Credit.'

'Christ, the British Government must be getting very generous these days, if folk on Universal Credit can walk into a showroom and buy a car in cash,' Logan said. 'Either that, or our Borys was up to no good. And the big pile of drugs on his dashboard would suggest the latter.'

'Wasn't drugs, sir,' Sinead said. She tapped a note on the board. 'It was sherbet.'

Logan followed her finger to the note. 'What? What do you mean? Like the sweetie? Like actual sherbet?'

'Actual sherbet, sir,' Sinead confirmed. 'No trace of narcotics of any kind.'

Logan sat back with his hands behind his head, giving this some thought. He'd pegged the white powder on the car's dashboard as heroin, though he hadn't looked too closely. If it wasn't, then what did that mean? Had someone placed it there on purpose, perhaps as some sort of message? Or, had Borys tried to pass it off as smack, only for the buyer to see through his deception and kill him for it?

'No record of him dealing at all?' he asked.

'No cautions or charges, no. Want me to talk to CID and see if he was on their radar?' Sinead asked.

'Aye. Worth a try,' Logan said, then he gestured to the board. 'Anything else on him?'

Hamza piped up, looking to make amends for his earlier slip-up. 'I've got an ANPR search running for his number plate over the past few weeks to see if we can get a bead on where he's been. They're going to call if they get a hit, but if he's stuck around Inverness then it's not likely. Unless he's passed a polis vehicle with a camera fitted, then we might get lucky.'

'Fingers crossed, then,' Logan said.

He got to his feet and Sinead stepped aside to give him the floor.

'So, report from the scene. It's a bit of an odd one, though I think we could all have guessed that ourselves. Palmer's team reckons the car was driven to the site two to three hours before they got there—there was still some residual heat in the engine, and less so in the brakes. He explained at great length about a calculation they do that can give them an approximate time-frame, but to be honest I tuned most of it out. Point is, we're looking at it being parked up at the school between five and six.'

'Five would be safer,' Sinead pointed out. 'It's nearly full daylight by six.'

'Aye, and the cover of darkness would've been helpful,' Logan said. 'The body isn't fresh, so he didn't drive himself. Which means someone else drove the car there, heaved him into the driver's seat, handcuffed him to the wheel, then fucked off.'

Sinead picked up her notepad and pen. 'Was the hand cut off at the scene, do we know?'

'Doesn't look like it, no, but we'll get confirmation after the PM.'

'Any prints or DNA found in the car?' Hamza asked.

'Palmer's taken it in for a full going over. Early signs are that it hasn't been wiped clean, though, so we might get lucky on prints. I stress "might", though. Whoever did this put some amount of planning into it. I'd be very surprised if they forgot to bring a pair of gloves with them,' Logan said. 'My gut instinct at the moment is that this is some sort of dealer rivalry.'

'Or could be another vigilante thing,' Hamza said. 'Given the history of that school, and everything...'

'Christ. I'm not even going to think about that for now,' Logan said, grimacing. 'I think another dealer's more likely.'

'You think Borys has moved in on someone else's territory?' asked Sinead.

Logan looked back at the board, his fingernails scraping through the stubble on his chin. 'It'd be nice and neat, but I don't know if it's that simple.'

'What are you thinking, sir?' Hamza asked.

'Why leave him there like that? Why take that risk of driving his car to a school, parking it up, and putting him in the driver's seat? If someone just wanted to stop him dealing on their patch, he'd be at the bottom of the Moray Firth, not on display for the whole world to see.'

'What if it wasn't for the world, sir? What if it was just for someone in particular to see?' Sinead suggested. 'Someone working at the school, maybe?'

'Or a pupil,' Hamza added.

Logan had come to the same conclusion back at the scene, but had filed it away to come back to later, hoping that something would come along to blow the theory out of the water. Nothing had.

It was too much of a coincidence for it not to be connected.

And his thoughts on coincidences were well known.

'Bosco Maximuke's daughter goes to that school,' he said.

Hamza sat up straighter at that. 'As in Bosco "Former Drug Kingpin Who Almost Killed Us All" Maximuke?'

'That's the one,' Logan confirmed. 'Maybe this is a message for Bosco. Maybe he's still trying to run things from the jail, and this is to warn him off. Make him think about what might happen to his daughter if he doesn't back off.'

'Want me to check if he's been getting any visitors lately?' Hamza asked.

'Go for it,' Logan said.

'He's in Bar-L, right?'

'Grampian,' Logan said, without missing a beat. 'I like to keep an eye on the bastard. He got moved last year to be closer to home, though the last I heard his family wants nothing to do with him.'

'Be a shame for his daughter if she gets dragged into all this because of something he's done,' Sinead said.

'She's a pretty tough kid, but aye, that would be rough,' Logan replied, then he checked his watch and reached for his coat. 'Right, Shona's due to be starting the PM. I'm going to go pay a visit to Bosco's family and see if they know anything. But first…' His eyes darted to the note on his monitor. 'I'd better go and face the dragon.'

Chapter 7

Detective Superintendent Mitchell was watering a plant on her windowsill when Logan knocked and entered her office. The plant was a short, stubby thing with dark, prickly leaves and an evolutionary design that favoured function over style.

He could see why Mitchell had been drawn to it.

'Ah, Jack. Glad you were finally able to fit me in,' she said, not turning. 'I'm sure you know why you're here.'

'I'm afraid not, ma'am.'

He did know. Or he had a damn good idea, at least.

Mitchell finished watering the plant, set down the little metal teapot she'd been using, and picked up a small green bottle with a dropper on the top. As she spoke, she unscrewed the cap and squeezed little dribbles of liquid onto the plant's many unattractive leaves.

'Right, we'll play it like that, then,' she said. 'What happened three days ago? Early afternoon?'

'Lunch?' Logan guessed, but the sigh from Mitchell told him to think again. 'Early afternoon three days ago? I don't recall, ma'am.'

He did recall. He very much recalled. But as he couldn't yet be sure how much the Detective Superintendent knew, it was safer to keep his cards close to his chest.

Mitchell finished dousing the leaves in whatever chemical compound was in the bottle, replaced the lid, then finally turned to face him. She did not smile. Not that she often did, of course, but her lack of humour was even more pronounced now than it usually was.

That wasn't a good sign.

'Allow me to jog your memory, then. That was the day that a former associate of ours—one Robert Hoon—was arrested on suspicion of assault. This was not your case, and yet you personally intervened. Correct?'

'That's correct,' Logan admitted.

Mitchell seemed surprised by the frankness of the response. 'Why?'

'Because he asked me to,' Logan said. 'And, given the potential for the force to be publicly embarrassed by the situation, I thought it prudent.'

'Oh, you thought it "prudent", did you?' Mitchell asked, her tone somewhere between outraged and mocking. She took her seat like she was settling in for a long conversation.

Logan, on the other hand, remained standing.

'There had been an altercation at a supermarket where Bob—where *Mr Hoon*—was working,' he explained. 'He intervened.'

'He assaulted a manager.'

'The manager was asking for it, ma'am.'

'Oh, and that's your professional opinion, is it?'

'It is,' Logan confirmed. 'In fact, when the gentleman had that pointed out to him, he agreed, and decided not to press charges.'

'And you didn't twist his arm? Just a little?'

Logan shook his head. 'No, ma'am. I made his options very clear to him. I made sure he was aware that, should he wish, we'd prosecute Mr Hoon to the full extent of the law.'

'But…?'

'But that the contents of the statement he himself had given would almost certainly lead to him facing charges of his own. He took a moment to reflect on that, then decided to put the whole thing down to a misunderstanding.'

'A misunderstanding that led to his nose being broken.'

'I wouldn't know, ma'am. I didn't see a medical report.'

'What then?' Mitchell asked.

'Ma'am?'

'You got him to drop the charges. What then?'

Logan frowned, like he still wasn't quite sure what was being asked of him. 'I took Mr Hoon home. Thought it best.'

'We're a chauffeur company now, are we?'

'No. But—'

'You thought you'd give your friend a lift?'

'I wouldn't call him my friend,' Logan was quick to reply. 'As I said, I felt there was a risk of embarrassment to the department if word got out, so I thought it best to take him home directly.'

Mitchell's chair gave a low, solemn creak as she leaned forward. 'One of the arresting officers claims Mr Hoon said you would get him off because "you owed him one". What did he mean by that?'

'No idea, ma'am.'

'Mr Hoon seemed to think he'd assisted in a recent case,' Mitchell continued. 'I've looked through the reports, but can't see any record of him. Mercifully, I must say, but strange. Why would he say that?'

'I don't know, ma'am,' Logan said. 'He could be referring to the Iceman case before Christmas. As he was involved in the original investigation, I asked him a few questions about that.'

'That's not in the report.'

Logan shook his head. 'He didn't provide any information that I felt was of consequence.'

Mitchell interlocked her fingers and tapped the tips of her thumbs together. 'What aren't you telling me, Jack?'

'Nothing, ma'am. That's it. That's all there is.'

'Mr Hoon's not going to pop up again today, is he? He's not going to *assist* in this investigation?'

'No, ma'am. Apparently, he's in London.'

'What's he doing in London? Is he even allowed in London?'

'I asked him the same question, ma'am. Seemingly, he is.'

He had called Logan two days ago, looking for a favour. It had not been a particularly big favour—a phone call to an old acquaintance in the Met—and so he'd done it just to get the bastard off the phone.

And then, he'd called back, asking for a second favour. And shortly after that, a third, which had involved Logan running the number plate of a stolen car. If the Detective Superintendent found out about that, Logan would be well and truly in the shit.

'And there's nothing else you're not telling me?' Mitchell pressed.

'Nothing, ma'am.'

Mitchell clicked her tongue against the roof of her mouth in time with her tapping thumbs, then sighed and took a slim silver pen from an organiser on her desk.

'Good. I'm going to choose to believe that, and also that it won't happen again. Should Mr Hoon find himself in trouble, he can find his own way back out of it. Understood?'

'Understood.'

Mitchell pressed the button on top of her pen, then turned her attention to a stack of paperwork on her desk. 'See yourself out, Jack,' she told him.

When she looked up just a few seconds later, he was already gone.

–

Ben Forde's knees cracked unpleasantly as he squatted down by the rack of magazines in the Co-op in the village of Corpach, just outside Fort William, and searched through that day's offerings.

There was no new *Love It!* out yet, which was a shame. They both enjoyed reading the ludicrous sob stories that publication offered, and the juxtaposition between the front page headlines and the magazine's screamingly positive title.

The rack held slim pickings today. And, after the day's previous highlights of 'I Lost My Foot to a Nazi Love Rat' and 'Granny Ate Our Dog' an afternoon spent leafing through the *People's Friend* struck him as disappointingly tame.

He found a *Woman's Own* hidden behind a copy of *The Beano*, and picked it up. He tucked it under his arm, started to stand, then stopped.

It had been years since he'd read *The Beano*. It had been years since he'd had the time, and even longer since he'd had the inclination. He picked it up, flicked through a few pages, then, after a quick detour to pick up a bar of Cadbury's Fruit and Nut, took both the magazine and the comic up to the counter.

'Aw. That for your grandson?' the server asked, as she bleeped the comic's barcode.

'Hmm? Oh. Aye. Something like that,' Ben said, hurriedly stuffing it into a bag.

He reached for his wallet once both publications and the chocolate had been rung through, then a thought struck him.

After a quick glance back to make sure nobody was behind him, lugging in, he leaned in closer and lowered his voice. 'Here,' he said, 'I don't suppose you do flowers, do you?'

–

In a cold, windowless room of Inverness's Raigmore Hospital, Shona Maguire was weighing a selection of internal organs. She had made it through the heart, lungs, kidneys, pancreas, and stomach so far, and was on course to have completed the set within the next twenty minutes.

For the past ten minutes, she had been quietly singing the song *Mr Loverman* by Shabba Ranks, substituting every instance of the word 'lover' for the word 'liver', and switching out the exclaimed 'Shabba!' for an equally enthusiastic 'Shona!'

This had taken her by surprise. While she often listened to music while working, she couldn't recall herself doing any mid-post-mortem singing before, and certainly none that involved substituting any of the lyrics with body parts or her own name.

It was unusual behaviour in anyone's book, she reckoned, and while it had confused her at first, she'd quickly come to recognise why it was happening.

She was happy.

Not at the job in front of her, of course. It would be inappropriate to derive happiness from that. Satisfaction, yes. A grim fascination, perhaps. But not happiness. Finding happiness in something like this would be weird.

'Mr Liverman. *Shona!*' she sang, as she finished washing a spleen and placed it on the scales. 'Oof. You're a big 'un,' she informed it, then she scribbled a note and turned back to the body on the table.

From where she was standing, she was looking directly at the soles of the victim's feet. She'd already gone over them when the body had first arrived, but there was a red mark between the first and second toe on the left foot that she hadn't noticed.

It was tiny—barely the size of a pimple—but something about the placement of it made her look more closely.

Fetching a magnifying eyepiece from a drawer, she got in close and studied the mark. It looked like a pinprick, with the faintest suggestion of a scab roughly the size of a midge's bollock crusting on top of it.

She pressed her thumb against the mark and gave a series of gentle squeezes, prodding the flesh surrounding the spot.

On the fourth press, she found a lump. It was long and thin like a grain of rice, and shifted around between her fingertips.

'Well, now,' she muttered, reaching for a scalpel. 'What do we have here?'

Chapter 8

From a distance, you'd be forgiven for thinking Lena Wozniak was somewhere in the lower end of her thirties. She had well-defined cheekbones, smooth, unblemished skin, and a slight build that was accentuated by her long limbs and short skirt.

Get much closer, however, and most of that fell apart.

The strong cheeks and flawless skin were the result of makeup so thick she must've scooped it on with a builder's trowel. It filled in all the cracks, and some careful use of colour and shading made her sagging face appear far more expertly sculpted than nature had ever achieved on its own.

Up close, she wasn't so much slim as haggard, her petite frame less to do with a healthy lifestyle and more to do with a lifetime of substance abuse, addiction, and very probably a variety of eating disorders.

Her teeth were the colour of old wood, the gums surrounding them a haunting palette of blacks and greys. She'd lived in Scotland for the better part of two decades, but her accent was unapologetically Polish, and the way she stumbled over her words suggested she'd invested only the bare minimum of time in picking up the local language.

Lena's flat was on the second floor in a block situated across the road from the Merkinch Community Centre in an area of the city best known as 'The Ferry'. It had been named after the boat service which had connected it to the Black Isle on the other side of the Moray Firth, and which had ended in 1982, after the bridge had been built.

The nickname had stuck, though, despite the countless far more disparaging alternatives that had been thrown at the area over the years.

Sinead and Hamza both sat perched right at the front of Lena's couch, avoiding the topographical map of stains that covered the back cushions. The arms of the couch were pock-marked with burns from neglected cigarettes and dropped hot rocks. At least one of them, Hamza had discovered, was also disconcertingly wet.

Lena had taken the news of her son's death fairly calmly, all things considered. There had been no crying, or wailing, or any great show of grief. Instead, she'd lit her third cigarette since the detectives had arrived, shaken her head for a few seconds, then had all-but knocked Sinead and Hamza onto their arses when she'd announced, 'I told him not to fuck little girls.'

Sinead blinked, shot Hamza a sideways look, then smiled politely. 'Sorry?'

'I told him, this is what happens when you are dirty fucking beast,' Lena said, waving her Marlboro like she was conducting an orchestra. 'When you screw around with schoolgirls, you open world of trouble. I tell him this, again and again.'

'Are you saying that Borys was in a sexual relationship with… what? A child?'

'He deny. Deny, deny, deny. "No way," he say. "It is just friends."' She pulled a face and took a draw on her cigarette. '*Just friends*. With girls half his age. Sure. That is normal. That is not weird in slightest. I do *not* think.' She blew two trails of smoke from her nostrils and fixed Sinead with a look. 'It is weird, yes?'

'Mrs Wozniak—' Hamza began, but she quickly set him straight.

'Miss. You see ring on this finger?' She waggled the finger in question in Hamza's direction. There was something vaguely suggestive about it. 'I do not have man. Not for lack of trying.'

'Sorry, *Miss* Wozniak,' Hamza said, steering the conversation right back on track. 'You're saying you believe your son was having sexual intercourse with schoolgirls?'

'No.'

'No?'

'I am saying he fuck little girls.'

'Oh, right. Thanks for clarifying,' Hamza said. 'How little are we talking?'

'How should I know? Five feet.'

'I meant... age,' Hamza said.

'Oh. I don't know. Twelve. Thirteen, maybe.'

Hamza scribbled a note. 'Do you know who they were?'

'No. No idea. But I see him with them. From window. I see them in car with him.'

'Having sex?'

'What? No. You have a dirty mind. Just passenger. Talking. Blah, blah, blah.'

'How many girls?' Sinead asked.

'I don't know. Only one at a time. I see maybe four or five times.'

Sinead pressed her. 'Could it have been the same girl?'

Lena shrugged. Her bones practically rattled in their sack of flesh and skin. 'Suppose. Maybe. I don't see their faces all the time. But I know they are young. Too young. Far too young for a grown man, even for Borys.'

'What do you mean? Why "even for Borys"?' Hamza asked.

Lena was halfway through her smoke now, and already getting the next one cued up. She waved the unlit cigarette around, while the other flapped up and down at the corner of her mouth in time with her reply.

'He was never good with people. He was... what is word? Loser. Or... loner? Loner. Never good at making friends, even as child. He cry non-stop when I try to make him. I thought he was fucking crazy, you know? Touched in head. Strange. What is the thing they have? Crazy kids. *Oddism*. That was him. Such an odd child. I thought he was *oddtistic*.'

'Did you ever get him diagnosed?' Sinead asked. When this drew a blank look, she added, 'By a doctor, I mean?'

'I don't trust doctors. They are fucking liars. I think to myself, he grow out of it.'

'And did he?' Hamza asked.

Lena's lips drew back over her teeth, like she'd necked a shot of something potent. 'He was fucking twelve-year-olds. What do you think?'

'When did you last see him?' Hamza asked.

'He never comes round anymore. Not since he got own place. I ask him to take me over and show me, but does he? No. No phone calls. No answers to text. I am ghosted by own fucking son!'

'So you haven't seen him or spoken to him recently?'

'Not for weeks. Ungrateful shit.'

'I don't suppose he ever mentioned a name?' Sinead asked. 'Of the girl, or girls that he was… involved with?'

Lena shook her head and started on her next cigarette. 'He tell me nothing. Full of secrets. I am his mother. I give him everything. Whole life. Split myself open, clunge to arsehole, pushing out his big fucking melon head, and little shit only hides things from me. Tells me lies. Screws with little girls like pervert.'

She shook her head and spat something black and blobby into an ashtray on the arm of the chair beside her. 'I warned him that this would happen. I told him, you fuck children, you face consequences. Well, good riddance!' she said, but her voice betrayed her, cracking for the first time since Sinead had broken the news.

A tear drew a line down her makeup. Her hand went to her mouth as the enormity of it all finally struck her.

'Oh, but my boy,' she whispered. 'My beautiful baby boy.'

Neither Hamza nor Sinead said a word until they were back in Hamza's car, and the doors were shut.

'Wow,' Sinead muttered. 'That was a bit...'

'Mental?' Hamza guessed.

It wasn't quite the word Sinead had been aiming for, but it would do the job.

Lena's quiet, dignified tears had risen to full-on sobs, then shouted accusations, then a foot through a television. Borys went from being a predatory paedophile to the innocent victim of some underage temptress who had cruelly taken advantage of his 'oddism'.

Eventually, she had screamed at the detectives to get out. They had suggested they wait until a friend or relative arrived, or a family liaison officer was brought in, but she had all but shoved them out onto the landing and slammed the door behind them.

They had listened to things being thrown around for a while, then everything had settled down into relative calm, and they'd left her to her grief.

'What do you think?' Sinead asked. 'About the relationship with the teenager, I mean, not about Lena.'

Hamza shook his head. His expression was drawn and haunted. 'Not sure. I'm still stuck back on "split me open, clunge to arsehole".'

'Aye, that was a vivid picture she painted, right enough,' Sinead agreed. She shuddered. 'But if she's right, if he was at it with an underage girl, what's the bets she goes to the school where his body was found? Got to be pretty high, right?'

'You'd think,' Hamza said.

'Could be a revenge thing. Maybe a parent found out and punished him for it.'

'Maybe.'

'Or one of those paedo hunter gangs. Though I've never heard about them taking anything this far before.'

'No,' Hamza agreed.

Sinead's forehead creased as she studied the DS. 'Any other ideas?'

'Not really,' Hamza said. He was facing front, looking ahead at the community centre across the road, but not really seeing it.

'Right. It's just I seem to be doing all the thinking today…'

'Yeah,' Hamza said, then he blinked. 'What? Oh. Sorry.'

'You all right? You've seemed a bit… I don't know, for the last couple of weeks. Distant.'

'It's nothing,' Hamza assured her. 'I've just… I've not been sleeping well.'

'Anything you want to talk about?'

He forced a smile, shook his head, then started the engine. 'Not really,' he told her. 'But thanks.'

The car pulled away from the block of flats. Sinead watched the DS for a while, then looked back at the building behind them. Lena Wozniak stood at the window of her flat, a cigarette in one hand, a glass of something in the other.

She watched them until the car rounded a bend, headed for the Waterloo Bridge and the city that stood beyond.

Once the flats were out of sight, Sinead took out her phone. 'Right, so our victim's a possible sex offender,' she said. 'Best call this one in to the boss.'

Chapter 9

Alexis Maximuke had met Logan a handful of times before, though never in the best of circumstances. Either she had been drunk or off her face on some narcotic or another, or he had been attempting to send her husband to prison.

He had never rated her highly as a human being, and even less so as a mother, given some of the things Olivia had let slip to Shona over the past couple of years of movie-and-popcorn nights. None of what the girl had said had been enough to warrant intervention by social services, but they had still painted the woman in a deeply unflattering light.

From the moment she opened the door, Logan could tell that something had changed. On each of their previous encounters, Alexis had looked a decade older than her age. This was despite her having spent substantial sums of her husband's illegally gotten gains on hairdressers, fake tan, and Botox. Not to mention, the ridiculous high heels and short, clingy dresses that made her look like she was auditioning for some am-dram production of *Pretty Woman*.

And not for the Julia Roberts role.

The Alexis who greeted Logan was a slightly frumpy forty-something dressed in a velour tracksuit and trainers, and she looked all the better for it.

Her skin, previously a radioactive shade of orange, now had a natural healthy glow about it. The dark rings below her eyes that she'd tried so hard to hide with makeup were virtually gone, and if she gave a damn about what was left, she wasn't showing it.

Unexpectedly, she smiled when she saw him. He assumed that meant she didn't recognise him, but was soon proven incorrect. Mostly.

'Detective… Wogan, wasn't it?'

'Close. It's Logan. Detective Chief Inspector. I wonder if I might have a few minutes of your time, Mrs Maximuke?'

'Of course! I've got spin class in an hour, but just pottering about until then.' She stepped aside and gave a tilt of her head, ushering him in.

The smell of baking swirled around him as he stepped into the hallway. The entrance to the kitchen stood along the hall from the front door, and he could hear the faint hum of an oven.

'Just making some baked oats for lunch. You want some?'

'I'm fine, thank you.'

She put the back of a hand to the side of her mouth and whispered to him. 'They've got Biscoff spread in them. But only a spoonful. They're still healthy.'

'Honestly, I'm fine,' Logan told her.

'Your loss!' Alexis trilled, then she set off at a trot into the kitchen, calling back over her shoulder as she went. 'I'm assuming this is about that useless shit of a husband of mine? What's he done this time?'

Logan followed her to the kitchen and immediately started to regret his refusal of food. The aroma from the oven made his stomach gurgle and his tongue flick across his lips. A jar of Biscoff biscuit spread and an enormous tub of fat-free yoghurt sat on one of the wooden worktops, alongside a plate and a spoon that had been set out in anticipation.

'Actually, I'm not sure,' Logan told her. 'It's possible Bosco doesn't have any involvement, but… well. I'm sure you heard what happened at the school.'

'School?'

'Aye. Olivia's school. Olivia didn't tell you?'

Alexis bent and peered through the glass front of the oven, then straightened and shook her head. 'No. She's still there. Doesn't get home until four-ish. Why? What happened?'

'Olivia didn't come home?' Logan glanced around the kitchen, as if he might find the girl lurking there somewhere. 'They closed the school. Everyone was turned away.'

'What? When?' Alexis asked, lines of concern writing themselves across her face. 'Why?'

'There was a body found in the car park this morning,' Logan told her. 'A man in his twenties.'

Alexis's jaw dropped. 'Oh, Lord. Oh, that's awful. What happened? Was it an accident?'

'We're still looking into it,' Logan told her. 'But we're quietly confident we can rule out natural causes. We believe he was murdered.'

'Oh, my goodness!' Alexis grasped at a silver crucifix she wore around her neck and kissed it. 'That poor young man. And you think Bosco was somehow involved? How could he be?'

'As I say, we're not sure. We're just asking questions at the moment, and seeing what comes out.' He raised his eyes to the ceiling. 'You're sure Olivia didn't come home?'

'I mean, I was out back doing the washing for a while, but she'd have said if she was back,' Alexis told him. She stepped out of the kitchen to the foot of the stairs and called up. 'Livvy? Livvy, you in, sweetheart?'

When no response came, she nodded like her point had been proven, then returned to the kitchen.

'She'd have said if she was back,' she reiterated, then a timer let out a series of chimes and she dived for the oven like every millisecond counted.

Logan inhaled deeply as Alexis took out a round ramekin about the size of a large cookie, something golden brown and cake-like, but with a nicely charred top, nestled within it.

'You sure you don't want a bit?' she asked, spooning a dollop of the biscuit spread on top, and finishing with a drizzle of yoghurt. 'It's just oats, really. Yummy, though. I hate the word, but it's very *moreish*. Father Conrad gave me the recipe.'

'Honestly, I'm fine,' Logan said, though his watering mouth very much begged to differ.

Alexis shrugged, set the hot ramekin on a plate, and took a seat with it at the kitchen's breakfast bar. 'So. This young man and Bosco.'

'Aye. Bosco. We've reason to believe the victim may have been involved in the local drugs trade. Given that his body was found at Olivia's school, we thought there might be some connection.'

He watched as the tip of a spoon broke the crust of the baked oats, and followed it all the way to Alexis's mouth. 'You think Bosco's still running things from inside?' she asked.

'Do you?'

Alexis shook her head. 'No. I mean, I think he'd like to, but he relied on the guys he had working for him, and most of them are banged up, too. Most of his other connections are down the road in Glasgow, and he burned his bridges there a long time ago.'

Alexis took another spoonful of the oats, this time dipping it into the melting blob of biscuit spread. The noise she made when she put it in her mouth bordered on the orgasmic, and Logan had to fight the urge to wrestle the spoon from her and get stuck in.

'Does the name Borys Wozniak mean anything to you?' he asked.

'No. Don't think he was one of Bosco's, was he?' she asked, wiping her mouth on the back of a hand. 'Oh, is he the dead lad? Wozniak. That's what, Polish? I can see why you'd make a connection to Bosco. Half his guys were Poles. And he was found at Olivia's school, you say?'

Logan confirmed that with a nod. 'He was. His body was found in a car. A black Peugeot SUV.'

'What's that? Like a sports car?'

'More like a small four-by-four,' Logan said, and he noted the way the next spoonful paused halfway to Alexis's mouth. 'That ringing a bell?'

'Hmm? Oh, no. I mean, maybe. I don't know. I saw a car like that on the street a couple of times recently. I suppose they're pretty common, though.'

'Don't suppose you happened to catch the registration?'

'Afraid not. I only saw it from the window. Sideways. Didn't see the number plate at all. And, to be honest, I'm not even sure it was the same one every time. There's a lot of cars up and down here, especially when the main road is busy. We're trying to get the council to put in speed bumps, but it's like getting blood out of a stone.' She shoved the oats in her mouth and chewed thoughtfully. 'You couldn't have a word, could you? Might help, coming from you.'

Logan offered a polite, 'I'll see what I can do,' knowing full well that there was no way in hell he was going to get dragged into the internal machinations of the Highland Council's road department. That way, madness lay.

'Was Olivia in a relationship, do you know?'

'A relationship? What, like a boyfriend?' Alexis shook her head. 'Not that she's mentioned, no. And I asked her. Just this morning, as it happens. But she's never really shown much interest. I've actually got my suspicions that she might be,'— she mouthed the words silently—'a lesbian. Not that there's anything wrong with that. Not really. Besides, it'd probably just be a phase, wouldn't it? They go through that at that age. It's just a fashion thing. Nothing serious.'

'Right. So… no boyfriends, then? You're sure?'

'Like I say, she's never mentioned anyone. And she's not even fourteen yet. Mind you, the things I was up to at her age, when I think back…' She pulled an exaggerated frown, then shoved another spoonful of her baked oats into her mouth to stop herself saying anything incriminating.

'She didn't mention anyone, then? Any male friends? Older, maybe?'

'No. How much older? What are you saying?' Alexis asked. 'Do you know something I don't?'

'No. Just building as full a picture as we can,' Logan said.

Then, before he could say anything more, there was a thud from the room directly above them. Alexis stopped chewing and forced down a swallow. 'Did you hear that?' she asked.

'I did, aye. You sure there's nobody upstairs?'

'You heard me shouting,' she replied. 'So no, not as far as I know.'

'What room is that?'

Alexis's gaze flicked across the ceiling and out into the hall as she mentally walked through the layout of the house.

'Olivia's bedroom.'

'Mind if I check it out?'

Alexis shook her head. 'Course not. Just… be careful.'

'Wait here,' Logan instructed, already heading for the stairs. 'And if you hear me shouting, call nine-nine-nine.'

He took the first half of the staircase two at a time, then slowed when he reached the top where a solid railing blocked his view of the landing above. He waited. Listened. But no other sounds came.

Sticking close to the wall, he sidled his way to the top, checked behind the railing to make sure the coast was clear, then headed for the room above the kitchen.

It was Olivia's bedroom. Had to be. A couple of film posters he knew that Shona had given to her were pinned on one of the walls—*Aliens* and *Ghostbusters 2*—and various items of clothing were spilling out of drawers and strewn like roadkill across the floor.

The window was open. A metal piggy bank in the shape of a horrifying pointy-headed clown lay on the floor where it had fallen.

Logan picked it up, muttered under his breath at the weight of the coins inside, then placed it back on the matching dust-free spot on the windowsill. He looked outside, saw the downpipe leading from the guttering above, and scanned the street for any sign of movement.

Nothing. The thud could've just been the wind knocking the bank off, although it would've had to be quite a gust to shift that thing. Even if it had been Olivia, though, she'd legged it and was now nowhere to be seen.

He had just shut the window when his phone rang. He felt a little flutter of excitement when he saw Shona's name, then had a quiet word with himself and pressed the button to answer.

–

Olivia Maximuke hugged her knees, held her breath, and remained absolutely still, the light through the slats in her cupboard door painting parallel lines across her face.

'Hey. I mean… hi. Hello,' Logan said, just a few feet away. 'How are…?'

There was silence as he listened. Olivia squinted, not moving, at him standing there in the middle of her bedroom. Her heart thudded like a drum, so loud that she thought he was bound to hear it, bound to turn, bound to pull open the door and find her hiding there.

She put her hands on her chest, like she might be able to muffle the thumping, or stop it beating, just for a moment. Just long enough.

The floorboards creaked as he shifted his weight. Olivia could hear the voice on the other end of the line, but it was tinny and distant and impossible to make out.

'Aye, that does sound weird,' Logan said, and the closeness and sudden boom of his voice made her jump. 'I'll be right there.'

Olivia bit her lip and tightened her grip on her legs as the detective ended the call and returned the phone to his pocket.

He didn't leave. Not yet. Instead, he rotated slowly on the spot, taking in the room's details. Through the downward angled slats, she saw his feet stopping, toes pointing in her direction. She felt the floor beneath her shift in time with his weight.

'Find anything?' her mother's voice called from downstairs.

The feet stopped a half-step from the cupboard door. Her lungs burned with the effort of not breathing as she watched them turn away.

'No. All clear,' he said.

Olivia listened to him leaving the room and making his way down the stairs. She heard him give over his contact details, and possibly something about a recipe, then the front door opened and closed behind him.

And only then, when she was sure he was gone, did she finally let herself breathe.

Chapter 10

It took Logan quarter of an hour of circling before he finally found a space in the car park at Raigmore. Even then, he'd had to lean out of the window and shout at some bastard in a Golf who'd tried to claim the space while the detective was lining up to reverse in.

A few minutes later, Logan strolled into Shona Maguire's office, got halfway through the 'Hi honey, I'm home!' line that he'd been rehearsing all the way through the building, then almost lost bladder control when a walking cadaver came bursting through the double doors that led to the mortuary.

'Jesus Christ! You nearly gave me a bloody heart attack, man!' Logan gasped, as Albert Rickett lowered himself into Shona's office chair.

Ricketts had once been the hospital's main pathologist, then had gone part-time, then had—as far as Logan knew—retired. Logan suspected this might have been for safety reasons, as, with his grey, papery skin and dark, sunken eyes, it was surely only a matter of time before he was mistaken for a corpse and shoved in one of the refrigerated drawers.

'Detective Chief Inspector,' Ricketts intoned, speaking the words like they were some sort of accusation. His voice was a hoarse and scratchy monotone that made Logan think of a long, dreary trudge through thick undergrowth. 'I assume you're here for the post-mortem findings?'

'Aye, that's the plan,' Logan said. He indicated the doors through which Ricketts had come. Through the circles of frosted glass, he could make out the shape of a figure moving inside. 'Dr Maguire through there, is she?'

'Last time I looked,' Ricketts confirmed. He allowed himself the tiniest of smiles, like he'd just made a joke. If he had, Logan was unable to pinpoint it. 'Would you like me to go in and ask if she's ready for you?'

'It's fine, I'll just go in,' Logan said.

Ricketts got up out of the chair surprisingly quickly for a man of his advanced years. 'No. I'm afraid I can't allow that, Detective Chief Inspector. The mortuary is a sacred space, not a… a… drop-in centre.'

Before Logan could offer a response, one of the doors swung open. Despite the mask covering the lower half of her face, and the goggles obscuring much of the top, Logan couldn't fail to notice her smile.

'Thought I heard your dulcet tones,' Shona said. 'Come away in and get the craic.'

Logan gave Ricketts a self-satisfied little nod, then headed for the mortuary, helping himself to a mask and gloves from the pack by the door.

'What's Herman Munster still doing knocking around?' he asked, once he had donned his PPE and stepped into the refrigerated room. 'He skint, or something? You'd think with two hundred years of contributions his pension would be in pretty good shape.'

'Albert? No, he doesn't need the money. Far from it. He's got property all over town. Minted, so he is.'

'Aye?' Logan glanced back at the door. 'Must be true what they say about money not buying happiness. Not sure I've ever seen the bastard crack a smile.'

'He's just helping out while we try to find a replacement,' Shona explained, her voice a little muffled by her mask. 'The bosses asked him to stay on until they could find someone to cover. Turns out the Highland region is not awash with pathologists. Or with people who have any interest in being pathologists, for that matter.' She shrugged. 'It's almost like people don't enjoy the thought of cutting open dead folk and poking around in their stomach contents.'

'Well, their loss,' Logan replied.

'Sure, especially on days like these.' She drummed her hands on the end of the table that currently held a sheet-covered corpse. 'What do you want first, the boring stuff or the big weird thing? Well, it's a little thing, but it's big-time weird.'

'Go for the weird thing,' Logan said, but Shona shook her head.

'Shouldn't have given you the option. I'm going to do it the other way and build up. Much more fun that way.'

'Fair enough.'

'Bad news first. Our fella here is a bit of a mystery,' she announced. 'I think we're going to have to count on the toxicology report to give us a lot of answers, but I'll go out on a limb and say he died of an opioid overdose, based on signs of cyanosis, and the frothy residue he had around his nose and mouth.'

'We thought the powder in his car was heroin, which would've fit, but it was—'

'Sherbet. I know. Geoff told me when he called to remind me about his gig tonight.'

'He's a trier, you've got to give him that,' Logan said.

'There are some track marks in his arm. The victim, I mean, not Geoff's,' Shona said, pulling back the sheet enough to reveal the arm with the missing hand. 'But I'd say all were done around the same time, so he's not a long-term user. It's possible that whoever killed him forcibly injected him with it. Bruising on the forearm suggests multiple hands holding him firmly.'

'How long ago was this?'

'I'm putting time of death as two days ago,' Shona said. 'I'd say he was injected around about that same time.'

'What about the hand?' Logan asked, flicking his gaze to the stump. It had been sewn up, the skin puckered and drawn tightly together like the end of a cheap sausage. Infection had set in, dappling the flesh with blooms of black.

'Removed around two to three weeks ago, I'd estimate. Something heavy.'

'And sharp, I hope?'

Shona winced behind her mask. 'Probably not as much as he'd have liked. Took three hits. Something like a small axe. Maybe a machete, though that's less likely, going by the markings. They stitched him up. Actually made a very good job of it, given the state of what they had to work with. It got infected, though. Must've been agony.'

'Jesus,' Logan muttered. 'He suffered, then?'

'Very much so,' Shona confirmed. She crossed to the large computer screen that was fixed to the wall, prodded at one corner, then stepped back as a grisly collage of photographs appeared. 'There were these burn marks on his back. Quite distinctive, actually.' She indicated one of the photos. 'Close-up there.'

Logan leaned in and studied the image. It showed a section of a ribcage, with a circular burn mark roughly the size of a ten pence piece. Looking closely, he could see the burn was actually made up of two circles, one within the other so it looked a bit like a bullseye on a dartboard.

'How many of these are there?' Logan asked, shifting his focus to the wider shot of the victim's back.

'Eighteen. Mostly his back, but also his buttocks and the backs of his thighs. One just inside the anus.' She led the DCI back to the table, and lifted the bottom of the sheet. 'And see these injuries around the ankle?'

'A shackle of some sort,' Logan said. He'd seen similar markings on kidnap victims before. 'Whoever killed him kept him chained up and tortured him.'

'For around two to three weeks,' Shona said. 'They fed him, but there were some lacerations to his throat, stomach, and intestines. A poke around in the stomach contents showed fragments of broken glass.'

Logan rocked back on his heels, taking it all in. When he had, the best response he could offer was a mumbled 'Bloody hell.'

'Oh, and… brace yourself.'

She pulled back the sheet with no further warning, revealing Borys' face. His eyes were open and staring. Then again, he didn't have much choice.

'Eyelids were cut off,' Shona said. She waited for Logan to finish flinching, then threw in another harrowing bit of detail. 'Small pair of scissors, I think. Like curved nail scissors.'

'God Almighty,' Logan muttered.

'You ready for the weird bit?'

'What, you mean we haven't done the weird bit yet?' Logan asked. 'There's more?'

'There is. Check this out,' Shona replied, fetching a small glass container from a worktop, and passing it over.

Logan turned the container over, and heard the ting of something moving around inside it. A label covered most of the outside, forcing him to hold it up and look through the bottom.

Something slightly smaller than a grain of rice sat inside the bottle. It looked a little like a pill of some sort—one half black, the other made of clear glass or plastic. There was something inside, he thought—components of some kind—but it was far too small for him to be able to make out the details.

'It was in the sole of his foot,' Shona said. Her tone was hushed and almost reverential, like this was a big, significant event. 'Almost missed it.'

'What the hell is it?' Logan wondered.

'It's a microchip,' Shona said.

Logan squinted at the bottom of the bottle. 'What do you mean? Like from a computer?'

Shona shook her head. 'No. Like from a dog.'

Logan side-eyed her like she'd lost her fucking mind. 'A dog? Since when did dogs have…?' Fortunately for his sake, the penny dropped just in time. 'Oh. Like vets put in, you mean? An ID chip?'

'I think so,' Shona said. Her eyes widened with excitement behind her goggles. 'Unless it's a tracking device. Like a spy thing. That'd be pretty cool.'

'Aye, well, only one way to find out, I suppose,' Logan replied. He pocketed the container and turned to the pathologist. 'Any idea where I can find the nearest vet?'

Chapter 11

Back at Burnett Road, Sinead sat listening to the outraged ramblings of the headteacher of the school where Borys' body had been found. He had taken the hump when she'd asked if it was possible that one or more of the younger girls could be involved in relationships with a man in his twenties, and was now ranting about 'duty of care' this, and 'rigorous supervision' that, while simultaneously making it clear that what pupils did outside of school was not his responsibility or, for that matter, business.

She had paid attention at the start, but had now resorted to the occasional, 'uh-huh,' and, 'I see,' while she waited for the tirade to lose some of its steam.

There were three messages from Tyler on her phone—one confirming that Harris had got off to school, one checking in on how her day was going, and another asking her to bring home a Creme Egg. They had all arrived roughly twenty minutes apart several hours earlier, but she hadn't had a chance to reply until now.

She mumbled another, 'Right, yes,' and typed out a reply that covered all the main points Tyler had raised, and revealed the location of an Emergency Creme Egg that she'd stashed away for just this sort of eventuality.

Ten seconds later, his reply arrived.

'*Ate that one days ago.*'

'Don't you think, Detective Constable?' said the voice in her ear.

Sinead auto-piloted out a 'yes,' then backtracked. 'Sorry, didn't catch that last part. What did you say?'

'That we need to get the school open as soon as possible so as not to further disrupt the children's learning?'

'We're doing everything we can,' Sinead assured him. 'We should be finished on site by tomorrow afternoon, and will then coordinate with you on reopening.'

The headteacher tutted. 'And what are we supposed to do until then?'

'That's easy. Stay closed,' Sinead said. It was an obvious, and if she was honest, a slightly petty answer. But she'd listened to his complaints for a full ten minutes now, and was feeling far less amicable towards him than she had at the start of the call. 'Like you explained to me several times during this conversation, the school prides itself on its educational standards, so I'm sure the kids will cope with a couple of extra days off.'

He made a sound that was part exasperation and part disbelief, but before he could say a word Sinead thanked him for his time, promised to keep him updated, then ended the call.

'God, he couldn't half go on,' she said, sitting back and breathing out.

Hamza looked up from where he'd been staring at his pad. 'Who was that?'

'Headmaster at the school. He categorically refuses to accept the idea that any of the younger girls could have been seeing any older men, but at the same time says it's not his responsibility to know what they get up to outside of school.' She shrugged. 'Which is fair enough, I suppose.'

Hamza nodded his agreement, then perked up a little as he remembered something. 'Oh. Tyler wants you to bring him a Creme Egg when you're going home.'

'He didn't text you, too, did he?'

'Aye. Said you hadn't replied, and he wanted to make sure you'd seen it.'

Sinead smiled and shook her head. 'I've replied now.'

'Wasn't about the emergency one, was it?' Hamza asked. 'Because—'

'He's already eaten it, I know. He'll just have to wait. It's already four, and there's no saying when we're going to get finished today.'

'No,' Hamza agreed, and the word seemed to weigh heavily on him.

Both detectives turned as the swing doors to the Incident Room were thrown open and Logan entered. He looked to the desk behind the door, where the Exhibits Officer usually sat. Dave Davidson had been filling the role for the past few months, but the uniformed constable was nowhere to be found.

'Who's dealing with evidence?' Logan asked.

'Eh... don't know,' Hamza said. 'But there's something on your desk from Palmer's team. A note they found in the glove box.'

Logan ignored the second part of Hamza's statement, the lines on his forehead shifting like some vast tectonic plate as he focused on the first thing the DS had said. 'What do you mean you don't know? Have you not sorted someone yet?'

'It's just that DI Forde usually arranges—' Hamza began, but Logan was having none of it.

'DI Forde isn't here, Detective Sergeant. You should've been on it. You should've been dealing.'

'Uh, yes. No. You're right. Sorry, sir,' Hamza replied. 'I should've done it. Want me to see if Dave's available?'

Logan regarded him for what felt to Hamza like a very long time. Finally, he shook his head. 'Sinead, you get onto that, will you? DS Khaled will be coming with me.'

'I'll get right on it, sir,' Sinead promised.

Logan stopped by his desk, picked up an evidence bag with a scrap of crumpled notepaper inside, and turned it over. It contained a list of words and numbers.

Boils – 350
Stumpy – 200

There were six or seven others, random words and figures. None of it meant anything to him yet, but he'd come back to it and give it some more thought later.

'Before you get onto Dave, do me a favour and stick this address up on the board,' Logan told Sinead, placing a sheet of headed notepaper on her desk with the words, 'Inshes Veterinary Centre', emblazoned in an arch across the top. An address out on the west side of the city had been written in neat block capitals below it.

'What's this, sir?' she asked, picking up the paper.

'Don't know yet,' Logan told her. 'It's from a microchip out of a dog.'

'A dog?' Sinead asked. 'I don't understand.'

'You and me both. It was found in Borys Wozniak's left foot. Under the skin, so it didn't get there by accident.'

'Someone chipped him?' asked Hamza, craning over to get a look at the address. 'Why would they do that?'

'No idea,' Logan said. He jabbed a thumb upwards, indicating Hamza should get up off his backside. 'But you and I, Detective Sergeant, are going to go and find out.'

—

'Right then. What's the problem?'

DS Khaled turned just briefly in the passenger seat, looked at Logan like he didn't understand the question, and said, 'Sir?'

'There's something bothering you, son. Spit it out.'

The address from the chip was on Ballifeary Road, near Bught Park. The name—M. Howden—didn't give much away, though Sinead had already texted through the details, identifying the owner as one Margaret Howden, a widow in her early eighties, who lived alone.

Unlikely to be the killer, then.

They'd picked the wrong time of day for it, with the late afternoon traffic clogging the city's streets and slowing their progress. It would've been quicker to have a patrol car swing by to check the address out, but Logan's curiosity had been piqued, and he wanted to get to the bottom of it himself.

Besides, the slow progress and confined space gave Hamza nowhere to go.

'I'm fine, sir. Honest.'

'Just…?'

He heard Hamza sigh quietly in the seat beside him. 'Honestly, it's daft. I'm being an idiot, that's all.'

'We're all guilty of that from time to time, son,' Logan assured him. 'Out with it.'

Hamza looked out through the side window at the passing streets. A fine drizzle was falling, the droplets so light they hung in the air like mist, and clung to the outside of the glass. People were making their way home from work, hoods up and heads down as they scurried along the pavement.

'It was that lassie,' Hamza said. His breath fogged the window. 'The one I found. Who'd killed herself.'

Logan said nothing, just listened.

'It was… I don't know. We see all sorts in this job. Worse than that. Way worse. But… I don't know. There was something about it. About her. Or the situation. Or…' He blew out his cheeks, said, 'I don't know,' for a third time, then fell back into silence.

'That was a tough one,' Logan said. 'You did well.'

Hamza turned then. 'How?' he asked. 'What did I do? Called it in. How did that help her?'

'You did everything you could.'

'But if I'd been there sooner. If I'd been quicker, I could've talked to her, or, shite, I don't know. Given her a hug, or something. Told her it was going to be OK.' He went back to gazing out at the drizzle. 'All I did was call it in. How did that help anyone?'

'We don't get to help everyone, son. Much as we might like to.'

67

'Do we help anyone, though?' Hamza wondered. His voice was so low that Logan suspected the question wasn't even aimed at him, but he answered it anyway.

'Aye. We do. We might not always arrive in the nick of time to pull off dramatic last-minute rescues, nice as that would be. That's not what we're here for. We're no' superheroes. We're here to bring closure. To give a wee bit of peace of mind to the families of the victims, letting them know that justice has been done, or that we're doing what we can to make sure that it gets done. We save the ones we can, we avenge the ones we can't. That's the job.'

Hamza's breath fogged the glass again. 'Aye, I suppose it is,' he said, sounding less than enthusiastic about this prospect. He gave himself a shake and sat up straighter in the seat. 'Sorry, sir. Just in a bit of a funk. I'll snap out of it.'

'Aye, well, happens to the best of us,' Logan told him. He tapped his fingers on the steering wheel, like he was building himself up to the next part. 'And, you know, there are people you can talk to. Professionals. In the building. It's all very discreet. And it can help. I'm told.'

Hamza smiled and shook his head. 'I'm not a basket case quite yet, sir,' he said. 'Honestly, I'll be fine.'

'Just… no point bottling it up,' Logan continued. 'Festering about these things never helps. Believe me.'

'Not festering, sir. Honest. Just having an off day,' Hamza insisted, and he looked relieved when he was able to point to a road ahead on the left. 'That's us down that way. Nearly there now.'

Logan decided not to press things further, and took the turning as directed, then the following right when Hamza pointed the way.

They pulled up outside a small bungalow with sandstone-coloured insulated cladding. A dilapidated conservatory grew from the side like some kind of tumour—malignant, probably, given the state of it.

The grass had been cut in the last few days, and lumps of it lay dotted around the front lawn and scattered over the path and driveway.

Logan pulled his BMW into the empty drive, and both detectives took a moment to appraise the house from the outside.

There were two windows on the front, one big bay window that was most likely the living room, and another smaller one that may have been a bedroom. Thanks to the difference in sizes, the house looked like it was winking at the passersby.

There was a much smaller Velux window in the roof, suggesting some sort of loft conversion had been undertaken at some point. The Velux was less than a foot square, though, so the amount of light it provided would've been minimal. There was no way anyone could use it as an emergency exit, either. Anyone who wasn't the size of a cat, anyway.

Blinds hung over the two downstairs windows—verticals in the living room, horizontals in the bedroom. The ones in the bedroom were closed, but those in the living room hadn't been pulled shut all the way. Unclipping their seatbelts, both men got out of the car and headed for the front door.

Logan knocked—a big, booming knock that would force anyone inside to sit up and take notice. It was a knock that said, 'You're in, I *know* you're in, and I'm not leaving here until you open the bloody door.'

But nobody did.

He knocked again, even more insistently. This time, he thought he heard a single faint wuff from somewhere further back in the house, but then silence came rushing back in.

Logan was about to ask DS Khaled if he'd heard anything, then saw him take a sudden step back from the living room window, which he'd been cupping his hands against and peering through.

'Shite!' Hamza ejected. 'In there. On the floor.'

Logan stepped onto the grass and made his way to the window. He cupped his hands just like Hamza had, and looked in through a gap in the blinds.

There was a shoe on the floor, lying on its side.

It took him a moment to spot that there was also a foot in it, attached to a dark-trousered leg. The rest of the body— *person*, he corrected, because it was too early to go making assumptions—lay out of sight behind a floral-patterned couch.

He ran back to the door without a word, checked the handle and found it locked. 'Get around the back,' he barked. 'See if it's open.'

Hamza hesitated, but only for a moment. As he set off running, Logan stepped back, squaring up to the door. There were no convenient glass panels that he could break to reach the lock, so he was doing it the old-fashioned way.

He angled his body, braced his shoulder, and launched himself at the door.

As well as being windowless—or possibly precisely because of this—it was a heavy, steadfast bastard of a thing, and didn't budge so much as a millimetre. If anything, it only seemed more determined than ever to keep him out.

Aye, well, he'd see about that.

He tried the shoulder again, hissed at the pain that went radiating through his ribs and up his back, and decided it might be best to try another approach.

Stepping back, he brought a foot up and fired it at the door, just as it was opened from the other side. He heard—and very much felt—his tendons stretching as he overshot the target, and DS Khaled jumped back just in time to avoid the heel of a size thirteen boot slamming directly into his groin.

'Fuck's sake! Bit of warning!' Logan hissed, limping into the house.

'Sorry, sir,' Hamza said. 'Back door was unlocked, so I just thought—'

Logan waved the apology away and went hurpling into the living room. A man lay on the floor, looking about as dead as

70

dead could be. His face resembled a sack of tatties, all bumps and lumps, and very few of them in the right places. It was the sort of face that would make the Elephant Man suck air in through his teeth and mutter, 'Look at the fucking state of that.'

Blood had congealed around his mouth and nose. It had also run from a gash around one eye socket so that it drew a snaking line down the side of his face and filled an ear.

A metal bar, like a metre-long piece of scaffolding, lay beside him and across one arm, suggesting it had been dropped after he'd hit the ground. The murder weapon, presumably, judging by the film of blood on it.

Hamza dropped to his knees, felt for a pulse, and took out his phone all in one fluid motion. He clearly had things in hand, so Logan backed out of the room. No point in them both contaminating the place any further. They'd dragged enough grass inside with them as it was, and Logan could almost picture Palmer's face, boiled beetroot red with rage.

Besides, there had been a bark, he was sure of it. High-pitched and muffled behind one of the bungalow's doors.

Logan crept through the L-shaped hallway, fishing gloves from his pocket and pulling them on. This was a crime scene, and he had to treat it as such, but first, he had to make sure there were no other surprises lurking inside the house.

The glass-panelled door to the kitchen through which Hamza had entered still stood open. The bark hadn't come from there, then. He tried one of the other doors, found only a cupboard containing a hot water tank, and moved on.

The moment he opened the next door, something knee-high and hairy came racing out at him, all yelps, and woofs, and whines. A dog, definitely, though it was of no obvious make and model. Its fur was a mongrel patchwork of white and gold up front, graduating to a muddy sort of brown colour by the time it reached the tip of its stubby tail, which was currently spinning like a propeller. Drop it in the North Sea, Logan reckoned, and it'd be in Norway before the day was out.

Its ears were raised and perky. Its tongue lolled around like it was three inches longer than it was meant to be, and five times as heavy. It sniffed experimentally at Logan's feet, barked twice at them, then pawed at his shin through his trousers.

It was young, he thought, judging by the way its paws looked too big for the rest of it, and its hair was as much fuzz as it was fur.

There was blood on the back of its neck from an inch-long wound that didn't currently seem to be causing it any problems. The microchip. Someone had cut the animal open so they could remove the microchip.

For reasons he couldn't quite explain, and despite everything he'd seen that day, this bothered him more than the rest of it. He reached down to pat the animal, but it skitted back into the room, yipping in fright.

Logan pushed the door the rest of the way open and followed, dropping his voice into a low, reassuring murmur.

'You're OK. Calm down. You're...'

The tang of stale urine filled the room, rising from dark spots on the carpet. There was another smell, too, though. Stronger. More nauseating.

She lay on top of the bed, a pillow over her face, the contents of her bladder and bowels staining the sheet around her. Her long, floral nightdress had been pulled up enough to reveal her wrinkled legs and varicose veins, but not so high that she was fully exposed.

He held his breath, carefully picked his way closer to the bed, then squatted so he could see beneath the pillow. The dog, thinking this was some sort of game, trotted over and tried to clamber up onto one of his knees.

'Aye, I see you. Piss off,' he said, gently pushing the animal back.

From the bed, a dead woman looked at him. Once the pressure on the pillow had been removed, her head must have fallen to the side, so he was staring straight into her glassy, empty eyes.

'Sir! Sir!' Hamza appeared in the doorway, his mobile jammed against his ear. 'He's alive. The guy in the living room, I've got a pulse.' He jumped back as the dog hurtled towards him like some hairy bullet. 'The fuck?'

Logan held a hand out, stopping the DS from coming any further. 'I'm glad yours is alive, son.' Logan sighed. 'Because mine sure as hell isn't.'

Chapter 12

Moira Corson sat in her chair by the living room window, complaining about the temperature, strength, and colour of her tea. It had been over a month now since her stroke, and while she was showing encouraging signs of recovery, she still wasn't able to do a whole lot for herself.

Ben had made the tea. He was starting to wish that he hadn't bothered.

His relationship with Moira was on the one hand simple, and on the other incredibly complicated.

It was simple because, all things considered, he barely knew the woman. She worked the front desk at the Fort William polis station, and seemed to live to make life difficult for everyone else in the building.

And woe betide any officers turning up from somewhere else—Inverness, say—looking to gain entry. It wasn't just that she insisted on all the correct paperwork being completed, Ben was sure she invented entirely new forms for them to complete, just to make it more of a challenge.

And that was where it all started to get a little more complicated.

He'd heard about her stroke during the last case, and when he'd discovered that nobody from the station had bothered their arse to visit her in hospital, he'd taken it upon himself to swing by and check on her.

She had seemed thoroughly annoyed to see him, but he had decades of experience of dealing with headstrong women, and had waited out the worst of her resentment. They had found common ground over one of the magazines he'd brought for her, and she'd even helped bring the team a step closer to solving their case.

When she was well enough, she'd been sent home to an empty house. A nurse and a home help both came in multiple times a day, but Moira wasn't exactly surrounded by friends and family, and Ben had felt compelled to book himself into a nearby hotel for a few days, and to help her settle back in.

She had not been pleased. So she'd told him, anyway. But she hadn't told him to go, and both the nurse and home help had privately told him that she was brighter than they'd ever seen her.

Given the dour look on her coupon, and the way she moaned about pretty much anything and everything in the world, Ben would've hated to see her on a bad day.

'You put the milk in first, didn't you?' Moira said, sniffing her tea like he might also have slipped some cyanide into it. 'That's what you've done. Well, I can't drink that.'

She started to set the mug down on the little folding table that had been slotted over the armrest of her chair, but her hand shook with the weight of it, and a big glug of it spilled into the cup-sized indent in the wood.

'Now look!' she spat, like this whole thing was somehow Ben's fault. 'It's gone everywhere.'

'Maybe if you'd just quit your bloody whinging and drink it, that wouldn't have happened,' Ben said.

Moira looked utterly aghast for a moment, then gave a grunt and a shrug of her uneven shoulders. 'Aye. Maybe,' she conceded.

'And no, I didn't put the milk in first,' Ben told her. He had discovered that, savage as she could be, she actually took quite well to him standing up to her. 'I'm no' a bloody animal. I do know how to make a cup of tea.'

'Not judging by this, you don't,' Moira told him.

'Aye, well, when you're up and about you can show me how it's done.'

Her lips thinned at that. She looked at the spillage on the tray, then further down to where one leg flopped limply against the side of the chair. '*Up and about.* Aye. We'll see.'

'The nurse says you're doing well,' Ben assured her.

'She's got no bloody right talking to you about any of it,' Moira retorted. 'I could have her fired for that if I wanted.'

Ben smiled. He was getting to know her. Like their relationship, she was straightforward on one level, but complex on so many others. 'Aye, but you don't.'

'Just as well for her sake,' Moira said. She raised her arm as Ben moved in with a cloth and mopped up the spilled tea.

'You'll no' be wanting another one, since that one was so bad,' he said.

'I'm trusting you can do better,' Moira replied. 'And that you don't put the milk in first this time.'

'I didn't put the bloody milk in—'

There was a look on her face that he rarely saw. It wasn't a smile—that would be stretching things into the realms of fantasy—but it was a precursor to one. It was an expression that anticipated the possibility of a smile at some point in the future.

'Right, fine. Wait here,' he said, getting up and heading for the kitchen.

Moira waited. Her options were pretty limited in that regard, anyway.

A few minutes later, the kettle clicked, liquid sloshed, and Ben returned with a tray containing a cup, a small teapot, and a half-full 500ml milk carton with a blue lid.

'Right, here we are,' he said, and she grumbled as he set the tray on her lap. 'Make it your bloody self.'

Something flashed behind Moira's eyes. Betrayal, maybe, or fear.

'How am I meant to do that? I've got no strength in my arm.'

'Aye, but you've got another one,' Ben pointed out.

Moira sniffed and turned her nose up at the tray. 'I'm not in the mood for tea now, anyway.'

'Don't talk shite, aye you are,' Ben said. He nodded to the contents of the tray. 'Come on.'

If looks could kill, DI Forde wouldn't just have died on the spot, he'd have been cut up, fed to pigs, then been poured as excrement into a shallow, unmarked grave. He shrugged the glare off, though, and tapped the side of the teapot.

'It's going to be stewed, if you don't get a shifty on.'

'And what happens if I spill it everywhere?'

'You'll get wet,' Ben said. He looked quite pleased with that reply, until a thought troubled him. 'And possibly scalded. Actually, maybe—'

He stopped, mid-reach, when she wrapped her fingers around the handle of the teapot. She was using her good arm, of course—the other had a long way to go until it was in any fit state to lift anything—but her movements were still clumsy, and concentration pushed her eyebrows down into a knot.

She gave the teapot a swirl, then carefully brought the spout closer to her cup.

'That's it. That's you,' Ben said.

This earned him a sharp look, and an even sharper, 'I don't need a bloody cheerleader!'

He mimed zipping his lip and then watched as Moira poured just over half a cup of tea. He saw the panic in her eyes then, and she tipped the pot back before she accidentally overfilled the cup.

Ben moved to take the teapot from her then, but she stuck out an elbow to fend him off, and managed to place it back on the tray without any help.

The milk was less of a struggle, being far lighter, and lacking that element of danger inherent in the boiling water.

'There you go!' Ben said. 'You did it. You managed.'

'Course I bloody managed. It was pouring a cup of tea, not building the pyramids,' Moira snapped, but Ben could tell she was pleased, even if she wasn't saying so. Or, for that matter, showing it in any way.

His phone buzzed in his pocket. Moira watched him as she sipped her milky tea.

'Jack, hello. How are…?'

Ben listened. The smile he'd had plastered on his face while watching Moira pouring her tea faded at the edges, then fell away completely.

'Aye. No. I understand,' he said. He checked his watch. 'About two hours.' He listened again, shot Moira a look of apology, then gave a nod. 'I'm on my way.'

–

Tyler stood over a kitchen worktop, inexpertly coating a small piece of chicken with a lot of breadcrumbs. This first involved dipping the chicken into some beaten egg, then into flour, then into egg again, before finally swiping it through the plate of Ruskoline.

Somehow, despite this being a fairly localised activity, the kitchen looked like a bomb had recently gone off in it.

The flour had been the main problem. There had been a small tear in the bottom of the bag that left a gunpowder trail across the kitchen floor from one end to the other. This would've been bad enough, but upon realising what was happening, Tyler had instinctively turned the bag upside down, forgetting that it was open at the top.

Things had not gone much better with the eggs.

And, cards on the table, there had been a mishap with the bottle of vegetable oil, too, which meant that roughly seventy percent of the kitchen floor was now an ice rink, and getting to the fridge would almost certainly require crampons.

'Is dinner nearly ready?' Harris called from the living room, where he was kneeling by the coffee table, doing that day's homework.

'Not long now, buddy!' Tyler called back. 'I've just got to finish prepping it. And then, you know, cook it.'

'Did you remember to put the oven on?'

'Of course!'

Tyler put the oven on.

From the living room, he heard the phone ringing.

'That's the phone,' Harris announced.

'I can hear that,' Tyler replied. He looked at his hands. The fingers of each were coated with a thick, congealing mixture of egg and flour. He shuffled to the sink and tried to turn on the tap, first with his elbows, then with his wrists.

The phone continued to ring.

'Want me to answer it?' Harris shouted through.

'Yes, please!'

He wrestled the tap on, turned the handle too far, and a jet of water thundered against the base of the sink, hit a bowl he'd dumped in there earlier, and went spraying in all directions.

'Fuck, fuck, fuck!'

Tyler shoved a hand under the running water until it stripped most of the gunk from his fingers, then turned off the tap. Water dripped from the metal window blinds and pooled on the worktop.

'Great,' he sighed, then he jumped with fright when Harris appeared at his back, holding the phone out to him.

'It's Sinead,' Harris said. 'She wants to talk to you.'

Tyler looked around for somewhere to dry his one clean hand, failed to find a towel, so wiped it on Harris's jumper, instead.

'Hey!' The boy laughed, shrugging him off.

Tyler grinned, took the phone, then pinned it between his shoulder and his ear. 'Hiya, what's up?'

As he listened to the reply, he looked around at the kitchen. The blizzard of flour. The slug-trail of egg. The puddles of water.

'Yeah, we're fine,' he said. 'I was just starting on dinner.'

He listened again, and this time the state of the kitchen was quickly forgotten.

'Bloody hell. Sounds major,' he said. 'So, I take it you're going to be late home? I can get...' He frowned, then looked down at himself. 'Me? I mean... aye. Aye, I'm fine. Just in the office. Aye. No, I can definitely do that.' His eyes flitted to where Harris stood listening in. 'She'll pick him up? OK! Well, I'll go jump in the shower, then. Or walk gingerly into the shower, I mean.'

He said his goodbyes, hung up the phone, then let out the sigh of a man thrilled to have been relieved of kitchen duties.

'Sorry, buddy, you're going to have to go stay with your Auntie Val tonight. She'll get you a KFC, or something.'

'Why?' Harris asked. 'Where are you going?'

'Me?' Tyler stood up straight, put his hands on his hips, and puffed out his chest. In an ideal world, the light reflecting off his toothy grin would've gone 'ting'. 'I'm going back to work!'

Chapter 13

Logan waited at the scene until the ambulance had left, and Shona had arrived to examine the dead woman in the bedroom. By then, the whole street was alive with spinning blue lights, webs of cordon tape, and legions of uniformed officers.

Faces peered out through the windows of neighbouring houses, all adopting an expression meant to suggest that they looked outside at this time every evening, and the fact that an army of polis was there was merely coincidental timing.

The SOC team had arrived just a few minutes before Shona. It was, to Logan's relief, lacking a Geoff Palmer. Palmer had always been a stickler for timekeeping, especially when it was for his own benefit. It was a very rare occasion when he'd tack an extra couple of hours onto the end of his shift, and if he had something else planned? Forget it.

Right now, he'd presumably be waiting in the wings at his comedy gig. The thought of his imminent humiliation had helped Logan stave off the worst of the cold from the cooling evening air.

A Uniform had taken the dog to the nearest vet to have the wound on the back of its neck looked at and stitched up. It had barked from the moment it was taken from Logan, to the moment it was returned to his side. At which point, it snuffled in circles for a few moments, licked one of his shoes, then sat down in front of him, looking up.

The vet had confirmed that the chip had been cut out of the animal. There had, as far as she could tell, been nothing in the way of anaesthetic used, though the blade that had made the cut had been surgery-sharp.

Once the machinations of a crime scene investigation were fully underway, Logan headed for his car, opened the door, and watched the little dog attempt to jump into the footwell.

'Where the hell do you think you're going?' he asked, as it stood on its hind legs and stretched its front paws up onto the car's door sill.

The dog tilted its head all the way back to look at him, and was temporarily blinded when its tongue flopped out so far it covered its eyes.

'You can't come with me,' Logan said. He bent and picked it up with one hand, and the dog shivered with excitement as he tucked it into the crook of his arm. 'Here, we'll find someone else to deal with you.'

He turned to look for someone to take the dog off his hands. Not the guys in the paper suits, obviously. Not Shona, either. She was still in the house going over the body, and would likely have a long night ahead of her.

Most of the Uniforms were already on door to door, and those who weren't were standing guard at cordons, or running around like chickens with their heads cut off.

'There must be some bugger who can hold onto you,' Logan said, which earned another quizzical head turn from the dog.

Logan looked down at the pup, sighed, then opened the back door of the car and set the animal down in the footwell. 'Right. Stay there. We'll find someone to deal with you back at the station.'

He closed the back door, opened the driver's one, and got in to find the dog sitting on the front passenger seat, panting happily.

'How the f—?' he asked, craning to look into the back, like he expected to find a second, identical dog sitting where he'd left it.

When he didn't, he pulled on his seatbelt and shot the animal a warning look. 'Aye, well, just you stay where you are while

I'm driving. And if you shite anywhere, yer bum's right oot the windae.'

By the time Logan was back in the Incident Room, Tyler and Ben had both arrived to make up the team's numbers. Logan started to apologise for calling them both in, but both men made a beeline for the dog and fussed over it so much it peed on the carpet through sheer excitement.

'Nicely done, gents,' Logan told them. 'I hope one of you is planning on cleaning that up?'

'Can't bend down boss,' Tyler said, cupping his groin.

'Aye, nor me,' said Ben, putting a hand on his back and wincing.

'You were both bending down patting the bloody thing two seconds ago!' Logan retorted, but both men just smiled and returned to their desks, each milking their respective 'disability' for all it was worth.

'Nice dog,' Tyler said, carefully lowering himself into his chair. 'Yours?'

'Course it's not mine,' Logan said, snorting like this was the single most ridiculous suggestion he'd ever heard. 'It was at the scene. Think it belonged to the female victim. Can't get rid of the bastard.'

'It's a bitch,' Ben said.

'Aye, it's that, all right,' Logan agreed.

'No, I mean the dug. It's no' a bastard, it's a bitch. It's female.'

Logan looked down at the dog. It stared adoringly up at him, as if hanging on his every word. 'How do you know that without looking?'

'I am looking.'

'I mean at the *key identifying elements*.'

'Well, I mean, you can tell, can't you?' Ben said, gesturing to the pup. 'Shape of the head. Size of the body. You can just see.'

Logan picked the dog up with one hand, turned it upside down, then set it down again.

'Aye, well, the genitalia would seem to disagree with your assessment there, Benjamin,' he said. 'On second thoughts, I'm no' sure we need your keen detective instincts here, after all.'

'You sure it's no' female? It looks female,' Ben insisted.

Logan picked the dog up again and presented its undercarriage for the DI to see. The puppy gave his hand a lick with its ridiculous tongue.

'Aye, that's a boy, right enough,' Ben conceded. He shrugged. 'It'll be a wee gay dog, though. Wait and see.'

'That's nobody's business but its own,' Logan said, setting the dog down again. Its stubby tail thumped against the floor a few times, like it was waiting for the ride to start again. 'Anyone fancy looking after it?'

'I'd love to, boss,' Tyler said. 'But mobility's not exactly my strong point right now. Maybe when I'm—'

'We're not getting a dog!' Sinead called out from over by the stationery cupboard. She emerged with a bundle of index cards and sticky notes, and headed for the Big Board.

'What about you, Ben?' Logan asked, but DI Forde was already shaking his head. Logan would not be deterred. 'Be a bit of company for you.'

'I'm quite happy with my own company, thank you very much,' Ben said. 'Besides, there's no saying what size it's going to get to. Could need a lot more walking than I'm capable of.'

'My arse. You could walk the length of bloody Britain,' Logan said, still trying to talk him round.

'Only if it was all downhill,' Ben said. 'They didn't put me on heart medication for the good of my health, you know.' He winced. 'I mean… that's exactly why they put me on it, obviously, but you know what I'm saying.'

'Hamza, how about—?'

'No can do, sir. Amira's terrified of them.'

'She'll grow out of that,' Logan insisted.

Hamza shook his head. 'I doubt that, sir. She's thirty-seven. Amira's my wife.'

Logan's eyes widened in horror, but he was prevented from digging the hole any deeper by the arrival of Constable Dave Davidson who chose that moment to throw open the double doors and wheel himself into the room.

'Relax, everyone, cavalry's here,' he announced.

Logan swooped down, picked up the puppy, and cradled it in his arms in a way designed to make it look as adorable as possible.

'Dave! The very man!' the DCI said. 'How would you like a dug?'

Dave stopped just inside the room, and the doors swung closed behind him. 'What sort of dug?'

Logan's flicked his gaze in the dog's direction. 'Well... this sort.'

Dave wheeled himself a little closer and squinted at the puppy. 'Nah,' he said, wrinkling his nose. 'Not interested.'

'Why not?'

'Looks a bit simple.'

'Simple?' Logan frowned. 'It's a dug. What's it meant to be doing? Calculus? He's smarter than he looks. He's a modern-day Taggart, this one.'

'Nah,' Dave said, not buying it. 'He looks thick as mince. And are you sure it's a "he"? Looks a bit feminine.'

'That's what I said,' Ben chipped in.

'But we've established you were wrong. He's definitely a "he",' Logan said.

'We think probably gay, though,' Ben added.

'No, *you* think he's gay!'

'What, you saying you don't?' Ben asked, looking highly doubtful.

'I'm saying it's... I mean... Can dogs even be gay?' Logan asked, then he pinched the bridge of his nose between finger and thumb, shook his head, and sighed. 'Jesus. Fine. Forget it.

We'll put him to the dog warden later. For now, just try and avoid standing on or rolling over the bugger.'

He placed the dog back down on the floor. It sat looking up at him for a few moments, then quickly got fed up of that and set off following a scent around the room.

'Right, first up, thank you to DI Forde and DC Neish for cutting short their time off, and for coming in at such short notice. Tyler in particular. Took a lot of balls for you to get up out of your sickbed, son.'

Tyler cracked a smile. 'Good one, boss.'

'Aye, took some stones that, right enough,' Dave agreed.

'Personally, I think he's nuts,' Hamza said.

Tyler sat back and made a beckoning motion for the jokes to keep coming. 'Right, let's get them out of the way,' he urged.

'Careful,' Ben warned. 'Sounds like he's starting to get a bit *testes*.'

From the door, there came the sound of a throat being cleared. Logan didn't have to look to recognise the unwelcome sound of Detective Superintendent Mitchell. He could sense her displeasure from here.

'I'm sure you don't need to be reminded that two people are dead, and one is in a critical condition in hospital,' Mitchell said. 'I hardly think now is the right time to be making jokes about DC Neish's recent medical procedure.'

Everyone else had carefully avoided turning to look at the Detective Superintendent, leaving it to Logan to offer a reply.

'No, ma'am. You're right, ma'am. Understood.'

'Good,' Mitchell said. 'Now, stop behaving like prize plums, and get back to it.'

There was silence as she left the room and the door swung closed behind her.

It was Tyler who eventually spoke.

'Did she just make a bollocks joke?'

'Oh, I don't know, son,' Logan said, taking a seat. 'For a first effort, I didn't think it was that bad…'

Chapter 14

He rose from the depths, gasping for the light. He couldn't get there. Couldn't reach it. Not now. Not yet.

And so, he retreated down into the dark. Waiting. Healing. Coming slowly back to life, minute by minute, day by day.

Getting stronger. Becoming whole.

No. Not whole. Not like he was. Not like before.

Nothing like before.

He saw flashes of movement. Heard words whispered in his ears. Understood none of it.

A word grew on his cracked and broken lips, but speech was still a long way off.

He opened his eyes, and it was night. Blinked, and it was morning.

There was sunshine. Rain. Days passed between wheezed breaths. Ghosts danced past his bed like a time-lapse video, leaving streaks of light that hung in the air behind them, and gradually faded back into shadow.

And the word on his lips continued to grow.

Sometimes, he didn't know what had woken him. Other times, like now, it was the pain. It burned and hissed and sizzled in his chest, up his throat, and spewed into his mouth and nose like he was vomiting some potent acid and swallowing it back down.

He tensed. Coiled. Thrashed. Opened his mouth to shout, but all that emerged was an animal squeal.

A hand—no, a claw—grasped at the darkness around him, searching for something that would end his suffering, make it stop. It found nothing. No one. Unoccupied space in an empty room.

He stretched further. Tried to, anyway. But a cuff on his wrist tightened, and another jolt of agony arched his back and cramped his lungs.

He coughed, spluttered, hacked, choking on the tubes that filled his airways and swelled in his throat. Breaths became short. Wet. Suffocating. He thrashed on the bed, some primal instinct to cling to life overriding the pain, blocking it out.

The world burst into light, bright, and brilliant, and agonising. He tried to close his eyes, but they wouldn't. Couldn't. His head snapped sideways, trying to get away from the burning ball of fire above him.

'Oh dear, someone's in a fine mess.'

He felt the voice more than heard it. Imagined it, possibly.

There was a pinprick, sharp in his arm.

Warmth, then. Peace.

And, as he succumbed to it, the word burst as a bubble of spit on his lips.

'*Ma…lysh…ka.*'

Chapter 15

It was almost seven by the time they were assembled in front of the Big Board. Technically, it was now two Big Boards, a second having been wheeled in from another Incident Room when one proved not enough to contain all the mounting information. Sinead had positioned them side by side, making one double-width board on which to lay everything out.

Tyler had made a couple of wisecracks about Hamza's mismatched shoes, to which Hamza had replied, 'Better my shoes than my bollocks' to some laughter from everyone, Tyler included.

Logan had then broken Tyler in gently by putting him in charge of phoning in pizzas, since none of them were getting home for a proper home-cooked meal anytime soon. He had handled the task admirably, and was officially welcomed back onto the team.

Everyone was now fully fed and watered, with the exception of Dave, who was still working his way through the leftovers, and the dog, who, despite his small stature, appeared to have a stomach like a bottomless pit.

Logan had urged the others not to feed him, or he'd 'only end up shiteing all over the floor.'

He had also asked them not to feed the dog, either.

After Logan's earlier comments where he'd tried to big up the dog's intelligence, they'd settled on Taggart as a name. It suited him fine, given that he was small, tenacious, and—as Dave had discovered when he'd first tried to pat him—could be a right vicious bastard, if provoked.

While Dave munched and the dog watched him hopefully, Sinead took to the floor in front of the Big Boards and started to spell out what they knew so far.

'So, latest news on the male victim found in the house on Ballifeary Road,' she began, glancing up from her notes to a photograph of the man she had pinned to the board. It had been taken at the scene, and showed the full horror show that was his face. 'He's stable, but critical. Still non-responsive, and it's not looking like we're going to get any answers from him anytime soon, if ever. Doctors say his injuries were the sort of thing they'd expect to see as the result of a car accident.'

'Christ, look at the nick of that,' said Dave, chewing noisily on a slice of Hawaiian.

'Poor bugger,' Ben remarked, quickly averting his gaze from the picture.

It would've been easier to look at if the man was dead—he wouldn't have thought twice about it then—but there was something about him being alive that made it harder to stomach. In this job, you learned to flick the switch that turned a dead body into a thing. An element in a puzzle to be solved.

That became much harder when the person was still alive. Knowing that this unfortunate bastard was still suffering made the photograph feel uncomfortably voyeuristic.

'Did they give you a list?' Logan asked, and the dog's tail thumped the floor at the sound of his voice.

Sinead flicked through her paperwork. 'They did, yeah,' she said, then she recounted the details the nurse at Raigmore had given her about his injuries. It took a full minute, then a further thirty seconds of silence while they all processed the information.

'Fuck,' Tyler muttered, which quite neatly summed up how the others were feeling.

'Do we have a name for him yet?' DI Forde asked.

'We do.' Sinead flicked pages again. 'Conrad Howden. Age thirty-nine. His mother's Margaret Howden. Maggie. Age eighty-one.'

'The woman in the bedroom?' Logan guessed.

'That's the one, sir,' Sinead confirmed. 'PM is scheduled for tomorrow morning, but initial examination suggests she was suffocated, probably around forty-eight to seventy-two hours ago.'

'Presumably the son was attacked at the same time?' said Ben. 'So he's been lying there all that time?'

'Potentially.'

'Still nothing from the neighbours?' Hamza asked. 'Nobody see anyone coming or going?'

Sinead deferred to Tyler with a nod and a point, following up with Uniform at the scene having been his second task, after the pizza order.

'Nothing concrete,' he said. 'Apparently the son is in and out most days, though. Mrs Howden herself didn't leave the house much in recent months.'

'Where did the dog come into it?' asked Logan, and the pup turned to look at him like he'd called it by name.

He pointedly ignored it. It was the only way the bugger was going to learn.

'Conrad brought it home a couple of weeks back, apparently. She told the woman next door about it. Said her son wanted her to have company when he wasn't around.'

'Was he meant to be going somewhere, like?' Tyler asked.

'No. Not that we know. But he didn't live with her, and apparently couldn't get over as often as he liked. He mentioned to one of the neighbours that his shifts are a bit all over the place. He's a labourer.' She anticipated the next question before anyone could come out with it. 'We haven't got a home address for him yet, but we're working on it. Expecting it any minute.'

Logan rose from his chair, which made the dog stand up, too. It followed him to the Big Boards, then lay down in the most awkward spot it could find, like it was deliberately trying to get itself stood on.

He brushed it out of the way with the side of a foot. Taggart didn't react other than to raise his head and look around at his new surroundings, then he curled himself up so the tip of his nose was resting on the base of his tail, and fell asleep.

'The timing's interesting,' Logan announced, studying the information pinned to the rectangle of cork. 'If we're saying Mrs Howden and her son were attacked forty-eight hours ago, that's pretty much the same time that Borys Wozniak was murdered.'

'Why's that interesting, boss?' Tyler asked.

'Well, presumably they cut the chip out of the dog either shortly before or shortly after they killed Mrs Howden. They then inserted it into Borys' foot. If Shona's estimates are right, that was all around the same time.'

'Busy afternoon for one man,' Ben remarked.

'We've already got multiple bastards in the frame,' Logan replied. 'Borys' injuries seem to have been inflicted by at least two people. Or... no. The stitches in his arm seem to have been applied by someone different to whoever inflicted the injuries. The injuries were frenzied and violent. The stitches were carefully applied by someone who knew what they were doing.'

'Could be a split personality, boss,' Tyler suggested. 'One guy, but different people, sort of thing.'

'*Or* just someone with a temper,' Sinead suggested, offering a less fantastical explanation. 'Inflicted the injuries in a blind rage, but did the first aid stuff when calmer.'

'Maybe,' Logan said. 'But Borys was held down by more than one set of hands while he was being injected.'

'Injected?' said Ben, who was still catching up on the case so far.

'Waiting on toxicology, but heroin, we think,' Logan explained. 'We thought there was a big bag of it in his car, but—'

'That was sherbet. Aye, I read that bit,' said Ben. He looked up, becoming lost in thought. 'God, when was the last time I had sherbet? Must be years.'

'Remember Dib Dabs?' Tyler asked the room at large. 'Wee bag of sherbet, but with the lolly stick thing that you licked?'

'What was the one with liquorice in it? It was yellow, I think, with a big sort of fuse of liquorice down the middle?'

'Sherbet Fountain,' said Dave, gnawing away at the crust of a leftover pizza slice.

Ben clapped and pointed at the constable. 'Yes! That's it! Sherbet Fountain!' he cried, then he shook his head. 'Hated those bloody things. Alice couldn't get enough of them, though. Them and those flying saucers. With the sherbet inside. The wee flying saucers. What were they called?'

'Flying Saucers,' said Tyler.

'Aye, what were they called, though?'

Logan cleared his throat with such force the dog stood up, barked once, then wandered over to see if Dave had dropped any bits of pizza on the floor. To Taggart's evident dismay, he had not.

'Can we…?' Logan said, indicating the boards with a thumb. He waited for everyone to look suitably contrite, before continuing. 'Thank you. So the microchip was clearly stuck in Borys for a reason. The killers wanted us to find Mrs Howden's address, which meant they wanted us to find her and her son. Why? What's the connection?'

There was no response from the rest of the team. Sinead turned over a few sheets on her clipboard, scanned her notes, then shook her head. 'Nothing obvious.'

'Then we get out our shovels and dig. The connection might not be obvious, but it's there somewhere. We just need to keep looking until we find it. Hamza, I want you taking lead.' He gave the DS a fraction of a second to consider this, then asked, 'You all right with that?'

'No problem, sir. I'll get right on it.'

'Good lad. Tyler's office-bound for obvious reasons, so use him where you can, but I want him looking into the note found in the first vic's car, too. I want to know what it means.'

'I don't have to just be in the office, boss,' Tyler said.

'What?' Sinead glared at him. 'Yes, you do.'

'Aye, no. I mean, I'm just saying... I can move around.'

'You walk like a hundred-year-old man who's just shat himself, son,' Logan pointed out. 'Can hardly have you pounding the beat in that state. You're here to be useful, and you're useful in here. Is that understood, Detective Constable?'

Tyler nodded. Given the narrow-eyed glare he was getting from Sinead, this may have been some long-dormant self-preservation instinct finally kicking in. 'Understood, boss.'

'Good. Sinead, you're with me. We're going back to the house to see what we can find. I doubt we'll be getting much back from Palmer's team or pathology tonight, so we'll have to rely on good old-fashioned detective work.'

'I'm great at that sort of stuff, boss,' Tyler ventured. 'You sure you don't want—?'

'Quite sure, DC Neish, quite sure,' Logan told him. 'And, for the record, you're no' that good at that sort of stuff. Or if you are, you've done a bloody good job of hiding it so far.'

With that, Logan went sweeping towards the door, forcing Sinead to hurry to keep up with his big strides.

Behind them, the puppy noticed Logan was leaving and set off in a scampering chase after him. Taggart dashed forward as the swing doors started to close, and gave a yip of triumph when he made it through the gap with half a second to spare.

A moment later, the door opened just enough for a hand to deposit the animal back inside the Incident Room, then turn it around so its nose was pointing towards the rest of the team.

Logan's voice boomed through the gap. 'And will somebody *please* keep an eye on this bloody dog?'

Chapter 16

Logan pulled the BMW up outside Maggie Howden's house. The street lights blazed along the road, fighting a losing battle against the ever-advancing night.

The cordon tape that had blocked the street earlier was now confined to the immediate surroundings of the house. A solitary Uniform stood close by the front door, using the slight protrusion of the building above him to shield himself from the big, fat drops of rain that had started to fall.

There were two polis cars parked directly ahead of where Logan had stopped, so presumably at least one other constable was roaming around somewhere, making sure things were in order. That's what they did, constables. They kept an eye on the status quo and helped to tip the world back towards it when required. This was either a very, very good thing, or a very, very bad one. It all depended on who you asked.

'This is us,' Logan announced, in case the lingering polis presence and the 'CRIME SCENE – DO NOT CROSS' tape wasn't enough of a hint. 'I'll head in. I want you to have a poke around out here first. Figure out which houses had the best view of this one. Check for any direct lines of sight.'

'Want me to look out the back, too?' Sinead suggested. 'There's a back garden. Would've been an easier way for the killer to get in and out.'

'Aye, check that out, see what you see, then come in and join me,' Logan instructed. 'Obviously, if you find anything, shout.'

'Obviously,' Sinead said. 'Same goes for you.'

Logan nodded. 'Right then, see you in there shortly,' he said, then he threw open the BMW's door, ducked under the cordon tape, and stormed off up the path.

Sinead got out of the car, fired off two quick texts—one to her Auntie Val, and the other to Harris reminding him to brush his teeth—then she crossed the street, took out her notepad, and set to work casing the joint.

There were no trees or bushes in front of the house, so the front door and windows were visible from at least four other houses on the other side of the street. Six, if the occupants were out in the garden. None of them had reported seeing anything unusual at the house. No strange vehicles. No strange men. No strangeness, full stop.

There were no driveways across from the bungalow, which meant getting any clear dashcam footage was unlikely. They'd already put out a call for anyone who'd been driving along the street around the estimated time of the attack to check their footage, but the chances of anything showing up were slim.

Still, it had helped before. Maybe they'd get lucky.

She took a couple of photos of the house from various angles, but with the night's darkness drawing in, they came out a little grainy. Clear enough for reference purposes, though.

With the photos taken, she had a quick scout around for any doorbell or security cameras on the neighbouring addresses, then concluded that she'd got about as much as she could from out front, and headed around the side of the house to the back.

The garden at the rear of the bungalow was boxed in by a high wooden fence that could've done with a lick of wood preserver. More accurately, it could've done with a lick of wood preserver about five or six years ago, and now could do with being dismantled before an errant fart anywhere in the immediate vicinity caused it to collapse.

The gate opened with a bit of shoogling and the light application of a shoulder. It led into a low maintenance garden area that was mostly stone chips, but with a few raised beds that were currently cultivating a lot of weeds.

There was a small shed that gave the fence a run for its money on the dilapidation front, three bins of different colours, and a couple of cheap folding metal chairs with mesh bases and backs.

The far end of the garden—thirty or so feet away—was untouched by chips, as if whoever had been laying them had just run out and decided not to bother going back for another load.

Instead, it was a jungle of bushes and shrubs. There was another garden beyond it, belonging to the house that backed onto this one, but the mass of greenery made it impossible to tell if a fence separated them.

Light spilled from one of the rooms in Margaret Howden's bungalow, and from an upstairs window of the other house out back, but otherwise, the garden was in darkness, no street lights casting their glow around this side of the building.

Clicking on her torch, she checked the shed. It was locked with a rusty old padlock, but a quick look through the grimy, cobwebbed window revealed nothing of interest.

She turned her attention to the other house. From its upper floor, it would have a perfect view of the garden and the back of the bungalow. Someone would have knocked and asked if anyone had seen anything, she was sure, but she scribbled a note to double-check.

She was checking out the bushes when she heard the creak of the gate behind her, and the crunch of footsteps on gravel.

She turned, only for the beam of a torch to hit her straight in the face, obliterating her night vision and forcing her to throw a hand up to shield her eyes.

'Who's there?' a male voice demanded. 'Police! What do you think you're doing?'

'Detective Constable Sinead Nei—Bell,' Sinead said, remembering at the last moment that she was hanging onto her maiden name for work purposes. Two *DC Neishes* in one office would just get confusing. 'Can you stop shining that torch in my face, please?'

The torch held steady. The man holding it said nothing for several seconds, then slowly lowered the beam from her face to her chest.

'Ha. Sinead! Fancy seeing you here!'

Sinead felt a tingling spread up the back of her neck and across her head, like spiders crawling over her scalp.

A figure stepped forward, and the light from the cottage window picked out the details of his police constable's uniform.

'It's me. It's Jason,' he announced, smiling at her like they were old friends.

And they were. Technically. Sinead had first met PC Jason Hall back when they'd been training at Tulliallan. He'd seemed like a nice enough guy, for the most part, and they'd mixed in a few of the same social groups.

In recent months, though, it had become clear that he was jealous of her move into plain clothes. He had gone from making the odd snidey comment to being a full-scale creepy bastard, to the extent that she knew she should probably have reported him.

She should *definitely* have reported him, in fact, but had decided to handle it herself. This had involved questioning his manhood, telling him to fuck off, and then hoping that he got the hint and stayed out of her way.

Unfortunately, Inverness wasn't a very big place. Avoiding anyone forever was difficult. When you worked the same job? Damn near impossible.

And so, here they were.

'Look, I know I've said this before, but I'm really sorry about the way things ended between us.'

'What do you mean *ended between us*?' Sinead asked. 'There was no *us* for it to end between!'

God, was that the root of his problem with her? Had he seen some spark of romance that had never been there?

'What? No! Shit, sorry. No. I didn't mean...' Jason smiled. The light spilling from his torch turned the expression into something vaguely sinister. 'I meant last time we spoke. I was acting like a bit of an arsehole.'

'Yes,' Sinead agreed. 'You were.'

'Holding my hands up. I was completely out of line,' he said, raising the non-torch hand like he was turning himself in. 'It was a wee bit provoked, maybe, but… I get it. I understand why you reacted the way you did. Why you felt the need to speak to me like that. You know, like I was a piece of shit.'

Sinead watched PC Hall's eyebrows dip and his forehead crease. He gave a little shake of his head before his apology could get away from him.

'Anyway. Just wanted to say that I'm sorry. I am. I'm really sorry.' He fell silent for a second or two, then completely ruined it. 'You don't have to say it back, by the way. If you don't want to.'

'I wasn't going to,' Sinead told him.

For a moment, he just smiled at her, the torchlight deepening the shadows on his face. 'Quite right,' he said, then he gave her a nod and touched the peak of his cap. 'I'll leave you to it, then. But just shout if you need me.'

'I won't,' Sinead said, glaring him down.

'Right. Well,' Jason stood framed in the gate for a moment, now just a dark silhouette against the street beyond. 'You have a nice night.'

And then, whistling quietly, he turned and walked off, leaving Sinead alone in the garden.

She jumped when the back door to the house opened, and turned to see Logan leaning out from within the kitchen.

'What are you doing, counting the gravel?' he asked. 'Come on inside and help me look around.'

Sinead glanced back at the gate. In the distance, she could still make out PC Hall's shrill, tuneless whistle growing fainter.

'Coming, sir,' she said. Shivering in the cool night air, she followed the DCI inside.

Chapter 17

Detective Inspector Ben Forde sat in his chair in front of the Big Board, enjoying a cup of tea and a doorstop-thick slice of Battenberg cake. He'd bought the Battenberg for Moira the day before, but it turned out she had an aversion to marzipan.

Not only did she not enjoy the taste, but she also refused to tolerate anyone else eating it in her presence, so Ben had been forced to return it to the carrier bag he'd excitedly produced it from, and settle for some slightly stale Rich Tea biscuits with the cuppa he'd made them.

He'd brought the cake into the station with the full intention of sharing it with everyone, but when it became clear that Logan and Sinead were going to be leaving, he'd made the decision to hold it back.

One Battenberg between four people was a decent split. Between six? It'd hardly be worth the effort.

Hamza and Tyler had so far come up short on finding any connections between Borys Wozniak and either Conrad or Margaret Howden. They lived on opposite sides of the city, had no apparent blood relatives in common, and were unlikely to move in the same social circles.

Ben had suggested a brainstorm in front of the board, and the lure of coffee and cake had turned the suggestion from a tempting offer into a downright irresistible one.

'Right. Back to the start,' he said, once they were all sitting together, their chairs and Dave's wheelchair forming the four corners of a square. 'Connections. First thoughts. Go.'

'Same guy killed them,' Tyler suggested.

'Or guys,' Hamza said. 'Plural.'

'Or *girls*, plural,' added Dave. 'Let's not be sexist here.'

'What about the dog?' asked Tyler.

They all looked down at Taggart. He sat in the centre of the square, his neck craning as he attempted to track the movements of every piece of cake in the room.

Ben took a bite of his Battenberg. The dog's eyes tracked the cake's progress from Ben's plate to his mouth and back again like its head was equipped with guided missile technology.

'What about it?' the DI asked through a mouthful of sponge and marzipan.

'Could that be the connection, boss?' Tyler wondered. 'Like… if they took the chip out of the dog, maybe there was some reason for it. Maybe the dog's the key to it.'

Taggart turned his head to look at Tyler, saw that his plate was now empty, and shifted his attention in Hamza's direction, instead. The animal stared, tongue hanging out so far it was practically resting on the carpet.

'Can dogs eat marzipan?' Hamza asked.

Ben crammed the rest of his cake into his mouth before replying. 'I think so, aye.'

'They can't eat chocolate,' Tyler announced.

Hamza glanced at his cake. 'It's not made of chocolate, though.'

'I know. I was just saying. For future reference.'

'A bit of Battenberg's not going to kill it,' Dave said, though Hamza noted that he'd already hoovered up his own slice of cake and was now licking the ends of his fingers so he could more effectively pick up the crumbs. 'And if it does, it's probably for the best. If a wee bit of cake is going to end you, I doubt you were going to last very long in the real world, anyway.'

'I'm sure it'll be fine,' Hamza said.

He picked up his one remaining square of pink sponge and tossed it to the floor in front of Taggart. The dog sniffed at it for several seconds, then turned its nose up and wandered off between their chairs.

'The little bastard,' Hamza muttered. 'I was enjoying that, too.'

Ben slapped both hands on his knees, getting everyone's attention. 'Right. This is getting us nowhere. Connections. Connections. What have we got?'

'Have we got any more details through on the guy still in hospital?' Tyler asked. 'Might be something there.'

'Conrad,' said Hamza. He rolled his chair over to his desk. 'Not sure, I'll see if anything's come in.'

As Hamza started clicking and tapping at his computer, there was a knock at the Incident Room door and a uniformed sergeant popped his head inside.

'Hiya. This the room dealing with the body at the school?'

'That's us,' Ben said.

'Got a woman and her son here. They've got information. Thought you'd want to hear it.'

'Oh, shit!' Hamza cried. He realised everyone was looking at him and gave a dismissive wave. 'Sorry, not the mother and son thing. Just reading something.'

Ben turned back to the sergeant. 'Right. Set them up in interview room two, will you? Get them a cup of tea, or whatever. A Ribena.'

'The kid's about sixteen, I think.'

'Maybe no' a Ribena, then,' Ben said. 'Pint of heavy. Just make them comfortable, and we'll be right there.'

'Will do.'

Hamza held his tongue until the sergeant had slipped out of the room, then blurted out the information in the email he'd received.

'Conrad Howden. We've got his address. And that's not all we've got. Turns out, he's got a criminal record. Guess what for.'

Hamza realised his mistake as soon as the answers started to come in.

'Public defecation,' Dave said.

'Sex with a car,' suggested Tyler, not wishing to be outdone.

Hamza cut the contest dead before it could escalate further. 'Impersonating a police officer,' he said. 'He was claiming to be in the polis to seduce women.'

Ben snorted. 'He'd have been on a short shrift to nothing with that,' he said, and there was some murmured agreement from the other men in the room.

'Apparently not, though,' Hamza said. 'Initial complaint came from a twenty-four-year-old woman who'd bought right into it. He was knocking her off for six months before she sussed something wasn't right. He did a four month stretch for it.'

'Don't suppose you've got the woman's address, have you?' asked Dave. He cleared his throat. 'Purely for professional purposes, you understand…?'

'Joking aside, worth checking in with her,' Ben said. 'Unlikely she was involved, but you never know.'

'Should I take a snoop around at Conrad's place, too? Maybe talk to the neighbours?' He checked his watch. 'Although maybe better leaving it until the morning.'

'Aye. We'll do both first thing,' Ben agreed. He got to his feet. 'Right, better go and see what this woman and her son want to—Jesus!'

Ben diverted, mid-step, narrowly avoiding stepping on a lightly steaming curl of dog shit on the floor. Taggart lay on his back a few feet away, all four paws in the air like he was pretending to be dead.

'You clarty wee bugger,' the DI said, wagging a finger. 'Can someone get rid of this?'

'The shite or the dug?' Dave asked.

'The shite for now, but we'll keep our options open,' Ben said, shooting the dog a look that he hoped conveyed it was skating on some very thin ice. 'Tyler, you're with me. I want you in on this interview.'

'Me, boss?'

'Aye,' Ben confirmed. A smirk tugged up one corner of his mouth. 'I want to make a good impression, and walking next to you makes me look ten years younger.'

–

Logan stood just outside the door of Margaret Howden's bedroom, saying nothing. He watched, hands buried in the pockets of his coat, as Sinead stood a few paces inside the room, studying the details.

'*See*,' he told her. 'Don't just look.'

Sinead glanced back at him, nodded, then turned her attention back to the room before her.

The bed had been stripped bare, and there were a few stickers on the wall and plastic tent-shaped markers on the carpet pointing out various spots of interest. Logan had told her to ignore those, and instead focus on her own instincts.

He waited as she held up a printout he'd brought of the scene as it had been before the body had been removed and the white suits had moved in. She lined herself and the picture up, so their viewing angles matched.

'Thoughts?' Logan asked, once he felt she'd had long enough to ponder.

'There's no sign of forced entry at the window, and nothing to indicate a struggle took place other than on the bed,' Sinead observed. 'Only one side slept in, I'd say. In the picture, a pillow's missing from the other side. The side not slept in. That's the one used to smother her.'

'We haven't had final confirmation that she died of suffocation, but aye,' Logan confirmed. 'Palmer's team is doing tests on it.'

Sinead took a step closer to the door and lined herself up like she was entering the room for the first time.

'Right. So the killer comes in through the door.'

'Just the one killer?'

Sinead looked back at him, then around the room in case she was missing something obvious. 'Can't say for sure,' she concluded. 'But probably just one. She was an old woman, and frail, so it wouldn't have taken more than one person to hold her down.'

'You'd be surprised. People can fair put up a fight when their life's in danger. But I think you're probably right that there was only one.' He nodded for her to continue. 'Then?'

'Then he goes to the bed, picks up the pillow, and puts it over her face.' Sinead thought back to the photographs she'd seen of the scene before the body had been removed. 'She hadn't moved, so either she was sleeping, or he came in too quickly for her to react.'

'Or?'

'Or...' Sinead stared at the bed like the answer might be scratched into the headboard. 'Or... I don't know.'

'Aye, you do,' Logan told her, then he shut his mouth and waited.

'Or...'

It took a moment, then a light went on behind the DC's eyes.

'She knew her killer. She didn't move because she had no reason to be afraid of him.'

'Well done,' Logan said. He rocked back on his heels. It was as close as he was ever likely to get to a celebratory dance. 'Of course, we don't yet have any way of knowing which, if any, of those scenarios is correct. But it's good that you're thinking.'

'Thanks, sir.'

'Come on, we'll take a look in the living room.'

Sinead followed him through, and they noted that there was no forced entry at the front door, either. Not even, Logan was a little disappointed to note, any damage to the frame from his attempts to shoulder-barge the door open.

'How's the post-mortem going for Mrs Howden?' Sinead asked as they entered the living room.

'That's happening tomorrow,' Logan told her. 'As you fine well know.'

Sinead smiled. It had seemed like a natural way to segue into the conversation, but he'd seen straight through it. The direct approach it was, then.

'So, you and Shona, then,' she prompted.

'Now's not the time, Detective Constable,' Logan replied, then he shot her a sideways look. 'But, yes. Me and Shona.'

'Good on you, sir. I really like her.'

'She does have her moments,' Logan said.

Having become almost fluent in 'Jack Logan' over the past couple of years, Sinead recognised this as more or less a declaration of undying love.

'I'm really happy for you.'

'Let's focus now,' Logan said, indicating the room before them with its bloodied carpet and crimson-spotted walls. There were so many of the triangular numbered evidence markers lying around that the floor looked like a campsite for toy soldiers. 'But thank you,' the DCI added quietly. 'You and me both.'

Chapter 18

Jonathan MacInally, it transpired, was not sixteen, but fourteen, though for a boy of that age, he was an absolute brute of a creature. He was sitting down when Ben and Tyler entered, but a dunt on the leg from his mum prompted him to stand and offer a sweaty hand out for the officers to shake.

When he was on his feet, he towered above both detectives. He wasn't as tall as Logan, but if he had another year of growing in him, he might yet get close.

His bulky, thick-set torso could have been composed of muscle or fat, meaning he was either out of shape or ridiculously in it. The whole lower half of his face was a bubbling morass of spots, boils, and pustules, with scar tissue filling what few gaps remained.

He had a boxer's nose that started well at the tip, took a sudden swing out to the right, then ended much flatter than it should've done between the thick foliage of his eyebrows.

It was the kind of face that only a mother could love. Except for the fact that his mother was sitting beside him now, and the look on her own face bordered on contempt.

Ben and Tyler introduced themselves, then sat down across the table from the mother and son. Tyler, still tender and off-balance, lowered himself slowly onto the chair while Jonathan and his mum watched with growing concern.

'Is he all right?' Mrs MacInally asked Ben.

'I'm fine,' Tyler said, answering for himself.

'You don't look fine.'

'You look like you shat yourself or something,' Jonathan said. He grinned for around a fifth of a second until his mum slapped him on the leg again, and he offered up a muted, 'Well, he does.'

'Sorry about him,' Mrs MacInally said, rolling her eyes. 'I don't know where he gets it.'

The detectives weren't quite sure what the 'it' was that she was referring to, but they both smiled and shook their heads to indicate they understood.

'Not a problem, Mrs MacInally,' Ben said.

'Sandra's fine,' she said.

'Sandra. Thank you. What is it we can do for you?'

Jonathan's mum couldn't be blamed for the boy's looks. Or, for that matter, for his scale. She was a full head shorter than he was, and two of her could hide behind him, standing shoulder to shoulder. Her skin wasn't exactly blemish-free, but it was a million miles from the pus-filled horror show taking place on the lower half of her son's face.

'You're investigating the dead body found at the school this morning. That's right, isn't it?'

'We are,' Ben confirmed.

Sandra sat back and folded her arms, then glared at the side of Jonathan's head. 'Right. Tell them, then.'

Both detectives shifted their gazes in Jonathan's direction. He squirmed, and his weight made the chair sing a grumbling little melody of complaint.

'Jonathan?' Ben prompted. 'What can you tell us?'

A nanosecond of silence was ended by Sandra giving her son another thwap to the thigh. 'Go on, then. Tell them what you told me. They haven't got all night.'

Jonathan winced, rubbed his leg, then shrugged. 'I just... the dead guy. Like, I came to school. When the police was there. I came in that way. Where the car was.'

'We live over the opposite side to the gates,' said Sandra, translating. 'He usually goes over the fence instead of walking all the way around. I've told him not to, but he doesn't bloody listen.'

'You jumped the fence this morning?' asked Tyler, and Jonathan nodded.

'What did you see?' asked Ben.

'Just, like, the car, mostly. But the door was open. There was a gap in the tent. Some lady was, like, poking about at him, or something. The guy.'

'The body,' Sandra clarified. 'He saw the body.'

'That must've been distressing,' Ben said.

'What? Nah. Stuff like that don't bother me. I even saw some guy online getting his head mangled one time.'

'Well, that sounds lovely,' Ben said. 'Still, there's a big difference between seeing something on a screen and seeing it in real life. I know several officers, even, who—'

'I recognised him. The dead guy,' Jonathan announced. The words blurted out of him like he physically couldn't contain them any longer. 'His car, too. I'd seen him around. Hanging about near the school.'

'Did you ever speak to him?' Tyler asked.

Jonathan shook his head. 'No. But I heard stuff. About him. Who he is.'

His mother leaned over and prodded an index finger against the tabletop. 'Russian Mafia!' she said, and Jonathan tutted like she'd stolen his thunder.

Neither Ben nor Tyler said anything for several seconds. Tyler, who had taken the lid off his biro, now put it back on.

'I see,' said DI Forde.

'Yeah. Russian Mafia,' Jonathan confirmed. 'That's what I heard.'

'You hear about it all the time, don't you?'

'Do you?' Tyler asked.

'Yes! The Russians. The poisoning thing a few years ago. That Putin is always up to something, isn't he?' Sandra said. 'He was dealing drugs. To children at that school!'

Ben frowned. 'Who, Putin?'

'Bold of him,' Tyler said. 'Well-known guy like him.'

'What? No, not… the fella. The man. The dead man. Him. He was dealing drugs to the pupils.'

'That's just what I heard,' Jonathan reiterated. 'I didn't see him doing it, or nothing.'

Technically, this was true. Jonathan had never spoken to Borys, or even seen him up close. But he knew all about him, and what he was capable of.

'Right. I see,' Ben said, smiling patiently. 'And who did you hear this from?'

Jonathan looked down at his hands. His fingers were writhing around like worms at an orgy, all twisting and knotting together.

'Go on, then!' his mum prompted. 'Tell them.'

Finally, Jonathan looked up. His face had flushed white, making the redness of his spots and boils look even more fiery and raw.

'Her name's Olivia,' he said. 'Olivia Maximuke.'

Both detectives remained almost perfectly still. 'I see,' said Ben.

'She's a psychotic little bitch that one,' Sandra snapped. 'Broke Jonathan's nose a few months back. Hit him with a brick. Then she attacked him in school, and almost killed him.'

'She didn't *almost kill me*,' Jonathan protested, looking mortified by the suggestion that a girl two thirds his size might be able to get the better of him physically.

'Yes, she did. You were in a right mess. I was the one who had to take you to hospital and listen to your blubbering. Your nose still turns my stomach when I look at it.' She regarded his face with an air of distaste, then turned her attention back to the detectives on the other side of the table. 'Do you want me to tell you what I think happened?'

They didn't really, but refrained from coming out and saying so. She took their silence as confirmation.

'I think that girl was working with the Russian. Dealing drugs. Her father used to be tied up in that sort of thing. So I've been told, anyway.'

'Is that a fact?' asked Ben, feigning ignorance.

'Yes. He was probably Mafia, too. I think his daughter followed in his footsteps, got tied up with the Russians, and then when things went wrong, she killed him.'

'Let me just get this straight. You think a thirteen-year-old girl murdered a member of the Russian Mafia and then left his partially dismembered body outside her own school building for the janitor to find?' Ben asked.

'Yes! Precisely! That's exactly what I'm saying,' Sandra cried, failing to grasp just quite how preposterous that sounded. 'Although I didn't know he'd been chopped up! God's sake. She's a bloody lunatic! She needs locking up. It's a miracle she didn't kill my Jonathan at the same time.'

'She couldn't kill me. I can handle myself!' the lad insisted.

'Come on, Johnny, you're a big lad, but you're hardly Russian Mafia material! If she could kill him, she can kill you. You told me yourself today that you were terrified of her.'

Jonathan blushed and went back to watching the live worm sex show that was his writhing fingers.

'You mark my words,' Sandra said, glaring at Ben and Tyler in turn. 'That nasty little bitch has done this. She's murdered that man. And if you don't stop her, my poor darling boy might be next!'

–

Ben was right. Compared to the hurpling Tyler, he walked like a man in the prime of his life. He offered the DC an arm as they headed back to the Incident Room, but Tyler politely declined and ignored the funny looks his wide-legged waddle earned from passing colleagues.

'You know what you look like?' Ben asked as they rounded the final corner.

'A man who recently had a testicle removed?' Tyler guessed.

'No. Well, aye, but that's no' what I was thinking. A cowboy,' Ben said. 'You know, like when the baddies came striding into town? I can just picture you in a leather waistcoat and matching chaps.'

Tyler side-eyed him. 'I'd rather you didn't, boss.'

By the time they reached the Incident Room, Tyler was huffing and puffing, but still refusing any help. He relented when Sinead came hurrying over, pushing his office chair before her, and lowered himself cautiously into it with a groan and a sigh.

'Cheers. That was starting to get a bit uncomfortable,' he wheezed. 'Aye, the conversation, I meant, not my goolies.'

Just then, Taggart bounded up into his lap. The dog raised his ears quizzically at the string of expletives that exploded from the Detective Constable, then woofed his objections when he was quickly picked up by Sinead and deposited back on the floor again.

'The wee bastard,' Tyler mumbled, nursing his groin. 'He did that on purpose.'

Logan emerged from the inner office, saw Tyler being wheeled across the floor with his hands cupped over his crotch, and reached the conclusion that it was high time every bugger was off home. They'd done all they could for the night. Tomorrow, they'd pick up the threads again.

He met DI Forde's gaze. 'Anything urgent come out in the interview?'

'Urgent? No,' Ben said, either reading Logan's mind or the bags below his eyes. 'Mostly shite. It can wait until the morning. You two find anything out?'

'Nothing new from the house, no,' Logan said. He addressed the room at large. 'Anyone else have anything that we need to be aware of or working on *right now*?'

'I've put everything you're not caught up on in an email to the shared inbox, sir,' Hamza said. 'And updated in HOLMES.'

Logan nodded his appreciation. This was more like it. This was *classic* Hamza—efficient, on the ball, and pretty much the only one in the office able to fully fathom the workings of the Home Office Large Major Enquiry System.

'I've printed the key stuff out and put it on your desk, Sinead,' the DS continued. 'You can stick it on the board tomorrow.'

'Cheers, Ham.'

'What about the dug?' asked Dave. 'What's happening with that?'

All eyes went to Taggart. The dog was sitting bolt upright on the floor, tongue lolling down to his chest. Feeling all the attention on him, his tail began to beat out a steady rhythm on the carpet.

'Technically, he's a witness,' Ben pointed out.

Logan grunted. 'Can't see his testimony standing up in court, can you?'

'Someone should take him home,' Sinead said.

'By all means, feel free,' Logan told her, but Tyler shook his head.

'No way. I think he might hate me,' he said. 'No way that ball shot was an accident.'

'Hamza can't take him, as we've already established,' Ben said. 'And I'm no' messing around with a puppy at my age. So...'

This time, all eyes went to Logan. 'You're not serious?' he said. 'We'll put him to the dog squad. They can watch him.'

Ben glanced at the clock. 'Bit late to be arranging that tonight, is it no'?'

'Jesus. Fine. I'll take him. But just for tonight. First thing tomorrow morning, we figure out what to do with him.' He looked down at the dog, tutted, then reached for his coat. 'Right, good work today, everyone. Be back here by seven.' He looked doubtfully at Tyler. 'You going to be fit enough?'

'Don't you worry about me, boss,' Tyler insisted. 'I'll be grand.' He looked over his shoulder at the door, then back to the towering DCI. 'But, eh, don't suppose you can give me a fireman's lift out to the car, can you?'

'Sorry, son,' Logan said. He bent down, and Taggart yelped in fright as he was snatched up off the floor. 'I've already got one pain in the arse to take with me as it is.'

–

This time, Logan stuck the dog in the boot of the car. He warned it several times to stay, using his best stern voice and raised index finger, then carefully lowered the boot lid and let it clunk closed.

He took out his phone as he walked around to the driver's side door, pulled up Shona's details, and slid in behind the steering wheel.

'The fu—?' he said when he saw Taggart already curled up on the front passenger seat. 'How the hell did you get there?'

'Eh, I drove. Why?'

There was a millisecond of confusion before Logan's brain processed the fact that the voice had come from the phone's earpiece.

'Everything OK?' Shona asked.

'What? Aye. Sorry. Just… I've been lumbered with a dug.'

There was a pause while Shona settled on the best line of questioning.

'In what sense?'

'In the sense that I'm stuck looking after the bloody thing tonight,' Logan told her. 'I can bring it round for you to see. Just if you're not busy.'

He heard her yawn, and knew what the answer was going to be before she said it.

'It's pretty late, and I need to be in early tomorrow for the PM on that other victim,' she said.

'Right, aye. Makes sense,' Logan said. If he was disappointed, he damn well wasn't showing it.

'Maybe you could bring it over tomorrow?' Shona suggested.

'With any luck, I'll be rid of the yappy wee bastard by then,' Logan said. 'But I'll see what I can do.'

There was some deeply awkward silence, neither of them quite sure what to say. It was Shona who finally broke the deadlock.

'Right, well, I'm dead on my feet here, so I'd better get to bed. See you tomorrow? I've got some*body* I'd like you to meet.' Logan could actually hear her grinning down the line. It was infectious. 'Get it? Like a dead—'

'I got it, thanks,' he said.

'Maybe I could sell that one to Geoff.'

Logan chuckled. 'Assuming he hasn't been torn limb from limb.'

'Which he probably has,' Shona said.

Logan nodded. 'Tragic loss. The world of comedy will never be… stop pissing on my seat!' he bellowed, slapping a hand down on the chair. If anything, this just made the contents of Taggart's bladder start evacuating at an even more impressive rate. 'Shite. I better go!'

'Go, go!' Shona urged. 'Goodnight!'

'Night,' Logan grunted, then he threw down the phone and hit the automatic window button with his elbow. Grabbing the still peeing dog, he thrust it outside through the gap in the door and held it there, three feet above the ground. They both maintained eye contact as the puppy concluded his business.

A car slowed on its way out of the car park. A passenger window slid down. 'Night, boss!' Tyler chirped, and the DC was still grinning when Sinead pulled them out of the car park, and off into the darkened streets of Inverness.

–

Shona thumbed the icon that ended the call, set her phone down on the arm of the couch, then shot it a guilty look. She hadn't lied to him. Not exactly. She *was* tired, and she *did* have an early start.

But neither of those things was why she had turned down his late-night visit. The real reason for that stood by the window, peeking out through the curtains into the darkness beyond.

'Right then, Olivia,' Shona said, offering the girl an encouraging smile. 'Why don't you sit down and tell me what all this is about?'

Chapter 19

She was scared. That much was obvious.

It had been nearly two years now since Olivia Maximuke had first come crashing into Shona's life, courtesy of their mutual acquaintance, one Detective Chief Inspector Jack Logan. Logan had brought her to Shona's for a movie and some popcorn.

That was how he'd pitched it to the pathologist, at least. In reality, they'd essentially kidnapped the girl, and were holding her against her will.

Mind you, she'd settled into the film quickly enough, and had apparently enjoyed the experience so much that she'd invited herself back again.

And again.

And again.

And Shona… hadn't hated it. Oh, sure, it had been uncomfortable at first, but Olivia had been escaping from a rough situation at home, and Shona didn't have the heart to deny her that.

Besides, she'd come to enjoy the girl's company, surly and sarcastic as she could sometimes be. She was a good kid, she'd just been dealt a tough hand with a drug-dealing dad and a messed-up mum.

Lately, though, her visits had become less frequent. She'd offered excuses to start with, then would frequently just fail to turn up. Even when she was there, she'd seemed distant and preoccupied, but no amount of coaxing had managed to get her to talk.

She had a job. That was the only explanation she would offer. She had a job and all the commitments that went with it. She'd love to sit around watching old movies all the time, but she had responsibilities now. Shona had tried very hard not to take that as some sort of dig, and despite her repeated asking, the nature of the job had never been revealed.

Tonight, she had arrived out of the blue, soaking wet from the rain, with mud covering her shoes and the bottom of her jeans. She wore a large black beanie and an oversized duffle coat that absolutely drowned her. The arms hung down to somewhere around her knees, and the bottom of the coat a little further still. Button it tightly, and she'd barely be able to walk beyond tiny micro-steps that would get her nowhere fast.

She had asked to come in, then glanced back over her shoulder like she was being chased, and squeezed past before Shona could step aside.

Shona had just finished fetching her a can of Irn Bru from the fridge when Logan phoned, and Olivia had pleaded with the pathologist not to mention that she was there.

There had been something about the way she'd asked— something in her voice, and in her eyes—that had made Shona do as she was asked. Something had clearly upset the girl, and if keeping her presence a secret was the only way she could find out what had happened, then so be it.

Besides, just because they were in a relationship, she didn't have to tell Jack *everything*. A woman had a right to a few secrets.

Olivia was still looking out through a tiny gap in the curtains, head bobbing left and right to give her the widest possible angle of view. Shona's house was on the other side of the Kessock Bridge, tucked back from the main road, so passing cars were few and far between. Whenever one did pass, Olivia would shrink back until the headlights had swept on by, before returning to her vigil.

Shona was already regretting not telling Jack everything.

'Did you hear me?' she asked, walking over to join the girl by the window. 'What's wrong? What's going on?'

'Nothing.'

'Then why are you freaking out at the window?' Shona pressed. 'And you're shaking. What is it? What's happened?'

Another car passed. Olivia leaned back, let the gap close, then whispered a three-count before opening the curtains a crack. The road was in darkness. The car had driven on by. She relaxed a little, like whatever danger she was in was passing.

'I'm sorry, I shouldn't have come here,' she said, finally turning from the window. 'I was... it's not... I'm sorry.'

She looked younger than she'd looked in a long time. Younger than Shona had ever seen her. Most of her face was pale, aside from her cheeks and the tip of her nose, which had been burnished red by the cold.

'Don't be silly. You're always welcome, you know that,' Shona told her. 'Sit down. Do you want a cup of tea? You look freezing.'

Olivia shook her head. 'No. I'm fine. I can't stay.'

'What do you mean you can't stay?' Shona asked. 'Why not? What's going on?'

Olivia dodged past her and crossed to the couch where they'd both spent long evenings watching dozens of movies and eating popcorn. Rather than jump back and sink into it like she'd always done before, she sat at the front, perched so she could leap to her feet in an instant.

Or maybe she could, if she didn't look quite so exhausted.

'Should I call your mum?' Shona asked.

Olivia shook her head. It was firm. Definitive. 'No. No, don't do that.'

'OK, then talk to me,' Shona told her. 'You're scaring me, and if you won't talk to me, I have to call someone.' She sat on the couch beside the girl and gave her hand a squeeze. Olivia didn't pull away. Her hand just sat there on the couch, limp and unmoving like all the many dead hands Shona had held before.

It was a little routine she had. One she'd never told anyone, and one she reserved for only the most tragic of cases. The murdered mother. The teenager killed in a car accident. The child cancer victim. Before making a single incision, she'd take one of their hands in hers, and she'd hold it, just for a moment.

She wasn't quite sure why she did it, exactly. It was an apology, perhaps, for what the world had done to them, or for what she was about to do. Maybe some offering of comfort for their onward journey. Or, it was possibly just a gesture of respect, from one human being to the other. A recognition of some shared connection, or collective pain.

Olivia's hand, cold from being outside, felt as lifeless as any of those.

'I shouldn't have come,' Olivia said, her voice fracturing under the strain. 'I just didn't know what else to do, or where to go.'

'Did you fall out with your mum?'

Olivia shook her head. A tear fell. The first of many. 'No,' she whispered. 'I don't know where she is.'

'What do you mean?' Shona asked, and she rubbed a little life back into the girl's hand. 'She's not back drinking again, is she?'

Another shake of the head. A strangled sob. Olivia gave an enormous sniff, like she might be able to suck all the tears back into her eyes, and pretend this had never happened.

'I think... I think someone's taken her,' she said, the words coming as a whimper of pain. 'Someone took her, and it's all my fault!'

–

It was earlier in the day, just past dinner time, and Alexis Maximuke didn't know where her daughter was. Worse than that—no, not worse, but *as bad*—she couldn't get hold of Father Conrad, either. She'd tried calling four times now, but he hadn't picked up.

Was she being ghosted? Could priests ghost people? Was that allowed?

Probably more permissible than them having sex, she supposed. Especially in the back of a Vauxhall Astra in the Poundstretcher car park.

There had been plenty of pounding going on that night! Not so much in the way of stretching, but then size wasn't everything, and to be fair to him, Olivia *had* been quite a big baby.

She tried Father Conrad's number again, listened to it ringing for thirty seconds, and then left another message asking him to call her, but stressing it wasn't important and that there was no rush. It wouldn't do to appear needy, after all.

Then she called Olivia. It went straight to voicemail. She didn't bother leaving one. Olivia never listened to them, anyway.

Alexis typed out a text—'Hey, where R U?'—and, for the sake of simplicity, sent it to both of them.

As she finished sending the message, she realised that her hands were shaking. Not much. Not yet. But it was the first time they'd trembled like this in months, and she had a horrible feeling that it was just the start.

Something coiled deep down in her stomach. Some dormant urge stirred and licked its lips.

She was stressed, that was all. The worry over Father Conrad and Olivia—she shook her head—over *Olivia and Father Conrad,* was agitating her anxieties. She just needed to breathe, that was all. To relax.

'This too shall pass,' she whispered. 'This too shall pass.'

It was a mantra that Father Conrad had taught her when they'd first started chatting online. It applied to both bad times and good, and was a tool with which to remind herself that she could get through the bad times, and should appreciate the good while they lasted.

She wasn't sure it was particularly effective, but it was less destructive than smothering her problems in a mound of white powder and hoping things looked better when she crawled out the other side.

This, here, now—this was one of the bad times. The shake of her hands and the twisting of her intestines made that clear. In the olden days, she'd have reached for a bottle already, and tried drowning the worries with a series of big, gulping glugs.

But that was then. That was the old Alexis. With Father Conrad's help, she'd shed that skin. She'd left that person behind.

So why could she hear her now, whispering below the kitchen door? Pleading to be let in.

Or let out.

But, no. That Alexis could beg all she liked. There was no booze left in the house. No drugs, either, beyond a few antihistamines and half a packet of Lemsip, and she had very little chance of getting wasted on that. A bit drowsy, maybe, but that was it.

The voice beneath the door called her a liar.

The voice beneath the door knew better.

There was one bottle. Tucked away. For emergencies.

She'd kept it for psychological reasons, she told herself. If there was no alcohol anywhere in the house, she'd obsess over it. Go crazy worrying about what would happen if she really couldn't manage, couldn't resist, couldn't abstain.

But if she kept just one bottle—a comfort blanket—she could rest easy. She could push it from her mind, and go about her day never giving it a second thought.

It was upstairs in her bedroom, tucked beneath the spare pillows way at the back of the big cupboard. Out of sight, out of mind.

But never out of reach.

She phoned both numbers again. Voicemail, both times.

Her hands shook. Her eyes raised to the ceiling, either seeking help from the divine, or plotting the quickest route to the booze.

She opened the kitchen door, making for the staircase, then stopped.

No, she wasn't doing this. She wouldn't. Not when she'd come this far. She wasn't slipping back into her old ways. She would fight. She would resist.

Besides, she had a *much* better idea.

–

'What do you mean, "someone took her"?' Shona asked. 'Who took her? Why?'

Olivia's tears were in full flow now. There was no sound with them, though. No screwing up of her face, or shaking of her shoulders. There were just the tears, dripping steadily, like someone hadn't quite shut a tap off all the way.

Shona found it concerning and disconcerting in roughly equal measures. These weren't grief tears, she thought. They were a manifestation of some sort of shock.

God, what had happened to her?

'I went back. I went home,' Olivia said, her voice modulating itself into a flat monotone. 'I'd snuck out earlier. I just… I didn't want to be around. I needed to think, and… and I did. I thought, and I was going home. To tell her. Everything. What I'd done. But she was… there was a note. She was gone, and there was a note.'

'What did it say?'

'I don't know. I didn't look.'

Shona frowned, but there was a suggestion of a smile there, too, like she'd just discovered a way to fix all this. 'Then it might have been anything! For all you know it said, "Going for milk, back in five minutes". You're probably worrying about nothing.'

Olivia shook her head. When the girl turned to her, the look in her eyes made the smile fall from Shona's face. She felt the ground opening up beneath where she sat. This—whatever this was—was far worse than she'd thought.

'I don't think it was from her,' Olivia said. 'I think it was from *him*.'

'Who?'

Olivia swallowed. She wiped away her tears, but they sprang back a moment later. She took a big breath, then another. Only then, did she start to explain.

'Remember before Christmas? All that stuff that happened. People being killed in freezers. The Iceman.'

Shona remembered it only too well. She'd worked the case, doing the PMs on the bodies.

The case had affected Olivia, too, of course. Had it not been for Logan's intervention, she could well have become one of the killer's victims herself.

'Sure, yeah. Why?'

'Remember the last body they found? Weeks afterwards. On the industrial estate.'

'I do. What about it?'

Olivia looked everywhere in the room except in Shona's direction. 'I put someone in there,' she said. 'In the freezer.'

The words were so quiet that Shona almost believed she'd imagined them, and had to ask to be sure. 'Sorry, did you say—?'

'He was my mum's... I don't know. Boyfriend,' Olivia said, blurting the words out like some floodgates had been thrown open. 'He was horrible. He made me... he made me do things.'

Shona's hand tightened on Olivia's. 'What? Oh, God. Oh, sweetheart—'

'Deal drugs,' Olivia said, which was not quite the turn Shona had thought the conversation was taking.

'Oh. Right. Oh. I see,' Shona said.

'Well, not deal them, exactly. Just bring them to people. People who worked for him.'

'He shouldn't have made you do that,' Shona said, which she quickly concluded was the single most obvious statement anyone had ever made. 'I mean... that's awful.'

Olivia nodded quickly, like she was heartened by the remark. 'And... and, I think he was going to do other stuff, too. He... he would come into my bedroom. Told me… said I was beautiful. Kept saying how grown-up I was getting.'

Shona held the girl's hand and opened her mouth to offer some words of support and comfort, but Olivia kept going. It was like she couldn't stop now, like her story had to be told.

'And… and I knew he would. Sooner or later. I knew he was going to do something to hurt me. And then, one day, he drove me out to that industrial estate. He took me to that place. With the freezer. And he showed me inside.' She lowered her head, and her voice became quieter. 'There was a man there. He was… I think he was dead. Frozen. And… and Oleg said that if I didn't do everything he told me, I'd be next. He'd put me in there, and leave me to die.'

'Oleg was your mum's boyfriend? That was his name?'

'I was so scared. I didn't want to do what he was making me do, but I didn't want to die.' She drew in a deep breath, steeled herself, then met Shona's eye. 'So, when he had his back to me, I pushed him in.'

'Into the freezer?'

Olivia nodded. 'I pushed him in, and I left him there. I left him there to die.'

Shona blinked, but tried not to show her shock. She'd been called in to do the PM after that freezer had been discovered, too. The cold had ravaged the man, then preserved what was left of him, and examining the body had been equal parts gruesome and fascinating.

Body. Singular.

'You must have made a mistake, Olivia,' the pathologist soothed. 'There was only one person in the freezer.'

'I know, but he was in there! I know he was. So he must've got out! Someone must've set him free. And now he's back. Now he's after me. He killed Borys, and now he's got my mum, and I don't know what to do!'

'OK, first, try to calm down,' Shona said. 'You're safe here. You're fine.'

They took a few breaths together. In. Out. The usual.

'Right. Now, we're going to phone Jack,' Shona said, which earned her nothing but a blank look. 'DCI Logan, I mean. He'll be able to help.'

'I don't want to get in trouble!' Olivia said.

'If what you're saying is true, then you're already in trouble, sweetheart,' Shona told her. 'But with the wrong people. Dangerous people. Jack will look after you. He'll see you right.'

Another year or two fell away from the girl, practically shrinking her right there before Shona's eyes. 'Will he find my mum?'

'Oh, of course he will. Of course,' Shona said, throwing her arms around Olivia and pulling her in close. The girl broke then, her silent tears becoming sobs that shook her shoulders in staccato jolts and jerks.

Shona held her until the worst of it had passed, then rubbed her back. 'There you go. You're all right. You're OK,' she said. 'How about I get you that cup of tea, then we give Jack a call?'

Olivia pulled free. It seemed to take all her effort, and she finally sunk back into the folds of the couch like a deflating balloon. 'OK. Thanks,' she muttered, sounding far away and absent.

Shona patted her leg, gave it a rub, then bounced up from the couch and headed for the kitchen. She filled the kettle, switched it on, and then rummaged in a drawer until she found a notepad and pen.

She had barely written three words when she heard Olivia's voice from the living room.

'Shona!'

Dropping the pad and pen, she hurried back to the living room and found Olivia standing a pace back from the window again. The curtains were drawn, but they weren't sitting right, like they'd recently been moved.

'Everything OK?'

'There was another car,' Olivia whispered. Her eyes were wide now. Alert. The tears were a thing of the past. 'I saw the lights.'

'It's fine. Cars pass here all the time,' Shona assured her. 'It's off the beaten track, but it's still only a couple of miles from Inverness. There's more traffic than you'd think. It'll just be someone passing, that's all. Nothing to—'

She caught one of the curtains by the outside corner and lifted it, creating a triangular gap between the pieces of fabric.

Headlights burned in the darkness, flecks of light rain swirling around them like fireflies. Olivia jumped back, eyes widening, tears racing down her cheeks once more.

As Shona watched, one of the lights went dark, then came back on. It took her a moment to realise why.

Someone had walked in front of it.

Someone was coming to the house.

She let the curtain fall back into place. A battle raged inside her—one part trying to keep calm for Olivia's sake, the other screaming at her to lock the door and call for help.

The creaking of her front gate being opened, and the clack of it swinging closed were enough to decide the battle. She stumbled out into the hall and reached the front door just as a shape appeared beyond the glass. A figure. A man.

Her hands—usually so steady and precise—became useless, clumsy things as she grasped for the lock and the chain.

She heard Olivia's feet on the floor behind her. Caught a reflection of her running for the kitchen.

And then a weight from the other side threw the door open before she could get the lock to turn, sending her stumbling backwards.

She turned. Ran to the kitchen, following Olivia. They could get weapons there. Protect themselves.

The back door stood open, the cold and the rain swirling in.

A hand caught Shona by the hair. Strong. Powerful. She cried out as it pulled her back, dragged her down.

And then his weight was on top of her. She slapped and gouged, fighting him off, pushing him away.

She tried to sit up. A fist hit her. It was a battering ram. A high-speed crash. A juggernaut of pain that filled her head with noise and light and chaos. She tasted blood. Choked on it. Drowned in it.

The racket in her head faded enough that she could hear more feet racing past, headed for the kitchen. Two men, maybe three. Big, like this one. They were talking. Shouting, maybe. Her brain couldn't figure it out, couldn't translate, couldn't understand what was happening.

She heard another sound. From the front door this time, she thought, though she couldn't be sure, and the weight of the man on top of her stopped her turning her head to look.

It was a wheeze. Or a gasp. Some short burst of moving air that ended with a click.

It was followed by a steady thunk and then a noise like something being dragged.

Thunk.

Drag.

Thunk.

Drag.

Louder and louder.

Closer and closer.

Another figure inched into view above her, leaning on a stick for support. Shona blinked away what she could of her tears, and looked straight into a face from a nightmare.

'Well, now,' he wheezed, and his voice echoed inside the plastic oxygen mask he wore strapped across his face. 'Aren't you just the prettiest little birdie I ever did see?'

Chapter 20

The night had been long and difficult. There had been whimpering. Scratching. Some angry shouting, and a complete loss of bladder control.

Finally, Logan had relented and let the bloody dog out of the kitchen, and onto his bed. It had been the only way either of them were going to get any sleep.

And it had worked. Aye, the dog had been a pain in the arse, practically draping himself over Logan's legs at every conceivable opportunity, but a furry knee warmer pinning his legs beneath the covers was infinitely preferable to all the howling, door scraping, and puddles of piss.

Logan was wakened by a tongue slipping into his mouth at just before six. He spent a confused but glorious half-second thinking his luck was in, then woke up enough to realise precisely what was going on.

'Jesus!' he cried, pushing the dog away, and drawing back so sharply that he stoated the back of his head off his bedside table.

For a moment, Taggart looked simultaneously flabbergasted and deeply offended by the rejection, like a rich older woman being turned down by the country club pool boy.

Then the dog jumped down off the bed, snuffled at the carpet, and spread his back legs as he prepared to pee on the floor.

'Don't you fucking dare!' Logan bellowed, throwing back the covers and leaping out of bed. He snatched up the dog before it could let rip, and raced naked through the house until he reached the front door.

It was, of course, locked, so he tucked the dog under an arm, turned the key, and practically threw Taggart out into the garden.

Two joggers turned to look as they went striding past, and Logan was forced to do a sort of standing sideways roll until he was hidden behind his door, all the while muttering darkly below his breath. He pushed the door closed with his foot, returned to his bedroom, and hurriedly pulled on some clothes.

He took a detour to the kitchen on his way back to the front door, stopping to fill the kettle and switch it on. Tea was his preferred morning tipple, but after last night, today was definitely a coffee day.

By the time he made it back to the door, Taggart had emptied his bladder and was now exploring. Logan's front garden wasn't big—just a few square metres of overgrown lawn he should probably get around to cutting soon—but to Taggart, it was an adventure playground.

Logan watched, yawning, as the young dog sniffed his way across the garden in an apparently random pattern that would, given enough time, cover every inch of the grass.

As he watched, he took out his phone, fired off a message to Shona announcing his dislike for dogs, then ended it with an 'x'.

Prior to very recently, it had been a long time since he'd ended a message with an 'x'. In fact, he wasn't sure that he ever had. He didn't quite know what that said about him. Probably nothing, but he wondered about it while waiting for a reply.

None came, not even by the time Taggart got bored of sniffing, and came over to sit on the doorstep, gazing up at Logan.

'She'll still be sleeping,' he told the animal. Taggart neither agreed nor disagreed with this statement, and instead just sat there looking gormless. 'Right, we should probably find you something to eat, I suppose. Not that you bloody deserve it.' He stepped aside. 'Come on.'

Taggart kept watching him as he trotted into the house, his back end wagging from the tip of his tail to about halfway up his torso.

He followed Logan into the kitchen and watched in rapt silence as the detective went through his cupboard.

It occurred to Logan that he wasn't very good at shopping. Or not very good at shopping for a small dog, at least. But then, it wasn't like he'd had time to prepare.

His cupboard, fridge, and freezer, were a bit of a No Man's Land when it came to fresh, dog-friendly food. Most of the contents were packaged convenience foods and ready meals—microwave lasagnes and chicken tikkas, boil in the bag rice dishes, and of course a couple of Pot Noodles in case Shona stopped by unexpectedly.

Those had been there for months.

He found a tin of tuna chunks in brine at the back of a cupboard and stood contemplating it for some time. Would that do? Could dogs eat tuna? Cats could, he knew, but then dogs—famously—weren't cats. They were the opposite of cats, in many respects.

He took out his phone to do a quick Google search, which also allowed him to check if he'd had a response yet from Shona.

He hadn't.

The Google search sent him down a rabbit hole of dog allergies and mercury poisoning. The general consensus seemed to be that the occasional tin of tuna wouldn't do a dog any harm, but eating it on a regular basis might eventually prove toxic.

Good enough.

Taggart sat drooling as Logan opened the tin, mashed the fish in a bowl, then placed it on the floor. The dog set about it in seconds, and had polished it off by the time Logan had refilled the bowl of water he'd put down the night before.

'Christ, you must've been starving,' Logan said, and he felt a pang of guilt that this had not occurred to him sooner.

Taggart sat down next to the bowl which had been completely licked clean, sniffed the air, and waited.

'There's nothing else,' Logan said.

The dog continued to watch him. Its head cocked to the right, and for a moment Logan was sure the little bastard shot a deliberate look at the fridge.

There was a pack of bacon in there. Thick cut, smoked. Just the way the DCI liked it.

The dog licked his lips. Technically, given the size of his tongue, he licked his nose, but the meaning was the same.

'God. Fine,' Logan said, fetching a frying pan from a cabinet. 'But just to be clear, you're not eating all of it.'

–

Logan met Sinead at Conrad Howden's house. It was a small, unassuming sort of place on a council estate out by Culloden— the middle in a terraced row of five, with a garden so small it made Logan's seem positively self-indulgent.

Sinead had done the required paperwork, and Uniform had fetched the keys from the hospital, where Conrad was still unresponsive. It was, Logan remarked, a nice change to be gaining entry to a property in a way that was completely above board, and didn't involve him having to break any windows or locks.

The house was far nicer on the inside than its drab exterior had suggested.

Actually, 'nicer' wasn't the right word, Logan thought, as much of the place was a bloody eyesore. It was more *ostentatious*.

In the living room, an enormous curved TV took up a third of one wall, an oversized reclining couch and matching armchair filled most of the available floor space, while what Sinead described as 'a big ol' plastic Jesus' stood in the corner like he was keeping an eye on the place.

The walls were painted in a dark, forest green. The curtains were thick, wide, and ruby red. The flooring was done in a herringbone style. Some sort of wooden laminate, Logan thought, but convincing enough that it could've been real wood.

'He's not short of a bob or two, is he?' Logan remarked, looking around at the smart speakers, iPads, and laptops that seemed to have been sprinkled randomly around the room with very little care. 'What did you say he did again?'

'Labourer, apparently.'

Logan studied the gentle curve of the TV. The screen was ludicrously thin, and flowed all the way to the edges, with no bezel around the outside. It had to be seventy inches, possibly more.

'Once again, it seems like we're in the wrong job, Detective Constable.'

There was a knock at the front door, then it opened.

'Hello?' Hamza called. 'Anyone…' He arrived in the living room and smiled. 'Aha. Hiya. Sorry I'm late. Had to drop the wee one in at nursery. Did you know the dog's barking at everyone that passes your car, sir?'

Logan told him that he was indeed aware of that. It was very hard not to be. For a little fella, Taggart was a noisy bugger, and his shrill bark carried far and wide.

Hamza looked around, appeared momentarily impressed by the TV, then pointed into the corner. 'That's a big Jesus.'

And it was. Well, it was big for an ornamental Jesus. At around four feet tall, it would've been quite short for an *actual* Jesus, even allowing for the changes in the average adult height over the centuries.

The counterfeit Christ had been made to look like it was fashioned from marble, but beyond using white plastic, very little effort had been put into making the illusion a convincing one. He looked suitably serene, with his hands clasped loosely in front of himself, and his head angled down like he was looking at something on the floor in front of him. Possibly some sort of lamb or small child accessory, Logan thought, that had presumably been sold separately.

'It's completely hollow,' Sinead said, giving the Son of God a rap on the noggin with her knuckles.

Logan was sure there was some sort of clever remark to be made there about religion in general, but decided he wasn't the man to make it. Instead, he got to work dishing out orders.

'Right, Hamza, we've got a lot of computer equipment here. I want you to start on that. See if anything is unlocked and easy to access. Check for the usual stuff, emails, web history...' His knowledge of computer terminology dropped off sharply there. 'You know the score.'

'No problem, sir,' Hamza said.

There was an efficient snap to the reply and a straightening of the back. He was overcompensating for his recent vagueness. Logan could see that. That wasn't exactly ideal, but it was better than the alternative. In the short term, at least.

'Sinead, I want you to start in his bedroom. Gloves and shoe coverings on. We don't know what we'll find.'

'Anything in particular you want me to keep an eye out for?'

Logan shook his head. 'If there's something to be found, you'll know it when you see it,' he told her. 'I'm going to go knock on a couple of doors and see what the neighbours are saying.'

Sinead and Hamza swapped glances.

'There a problem with that?' Logan asked.

'No, sir,' Hamza began. 'It's just...'

'It's just what, Detective Sergeant?'

Sinead threw herself into the line of fire. 'It's just that you don't usually like talking to people, if you can avoid it, sir,' she said. 'You don't usually like people at all, in fact.'

'I like people,' Logan protested. 'Not all of them, obviously. I mean, some of them are bastards. *Many* of them are bastards, in fact. But I like... some people.' He thought this through a little further. 'Sometimes.'

Sinead raised her eyebrows and formed her mouth into a thin smile. 'Want me to go talk to the neighbours?'

'Aye. Aye, that's maybe for the best,' Logan admitted. 'I'll snoop around and see what I can see. You can start in another room when you get back.'

'Will do, sir,' Sinead said, turning towards the door.

'Oh, and Sinead, while you're out there?' he said. He tossed her his car keys. 'Check on that bloody dog, will you?'

Chapter 21

'Who was that you were on the phone to, boss?' asked Tyler, John-Wayneing his way across the Incident Room with his legs splayed wide. 'Something come through on the case?'

Ben looked guiltily at his desk phone, the display screen still illuminated from the recent call to Moira down in Fort William.

'Uh, no. Personal matter,' he said, then he swiftly switched subjects. 'I want you to give Borys Wozniak's mother a call this morning. The Russian Mafia stuff is almost certainly nonsense, but worth a quick chat. If he's been supplying drugs, he must've been getting them from somewhere. Let's see if we can find the links in the chain.'

'Aye, I was thinking about that last night, boss,' Tyler said. He held his breath as he eased himself down onto his chair. 'He wasn't on the drug squad's radar—not seriously, anyway—so he could've been quite new to the game. If he's moved in on someone else's patch, then surely that's our line of inquiry? Stands to reason someone would want to kill him.'

'True,' Ben said. 'But the microchip and the location complicate things, don't they? Aye, if he was just found in a car in the middle of nowhere, or in his house, or whatever, then that would be one thing. But the school? There's a connection there. And the fact the address on the chip led to the other victims?' He shook his head. 'This isn't as neat as a rival thinning out the competition. This is something more.'

'Aye. I know. I was thinking about that, too, though,' Tyler said. He smiled, almost apologetically. 'Couldn't sleep. Mind was racing.'

'I know what that's like,' Ben said. 'What did you come up with?'

'Right, well, we know Bosco Maximuke was the main supplier for this whole area for a few years, before we banged him up.'

'We do,' Ben confirmed.

'And we know his daughter goes to that school.'

'She does.'

'OK, so, I'm thinking either Borys was working for Bosco, and someone looking to take over Bosco's turf killed him, *or* Borys was working for one of the guys moving in to take over Bosco's turf, and it was Bosco who had him killed.'

Ben frowned. 'So it was either Bosco or...'

'Or it *wasn't* Bosco. Exactly,' Tyler said. He held his hands out at his side like he was expecting cheering and applause. 'Narrows it down a bit, eh?'

'Does it, though?' Ben asked. 'Is saying "it was Bosco or it was someone else who isn't Bosco" really narrowing it down all that much?'

'Well, I mean, we know it's either...' The sound of the words fell away, but Tyler's lips continued to move, silently playing out the conclusion of the sentence.

Ben saw the moment that the penny dropped, and almost felt sorry for the lad. He'd tried. And, to be fair to him, he did have a lot on his mind.

'No, I suppose it doesn't really cut down the list of suspects very much, does it?' Tyler admitted. He smiled weakly, then pointed to his phone. 'I'll just jump on that call, boss.'

'Aye, you do that, son,' Ben said. 'But keep up with the whole thinking thing. I'm sure it'll pay off, eventually.'

–

The bedroom was even more lavish than the living room had been, to the point it crossed the line into gaudy. The bed was a four-poster, styled like an antique, but nowhere near as sturdy.

It had the same red drapes as in the living room, tied back at each of the legs.

The sheets and covers were a shiny satin gold, made from the sort of material that would shoot you right out of the bed if you made any sudden movements during the night.

One of the walls running parallel with the bed was a row of mirrored doors—perfect for anyone who wanted to watch the live show of their own sexual exploits.

The doors slid open almost silently on their runners, revealing some well-planned storage space. One of the cupboards contained a rack of cube-shaped shelving, on which various pairs of jeans, trousers, and shorts had all been stored. Given the area's usual climate, the shorts seemed optimistic. And, sure enough, when Logan checked, most of them still had their label on.

The next cupboard along had the same sort of shelves, but this time they held trainers and shoes. Logan had a poke around, but found nothing of any immediate or obvious interest.

He slid that door shut, and moved on to the next.

Shirts and suits this time, all hanging from a rack. Plenty of them, too. Even if he totalled up all the shirts he'd ever owned, Logan wasn't convinced it would equal the number hanging in Conrad Howden's wardrobe.

It was all expensive stuff, too. The jeans had been designer brands. The shoes and trainers wouldn't have been cheap, either. Conrad would have expensive tastes for a London banker, never mind a labourer from Inverness.

Logan looked through a few of the suits, then stopped.

'Hello,' he muttered, unhooking a hanger.

He looked at the suit—the trousers threaded through a slot in the plastic hanger, the jacket hung over it at the shoulders. It was black, plain, and largely uninteresting.

But it wasn't the suit itself that had caught his attention. It was the white priest's dog collar wrapped around the hanger's metal hook.

First a big ol' plastic Jesus, and now this. Logan checked the pockets of the suit, found nothing, then hung it from the top of the bedroom door to look at later.

Finding nothing more of interest in the cupboards, he turned his attention to the bed. The bedclothes had mostly been made, but they were a little rumpled, like someone had gone for a quick nap on top of the covers, or possibly just sat down near the bottom end for a while.

He slid a gloved hand under the satin-covered pillows, found nothing, then peeled back a corner of the duvet to get a look below.

Nothing there, either.

Dropping to his knees, he brought the side of his face down close to the floor, lifted the valance sheet, and shone his torch into the space beneath the bed.

The first thing he saw was a tote bag up near the head of the bed, placed so it was within easy reach of anyone lying on the mattress above.

The second thing he spotted was the alarmingly detailed plastic penis that protruded from the top of the bag, clearly far too large to fit in all the way.

The third thing he noticed was the bomb.

–

'Here, boss. You got a minute?'

Ben looked up from the report he was reading, considered summoning Tyler to his desk, then remembered the lad was walking like he'd recently lost his horse. He got up, lifted his half-drunk cup of tea, and sauntered over to find the DC looking down at a page in an A4 notepad that was blank aside from a solitary word.

'Boils.'

Tyler had ringed the word three times, then added a question mark after it.

'I've been thinking, boss. Like you said.'

'Looks like you've been hard at it, right enough,' Ben replied.

Tyler, completely missing the sarcasm, continued. 'Remember that note found in Borys' car?'

Ben pointed to the evidence bag on the desk between them. 'That note?'

'Aye! That's the one,' Tyler confirmed. 'First word on it is "boils", right? "Boils, three-hundred-and-fifty". I've been thinking about that.'

'And?'

'Right, well, here's my thinking. I Googled to see if there's anything that reaches boiling point at three-hundred-and-fifty degrees. And there is. It's called…' He flipped back a page on his notebook, frowned, tried a silent first pass at the word, then attempted to speak it out loud. 'Try… Triethanolamine.' That didn't sound quite right, so he pronounced it differently on his second and third attempts, then just shrugged to indicate he didn't know which was correct. 'Anyway, that boils at three-fifty.'

Ben took a slurp of his tea. 'What is it?'

Tyler turned his attention to his computer. 'According to Wikipedia it's…' He clicked through several different browser windows, searching for the correct one. 'One sec. It's… here we go. It's "a viscous organic compound that is both a tertiary amine and a triol".'

He swivelled his chair a little so he was looking up at the Detective Inspector. Ben raised his eyebrows. 'What does that mean?'

'I have no idea,' Tyler admitted. 'But it doesn't matter, because I think I was barking up the wrong tree.'

'Thank Christ for that,' Ben said.

'I think it's a nickname, boss,' Tyler said.

Ben's raised eyebrows travelled in the opposite direction. 'What, *try-e-thingamajiggy*?'

'No. Boils. I think it's a nickname. I think they're all nick-names. Look at the list.' Tyler picked up the evidence bag and

held it up. 'We've got Boils, Stumpy, Brace, Ginger, Ratty…
They're like playground insults. Based on physical appearances.'

'You think these are all people?' Ben asked.

'I think they're all kids, boss. At that school. And I reckon
the numbers are money owed, or something.'

'You think they were buying from Borys?'

'Or selling for him.' He leaned back in his chair. 'And if
the names are based on physical traits, like they seem to be,' he
said. 'Then I'll give you three guesses who I'm thinking "Boils"
could be. And the first two don't count.'

Chapter 22

Logan's initial instinct was to get clear, get everyone a safe distance from the house, and then call in the bomb squad to deal with the device beneath Conrad Howden's bed.

But he didn't.

Instead, he took some more time to study the thing. There was nothing to indicate that it was going to detonate any time soon, so he allowed himself a minute or two to examine it.

It was about the size and shape of a small briefcase, with four wires running up towards each corner of the bed. Pressure pads, maybe? Sensors rigged to detonate when anyone lay on the bed?

A small screen, roughly the size of a compact mobile phone, was fixed to the side facing him. The screen was darkened, like there was no power getting to it.

The device itself had power, though. A single orange light pulsed slowly on what looked like a button of some sort that had been built into the plastic casing.

It was very neat for a bomb. In Logan's experience, they tended to be quite messy things. Even the more professional versions had a real homemade feel to them that this device lacked.

'All right, sir?'

Logan drew back suddenly, sucked in what he momentarily thought would be his last breath, then let it out again as a sigh. 'Jesus Christ, Hamza! I thought I was a bloody goner there!'

Hamza stood in the doorway, looking thoroughly confused. 'Why's that, sir?'

Logan beckoned with his head. 'Check this out. But slowly, and don't touch the bed.'

Hamza hesitated, then carefully lowered himself onto his hands and knees. Logan flexed his fingers, steadied his hand, then began to raise the valance sheet to give the Detective Sergeant a look at what they were dealing with.

'What's all this?' asked Sinead, joining them in the room, and this time both men jumped.

'Jesus fuck!' Logan yelped. 'I'm going to put bloody bells on you lot!' He indicated the bed with a nod. 'I think there might be a bomb.'

'A bomb?' Sinead gasped.

'Cheers for telling me before I got down here with my face right next to it, sir,' Hamza said.

'I'm not... I don't actually think it is,' Logan explained. 'I mean, I thought it might be, but now I'm not sure. I want you to have a look at it. See what you think. You ready?'

Hamza inhaled through his nose, then nodded. 'Ready.'

Sinead retreated into the hall as Logan slowly lifted the trailing sheet, giving Hamza a view of the device below the bed.

'Aye, that's not a bomb. It's a computer,' the DS said.

'You sure?' Logan asked.

'Aye. It's plugged into a wall socket, for one thing, and... hang on.'

He got up, went around to the other side of the bed, and his face appeared when he lifted the valance. 'Those cables are to a USB hub at the back. Tap the screen. What does it say?'

'You sure?' Logan asked. 'It's definitely no' a bomb?'

Hamza shrugged. 'I mean, technically it could be, but if it is, then it's a bomb in a pretty convincing disguise. It should be fine.'

Logan didn't feel entirely comfortable with the 'should' in that sentence. Nevertheless, he cautiously reached a hand under the bed and gave the screen a single light tap.

'There's numbers.' He groaned. 'There's numbers counting.'

Hamza swallowed. Both men held eye contact below the bed.

'Up or down?' he asked.

Logan checked.

'Up,' he said, and they both relaxed a little. Bombs rarely came with a count-up function.

'I think I know what this is,' Hamza said.

His face vanished, and Logan resurfaced to find the DS searching one of the bedposts. Hamza ran his fingers across the spiral of wood, then poked around in the drapes at the top.

'Haha. I knew it! Dirty bastard,' he announced, pulling the curtain part-way aside. 'He's put cameras in! Four of them, I bet, multiple angles. Motion-activated. He's a shagger, and he's been filming everything he got up to.'

'Ugh,' Sinead muttered, returning to the room. 'I think I'd have preferred it to be a bomb. Ties in with what the neighbours said, though. Lot of women came and went. All times of the day and night. The couple through the wall said he was—and I quote—"at it twenty-four-seven." The husband seemed the most bothered by it. Wife said she didn't really notice.'

'Right, so we're building a picture,' Logan said. 'Well done. And good detective work there, Hamza, finding those cameras.'

Hamza smiled and scratched the back of his head. 'Aye, well, I was sort of cheating a bit, sir,' he admitted. 'See, one of Conrad's laptops was unlocked, and I found some video footage on there. A *lot* of video footage. Taken from these cameras.'

'I can see why that might've given you a bit of a heads up, right enough,' Logan said. 'What's the footage like?'

'Pretty high quality. Cameras must be 4k. Impressive, given the size of them.'

'I meant, what's the content like? What are we looking at?' Logan clarified.

'Oh. Right. Aye, well, some of it, from what I can gather, is just him… pleasuring himself. In some quite *creative* ways.'

His gaze went to a spot below the head of the bed, and Logan knew exactly what the Detective Sergeant was getting at.

'Anything else?'

'Plenty, sir, aye. Too much to wade through, even if I wanted to, which I very much do not,' Hamza said. 'They go back months. There's one woman showing up a lot recently, though. Come on through.'

He led the way into the living room. Sinead hung back a moment, regarded the bedposts with a look of mild disgust, then followed the other detectives.

Hamza presented Logan with an open laptop. There were half a dozen video windows open on the screen, each one partly obscuring the one below, so Logan only got hints of what was going on in them. A cheeky glimpse of a bare arse. A wee swatch of a snatch.

The topmost video was paused early enough in proceedings that both 'performers' were fully clothed. Conrad Howden lay on his left side, resting his head on one hand. He was dressed like he'd been out jogging, just like the woman lying flat on her back beside him.

Her eyes were closed, her head tilted back and to the side as Conrad's free hand fiddled down the front of her velour tracksuit bottoms.

The quality of the image really was very good, Logan had to admit. It showed every detail in vivid Ultra HD, and allowed him to easily recognise the woman in the video.

It wasn't difficult. He'd seen her wearing a near-identical outfit just the day before.

'That's Bosco Maximuke's wife,' he announced. 'Conrad Howden was shagging Alexis Maximuke!'

'She's in loads of them,' Hamza said. 'Not just the bedroom, either. There's footage taken from inside a car of them, too. And mobile phone recordings in a park somewhere.'

'So… a body of a suspected dealer turns up at Bosco's daughter's school, and then the guy who was having sex with his wife is nearly beaten to death, and his mum killed?' said Sinead. 'It's got to be tied to Bosco, right? He's got to be involved.'

'Aye, it's looking like it,' Logan said. He checked his phone. Still no messages from Shona. She should be in the post-mortem by now. Strange that he hadn't heard. 'Hamza, keep going here. See what else you can find. Call in whoever you need.'

'Will do, sir.'

'Sinead, I want you to head to Alexis Maximuke's house. I had a chat with her yesterday, but I want her brought into the station. Don't tell her any details, but imply that she's in the shit. She can sit there stewing on that until I get there.'

'Where you going, sir?' Sinead asked.

'Mortuary,' Logan said. He stole one last glance at his phone. Still nothing.

'You checking in on the PM for Conrad's mum?' Sinead asked.

'Aye,' said Logan, shoving his hands deep down into his pockets and heading for the door. 'Something like that.'

—

Sinead knocked for a third time, then stepped back from the door and looked up at the upstairs windows. The curtains were all open, just like those on the ground floor.

She knocked again, then pushed open the letterbox and called inside. 'Mrs Maximuke? Can I have a word?'

There was no reply from within the house. Sinead let the letterbox close, then frowned, and opened it again. The front door offered a view straight along the hallway and into the kitchen. It was hard to be sure from that distance, but the back door looked like it might be ajar.

Straightening, Sinead tried the front door handle, but it was locked. She returned to the street, strolled past half a dozen parked cars, including her own, then hung a left down an alleyway that led to the backs of the row of houses.

The back fence was high and shoogly, like it was just waiting for the right moment to fall on some unsuspecting passerby. It wobbled precariously when Sinead opened the gate and entered the cluttered, overgrown back garden.

Clothes hung from a whirligig washing line, the arms hanging down like they were desperately trying to reach the ground.

From there, it was clear that the door was open. If Sinead had hoped to find Alexis Maximuke out there, though, she was disappointed.

Around the front of the house, a car door opened, then closed.

'Hello?' Sinead called, nudging the back door open a little further.

The house remained stoically silent, and she took a faltering step inside.

Her foot splashed down into a puddle. Milk. A plastic carton lay open on the floor.

She tracked its trajectory from the worktop above. A cup sat there, a teabag ready and waiting at the bottom. Sinead touched the kettle with the back of her hand. Cold.

'Mrs Maximuke? Alexis?' she said. 'Olivia? Is anyone here? This is Detective Constable Sinead Bell. This is the police. If you're here, please make yourself known.'

She waited. Listened. Heard nothing.

'Bollocks.'

She had just taken out her phone to call Logan when she saw a folded sheet of notepaper stuck to the door of the fridge. A single word had been written on the side she could see— 'Olivia.'

Sinead reached for the note, then stopped herself just in time. She took a couple of photographs of it in situ, then took a pair of protective gloves from her pocket and pulled them on.

First, she very carefully removed the magnet, plucked the paper from under it, then returned the magnet to its original position.

She unfolded the page and found a short message written on the paper. She read it in silence, then took out her phone to call Logan. The gloves rendered the touch-screen unresponsive, so she returned the note to the fridge, snapped one of the gloves off, and swiped to her contacts.

Behind her, a foot splashed in the puddle of milk.

Chapter 23

'What are you doing here?' Logan asked, scowling at the skeletal specimen standing before him. 'I thought you were just part-time?'

Albert Rickett raised his plastic visor to reply. The visor was transparent and not remotely soundproof, so this was completely unnecessary.

'You and me both, Detective Chief Inspector,' he said, in his dry monotone. 'I wasn't supposed to be back in to provide cover until the weekend. And yet, here we are.'

Logan looked past him to the swing doors of the mortuary. 'Right, aye,' he said, already boring of the conversation.

'I'm also just meant to be providing administrative support, not *getting my hands dirty*, so to speak.'

'Aye, I think Shona said… wait, what?' Logan asked. 'You're doing the PM? Why? Where's Shona?'

'Your guess is as good as mine,' Ricketts replied. 'I mean, I actually assumed that your guess would be better than mine, since you seem to have become so… friendly. But, judging by your face, I can see that you don't know where she is, either.'

'She didn't come in?'

Ricketts shook his head. Given his advanced years, this was a pretty risky move. 'She did not.'

'And nobody thought to get in touch?' Logan demanded, already taking out his phone. 'You didn't phone her?'

'I'm sure someone tried,' Ricketts said. 'But not me personally, no. That's not really something I would consider to be an essential part of my—'

'Aye, aye, shut up,' Logan snapped. He listened to the ringing tone from his mobile, then grimaced when Shona's voicemail started to play. 'Hiya, it's me,' he said, once the bleep had sounded. 'Give me a ring when you get this. I'm, eh, I'm heading over.'

'Is everything all right?' asked Ricketts.

'Eh, aye. Yes. Fine,' Logan said, backing towards the door. He jabbed a finger in the direction of the morgue doors. 'Just get me those PM results.'

Ricketts didn't bother replying. Even if he'd had something noteworthy to say, the DCI had already left.

Instead, he just stared at the office door until the slow-closing hinge had finally allowed it to clunk shut, then shook his head and lowered his plastic visor down over his face once more.

'Very good, sir. As you wish, sir,' he muttered, adopting the tone of a Royal butler.

And with that, he set to work.

—

Logan tried calling half a dozen more times between Raigmore and the Kessock Bridge. Traffic was flowing fairly smoothly, but he fired up the siren and lights, and bullied his way across the city, dread gnawing like rats at his insides, while Taggart barked furiously at the sound of the screaming sirens.

Shona would be fine, of course. She'd have overslept. Or…

Or what? What other explanation was there that allowed her to be 'fine'? Even if she'd just decided not to come in, that suggested something was far wrong. She wouldn't do that. Not the Shona he knew.

Still, he'd take that over many of the alternatives that were swirling around his head by the time he was flying along the A9 and across the Longman roundabout.

He hadn't called in backup. What would he have said? 'Shona's late for work, send in Armed Response'?

He reached the other side of the bridge in moments, powered past a couple of caravans, then took the turn-off so fast his tyres screeched their displeasure.

Shona's bungalow looked unremarkable enough from the outside. It was still standing, proving his worries about fire or localised earthquake unfounded, and her car was parked out front, so she hadn't just driven away somewhere and left her old life behind.

There was no movement from the windows. The curtains in the living room were shut, aside from a narrow gap down the middle.

He ordered the dog to stay, ran up the path to the front door, knocked once, and entered. He briefly registered the fact that the door was unlocked, but didn't have enough information to decide if this was good news or bad.

'Hello? Shona? You here?'

He and the house both seemed to hold their breath.

He checked the living room first. No sign of her in there.

The bedroom next, a knock on the door, then a look inside. The bed had been made in her usual half-hearted style. He put a hand on the side she slept in, but found no trace of her body heat on the sheet or pillow.

The bathroom door was ajar. He called her name again, then peeked inside, half-expecting to find her on the floor. That had been one of the many scenarios that had played out in his head on the way over. She'd slipped getting out of the shower, cracked her head on the sink or toilet, and was lying there, unconscious.

But, no. The bathroom was empty, the shower floor dry.

The first thing that drew his eye in the kitchen was the back door, which wasn't quite on its latch. A breeze blew against it from the other side, moving it a few millimetres each time, and making it dunt against the frame.

He opened it, stepped out onto the uneven paving stones of the back garden, and called her name again.

'Shona? You here?'

She wasn't.

He returned to the kitchen, and saw a pen on the worktop, the lid beside it. From there, his eyes went down to the floor, eventually settling on a small ring-bound notebook that had fallen so it was propped up against the front of a cabinet.

Bending, he picked it up by one of the metal coils, and placed it on the worktop beside the pen, face-up.

There were three words written on the pad.

Olivia

Iceman

Ole

He read them again and again, each jarring him in its own way.

Olivia meant Shona's disappearance could be connected to the case.

The Iceman case was closed. Had been for months. So why was the name written here?

And as for the 'Ole,' he was at a complete loss. What the hell was that supposed to…?

Something else on the kitchen floor pulled his attention away from the notepad. Something so small, that he'd almost missed it.

A spot of red on the black-and-white lino. A splash of blood. Even from that distance, he was sure that's what it was.

The polisman in him stepped in and took over then.

He snapped a photo of the notepad, then returned it to the place he'd found it. That done, he retreated from the kitchen in as few steps as possible, doing his best not to contaminate the scene any more than he already had.

He returned to his car to call in the report. Kept his voice steady until he'd relayed all the necessary information and made sure it had all been understood.

Then he punched the living shit out of his steering wheel, and shook it so hard he almost ripped it right out of the dash.

He roared. Not a shout. Not a scream. Something savage and primal that he couldn't hold back, even if he'd tried.

She had been taken. She had been hurt, and she had been taken. He had no idea who by. No clue as to why. But he did have one lead. One thread to pull at. A thread that was tangled around every part of this case.

Olivia.

Throwing open the car door, he forced his feet and hands into protective coverings and returned to the house. It could be an hour or more until Palmer's team got there, and he needed to know now what had happened to her. Or start to figure it out, at least.

He stopped at the threshold, swallowed down the heaving ball of emotion that threatened to choke him, and stepped inside.

His mind raced at the possibilities, all his fears rushing to make themselves known, dragging his attention this way and that.

He closed his eyes. Shut the thoughts out. Now was not the time to crumble. Now, perhaps more than ever, was the time for him to do what he had been trained for. And for that, he needed a level head.

'See,' he reminded himself. 'Don't just look.'

His eyes opened. And he saw.

He saw a dent on the wall behind the front door that lined up with the handle. He saw plaster dust on the skirting directly below it, which told him the damage was recent.

No damage to the catch or the doorframe, so it hadn't been locked. A struggle, maybe? Shona had been trying to hold it closed, but the person on the other side had been bigger and stronger than she was.

What next? The door was open, her attacker would have been inside. In here. With her.

The kitchen, then. She'd run to the back door to get out that way. Had someone come in? Was that why it was open?

Or had someone gone out?

He saw the blood droplet again, and this time found a couple of smaller spots and a smear on one of the black tiles closer to the door that led back to the hallway.

There was no blood by the back door, suggesting she hadn't made it that far. So, she'd been grabbed from behind, or blocked from the front. Pulled or pushed to the ground, possibly. Struck, probably no more than once, given the limited blood splatter.

The smear suggested something had been dragged through it, back in the direction of the hall. He traced the most likely route and found two more small streaks of blood on the scuffed wooden flooring.

Back to the kitchen. *See, don't just look.*

There was part of a footprint on one of the black tiles nearer to the door, a muddy imprint of the edge of a shoe. There wasn't enough for him to accurately judge the size, but it was substantially smaller than his own.

Then again, most feet were.

He saw the pen on the kitchen counter. Odd angle, like it had been set down in a hurry, or—yes, there was a spot of ink on the worktop. Dropped. The pad, too, probably.

She'd been in the kitchen writing in the pad when the attacker had arrived. He looked to the back door. Had someone come in there first, maybe? She'd run to the front to get out, and then…

No. That didn't work. The force the front door had been thrown open with suggested a struggle. Brute strength had been used. If an attacker was already there in the house with her, why would she fight to keep the front door closed?

So, she'd been writing. Something had alerted her to the attacker approaching the front of the house. She'd run to the door to try to keep him out, rather than running straight out the back.

He glanced at the kitchen window. It faced out to the back of the house, so there was no way she could have seen anyone coming up the front path from there.

Someone else *had* been in the house. Someone who had warned her. She'd dropped the pen and the pad, then gone running to the door to block it. The attacker had forced their way inside, she'd run to the kitchen to escape, and hadn't made it.

That fit.

She'd seemed a little off when he'd spoken with her the night before. Someone could have been with her then. Someone she didn't want him knowing about.

He took out his phone, removed a glove, then tried calling her number again. It rang in his ear, then a moment later, Bon Jovi's *Blaze of Glory* came belting from elsewhere in the bungalow.

Watching where he stepped, Logan followed the sound and found Shona's phone in the living room, sitting on the arm of her couch. He pressed the 'end call' button on his phone, and the music shut off. Silence returned, even more oppressive and smothering than it had felt just a moment before.

There were missed calls and some texts on the home screen of Shona's phone. The caller and sender details were hidden, but the time stamps were enough to tell him that his number would be responsible for most of them.

There was a can of Irn Bru on the table next to the armchair. Mud on the floor and near the base of the chair at the front. Someone *had* been there, then. Someone had come in from outside, sat down, opened a can of Irn Bru, and then done very little with it, judging by the amount of the vibrant orange liquid that was left in the can.

He noticed something on the floor beside the armchair and bent down to get a better look. It was a hat. A knitted black beanie that, when he touched it, left a suggestion of moisture on the fingertips of his gloves.

There were some hairs stuck to the fibres. Longer than Shona's. Lighter, too.

There was only one way this was pointing.

Olivia had been here, and either by accident or design, Shona's attackers had come with her.

Olivia was the key to it all. Find her, and he might find Shona, might be able to save her.

The rats of dread began to gnaw away at him again.

Assuming he wasn't too late.

Chapter 24

Shona hissed as the hood was pulled off, and the beam of a head torch shone straight into her light-starved eyes.

She had blacked out for a while. She thought so, anyway, but it had been hard to tell in the darkness of the hood. There were periods without sound, though, she thought. Without panic. Without pain.

She had been in a car. There had been men. Silent types, who had ignored her babbled pleas, and her cries for help. She could smell them, even through the hood, the musk of their sweat, the stink of their cheap cologne. She could feel them, too, one on each side, boxing her in, squashing her between them.

There was the occasional muttered remark, but she couldn't make out the words, or maybe couldn't understand the language.

The car had headed back to the city. She could tell by the bumps of the bridge beneath the wheels, and the shrill whistling of the wind between its cables.

She tried to keep track from there, but was soon lost among the twists and turns of the city.

They could've been anywhere when the car finally stopped. When the doors opened. When the hands grabbed at her and dragged her out, kicking and screaming.

There had been a satisfying thunk when her foot found a target, but then hands had pawed at her breasts, grabbing them, squeezing them until she had cried out in pain. A roar of laughter had rung out, several male voices joining in the chorus. She hadn't dared try anything else.

They'd stuck her in a padded chair of some kind, and tied her wrists to the furniture's wooden arms. She had listened to their footsteps retreating, growing distant, and then the only sound she could hear was the rasp of her own breathing inside the hood, and the twenty-one-gun salute of her heartbeat.

How long had she sat there? How often had she sunk down into stolen snatches of sleep? Time had no meaning beneath the hood, and when it was finally pulled free, she had no idea how much of it had passed.

The room she was in was a… what? A warehouse? A store-room? A cupboard? The only light shone directly into her face, and she had no idea how far the ocean of darkness extended. Five feet? Fifty? She couldn't say, but the darkness felt endless and infinite, like there was nothing else left of the world but this spot. This place. This time.

'Who… who are you?' she asked the man with the head torch. She didn't want to look at him, but she didn't dare not. 'What do you want?'

The man with the head torch—if, indeed, it was a man, the direction of the light making it impossible to tell—remained silent. Another voice replied, its words muffled, and slightly echoing.

'Where is the girl?' it asked.

Shona tried to turn in the voice's direction, but it was behind her somewhere, and her restraints stopped her before she could get a glimpse of whoever had spoken.

She could hear him, though. His breathing was a wheeze and a click, like a budget Darth Vader. When he moved, it was with the same thudding and dragging she'd heard back at her house.

'Where is Olivia?'

'I don't… I don't know.'

The next wheezed breath was deeper, like a gasp, but not a gasp. A sigh, perhaps.

'Please, do not try to be brave,' the man in the shadows told her. The voice was light, and the warning sounded quite friendly. 'Bravery will hurt. A lot. This, I can guarantee.'

He gave that some time to sink in, then tried again.

'Where is Olivia?' he asked, this time from somewhere over her other shoulder. The man with the head torch continued to sit there in silence, staring and dazzling her. 'She came to see you, did she not?'

There was an accent there, Shona thought, buried in all the dry, throaty rasping.

'I don't know where she is,' Shona said. 'She came to see me, but she left. She's gone. I don't know where she went.'

'Ha!' said the voice, then it fell away into a silence that begged to be filled.

'Please, I don't know what this is about, but we can talk about this,' Shona obliged. 'Please, you don't have to do this. Any of this. We can talk, OK? We can talk.'

'Oh? And what would we talk about? You and I? What would we discuss?'

'I don't know. I don't know, whatever you want. Maybe I can, I don't know, help?'

'Help me?' His voice was in front of her now, just beside the man with the torch. He leaned in, and for a moment the edge of the light picked out a face straight out of a horror movie. 'I'd like to see you try,' he whispered, then he returned once more to the shadows.

Shona sat there, not speaking, shaken as much by those eyes and that face as by everything else that was happening to her.

'She took something from me. Olivia,' the voice continued. 'You could say, she took *everything* from me. I have been repaying the favour. Bit by bit. Day by day. But now, I wish this suffering to end. My suffering, I mean. Not hers. Hers…' He drew a deep breath in through his oxygen mask. '…is only just beginning.'

Chapter 25

Tyler's mobile was in his hand when it buzzed, almost making him drop the thing in fright.

'It's the boss,' he announced, and Ben came hurrying over to listen in.

'Put him on speakerphone,' the DI said.

'All right, boss? You're on speaker,' Tyler said. 'Uniform should be with you any minute.'

'How you doing, Jack?' Ben asked, leaning in far closer to the phone than was necessary.

Logan didn't answer, and instead skipped straight to his point. 'On my way back. Has Sinead brought Alexis Maximuke in yet?'

'Eh, not yet, boss, no,' Tyler said. He looked at Ben, who shrugged. 'Didn't know she was meant to be.'

'She's round there now. Alexis was at it with Conrad Howden. She called him "Father Conrad" when I spoke to her yesterday, so she might think he's a priest.'

'Why would she think that, boss?'

'Because he dressed up as one,' Logan replied. 'He was running a con on her.'

'I'll get an Interview Room prepped for Alexis,' Ben said.

'I don't care about the other stuff right now,' Logan said. Judging by the noise in the background, he was driving. 'Conrad Howden, their relationship, whatever. I'm not interested. I just want to know where her daughter is. You get onto Sinead and find out what's taking so bloody long. Tell her to get Alexis, and find out where Olivia is, all right?'

'When did she set off?' Ben asked.

'I don't know. A bit after ten,' Logan said. 'Thereabouts.'

Hunched over Tyler's desk, both detectives checked their watches. 'That's over two hours ago, boss.'

'And you've no' heard a thing from her since then?' asked Ben.

There was silence from the other end of the line, other than the interwoven rumblings of an engine and the wind.

'Right, check with Hamza. Maybe he's heard from her. Get Uniform round there,' Logan instructed.

Tyler stood up, all pain and discomfort momentarily forgotten. 'What? Why? What's happened?'

'I'm not... I don't know.'

'Boss?' Tyler asked, his voice rising half an octave. 'Where is she? Why are we sending Uniform? What's going on?'

'I don't know, Tyler!' Logan snapped. He flicked the switch that ignited the blazing blue lights behind the BMW's front grille and set the siren wailing. 'It might... it's probably nothing. Just get someone over there, pronto. I'm heading there now.'

'Boss?' Tyler said, but the screen of his phone turned dark as the call was cut off.

DI Forde stared at the mobile for a few seconds, then straightened up. 'Right, Uniform. Let's get a call out to—'

'It's not far,' Tyler said. 'I'm going. Give me your keys, boss.'

'No, I bloody well will not! You're not going anywhere in your condition. I'll never hear the end of it if you go and—'

'Ben!' Tyler barked, cutting him off. And then—for that moment—his affable boyish air was gone. 'Give me your keys,' he said. 'So I can go and find my wife!'

The battle that raged inside Ben was there on his face for all to see. Eventually, he sighed and fished out his keys. 'Fine,' he said. 'But for once in your bloody life, don't do anything stupid.'

Tyler's balls thrummed with pain as he tore along the Longman estate in Ben's car. Well, his *ball*, technically. It ached with that singularly unique sort of ache that could only be caused by testicle trauma—that dull, nauseating sensation that clawed its way up into the lower intestine and set up camp there until you wished you'd never been born.

He ignored it. It didn't matter. Not now.

He'd tried calling her twice since leaving the station, once as he'd lurched, Igor-like, across the foyer, and again once he'd heaved himself into the driver's seat.

Straight to voicemail, both times.

Cars slowed for the red lights ahead. He slammed a hand down on the horn, adding to the cacophony of the sirens. 'Move! Fucking move!'

There was no way past but the pavement. He let out a gasp as the wheels mounted the kerb and his one remaining gonad was pancaked against the seat.

Forget it. Ignore it. Move on.

Brakes and tyres screeched. There was the sedate crunch of a slow but significant impact.

He ignored that, too, and went powering through the junction, swerving onto the wrong side of the road to pass some slow-moving bastard who hadn't pulled over in time.

She was probably fine. There was almost certainly nothing to worry about.

And yet, something about the timbre of Logan's voice had filled him with fear all the way down to the bones.

She could be hurt. She could be worse.

And *that* was something he couldn't ignore.

–

Hamza had waded through thirty or forty hours of Conrad Howden's past sexual exploits now. Thankfully, he hadn't been forced to relive every minute, and had instead scrubbed through them at high speed, skimming for anything of interest to the investigation.

There had still been hundreds of video clips to go when he'd decided that he'd had quite enough, and that this felt like a task that could be safely dingied off onto someone at a more junior level.

He had been about to pack up when a thought had occurred to him. The footage on the laptop had been saved by Conrad—a hand-picked selection of his favourite intimate moments. The footage on the hard drive of the computer under the bed, on the other hand, would be more recent, and untouched.

It had taken him just a few minutes to find a cable, plug in the laptop, and access the storage. There, he'd found eighty-four videos taken in the last few days, plus four separate ongoing recordings that he'd triggered by getting close to the bed.

The four videos before that all started with Logan at the bottom of the frame. They lasted several minutes, presumably until the detectives had left the room again. A quick scrub forward confirmed this, and Hamza closed down those files.

There was a five-day gap between those videos and the previous recordings. By Hamza's reckoning, that meant they had been captured the day before Conrad was attacked. He double-clicked the first file, waited for it to load, then whispered an 'oh, shit,' at what played out on the screen.

His phone rang. He reached for it, still transfixed by the video, and didn't even bother to check who was calling before he answered.

'DS Khaled,' he said. The worry in DI Forde's voice finally grabbed his full attention. 'Wait, wait, hold on, sir, say that again.' He paused the video. '*What*'s happened?'

He listened. Nodded. Closed the laptop's lid.

'Right, sir,' he announced. 'I'm on my way.'

–

Two uniformed officers were already standing on guard at the front door of Alexis and Olivia Maximuke's house. One of them made the mistake of trying to intercept Tyler as he came lumbering up the path, but a flash of a warrant card and a warning look made him give way.

'I'd be careful, though,' the Uniform said, as Tyler made for the door. 'There's a lot of blood.'

The words stopped him. Jerked him back. The door was no longer an entrance, but a barrier. Not a way in, but a blockade keeping him out. Saving him from whatever waited inside.

Sinead's car was along the street. He'd passed it on the way in. She hadn't left. Not the way she'd arrived, at least.

'Is there… is anyone in there?' he asked.

'Not that we saw,' the other Uniform replied. She shrugged. 'Didn't want to go traipsing through the place, though. Not until someone more senior gave the order.'

Both constables looked Tyler up and down, decided he didn't qualify, and so shut their mouths.

Tyler had the presence of mind—but only just—to pull on gloves before turning the handle. The door relented inwards, and the hallway seemed to stretch into infinity before him.

He spotted the blood right away. It was hard to miss. It painted one of the top cabinets in the kitchen at the far end of the hall, and was in the process of dripping onto the worktop below.

Plop. Plop. Plop.

Tyler forced his legs over the threshold. His heart was racing so fast it felt like a solid thrum vibrating outwards from his chest. That explained the shaking as he moved along the narrow hallway, his eyes both drawn to, and yet refusing to look at, the kitchen floor as it came into view, afraid of what they might find there.

He tried to say her name, but his throat was too tight for the word to emerge. All he could do was walk, and wait, and hope.

A lifetime later, he finally reached the kitchen. No Sinead. No anyone. He didn't know whether to laugh or cry and so, for just a moment, he did both.

'Tyler?'

Hamza's voice came from out on the front step. Tyler heard the snap of his gloves being pulled on.

'Is she there? Is she in there?'

'I don't… she's not in here. In the kitchen, I mean, I don't…'

Hamza was already talking, but this time not to him. 'Did you check out the back?'

There was an awkward silence, then one of the uniformed constables admitted that no, they hadn't.

'Then what are you bloody waiting for?' Hamza demanded. 'One of you get round there. See what's what. Don't go trampling around, just look. And you, get onto dispatch. I want more officers here.'

'And the crime scene guys,' Tyler said. He looked back over his shoulder and met the wide, worried eyes of DS Khaled. 'There's blood, Ham. There's blood everywhere.'

Chapter 26

It was later. How much later, Logan wasn't sure. Time had lost much of its meaning in the past few hours, or minutes, or days.

They were gathered in the Incident Room. Those who remained, at least. The atmosphere wasn't so much subdued as morose. Even Taggart had tucked himself into a ball beneath Logan's desk, after Hamza had sourced some food for him from the dog unit.

Both houses—Shona's and Alexis Maximuke's—had been combed over by Palmer's team, and the evidence was now being catalogued and sent over in dribs and drabs.

The results of the tests on the blood were mixed. The blood on the floor of the cottage across the Kessock bridge was a match for Shona's. The more significant amount of the stuff in Alexis Maximuke's kitchen was made up of two types, neither of which was Sinead's. That news had heartened all of them, but done nothing to tell them where she was, or what had happened to her.

There had been a struggle in the kitchen. Possibly more than one. A puddle of milk on the floor had turned pink with the aftermath of a fight. A note had fallen into it, and become so sodden and stained that whatever had been written there was now completely illegible.

There had been a knife involved in the blood-letting—a small paring knife that one of Palmer's guys had found on the floor under the kitchen table.

The knife had blood on the blade that matched a spray on the front of the fridge. The blood on the top cupboard had arrived there courtesy of someone else. Judging by the splatter, someone's face had either been smashed against the cupboard door, or vice versa. The cupboards were reasonably low, but the point of impact suggested someone around six feet tall, and almost certainly now in possession of a broken nose.

According to the blood patterns, both injuries had been inflicted at approximately the same time, give or take a few seconds, which meant it had all kicked off in the kitchen, and two currently unidentified individuals were now paying the price.

Samples had been taken from both spillages and were being fast-tracked through DNA profiling. Even with Logan applying pressure, though, it was going to take eight to ten hours to get even a whiff of feedback from the lab. Eight to ten hours that they couldn't afford to waste.

One of the neighbours had given them something useful. She'd seen two men getting out of a dark blue or grey van and entering the house. Several minutes later, one had returned to the van and collected some sort of large plastic bin—for compost, she thought, though she confessed that she wasn't a gardener.

She hadn't seen them come back out, but when she'd looked twenty minutes later, the van, and the men, she assumed, were gone.

Sadly, she hadn't thought to take a note of the number plate, but she would swear that the van was dark blue, grey, or maybe black. Possibly a deep navy blue.

So, helpful, but not overly so.

'Right, CID and Uniform are gathering downstairs for the briefing,' Ben said. 'All leave has been cancelled, and everyone brought back in. It's all hands on deck.'

He looked at Tyler then, hoping this would offer the lad some comfort, but if it did, the Detective Constable didn't show it.

'Mitchell also wants a press briefing, on both Shona and Sinead,' Ben continued. 'She wants their pictures everywhere. And, eh, she wants you to talk to the media, Jack.'

Logan nodded. 'Fine.'

'You sure you're all right with that? You're not going to lose the rag with them or—'

'I said it's fine, Ben. I'll talk to them. Whatever it takes.'

'Is this all we've got?' Tyler asked. He'd been tapping out a message on his phone, but now threw it down onto his desk. 'Is that it? Ask people to keep a lookout for her? Them. Is that the best we've got?'

'I'm getting a trace done on Sinead's phone. Should be through any minute,' Hamza said. 'We'll find her, mate. We'll find both of them.'

'In the meantime, I suggest we continue with what we've got,' Ben said. 'We bring that spotty-faced lad back in. Tyler had an idea he might be involved with Borys. Dealing for him. Worth putting the pressure on him a bit to see if he's holding out on us.'

'What, *now*?' Tyler asked. 'We're worrying about that now?'

'It's all connected,' Logan said. He didn't look at the Detective Constable. He couldn't. 'We've got a lot of questions in front of us. The more of them we can answer, the better chance we have of getting Sinead and Shona back. We do the work. We figure it out. It's the only way this ends.'

Tyler begrudgingly conceded the point with a shrug and a grimace.

'Ricketts should be finished the PM of the second victim,' Ben said. 'No change in Conrad Howden's condition yet.'

'Oh!' Hamza sat up straight. 'Shite, I found something at Conrad's house. Camera footage. With everything going on, I forgot.'

'What was it?' asked Tyler.

'Here, I'll show you,' Hamza said.

He hooked the laptop up to the big flat-screen TV that spent most of its life tucked away in a corner of the Incident Room, while the others gathered round to watch.

'Recorded the day before we think Conrad was attacked,' Hamza said.

On the TV, the image on-screen mirrored what was happening on the computer desktop. The other detectives watched as he opened up a video file, and an overhead view of Conrad Howden's bed appeared.

'This is the best view, though it doesn't show much. The cameras are motion-activated, but very sensitive. Shadows set them off, or just the shake of the bed if someone walks too close to it,' Hamza said.

'Nothing's happening,' Logan pointed out.

'He's not started it yet,' Ben said. 'It's paused.'

'No, it's playing,' Hamza said.

'Is it?' Ben squinted over the top of his glasses. 'Are you sure? Nothing's moving.'

'That's because there's no bugger in the room,' Logan said.

'Actually, there is, sir. Wait for it…'

Hamza pointed to the left of the screen, which showed part of the floor at the side of the bed. The camera the footage was from seemed to be the one on the bottom right of the bed, were you to look down on it from above, and the angle offered the clearest view of that particular section of floor.

'…there.'

The bottom half of a figure shuffled into the room, leaning on a walking stick for support. He was an old man, judging by the stiffness of his joints. He wore a black glove on the one hand that the detective could see. It gripped the top of his cane, almost fully encasing the metal ball that formed the handle.

'Who's this?' Logan asked.

'No idea, sir. But he's not alone.'

Even as Hamza said the words, two other men entered the frame. Well, the legs of one and one foot of another, at least.

The voice, when it spoke, took Logan by surprise. He was so used to CCTV and security camera footage that it hadn't occurred to him that the place would've been rigged for sound.

'He is not here.'

It was one of the new arrivals who spoke, he thought. The accent was from somewhere in the former Soviet block. That didn't come as too much of a surprise, given how mixed up the Maximuke clan seemed to be in all of this.

'Find him,' said the man at the front. 'Check the usual places.'

'What's up with this voice?' Tyler asked.

'Sounds muffled,' Ben said.

Hamza turned his attention back to the laptop. 'Aye. Wait until you see this,' he said, pausing the video and opening another. 'They basically just leave after that, but I can show you it from a different angle.'

The second video played, but this time the footage came from the camera diagonally across from the first. This one had been angled a little more steeply so it was aiming at the mirror cupboard doors that ran alongside the bed. It was a sneaky way of getting a good wide-angle view of any bed-based action, without having the camera in sight.

Unfortunately, as the intention was specifically to film events taking place on the bed, the angle didn't offer much of a view of the rest of the room, so very little more was revealed of the three men who entered.

'Wait for it again…' Hamza said, then he hit the pause button just as the man with the walking stick positioned himself so the bottom two-thirds of his face was in view. 'There he is. It's just for a second, but you can see what's up with his voice.'

'Is that an oxygen mask?' Logan muttered.

'That's what it looks like to me, sir, aye.'

'Who is he?' Tyler asked.

'No idea,' Hamza admitted. 'He's too small in the image to make out much apart from the mask, but it looks like there's something wrong with his skin. Eczema, or really bad acne, maybe. Something's not right, anyway.'

Logan was staring at the screen, so deep in thought that his eyebrows looked like two caterpillars squaring up for a scrap.

'Go back to the first view,' he instructed. 'I want to see him coming in.'

Hamza did as he was told, scrubbed backwards through the footage, and played the arrival of the man in the mask.

'Right, pause there,' Logan said, just as the feet entered the frame. He got up from his chair and crossed to the screen to get a better view.

'What is it?' asked Ben. 'His shoes?'

Logan shook his head. 'The cane. The walking stick. The bottom few inches there, that's metal.'

'Aye. Not uncommon,' DI Forde said.

'Borys had burn marks inflicted on him before he died. Little round ones, about yon size.' He formed a circle a little smaller than a ten pence piece with a curled finger and thumb. 'I reckon if you were to heat that metal up, it would do the job.'

'You think the stick would match the burns?' asked Hamza.

'I'd put money on it,' Logan replied. He prodded the feet on screen. 'We find this bastard. Whoever he is, he's slap bang in the middle of it. Him and Olivia Maximuke. And we need to go back over the Iceman case. I think it might be connected.'

'The Iceman, boss?' Tyler asked. 'What makes you say that?'

Logan told them about the hand-written list on the worktop in Shona's cottage, which was currently being checked over by Palmer's team.

'Olé?' Ben asked. 'That's Spanish, isn't it?'

'Aye, but it didn't have the accent, so it must just be "ole", like in "This Ole House".'

'Shakin' Stevens,' Ben said. He looked momentarily pleased with himself, then quietly cleared his throat and made a note in his pad. 'The Iceman, eh? That's what she wrote?'

Logan nodded. 'Aye. "Olivia. Iceman. Ole." Or 'Olé", I can't be sure.'

'What does it mean?' Hamza asked.

Logan blew out his cheeks. 'I don't know. Yet. That's why we need to go over everything from the Iceman case.'

'That's years of files and reports, Jack. It's going to take time,' Ben reasoned. 'It's one thing having the manpower, but they need to know what they're looking for. This isn't a job for Uniform. This is specialist stuff.'

'Aye, well, we'd better get a move on, then, before—'

'DCI Logan?'

Detective Superintendent Mitchell had managed to appear in the doorway again without any of them noticing her arrival. At least this time they hadn't been caught making jokes at the expense of Tyler's testicles, but quite frankly Logan didn't have time for her shite right now.

Nor did Taggart, apparently. He emerged from under Logan's desk to fire out a couple of barks and a howl that must've sounded disappointing even to him, then stood glaring at the Detective Superintendent like he might rip her throat out at any moment, or at least have a nip at her ankles.

Mitchell regarded the dog coolly for several seconds, after which Taggart rolled onto his back and stuck his legs in the air like he was dead.

'I'd like a word in my office,' Mitchell told Logan.

'Sorry, ma'am. We're deep in the middle of something at the moment.'

'It wasn't a request,' Mitchell said. She inched the door open a little further, making very clear what his next actions should be.

Logan briefly contemplated telling her to ram her office up her arse, then concluded that it would be in everyone's best interest to keep the station's senior management on-side. They were the ones who signed off on the overtime, after all, and until this case was closed, everyone was safely back home, and justice had been done, he was determined that no bastard was taking so much as a smoking break.

'Ben, you've got the room. Let's crack on with this, and I'll be back in two minutes.' Logan put emphasis on that last part for Mitchell's benefit, then got to his feet and followed her out of the room.

–

Just over three minutes later, Logan could not believe what he was hearing. He leaned forward in his chair until his shadow covered most of the desk.

'Sorry, ma'am. You're going to have to say that again.'

'Why? Didn't you hear what I said, Detective Chief Inspector?'

'Oh, I heard what you said, all right, but with all due respect, I can't quite grasp the absolute fucking stupidity of the idea, and I wanted to make sure that I didn't imagine it.'

Across the desk, the Detective Superintendent became very still. So still, in fact, that Logan could've swapped her out for a cardboard cutout, and nobody coming into the office would've been any the wiser.

Under a microscope, it might be possible to make out some sort of movement. An incremental flaring of the nostrils, perhaps. A standing on end of the hair on the back of her neck. A clenching of a dark-skinned jawline that was impressively taut for someone her age.

Truthfully, Logan had expected more of a reaction to his outburst, even as the words were lining up to be deployed. Her predecessor would already have stapled Logan's tongue to the desk for such a remark, and would now be in the process of driving both thumbs deep into his eye sockets.

It would've been worth it, though. What had just come out of Mitchell's mouth had, without question, been ridiculous enough to merit his reaction.

What was worse was that now, several seconds later, she still hadn't taken it back. He'd actually hoped she might be joking, but nothing she'd done since suggested that was the case.

'You aren't serious?' he asked, a little perturbed by her stillness. He'd seen snakes and other venomous creatures freeze like that in nature documentaries. It rarely boded well for anything within striking range. 'You can't really be taking him off the case? We need all the help we can get and, though I never thought I'd say it, he's one of my best officers.'

'He's also married to what we have to assume is a victim.'

'I'm aware of that. I was at the wedding, but—'

'Good. Then you appreciate why it's completely inappropriate for him to be involved in the investigation.'

'No! I don't!'

'The regulations are very clear on the matter. If an officer—'

'Fuck the regulations!' Logan snapped, not even bothering with the 'all due respect' part this time. 'Tyler can help. The poor bastard *needs* to help. It's the only way he's getting through this with his sanity in one piece.'

Mitchell clasped her hands so everything from the middle fingers to the pinkies were interlocked. Both index fingers pressed together, pointing in Logan's direction.

'I appreciate your frustration, Jack. And if we were running a mental health charity, he could absolutely stay on the case. But we're the constabulary. There are rules. Strict ones. There have to be, or it all falls down around our ears.'

'He's a good officer,' Logan protested. 'He'll help us get them back. He'll help us crack this.'

'Oh, Jack, for God's sake, grow up! Face facts!' Mitchell said, raising her voice to match his own. 'He can't be on the team for this investigation. He's too close to it.'

'I'm not taking him off this case!'

'He's compromised!'

Logan slapped the desk, frustration bubbling over into anger. 'If he's compromised, then so am I!'

The words were out of him before he could stop them. They'd been intended as a defence of Tyler, but he'd realised too late that they were something else, too. They were an indictment of himself.

'What are you talking about?' Mitchell asked.

'Nothing. I didn't mean anything,' Logan said. 'I just meant… we're all close to Sinead, so we're all—'

It was no use. He could see that. Across the desk, the Detective Superintendent had closed her eyes, and was emitting a noise not unlike the creaking of old, well-weathered wood.

'The pathologist, Dr Maguire,' Mitchell muttered. 'You're in a relationship.'

'It's not—'

'Don't, Jack!' Mitchell warned, and there was a fire in her eyes when they snapped back open that told him to hold his tongue. 'Just… just don't say another bloody word.'

And so, he didn't. He just sat there, waiting, while she stared back at him, fingers tapping the desktop, brain knitting her thoughts into something neat and coherent.

Finally, with a sigh, she nodded. 'Fine. I don't like it, but you're right,' she said.

'Thank you,' Logan said, bouncing to his feet. 'You won't regret it, ma'am. Tyler's going to be a major part of—'

'You misunderstand me, Jack,' Mitchell told him. 'I don't mean you're right about DC Neish's involvement in the investigation. I mean you're right about yours.'

Logan frowned. 'Ma'am?'

'You're both compromised by your relationships to the victims,' Mitchell told him. 'Like I say, I don't like it, but I'm afraid you're both off the case.'

'What?' Logan almost laughed. Emphasis on the 'almost.' 'You're not… you can't be serious?'

'It's completely inappropriate for you to have any involvement. Either of you. DI Forde can act as S.O. until we can bring in additional resource.'

Logan was on his feet. He couldn't quite remember how or when that had happened, but he was looming large over the seated Detective Superintendent now. To her credit, she didn't so much as blink.

'Now wait a bloody minute, *ma'am*,' he said, making the title sound like an insult. 'You know as well as I do that we need the full team assembled for this. One of our own—hell, *two* of our own—are missing. There are clear signs of injury, and we've got reason to believe the case is connected to the Iceman investigation from late last year—an investigation that both Tyler and myself were both heavily and directly involved in.'

'Yes. DC Neish almost died, didn't he?' Mitchell asked, knowing full bloody well what the answer was. 'So, again, his involvement is too personal.'

'It's *all* personal!' Logan cried. 'Every case we work. Every victim we have to mourn. Every loved-up one whose eyes we have to look in. Every bastard we hunt down and throw behind bars. Every one of them is personal, and don't you dare try to pretend you think otherwise, or you wouldn't have your arse in that fucking seat.'

'That's enough, Detective Chief Inspector.'

'Enough? You're trying to pull me off this case. I've no' even got started!'

'I said *that's enough*!'

This time, it was Mitchell who struck the desk. She used a ring binder for added effect, and the sound was like a whip crack in the confines of the office.

'Go home, Detective Chief Inspector. Go home and cool off. Call me tomorrow, and we'll see if it's appropriate for you and DC Neish to be reassigned, or if it's best you take some leave.'

'Leave?' Logan said, but the fires of his rage had burned down to embers now. This was an argument he was unlikely to win, and every hurled accusation or shouted insult only reduced his chances further. 'We've cancelled everyone's leave. We've brought them all back in.'

'Yes, well.' Mitchell replaced the binder on her desk and lined it up with the others. 'None of them are in relationships with the victims, are they?'

'Well, no, but—'

'Take DC Neish and go home, Jack,' Mitchell said, already reaching for the phone to start making arrangements. 'And be sure to take that dog with you.'

Chapter 27

Tyler had protested. Of course he had. Logan would've been disappointed if he hadn't. He'd wanted to go hobbling into Mitchell's office and confront the Detective Superintendent himself. He could make her see sense, he was sure of it.

Logan had talked him down. Mitchell wasn't going to budge, no matter how much they cajoled, threatened, or begged. Her mind was made up. They were off the case, and that was that.

They sat in Logan's BMW, both numbed into silence. Ben had stepped up, of course, like he always did. Hamza, too, the DS having apparently shaken off his recent hang-ups enough so that he no longer looked one wrong word away from taking early retirement.

They all just wanted Sinead back. And Shona. And they were going to do whatever it took to make that happen.

Officially, Logan and Tyler were off the investigation, but Hamza was conveniently going to forget to remove them from the team's email inbox, and Ben was going to share any developments as they came in. It wasn't the same as being there in the heart of it, of course, but it was better than nothing.

'What do we do now, boss?' Tyler asked. Taggart was sitting upright on his lap, tongue flapping around, one front leg dangerously close to the DC's injured crotch. 'I don't think I can go home. Not when Sinead might be... not when she's still out there somewhere, missing.'

Logan, who had been lost in thought, turned at the sound of the younger detective's voice. 'No,' he agreed. 'No, I won't be able to sit still.'

'So… what do we do?' Tyler asked. 'Do we go back in and just tell her we're not letting her take us off the case? Do we just go in and say it?'

'Only if you want to lose your job, son,' Logan told him. 'She'll have you shifted back over to Uniform before you can say "crabbit bastard".'

'So, what then? We can't just keep out of it. We can't just wait for someone to tell us what's happening,' Tyler said. He winced, like the very notion of this caused him physical pain. 'Can we?'

Logan drummed his fingers on the steering wheel and looked up at the Burnett Road station. He could see the Incident Room from there. *His* Incident Room. The case was in Ben's hands for now, and there was nobody Logan trusted more.

But Ben's role as senior investigating officer wasn't permanent. Mitchell had mentioned bringing someone else in to head up the case. Someone else who would have responsibility not just for finding a cold-blooded killer, but safely returning two of the most important people in Logan's life.

Who else did he trust to do that, besides Ben? Who else could he count on?

Just a handful of people, he decided. And two of them were sitting in this car.

Logan pressed the button that started the engine, then pulled on his seatbelt.

'Right, then, son,' he announced. 'Stick that dog in the back, and then strap yourself in. You and me are going on a little road trip.'

—

They made it all the way to the coastal town of Banff before the dog pissed on the back seats, and Tyler threw up in his mouth. That was a far better result than Logan had been bracing himself for.

179

They took a short break then, Tyler walking the dog along the beach of the bay that separated the town from the North Sea, while Logan sprayed and scrubbed the upholstery with a selection of cleaning products he'd bought from the Co-op just around the corner.

Logan had been quick to point out that walking wasn't exactly Tyler's strong point at the moment, but Tyler had countered that, given his current nausea levels, nor was getting stuck into cleaning up dog piss, and doing so would likely result in more mess in Logan's car, rather than less.

Once the car was scrubbed clean and the aroma of dog-urine no longer filled the cabin, Tyler came waddling back with a squirming Taggart in his arms.

'The idea is the dog's meant to get a walk, too,' Logan remarked, as the DC made his way up from the beach. 'Carrying it sort of defeats the point.'

'It kept trying to have a go at the jellyfish, boss,' Tyler said. 'I thought it was eating one at one point, but turned out some dirty bastard had left a condom lying on the sand.'

Logan regarded Tyler, then the dog. He shook his head. 'I don't know if that's better or worse.'

'Well, it wasn't a barrel of laughs trying to get it off him, I'll say that,' Tyler replied, and the look on his face was the thousand-yard stare of a man who'd seen too much. He gagged violently, and Logan's eyes narrowed.

'You'd better not be sick in my car again,' he warned.

Tyler shook his head. 'No worries on that front, boss. After what I've just been through, there's nothing left in me to come up. I just hope the tide comes in and washes it all away soon, before some poor bugger stands in it.'

'Jesus,' Logan muttered. He shook his head and opened the back door for Tyler to deposit the dog. 'Right, get that bastard in there, and let's crack on.'

Tyler sat Taggart on the back seat, then both men hurried around to the front before the dog could beat them there.

They both checked their phones before setting off, each hoping for good news, but both disappointed.

It would've been easy to sit and fret. To pace anxiously, the imagination conjuring up all sorts of increasingly terrible scenarios with which to torment itself. That's what Mitchell's orders would have condemned them to. Logan doubted that had been her intention, but it would have been the result—too much free time and zero purpose was fertile ground from which all sorts of nasty thoughts grew.

And so, Logan had given them a purpose. Officially, they may have been off the case, but that allowed them a certain amount of freedom to do things their way.

His way.

One way or another, they were getting Shona and Sinead back.

And to do that, he'd have to turn to one of his oldest enemies.

From the corner of his eye, he saw Tyler checking his phone again, and sensed the frustration and disappointment radiating off him.

'What do you make of the note in Shona's?' he asked, filling the silence in the car.

Tyler returned his mobile to his pocket. 'What was it again?'

Logan rattled off the three words that had been written on the pad.

'Well, I mean, "Olivia" has got to be Olivia Maximuke, hasn't it?' Tyler said. 'Be weird if it wasn't.'

'I'm positive it is,' Logan said. 'There was a beanie hat at Shona's. Hair length and colour were a match for Olivia. I think she was there when Shona was taken.'

'You think she's behind it? She's only a kid.'

'I don't know. Maybe. Maybe not. She's deep in it, somehow, though.' He moved on to the next item on the list. 'What do you make of "Iceman" being there?'

Tyler's head snapped to his right. 'What, he was at the house, too?'

'On the list,' Logan said.

'Oh. Right. Aye. Sorry, boss,' Tyler said. 'Eh… I don't know. I thought that was all dealt with, wasn't it? I thought the Iceman was gone.'

'Aye, but we thought that before,' Logan reasoned. 'There was more than one of the bastards. What if there's still one out there?'

'Like the main one you mean? Like a boss level Iceman?'

Logan shrugged. 'Don't know about that.'

'But he was a vigilante. He had a big list of criminals he targeted,' Tyler said. 'Why would he have targeted Sinead and Shona?'

Logan ground his teeth for a moment, considering his answer. 'There was another list found way back when. On the original case. Ben and Hoon were on it. Hamza, too.'

'What? He was coming after polis?'

'He never did it, just made a list. But, after last time, it's not impossible that the rest of us would've ended up on it, too. Even Shona, potentially.'

'Jesus Christ!' Tyler cried. He had personal experience of being shut in one of the Iceman's freezers. Even now, several months later, he could almost feel the stabbing blades of cold burying themselves in his flesh. 'You think they might be in a freezer somewhere? You think that's what's happened to them?'

'I don't know, son. I wish I did,' Logan replied. 'But we're going to work it out. We're going to find them. All right?' Tyler said nothing, so Logan shot him a sideways glare. 'I said, *all right*?'

'Aye. Sure, boss,' Tyler muttered. 'Whatever you say.' He fidgeted. Chewed his lip. 'But what if we don't?'

'We will.'

'Aye, it's easy to say that. 'We will.' And I know we should be thinking it. But… what if we don't? What if we're too late? What if—'

He choked on the words. Swallowed them back down. He wasn't going to say.

Even if they were both thinking it.

'What if?'

Logan watched the road ahead. 'If that's the case,' he intoned. 'Then we will find the people responsible. You and me. And we will set them on fire and dance around them while they burn.'

Tyler nodded at that. 'Works for me,' he said. He, too, stared straight ahead at the oncoming road. 'But we'll find them, boss,' he said. 'Won't we?'

'Aye, son,' Logan replied. 'We will.'

Chapter 28

There were voices. Male. Talking in a language Sinead couldn't understand.

They were somewhere on her left. Instinctively, she tried to turn, but her head wouldn't move, tried to sit up, but her limbs felt impossibly heavy.

No, not heavy. Gone. Her brain was sending the signals, but there was nothing at the other end to receive them.

What had happened to her? Why couldn't she feel her arms or legs? Why couldn't she feel *anything*, not even the sensation of panic that should be burning like a supernova in her chest right about now?

Oh, God.

Oh, God, what had they done?

She fought to remain calm, but it was like struggling against quicksand. Panic pulled at her, dragged her down into its smothering grasp.

She'd suffered from night terrors before, shortly after her parents had been killed in the crash, and she'd been the first officer on the scene. This felt just like those occasions—a pressure on her chest pinning her to the bed, a growing sense of dread that she might be stuck like this. That there might be no way back.

And that no matter how hard she tried, and how much she wanted to, she couldn't scream.

The first time it had happened, she'd been terrified. Several notches beyond terrified, in fact, and deep into previously uncharted regions of fear.

The next few times hadn't been much better, but she'd known what was happening, at least. She was better equipped to ride it out. It was still always frightening, but the trauma of it became less and less, until one night it was nothing more than an inconvenience, and the next night, it was gone.

She harked back to some of the calming techniques she'd taught herself back then. Don't panic. That was the main one. Don't lose control. *Think*. Reason it out. Don't stress out about what you can't do, focus on what little you can.

Her eyes. She could move those. It wasn't easy, and there was a delay between her moving them and the picture updating, but it was something. It was a start.

She tried to look in the direction of the voices. She might not be able to understand the words, but she could tell they were angry. Something—paranoia, maybe—told her they were talking about her.

If so, they probably had every right to be angry, assuming they were the same men she'd encountered in Alexis Maximuke's kitchen. She'd smashed one in the face with a cabinet door, and slashed another across the thigh with a kitchen knife before she'd been pinned to the table, punched three times in the kidneys, then had a bag pulled roughly over her head.

After that…?

After that, it all got hazy. She remembered a pain in the back of her head. She remembered the smell of diesel, and something else, too. What was it? Something familiar that she'd recognised in a fleeting moment of lucidity.

Plastic, that was it. She'd been in some sort of container.

It came rushing back to her then. The echo of her breathing in the cramped space. The sound of an engine. The lurching movement of a vehicle.

A van. Had to be.

She'd heard the same voices then, she thought, though they'd been muffled by the plastic and the coughing of the engine.

There had been a touch of panic to one of them. Probably the one with the blood gushing from his leg.

Something twitched. A toe. She felt the spasm go through her foot. If she could speak, she would've cheered. She had a foot, which meant she had a leg. And if she had one limb that was starting to wake up, she may well have them all.

She focused all her efforts on her left hand. Her brain was still firing signals into empty space at the moment, but if she really concentrated, she thought she could get an impression of her arm. The merest suggestion of it lying at her side.

If it was still there, it wasn't ready to respond. Not yet.

All the brain activity was helping, though. She could feel her mind becoming sharper, and more alert. It presented her with another piece of information that should've been obvious from the moment she woke up.

The lights were on. She was no longer in darkness. No longer stuffed into a container.

The room was small, she thought, though her eyes could only move far enough to see the wall on one side. It was an unpleasant yellowing white that nobody would ever choose on purpose. There were a few lighter-coloured squares of various sizes dotted across the wall that confirmed her suspicions that people had smoked here. A lot of people, probably, and for a long time. Pictures had once been hung on the wall, shielding the areas behind from nicotine staining.

She realised then that something was different about the room. Something had changed in the past few seconds.

The voices had stopped.

'Good afternoon.'

He appeared in her field of view from over on the right, cast mostly into silhouette by the bare light bulb hanging from the ceiling behind him. He had an accent like the other men, but nowhere near as strong. Unlike them, his voice was a haggard, battle-ravaged thing, like it had been forced to fight its way out through the post-apocalyptic wasteland of his throat.

What she could make out of his face didn't make much sense. It was wrong. All of it.

He was right at the limit of her peripheral vision, and she blamed her imagination for filling in the blanks. Nobody actually looked like that. Nobody real, anyway.

'You are awake,' he said. It felt like a warning, almost, as if he was making it clear to her that this wasn't a nightmare, and was only too real. 'You were a little… feisty, and so you understand that we had to subdue you.'

He leaned a little closer. His stench—antiseptic cream on rotten meat—snagged at the back of Sinead's throat.

'Who are you?' he asked. It didn't sound like a direct question that she was expected to answer. Just as well, given that she still couldn't utter a sound. 'We know your name, and what you do, but who are you *to her*? Will she care what happens to you? Will your suffering bring her pain? Or were you simply in the wrong place at the wrong time?'

She felt his hand on her arm. The weight of it, if not the touch. It was a disturbingly alien sensation, but it was significant.

Her arm. She could feel her arm.

Whatever was affecting her was wearing off. With great effort, she was able to shift her head a few millimetres to the right, bringing more of his face into view. She still couldn't see much of him, but the light reflected off a head mostly devoid of hair. A few short, wiry tufts sprouted here and there. Combine them all, and you might have enough for a half-decent moustache, but there wouldn't be much, if anything, left over.

'Will she mourn, when she watches you die?' he asked, and the voice was a serpentine thing slithering into her ears and through her brain. He smiled. At least, she thought that's what the arrangement of his shadowed features was suggesting. 'I suppose we will find out, soon enough.'

187

Chapter 29

Ben stood at the head of the Briefing Room, looking out at a few dozen uniformed officers, and a handful of detectives from CID. He recognised most of them. Unlike Logan, DI Forde took a real interest in people and had spoken at least once or twice to everyone in the room.

He couldn't remember half their names, of course—his memory was a bugger like that—but he knew them all to some extent, and they all knew him, too.

They had listened in near-silence while he'd filled them in on the pertinent parts of the case. Mostly, they were going to be focused on the search for Sinead, Shona, and Alexis Maximuke. And while, in theory, equal weight would be given to all three, Ben knew what most of the officers' order of priority would be.

'We find one, there's a good chance we find all of them,' he said. 'My team—' He shot the watching Detective Super-intendent Mitchell a meaningful look. '—what's left of it—is going to be focusing most of its attention on finding Alexis's daughter, Olivia Maximuke, who is of significant interest to the investigation. You'll all be given her details, but anything comes up in connection with her, you don't investigate, but bring it straight to me.'

He indicated the photographs of the three women being projected onto the screen behind him. 'Find anything related to Detective Constable Bell, Dr Maguire, or Mrs Maximuke, you get your teeth into it and you don't let go. Exhaust every line of inquiry. Be tenacious. Everyone you talk to from the moment you leave this room is a potential witness and a potential suspect, so eyes and ears open, full alert. Any questions?'

A uniformed arm went up somewhere near the back of the room. As with many of them, Ben recognised the man's face, but couldn't place the name. 'Any result from the media shout, sir?' the constable asked.

Ben nodded. 'We've got one or two leads coming in.'

'I'd like to volunteer to follow-up on any regarding Sinead, sir,' the constable continued, his arm still raised. 'She and I went to Tulliallan together. We go way back.'

'Right. Good. Thanks for your enthusiasm. Inspector Hawthorne will be coordinating that,' Ben said, indicating one of his Uniform counterparts at the back of the room. 'So talk to him when the briefing is over.'

'Where's Logan?' asked one of the CID boys. The way he avoided looking in Mitchell's direction while asking the question told Ben that the rumour mill had already started turning.

He cleared his throat before answering. 'DCI Logan will not be involved in the case going forward. Nor will DC Neish. It was felt—not by me—that they were too closely connected to the investigation, since DC Neish and DC Bell are married, and DCI Logan is in a relationship with Dr Maguire.'

Ben snapped his mouth shut half a sentence too late. So much for keeping Jack and Shona's relationship quiet. Still, judging by the lack of reaction in the room, either everyone already knew, or nobody cared.

Detective Superintendent Mitchell stood up and addressed the audience. 'I took the decision to remove them from the investigation because it was the only decision there was to be made on the matter. I have requested additional resource from MIT in Glasgow. In the meantime, DI Forde is taking lead. I expect everyone, regardless of rank, to respect his authority on this. Understood?'

A murmured agreement made its way around the Briefing Room. Mitchell waited until it had completed the full circuit, then checked her watch and leaned closer to Ben, lowering her voice so the others wouldn't hear.

'You'll have to excuse me. I've arranged a full press conference for an hour from now. I want you there.'

'Me? I'm no good at that sort of thing,' Ben told her. 'I've no' got a face for the telly.'

'It's not *Britain's Next Top Model*, Detective Inspector. It's the news. Nobody's going to be paying attention to how you look. One hour. I expect you to be there.'

Her stare bored into him until he relented with a nod.

'Good,' she said. Her gaze flitted down for a fraction of a second. 'And fix your tie before we go on.'

'I thought you said nobody would be paying attention to how I looked?' Ben countered.

'Nobody but me,' Mitchell replied.

With that, and a final nod in the direction of the audience, she picked up her folders and marched out of the room.

Ben looked across to where Hamza sat in the front row. DS Khaled offered a supportive shrug and a half-smile, but said nothing.

'Right, then,' Ben said, turning back to his notes. 'Where were we…?'

–

It had been a long time, Logan thought. A long time since he'd sat across from the man on the other side of the table. A long time since he'd seen that smirk. Since he'd breathed the same air.

Not long enough.

Prison seemed to be treating him well. He'd been podgy and overweight on the outside, but free time, free gym membership, and several dozen hardy bastards who wanted to leather shite out of him for no particular reason, had helped him sculpt the flab away.

It hadn't done much for his height or his baldness, of course, but he exuded an air of danger as he sat there leaning one arm over the back of his seat—even more so than he'd done as a free man.

'You're looking well, Bosco,' Logan said.

Bosco Maximuke glanced down at himself, then nodded admiringly, like he was seeing his physique for the first time. 'You are right. I am—what is word? Ripped as fuck,' he said.

He hadn't lost the Russian accent, then.

'See?'

He lifted the front of his sweat-stained grey t-shirt to reveal something that, under the right lighting condition, might be considered an ab.

'Aye, getting there,' Logan said. 'Another six months and you'll have them muscle tits all the bodybuilders have. Instead of, you know, just the normal tits you used to have.'

Across the table, Bosco chuckled and wagged a finger. It made the chains holding him to the tabletop rattle and clank. 'You are still funny guy, Jack. You still make me laugh.'

Bosco's gaze shifted sideways to where Tyler leaned against the wall by the interview room door. 'I know you,' he said. 'We have met, yes?'

'*Met*?' Tyler spat. 'You tried to kill me!'

Bosco shrugged. 'I have tried to kill lot of people. Their faces all become blur to me. But you… you, I remember.'

'Ah, come on now, don't be modest, Tyler,' Logan said, though he didn't take his eyes off the man across the table. 'Detective Constable Neish was your arresting officer, Bosco. He's the man who brought you to justice. He was just going to kill you, but we talked him round.'

The insidious little smile that had been bending up the corners of Bosco's mouth fell away, his expression darkening as he was reminded of why the Detective Constable was quite so familiar.

'Ah, yes. That one,' Bosco muttered. He tried to stare the younger man down, but Tyler was in no mood to relent, and returned the glare.

It helped, of course, that Bosco was currently restrained, and separated from Tyler by the much larger Logan. But Tyler held the stare, and that was the main thing.

'You're probably wondering why we're here, Bosco,' Logan said.

'Oh, not social visit?' Bosco asked, feigning hurt. 'I thought old friend just pop by for chat.'

'Your daughter's missing, Bosco,' Logan said. 'Your wife, too.'

There was a change to the man across the table then. It wasn't one obvious thing, but a thousand subtle little tweaks to his face and body language that all added up to a seismic shift in the atmosphere around him.

There had always been a sort of *roundness* to Bosco, both physically and in terms of his personality. Aye, he'd always been a dangerous bastard, but he played the role of the jovial stranger in a strange land, laughing and joking with you as he had your kneecaps broken and your thumbs removed.

The roundness was gone now. Something hard and sharp had replaced it.

'When?' he asked.

'We don't know,' Logan admitted. 'We think Olivia may have been last seen late yesterday evening. Alexis sometime yesterday, earlier in the day.'

'Who took them?'

'We don't know that, either,' Logan said. 'That's why we're here. We don't actually know for a fact that they *have* been taken. They might just be on the run somewhere.'

'From what?' Bosco asked.

'You tell me,' Logan urged. 'You must have a lot of enemies, Bosco. Maybe someone's trying to get at you.' He leaned closer. 'Or maybe you're trying to get at them.'

'What fuck is that meant to mean?' Bosco spat.

'Right now, I'm looking at two homicides and one attempted, all connected to your family,' Logan said. 'You know Alexis was seeing someone? Shagging him, I mean.'

Bosco said nothing.

'Aye. Thought so,' Logan said. 'Nothing gets past you, does it, Bosco? No' even in here.'

'She is healthy woman. She has needs.'

'Oh, come on, Bosco!' Logan laughed. 'Don't try and tell me you're fine with your wife being humped twice a night by some smooth-talking no-mark. No way Bosco Maximuke tolerates that. No way that goes unpunished.' Logan sucked air in through his teeth. 'Killing his mother, though? I mean, Jesus, that's extreme, even for you.'

'I have no idea what you are talking about,' Bosco replied. 'I do not touch this man, or his mother.'

'Maybe not you personally, no,' Logan conceded. 'But a wee phone call could get it done. A wee word in someone's ear.'

'You know Borys Wozniak?' asked Tyler, hurrying things along.

Bosco packed a lot of contempt into the fleeting look he shot in the DC's direction, then addressed the answer to Logan. 'Never heard of him.'

'Funny that,' Logan said. 'We think he and your daughter were dealing together.'

Bosco's chain gave a rattle as his muscles tensed. He shook his head. 'Olivia does not do that. She is not part of business.' The tip of his tongue flicked across his dry lips. 'Of *old* business. She is child, nothing more.'

'Aye, well, she's growing up fast, by the sounds of things,' Logan said. 'We've got a witness who tells us she and Borys were supplying to kids at her new school.'

'At *school*?' Bosco gasped, sounding genuinely horrified. 'She is dealing at school? Who is this fuck? *Borys*. Who the fuck is he?'

'He's dead. Body found earlier this week in his car,' Logan said. 'In the car park of Olivia's school, no less. Seems to me like someone is sending a message, Bosco. I just can't figure out if you're the one sending it, or if you're the one the message is meant for. Either way, I think you're mixed up in it.'

'You think wrong.'

'What about the Iceman?' Tyler asked.

Logan had briefed him on when to ask the question while they waited for Bosco to be brought across from his cell. With Tyler doing the asking, it left Logan free to focus on the answer—or lack of one—and to try to figure out how much of it was the truth.

While briefing Tyler on what to say, he had also stressed the things he should *not* mention—namely, the fact that Sinead and Shona were missing, and that the detectives had a personal involvement in the case as a result. That information would give the bastard power.

And Bosco was a man who could wield power to devastating effect.

'Iceman? You mean like from comic books?' Bosco asked.

'Cut your shit,' Tyler warned. 'You know who I mean. The vigilante killer.'

Bosco's smirk returned. 'Ah. That one. What about him?'

'What do you know about him?' Tyler pressed.

'Why is monkey now asking questions, and not organ grinder?' Bosco asked Logan. 'I do not want to waste breath on fucking... junior club. I talk to you. Just you.'

'Fine. Talk to me, then,' Logan said. 'The Iceman. What's your connection?'

'None! No connection. I mean, I read in paper he kill a few people I know, but then I hear he is stopped by fine men and women of Police Scotland.' He raised his arms as high as the chains would allow and shook them in celebration. 'Day is saved! Streets are safe for dealers once more! You are true champion of the people!'

'I'm rapidly tiring of this conversation, Bosco,' Logan said.

'Good. Then get the fuck out there and find my daughter.'

Logan gave the rest of the sentence a few seconds to come along. When it didn't, he finished it off for him. 'And your wife.'

'What? Yes. And wife. Of course, wife.'

'If Olivia was to run away, do you have any idea where she'd go?' Logan asked. 'Any special place you can think of where she might feel safe?'

There was silence for a moment, then a long, slow creak as Bosco leaned his not-inconsiderable weight back on the plastic chair.

'What is worth?'

'Excuse me?' Logan asked.

'You want information. I also want things. Make life in here more comfortable. Bigger cell. More privacy, maybe. What is information worth to you?'

Tyler stepped away from where he'd been leaning on the wall. 'Are you… are you bargaining with your own daughter's life?' he asked. 'Is that really what's happening right now?'

Bosco gave the questions but a moment's thought before nodding. 'I think, yes, it is,' he said. 'You are "good guys". Yes? You need my help for this. So that you can be heroes. So that you can find her.' He paused, just for a beat. 'Find *everyone*.'

'What do you mean "everyone"?' Tyler demanded, moving closer. 'What do you know?'

'Back off, Detective Constable,' Logan warned.

'He knows something, boss. He knows more than he's saying.'

Bosco gave an innocent little shrug of his big, powerful shoulders. 'Maybe yes, maybe no. Perhaps little birdies tell me things. Cheep, cheep. In my ears.'

'He's messing with your head, Tyler. He doesn't know anything. Back up.'

'Where's Sinead?' Tyler demanded, lunging towards the table. 'What have you done with her? Where is she?'

Bosco's eyes lit up. His smirk was instantly upgraded to a grin. '*Sinead*. Now, that is pretty name. She is missing, too, yes?

She is someone important to monkey. And organ grinder, too, I think.'

'She's an officer who was trying to help Olivia and Alexis,' Logan said, doing his best to recover the situation. 'We believe she was attacked while attending their house, and taken away by two men.'

'Oh. How heartbreaking,' Bosco said, but his grin had gone nowhere.

'You sick fucking—'

Tyler threw himself at the prisoner, only to be blocked by Logan, who rose to his feet.

'DC Neish! Outside. Now!' the DCI barked.

'But, boss!'

'Out, before I bloody throw you out!'

He glowered down at the younger man, then pointed to the door. Behind him, Bosco gave a little wave, then the Russian sniggered as the Detective Constable pulled an about-turn, hammered on the door to be let out, then left the room without another word.

'Kids today, all piss and vinegar,' Bosco said. 'They don't know they are—'

'Shut your fucking mouth and listen to me,' Logan said, turning on the other man. 'I think your daughter's got herself into some deep shite, Bosco. I think she's mixed up with the wrong people, and right now, I'm the best chance she's got of going on to live a full and fulfilling life, with all her bits and pieces intact. Because I've seen what these people do, Bosco. I always thought you were a sick fuck, but these guys? The things they do to people? It'd turn even your stomach.'

He returned to his seat and pulled it in closer to the table.

'They've probably got your wife,' Logan continued. 'They might have your daughter, too, but there's a chance they don't, Bosco. There's a chance we can find her. Protect her. And if that means getting you extra fucking helpings at lunchtime, or a soap on a rope that you can't drop in the shower, then fine. I will. But that's going to take time, and time's something Olivia might not have.'

Across the table, Bosco ran his tongue across the front of his teeth, like he was checking if he'd brushed them that morning.

Finally, after several seconds of this, he shrugged. 'I do not know where she would go.'

'What about friends? Family?'

'She was never social girl. Friends? No. Family? Unless she can travel to Russia, then only other family she has is…' He shook his head. 'No. She would not go to him.'

'Who?'

'Nephew. Sort of. Or… cousin's boy. Relationship is shaky, but he is family of sort. Brought up here. But I hear he is dead. Missing for long time.'

'What's his name?'

'It is irrelevant. Even if alive, she would not go near, I am sure. He is… what is word?' His fingers twitched like he was physically grasping for the word. 'Psychopath. Very dangerous.'

'Coming from you? Jesus. What's his name, Bosco?'

Bosco partly opened his mouth, frowned, then closed it again.

It was a strange sight, Logan thought. Bosco Maximuke, once a giant in the Scottish illegal narcotics industry, now apparently afraid to say the name of his own sort-of-nephew.

'Olivia's time could be running out here, Bosco,' Logan stressed. 'What's his name?'

'Oleg. His name… he is Oleg Ivanov,' Bosco said, and the word seemed to drain him of strength, like the very act of saying it aloud had knocked the wind out of him.

The name immediately became an itch inside Logan's head. It meant something. It was connected to something he'd heard or seen. It was…

'Wait a minute!' he barked, pulling his phone from his pocket. He tapped furiously at the screen until it woke up, then opened the photos app and presented Bosco with the picture of the list Shona had been writing. 'The person we think last saw Olivia was writing this list. That last word, I thought it was finished, but what if it isn't? What if she didn't get to write the final letter?'

Bosco stared at the screen, his head tick-tocking from side to side like it was denying what his eyes were seeing. 'No. Cannot be him. Cannot be Oleg. I heard he is dead. I heard…' He swallowed as he considered the significance of the second word on the list. 'I heard Iceman killed him.'

'We found several of the Iceman's victims, and we've identified all of them. None of them was anyone named Oleg,' Logan said. 'Assuming he's still alive, what would stop her going to him?'

'Oleg is… different. Always has been. Charming on outside, but inside? Like rotten fruit.'

'Must run in the family.'

'No. Me, I have done bad things, yes. But the things I hear Oleg has done? The things I see? It is not the same. It does not compare. When I came in here, I got message to him. "Stay away from my family." I warn him, do not go near. What does he do? He fuck my wife.'

'Well, like you said yourself, Bosco, she's got needs…'

Bosco lunged across the table, but the restraints snapped tight, stopping him a few inches from the unblinking detective.

'You think funny? Maybe I make joke about your missing colleague? About her being tortured to death. See if you laugh then.'

Logan stretched out the fingers on one hand, like he was fighting the urge to ball them into a fist. Otherwise, he managed to not react.

'I was over fucking moon at the thought that piece of shit was dead,' Bosco said. 'I do Cossack dance across yard. You know? Squatting one, with big arms. *Oi!*'

'I know the one you mean,' Logan said, keen to crack on. 'So, Olivia would be aware of him? She'd know where to find him?'

'Perhaps.'

'Then she could be hiding with him, then.'

Bosco's hands banged down on the table like the crack of a pistol. 'No! Olivia is not idiot. Not like wife. She will see him for what he really is. Never in hundred years would she go there. He is last person she would run to.'

Logan sat back, giving this some thought. 'If Oleg was knocking off your missus, then found out she was with someone else—that she was cheating on him, what would he do?'

'Hard to say. But I would not like to be in other man's shoes.'

'You think he'd kill him?'

Bosco laughed at that. 'Not right away. But eventually.'

'And if Oleg was trying to stake his claim to your territory, and found someone else trying to do the same? Borys Wozniak, for example.'

'He would not be happy. And an unhappy Oleg is not someone you want to get on wrong side of.'

Logan sat forward again. 'You say Olivia wouldn't run *to* Oleg. What if she's running *from* him? What if he's got wind of her and Borys' little enterprise, and is taking out the competition?'

Across the table, Bosco's jaw clenched. His eyes blurred, and Logan realised—to his utter amazement—that the bastard was fighting back tears.

'Then you must find her. You must find my daughter. Find Olivia. Please,' he said, his voice descending into a throaty croak. 'Find her before he does.'

Chapter 30

Ben stood out of sight behind a stationery cupboard, listening to the murmurs of the assembled members of the press. The table had been set up with two microphones, two glasses, and a big jug of water that he already had visions of himself spilling in front of the cameras.

He and Detective Superintendent Mitchell were sharing top billing at the press conference. Mitchell would do the higher level stuff and the introduction, he'd take over with more detail and the appeal.

He'd been involved in press conferences a few times over the years, but usually just to show face, or offer a few nuggets of information. This wasn't his first time being the main event, even, yet he had a horrible nagging feeling that he was about to make a right arse of it.

It didn't help, of course, that Sinead and Shona's lives might depend on it going well. If he could find just the right words, say them in just the right way, it might prompt someone to come forward with the nugget of information they needed to crack the case. To get everyone home safely.

Great. He was overthinking it again.

He stole a look out from behind his cover. The room was filling up now. There were fifteen or so journalists taking their seats, four video cameras mounted on tripods, and a cluster of photographers kneeling down at the front.

A couple of the photographers angled towards him, so he quickly ducked back out of sight, and almost collided with

Detective Superintendent Mitchell, who chose that moment to come striding through the door beside him.

'Everything all right, Ben?' she asked. A couple of cameras flashed. She ignored them.

'What? Oh, aye. Aye. I'm fine,' Ben said, drawing himself up to his full height. 'I was just checking the turn-out. Going over what I'm going to say.'

'Good. Happy?'

Ben was not happy. Not even close.

'As Larry,' he said, not giving her the satisfaction. 'When do we go on?'

'Now, if you're ready.'

Ben swallowed. Nodded. 'Aye. I'm raring to go,' he said, lying through his teeth. 'Just you lead the way.'

Mitchell nodded curtly, adjusted his tie for him, then went striding onto the small stage.

Out of habit, and partly as some small act of rebellion, Ben loosened his tie again, took a deep breath, then felt his phone buzzing in his pocket.

He probably shouldn't have, but he checked it. Logan's name filled the screen.

On stage, Mitchell was staring. Her mouth drew into a razor-thin line as Ben held up his index finger, signalling for her to wait, then he turned away and pressed the phone to his ear.

'Jack? Not a good time. I'm about to do the press conference.'

'Stall it,' came the reply. By the sounds of things, Logan was driving. And driving fast.

'I can't stall it! Mitchell's on stage waiting for me!'

'Get her off the stage, then. New information's come up,' Logan told him. 'We need to consider our next move before we say anything to the media.'

'Consider our...? What are you on about? What's happened?'

And so, Logan told him about the conversation with Bosco. About Oleg, and all the things he might have done.

And all the things he was capable of.

Logan was right. They couldn't go out and deliver the press conference they had planned. Not without strategising first. There was only one shot at making a first impression when it came to these things, and a muddled message wouldn't bring results.

Worse than that, even, it might do more harm than good.

'Shite. I need to get her off the stage,' Ben muttered. He glanced back at Mitchell, who was now glowering at him with a face like thunder. 'Where do I tell her we got this information from? I can't say it came from you.'

'Aye, you can.'

'You're meant to be off the case! She'll have your job!'

'Fuck the job, Ben,' Logan said. 'Right now, that doesn't matter. All that matters is—'

'I know,' Ben said. 'And you're right. I'll call you back shortly.'

He hung up. He took a deep breath. 'Fuck the job,' he told himself, then he walked onto the stage, bent to the microphone that had been set out for him, and announced there would be a short delay.

Mitchell covered her own microphone with a hand. 'What's going on?' she demanded.

'We've, eh, we've had a bit of an update, ma'am,' Ben said. 'From Jack.'

'An update? From *Jack*?' The Detective Superintendent's nostrils flared. 'Unless it's concerning who won today's episode of Bargain Hunt, I don't think I like where this is going, Detective Inspector.'

'No, you probably won't, ma'am,' Ben admitted. He shot a sideways look at the journalists, who were all leaning forwards, desperately trying to listen in. 'So, since I suspect you're about to do a lot of shouting, maybe we can go somewhere more private?'

By and large, DS Hamza Khaled considered himself to be a patient man. He had to be, with a young child at home, and a mother-in-law like his. Patience became second nature. It was that, or suffer a stress-induced cardiac arrest at the age of thirty-five, which did not particularly appeal.

But, by God, Albert Rickett was slow.

It had taken him ten minutes now to explain that Mrs Howden—Conrad's mother—had been suffocated. Given that this had been Hamza's assumption before even entering the room, it had felt like a *long* ten minutes, too.

There were no real surprises in anything Ricketts had to say. A pillow had been applied to her face, then forcibly pinned down until she was unable to breathe. She hadn't fought back in any substantial way, but then her arms were too frail to have done much harm to anyone, so it may not have been for want of trying.

She had a tumour in one of her lungs that would've killed her in a month or two, anyway. Ricketts had pulled her medical records, and it turned out that she'd been aware of the cancer, but had refused treatment for it.

Her health, in general, had not been good for a number of years, and her medical records were a litany of debilitating complaints, from advanced COPD to herniated disks.

'You could've thrown a dart at her and you'd be guaranteed to hit something that was failing,' Ricketts explained. He flipped quickly through the folder of medical notes like it was an international bestseller. 'Macular degeneration. Alopecia. Haemorrhoids. Fungal nail infections. Eczema. The woman was falling apart. The family and her GP had concerns about dementia, too. Hadn't been investigated fully yet, though.'

'The family?' Hamza asked.

'Well, her son. He's the next of kin. Seems to have been doing everything,' Ricketts said. He snapped the folder closed and placed it on the stainless steel worktop beside him. 'You ask me, she might be better off where she is. Not that you'd ask me, of course.'

Hamza scribbled a few quick notes about Mrs Howden's medical history, then turned back to the pathologist. 'Time of death? We still saying between forty-eight and seventy-two hours ago, as per the initial estimate?'

Ricketts sniffed. 'Well, far be it from me to dispute Dr Maguire's opinion, but I'm afraid I have to do so,' he droned. 'I'd say she's been dead for longer, although it was hard to tell without getting her opened up, given her natural state of decay.'

Hamza's eyes were drawn to the double doors of the mortuary. 'How long are we talking?'

'Five days. Well, six, as of today. Maybe as long as a week.'

'That doesn't fit,' Hamza said, flipping back a few pages in his notepad. 'We've got Conrad Howden on video five days ago. At home.'

Ricketts raised an unkempt eyebrow. 'And?'

'And we assumed he and his mum were attacked at the same time. But if what you're saying is right.'

'It is,' Ricketts said.

'Then they can't have been. She must've been dead before he went to the house.'

'That's for you to worry about, Detective Sergeant, not me. I just tell you the science, and the science says she's been dead for at least six days.'

'Right. Aye. Thanks,' Hamza said, getting up from the stool he'd been perched on. 'There's nothing else, I take it?'

Ricketts shook his head. 'Nothing at present. If any blood work comes back, I'll be sure to let you know. Or… DCI Logan?'

The old bastard was fishing, Hamza could tell. No harm in telling him, though. 'DCI Logan isn't currently involved in this case.'

'Why ever not?' Ricketts asked. 'I've never taken to the man, but he seems to know what he's doing.'

'What, unlike the rest of us, you mean?'

'That is not what I meant.'

Hamza shook his head and sighed. 'No. Sorry. Long week,' he said. 'It was felt that DCI Logan's... personal connection to the case might hinder the investigation.'

Ricketts' raised eyebrows went the other way. 'Personal connection?'

'Aye. You know. With Shona. With Dr Maguire.'

Something—either the stool he was sitting on, or Ricketts himself—creaked as he stood up. 'What does Dr Maguire have to do with the case?'

'What...? You didn't hear?'

'Hear what?'

'It went out on local radio a couple of hours ago.'

'I don't listen to *local radio*,' Ricketts said, practically vomiting out those final two words in disgust. 'What has happened? Explain!'

'We think Shona was abducted from her home last night,' Hamza said. 'Her and a friend of— her and one of my *fellow officers* are both missing. We believe it's all connected. The victim in the car at the school, Mrs Howden and her son, and now this.'

'Connected? Why would it be connected? How are those things connected?' the pathologist asked. He brought up an arm that could've been made entirely of elbows, and ran a hand through what was left of his powder-white hair. 'Why would anyone want to take Shona? She's not involved in anything.'

'We think they may have been after someone else,' Hamza said.

'Have there been any demands?'

'Demands?'

'Yes! Ransom. Or... demands. Kidnappers make demands, don't they? That's the norm, isn't it?'

'Oh. Aye. No. Nothing yet,' Hamza said.

'God. OK.' Ricketts wheezed out a long breath, leaning on the worktop for support. 'Sorry I snapped, I just… I hadn't heard. I didn't know what had happened.'

'No apology necessary,' Hamza said. 'I understand. We're all a bit emotional at the moment. Everyone's a bit on edge.'

'Yes,' Ricketts agreed. He sat on the stool and felt for the pulse on his wrist, breathing steadily to bring his spiking heartbeat back under control. 'Yes, I'd imagine everyone is.'

–

Ben had been right about the shouting. There hadn't been as much of it as he'd expected, but the volume and intensity of it had more than made up for that.

Mitchell had just launched into a particularly venomous rant about *arrogant, self-aggrandising idiots* thinking they knew better than to follow orders, when Ben had done something quite unexpected. So unexpected, in fact, that he wasn't aware of it until he saw the look of shock on Mitchell's face.

He'd shouted back.

'Don't you talk about them like that!' he'd bellowed. 'Jack and Tyler are good men, who should never have been taken off this bloody case! They're not "compromised" by their personal involvement, they're driven by it. Nobody in this station— nobody on the face of this bloody *planet*—is going to work harder than those two to solve this thing and bring everyone home safely. The only person compromising the investigation is you, by sticking your bloody nose in!'

He'd stopped then, his survival instinct and plain common sense alerting him to the fact that he really ought to shut his mouth.

Mitchell had stared, her mouth slightly open, her eyes two circles of surprise.

Finally, after the initial shock of Ben's outburst had faded, she smoothed down the front of her shirt, then took her seat behind her desk. 'I'm going to give you an opportunity to apologise for that, Detective Inspector.'

'Aye, well, you'll have a bloody long wait,' Ben snapped back. 'I shouldn't have raised my voice, but I stand by every word. Taking them off the case was a mistake. And, frankly, it was never going to happen. They were never going to stop. All you've done is untied their hands, and freed them to go out and dig around on their own. And thank God they are, because they've already found us a suspect.'

He saw it then—a tiny, self-satisfied little smirk on the Detective Superintendent's face that he could *almost* be convinced he was imagining.

'You knew,' he said. 'You knew full bloody well that's what would happen. That they'd start digging.'

Mitchell clasped her hands on the desk. 'I'm sure I knew nothing of the sort, Detective Inspector. DCI Logan and DC Neish had clear instructions. They were told in no uncertain terms that they were no longer on the case.' She opened her hands again and shrugged. 'What they chose to do after that? That's their responsibility, not mine. And I'm sure they'll be prepared for the consequences, should they arise.'

'Eh, aye. Yes, I'm sure they will,' Ben agreed. He gave her a nod. She deserved that much, at least. 'Ma'am.'

'Good. I'm glad we're on the same page. So let's not allow the press to linger on the premises any longer than we have to,' Mitchell said. 'Tell me what we've got.'

The dispatch office at Burnett Road was always a hive of activity, but today the whole room hummed with the murmurs of a dozen voices all talking at once. Calls had been coming in from all over—sightings of the missing women, for the most part.

A few guys had called up claiming to have information on Oleg. Then, once questioned on it, they had broken into the voice of that bloody meerkat from the insurance comparison site advert on the telly, and hung up laughing.

They'd got one of the bastards' numbers, though. As soon as the current emergency was over, Uniform would be paying them a visit.

Erin Powis should have finished her shift an hour ago. But how could she go home at a time like this? How could she abandon her post when one of their own was in trouble? She couldn't.

She literally couldn't. The sergeant currently supervising the room had made that very clear. Compulsory overtime all round, until they got a happy ending.

She had a list of reports in front of her, and was doing her best to prioritise them. Most of them would be nothing, of course, but one or two might be genuine leads. The problem was, it was impossible to say from here which was which, so everything had to be investigated.

'Right, what's next?' she muttered, before taking a swig from her third Red Bull can of the day. She hated the taste, and felt like the caffeine was having zero effect now, but she persevered, more out of habit than anything else.

There'd been a sighting of Olivia Maximuke, or someone that might generously be described as 'matching her description' at the Eastgate Centre food court earlier that day. The only description the caller had offered was 'a girl in a school uniform', so the chances of it being Olivia were so slim as to be almost non-existent.

Erin sent a unit to check it out, and to gather up any CCTV footage.

Next was from a woman who claimed she was psychic, and that the spirits had told her all the missing women were dead. Erin finished off the rest of her energy drink, then bumped that report way down to the bottom of the list.

Moving on.

She tabbed down a line and read the details of the next call. This one was a report of two men carrying a box.

'What, is that it? That can't be it. A bloody box?'

She clicked in for further information but found very little worth mentioning. Two males, one with a possible limp, carrying a large box or plastic container into an old farmhouse out by Newton of Leys. An old couple who lived in the closest house had called it in. Said that they'd found it 'suspicious'.

Erin looked up the addresses on Google Maps, and noted the two houses were about a third of a mile apart. Presumably, the neighbours' suspicions had first been aroused when they'd been watching the farmhouse door through a bloody telescope.

She put out a shout, and a constable quickly volunteered to swing by and check it out. She thanked him, then logged his details on the case notes, whispering his name as she typed it.

'PC Jason Hall,' she said, then she cracked open another can of Red Bull and continued down her list.

Chapter 31

By the time Logan and Tyler were halfway back to Inverness, Oleg's face was everywhere. Tyler had watched the press conference on his phone, the footage stuttering as they'd passed through areas of low reception, and pausing completely when they'd encountered one of the many coverage blackspots along the coast.

They'd got the gist, though. Word was out. Oleg Ivanov had been identified as the chief suspect in the investigation, and with two dead, plus three women and one teenage girl missing, that made him the most wanted man in Scotland.

Hamza had been sending a lot of information to the shared inbox, which Tyler had picked up. Reading while travelling usually made him car sick, but he fought off the creeping nausea through sheer willpower alone, and persevered through DS Khaled's notes.

Even Taggart seemed to understand the urgency of the situation. He'd curled up on one of the back seats, and had snored gently for the entirety of the journey, and—so far, at least—there had been no need to stop for a toilet break.

'He's got a history, boss,' Tyler said, as they closed in on Nairn and the final leg of the drive home. 'Quite a few assault and domestic abuse charges. Some drug stuff. Burglary. Only thing he's ever been convicted of is possession of a Class B, though. Got a fine for it, no jail time.'

'Sounds like a right charmer,' Logan said.

'Aye, but maybe not as bad as Bosco made out,' Tyler replied. There was a note of hope to it. A pleading tone, almost, like he wanted reassurance that Sinead wasn't trapped with the monster that Bosco had described.

'Aye, maybe,' Logan conceded, and he pushed the accelerator pedal a little further towards the floor.

They were approaching the airport roundabout when the email dropped about Oleg's last known whereabouts. Given everything that Bosco had said, it didn't come as much of a surprise. He'd been living in Inverness, in a rented flat that Uniform had already gone to check out. It had since been let out to new tenants, who had seemed alarmed by the sudden appearance of four burly polis bastards at their front door.

None of the current occupants knew anything about the previous tenant. Uniform was following up with the letting agency, though Logan thought it unlikely he'd have gone to the bother of leaving a forwarding address.

Bank accounts and phone records were being checked for recent activity, but the information hadn't come back yet. Hamza insisted it would be soon, though. Mitchell had got the higher-ups involved, which was speeding things up immensely. If Oleg had so much as switched on his mobile or used his debit card to buy a Mars Bar in recent weeks, they'd soon know about it.

It wasn't all positive news, though. They had very little information about any of Oleg's past associates. His parents were dead, he had no siblings, and while he might have had a wide and varied social circle, he'd never regaled any interviewing officers with tales of it.

The only connections they had to him were Bosco—who didn't know where he was—Alexis and Olivia—who were both missing themselves—and the firm of solicitors who had managed to help him evade justice on several occasions.

They, apparently, didn't know where he was, either.

'This is interesting, boss,' Tyler said, reading another report in the inbox while simultaneously swallowing back the urge to vomit. 'PM for Conrad Howden's mother. Turns out she died earlier than we thought.'

Logan shot the younger officer a sideways glance. 'What? How much earlier?'

'Two, three days.'

Logan's eyes narrowed. They were speeding towards the big retail park at Eastfield Way now, the Tesco sign rising into view just above the top of a row of delivery trucks that he had no intention of getting stuck behind.

He fired up the lights and sirens and heard Tyler hiss in fear as he powered into the middle of the road and forced both lanes of traffic to swerve outwards to make a path.

'She died before Conrad was attacked, then,' Logan said. 'Days before.'

'Maybe Conrad turned up, and the killer was still there. Like, living there. With the body,' Tyler suggested. He shuddered, already fully committed to this version of events. 'The creepy bastard.'

Logan shook his head. He jerked the wheel, pulling back into the left-hand lane ahead of the now-stationary trucks, just in time to go screaming across the roundabout and onto the dual carriageway.

'There'd be more physical evidence if someone else had been there that long.'

'Maybe the killer was watching from nearby, then. He waited until Conrad came to visit, then followed him in.'

Logan threw a thumb back over his shoulder. 'What about the dog?'

Tyler twisted to look at the animal, but a sudden shooting pain in his testicles made him abort. 'What about it, boss?'

'It hadn't been starved. Vet said there were no signs of dehydration.'

'Maybe…' Tyler went through the options, then settled on the only one that made sense. 'Maybe the dog was with Conrad the whole time. He brought it from home.'

'It was her address on the chip,' Logan reminded him.

'Aye, but I'm looking at her medical records here, and she's in no fit state to look after a dog,' Tyler said. 'I mean, Christ, with the time she must've had left, I'd have been wary of getting her a goldfish.'

'She was in a bad way?'

'Aye, you can say that again,' Tyler replied. 'There's a copy of her repeat prescription here. It's sixteen pages. You'd be quicker walking into Boots and saying, "just give me one of everything".'

'She got painkillers on there?'

'Eh, aye. I think so.' He swiped through a few pages. 'Tramadol. That's one, isn't it?'

'Aye.'

'There's also paracetamol and aspirin, and… I mean, half of these I've never heard of, so there might be more.'

'Conrad still unconscious?'

'Aye, I think so. Why?'

'Doesn't matter,' Logan said. 'We can go over all that later. Right now, we've got bigger worries.'

'Turn off to the station's that way, boss,' Tyler said, pointing to the junction that would take them towards Burnett Road, just as they went flying past it.

'Aye, I know,' Logan replied. 'But we're no' going to the station.'

'Oh. Right.' Tyler looked at the road ahead, then back at the driver. 'Then where is it we're headed?'

–

The house once owned by Bosco Maximuke, and which was now the property of the Crown, did not hold happy memories for DC Neish. The mere sight of the place, in fact—and in particular the high metal fence—had made his face go pale and his breathing become so laboured that Logan had instructed him to wait in the car and keep an eye on the dog.

To be fair to the lad, being here had been the precursor to the worst few hours of his life. Maybe of any of their lives.

Until now, at least.

The place had been a fortress even before it had been boarded up and secured against squatters and other intruders. It was due to be sold eventually, but if the wheels of justice turned slowly, then the stabilisers of justice-related real estate administration were positively glacial.

Just as well. A new owner would've made everything Logan was about to do that much more difficult.

He had a scout around the outside first, hoping to find some flaw in the boards. Some sign that he wasn't the first person to have broken into the place.

A door around the back of the house provided just what he was looking for. The bottom right corner of the plywood had been prised away from the frame. The window in the door behind it had been broken, giving relatively easy access to the kitchen.

Fragments of glass crunched beneath his boots as he entered. A flick of the switches revealed that the power was off, so he found his torch in one of his coat pockets and painted the walls with the LED beam.

Bosco's kitchen was huge. Ridiculously huge. There were probably sports arenas that were smaller, and certainly less lavishly decorated.

'And they say crime doesn't pay,' Logan muttered, taking solace from the fact that at least the owner was in no position to enjoy all the expensive fittings and marble worktops.

Logan wasn't familiar with the layout of the house, but it didn't take him long to find the door that led down to the basement. It opened to reveal a shonky-looking wooden staircase that gave a sharp squeal of panic when his weight was applied to it.

Basements were unusual in this part of the world. Logan had very rarely been in a house that had one. Then again, he'd very rarely been in a house with gold taps and a kitchen the size of Wales, either, so nothing came as a surprise at this point.

The basement ran under the whole of the house and was subdivided into a number of rooms. Unlike the immaculate decor of the floor above, everything down here below the surface was grubby and cheap—the perfect metaphor for Bosco himself.

Logan traced the route that Bosco had given him. *Second entrance on the left. Through the door at the back of the room, then hang a right.*

It led him to what looked like a small storeroom, with shelving on two of the four walls. The shelves were empty. Anything that had been stored here would've been seized at the same time as the house. It was probably packed up in a storeroom somewhere at the taxpayers' expense, biding its time until it was sold at auction.

Logan swept the torchlight across the shelves, comparing their widths. He settled on the narrower of the two sets, as instructed, then ran a hand below the bottom shelf until he found a thick length of wire, like the emergency stop cord on a train.

He stopped then, not yet pulling it.

He and Bosco went way back. He'd known the bastard for years, and he knew just how treacherous he could be.

What if he'd set him up? What if this was a trap? What if pulling this cord would blow the whole bloody place sky high?

He thought of Shona and Sinead.

The decision was easy.

The wire gave a clunk as he pulled it until he met resistance. The wall with the shelves on it inched inwards, revealing more darkness beyond. A room, maybe. Possibly a corridor. Bosco hadn't been too clear on that.

He pushed the secret door open the rest of the way. The thin beam of torchlight did little to cut through the gloom of the space on the other side.

A floorboard creaked as he stepped inside. A shape moved somewhere up ahead, something dark detaching itself from the shadows.

'Hello?' he said.

There was a flash—a bright, brilliant flame that flowered briefly in the darkness.

There was a bang—a deafening roar that filled all the space and changed the texture of the air.

And then there was nothing but the shrill, ringing silence, and the cold, suffocating dark.

Chapter 32

On the back seat of DCI Logan's BMW, Taggart woke with a start, raised his head, and uttered a quizzical whuff.

'What is it?' Tyler asked, wriggling himself around in his seat so he could see into the back with as little discomfort as possible. 'What's the matter?'

The dog was up on his feet now, head cocked as he stared out through the side window in the direction of the house. Taggart's ears were raised. They angled themselves like little satellite dishes, shifting left and right as if trying to get a signal.

'You hear something?' Tyler asked. He turned back to his left and looked over in the direction of the house.

There had been a dog involved the last time Tyler had been here, too. That one had been significantly larger and meaner than Taggart, though. Even then, it had turned out to be the least of his worries, although it hadn't much felt like that when it had been chewing up the ground behind him while he'd run for his life.

Tyler checked his phone, but found no messages. He was under strict instructions not to call Logan unless there was an emergency. The dog taking an interest in the house was unlikely to qualify, he thought, regardless of how sudden that interest was.

'Did you hear something, boy?'

Tyler wasn't exactly sure why he asked the question again. It wasn't like the dog was just being stubborn by not replying the first time. But he didn't know what else to do, and reiterating his question to the dog felt like he was doing something, at least.

Actually, that was a lie. He did know what to do. There was only one thing *to* do.

He got out of the car, opened the back door, then watched as Taggart raced through the open gate and went tearing across the grass.

'Here, you wee shite!' Tyler called after him, breaking into the speediest waddle he was capable of. 'Wait for me!'

A moment before, there had been nothing. No thought. No pain. No fear.

And now, all of a sudden, there was something. Something far off. A snatch of a sound, maybe, like the final shout of a drowning man. There one moment, gone the next.

She awoke into the same dead state as before, her mind rising from its slumber, but her body still not her own.

Her eyes were open. Maybe they always had been. She could see the same ceiling as last time, the same nicotine-stained walls. It was brighter now, and the light streaming in through the net curtained window ached at the back of her eyes.

How long had she been out for? Hours? Days? There was no way of knowing.

She concentrated on what she *did* know. She was awake. She was paralysed. She was alone.

Or she seemed to be, anyway. There was a chance that someone was sitting in the corner of the room, or even standing on her right-hand side, beyond the reach of her peripheral vision. There could be a whole crowd of them there, watching her, leering over her, their faces twisting into monstrous visions of—

She was letting her imagination get away from her. It was hard not to, in this state. Her brain, deprived of all its usual stimulus, was filling in the blanks, and tapping into her worst nightmares for inspiration.

She had to stay calm. Focus on what she knew to be true. To be real.

She was lying down. She had been drugged. She was in a house. It was daytime. She was *probably* alone in the room.

And there had been a sound.

And now, there were more. A car door closing. Footsteps on gravel. A clearing of a throat.

A knocking, somewhere down beyond her feet, where she couldn't possibly see. It was a heavy, impertinent knock. A polis knock, if ever she'd heard one.

'Hello? Police. Anyone home?'

Sinead tried to speak, but her mouth wouldn't obey, and the most she could manage was a soft gargle at the back of her throat. She tried to move, to sit up, but the link between her brain and her muscles had been numbed into non-existence, and she didn't so much as twitch.

'Hello, anyone there?'

Another knock. Harder this time.

Please, let her speak. Just let her speak!

She managed a wheeze, but nothing more.

Outside, the footsteps crunched on the gravel.

No! No, don't go. Please, don't go!

She listened to the sound fading away until all she could hear was the rasping of her own breath, and the pulsing of her blood as it went whooshing through her veins.

Tears fell, unnoticed, down the sides of her cheeks and into her hair. Salvation had been so close. Someone had been right there. Right outside. Just a few metres from where she lay.

And now, it was gone. Now, she was on her own, and—

A shadow passed over her. She heard a scuffing against the glass of the window, and then a muttered 'what the fuck?'

A fist banged on the glass, shaking it in the frame. She couldn't turn to look, but felt a surge of hope as the footsteps went racing across the gravel again.

Another window smashed, throwing glass onto the floor. She heard the rattling of a lock, footsteps, then the sound of the door to the room swinging inwards.

'Jesus Christ!'

Someone was here. Someone had found her! A sob formed in her chest, but she was still too immobile for it to go anywhere.

'Sinead? Jesus. Is that…?'

He moved closer, forcing his way into her limited field of view. She saw the uniform first—the cap and the high-vis jacket.

And then, she saw him. Looking down at her as she lay there, helpless.

PC Jason Hall.

'What the fuck happened? Are you…?' He clicked his fingers above her face. It took all her concentration to blink, to let him know that she was in there. That she was alive and awake. 'Jesus Christ Almighty. What have they got you hooked up to?' he asked, and he disappeared for a moment while he looked at something beyond her line of sight.

He reappeared a few seconds later on her other side, closer now. One thumb was pressing down on the call button of the radio on his shoulder, but he hadn't said anything to dispatch yet.

'Are you… are you, like, completely frozen?' he whispered. He prodded her on the side of her face. Had it not been for the way it moved her head, she'd never have known. 'Wow. That's crazy. That's…'

She could only watch as he looked her up and down, his gaze going all the way to her feet and back again. Something flashed behind his eyes. Something hungry.

With a click, his thumb came off the call button.

'Look at you. How the mighty have fallen, eh?' he said, and he was smiling now. *Smiling*. 'At least you're not acting like the big I am now, are you? Not being all high and mighty. Like you're better than the rest of us. That's something, I suppose. Makes a nice fucking change.'

He ran a hand across her forehead, sweeping back a strand of her hair, then wiped a tear from her cheek with his thumb. She felt none of it, but saw it all. It was like it was happening to someone else. Some stranger she'd never met, and couldn't possibly help.

He disappeared for a moment, moving down her body until she couldn't see him. She could hear him, though. Sniffing. At her.

'You know you've pissed yourself?' he told her. 'Still warm, too.'

He reappeared, smelling his fingers, dabbing them against his tongue. He stared down at her. Just stared, head tilted to one side, eyes studying her face, before inching down to her chest.

Sinead managed a gasp. It made his eyes snap back up to her face, but then they went wandering down again and settled on her breasts.

He put his hands on them, first one, then the other. She couldn't feel his touch, could only watch first the anticipation, then the growing glee on his face, and the way he chewed on his bottom lip as he stroked, and kneaded, and squeezed.

'Mmm. Wow,' he whispered. 'God, they're bigger than they look, aren't they? They're really... they're really nice. Jesus.'

She forced her throat to make another sound. Almost a grunt this time. It snapped him to his senses and made him pull his hands away in fright.

There was a moment of clarity then. He clutched at his hair and shook his head, unable to believe what he'd been doing.

'Fuck! Fuck, sorry, Jesus. I'm sorry, I'm sorry, I'm sorry!' he babbled, bouncing from foot to foot. 'I shouldn't have done that... I didn't mean to... It wasn't—'

He bent forward suddenly, throwing himself at her, his hands grabbing her face. And then his lips were on hers, his tongue exploring her lifeless mouth, his breathing becoming a series of increasingly animalistic grunts.

Sinead lay there, motionless. Trapped. Screaming inside.

Panic wouldn't come, though. There was no sudden rush of adrenaline, no knotting of her gut, no reactionary jolting of muscles. There was just the same numb terror. The same rigid shock.

The same cold dread as he pulled away from her, vanished out of sight, and quietly closed the door.

Chapter 33

The torchlight swung, picked out the shape of the girl and the gun, and then Logan dodged sideways just as she opened fire again. The handgun jerked in her grip, and the bullet exploded through plaster somewhere up near the ceiling, the roar and the ring of it driving the silence from the confined space of the safe room.

Logan threw himself at her, grabbing for her hands, forcing the weapon up above her head.

A knee came up and caught him in the bollocks. Once. Twice.

'Ow! Fucking quit that!' he bellowed, before finally wrenching the weapon from the girl's grasp and pushing her back beyond kneeing distance.

'D–don't kill me.'

Logan shone his torch into his own face. The spooky lit-from-below look didn't quite have the calming effect he was hoping for, but after her initial squeal of terror, Olivia realised who she was looking at.

Arms were flung around him. His testicles retracted in anticipation of another full-scale assault, but the girl just buried her face into his chest and wept. He patted her back with one hand, while trying to find somewhere safe to put the gun with the other.

There was a rack of shelving beside them. He shoved it up on top of that, well beyond anyone's reach but his own.

And then, for a while, he just stood there, saying nothing, letting her get her tears out.

Only once the girl's sobs had finally faded, did he ask the obvious question. 'What the hell did you think you were doing? You could've bloody killed me.'

'I thought you were... someone else,' Olivia whispered. 'I'm sorry, I didn't think that...'

Behind Logan, a dog went whuff, making both him and Olivia jump.

'Jesus!'

'You all right, boss?' Tyler asked, hobbling into the adjoining room on the other side of the false door. 'We thought we heard something.'

'Oh, did you now?' Logan grunted. 'You and them sensitive ears of yours, you mean?'

'Aye, well, it was mostly the dog, right enough,' Tyler said.

There was a click as he found a light switch. A fluorescent strip light illuminated overhead, and everyone blinked in the sudden brightness of it.

The space they were in, just like Bosco had told him, wasn't so much a room as a bunker. There was a tiny kitchen area made up of a single-ring electric stove, two dented metal pots, and a can opener. A toilet was partly hidden by a folding screen, while a single tap above a sink the size of a soup plate provided a source of water.

The shelving rack Logan had set the gun on top of contained various tins and packets of food. There was enough of it to survive on for weeks, provided you weren't too fussed about a varied or balanced diet.

'How did you find me?' Olivia asked.

Her skin and clothes were dirty, her hair tangled in knots. Despite the little oil radiator pumping out heat in the corner, she looked cold—the sort of cold that got into your bones and gnawed on them until there was nothing left but marrow and gristle.

'Your dad told me about this place,' Logan said. 'Didn't tell me you'd be armed, though. Where the hell did you get that gun?'

Olivia pointed to a space on one of the shelves. 'It was there. I just… I'm sorry. I thought you were someone else.'

'Oleg,' Logan said, and the girl physically recoiled like he'd slapped her.

'How do you know about Oleg?' she asked, her voice becoming a whisper.

'I know a lot of things, Olivia,' Logan said. 'But I don't know everything. I can help you. I can help everyone. But I need you to fill in the blanks for me. About Oleg. About Borys.' He hesitated, then took the chance. 'About the Iceman.'

She didn't react. No surprise, no confusion, no denial. She just looked tired. Defeated. Small.

Olivia sat down on the safe room's only chair. It was a folding canvas and wood number, the sort of thing Hollywood directors used.

'I can't,' she said, shaking her head. 'I can't, it's too… I can't.'

Logan crouched in front of her. 'Shona's missing, Olivia. So's your mum, and see Tyler there? His wife has been taken, too.'

A tear rolled down Olivia's cheek. She focused on her clasped hands, not looking at him.

'And we can do it. We can get them back. Whatever's happened, whatever's wrong, we can sort this all out.'

She sniffed, shook her head, almost choked on another sob. 'You can't.'

'I can, Olivia. We can. Us, together,' Logan promised her. 'But I need you to work with me. I need you to tell me everything.'

'He'll find me. He'll come get me for what I did.'

Logan stood, rising like a giant from the deep. From where Olivia sat, he almost reached the ceiling, nearly filled the room.

'He'll have to get through me first,' he told her. 'And I do not fancy the bastard's chances.'

'Please, Olivia,' Tyler said. 'Please, tell us. Help us get everyone back safe.'

Taggart sniffed experimentally at her feet, then brought his front paws up so they were resting on her knee. She pushed him down, but when he repeated the exercise she relented and patted him on the head.

'OK,' she said, her eyes darting between the detectives. She swallowed. 'What do you want to know?'

–

Sinead's trousers were on the floor. She'd been jostled around as he'd worked them down over her hips and knees. She'd watched them being pulled off her, and then discarded. She'd heard the clinking of Jason's belt, and the rustling of fabric as he'd slid his own trousers down around his ankles.

He was kissing her again now, all tongue, and gums, and slevvers on her mouth, and on her throat, and on her neck. His breathing was short and shallow, one arm pumping back and forth as he struggled to get himself ready. Get himself hard.

'Oh, fuck. Sinead. Fuck, you don't know how often I've thought about this,' he whispered to her.

His free hand went to her breasts again, pawing at them through her shirt. She couldn't feel his touch, exactly, but there was… something now. The slightest suggestion of pressure on her chest, as her nervous system started to shake off whatever had been pumped into her.

Another few minutes, and maybe she could move. Another half-hour, and perhaps she could fight him, claw at him, push him away.

But all she could do was lie there. All she could do was wait.

He stepped back from her, and looked down at the hand that was still pumping back and forth, priming himself. It was out of her eye-line. A small mercy.

'Right, that's more like it,' he muttered, looking down at himself.

The bed tilted a little as he put his weight on it, adjusting her angle and giving her a better view out into the hall.

She caught a glimpse of a shape out there. Of movement. But then Jason was on top of her, blocking her view, his leering face just inches from her own.

'Right, you stuck-up slut,' he whispered, the words bubbling out of him like a giggle. 'Let's see how you like—'

He stopped talking. His eyes bulged, as a wire was looped around his throat from behind. Jason gargled as he was dragged backwards off the bed, and was lost to the blur just beyond Sinead's field of view.

She heard him gasp. Choke. Wheeze.

She heard the thudding of his heels against the wooden floor as he frantically tried to find purchase. Tried to fight back.

She heard the struggle become fainter. Weaker. Quieter.

And then she heard the thump of his head falling back, and the fast, unsteady breathing of someone who had just expended a lot of effort.

There was a creaking of floorboards, and a rustling of material as the newcomer got to his feet. He was still out there in the empty space beyond where her vision reached, but Sinead got an impression of a man right at the limit of her peripherals.

'Oh, God,' he muttered. 'Oh God, what has he done?'

Chapter 34

Logan strode into the Incident Room, held the door open, and waited in silence for Tyler to catch up. Ben, Hamza, and Dave Davidson sat listening to the grunting and wheezing of DC Neish's progress along the corridor, but said nothing until he'd finally joined them in the room.

'Eh, you know you're not meant to be here, Jack,' Ben said.

'Aye, good to see you, too, Benjamin,' Logan retorted, and the older man smiled.

'That's me said my piece. You all heard it. No bugger can say I didn't try,' he announced. 'You know if Mitchell finds out you're here, though, there'll be—'

'Get her,' Logan said. 'Call her in here.'

'Bold! I like it!' said Dave.

'Get her in? Are you mental?' Ben asked. 'She knows you've been digging into the case. She's going to have something to say about that.'

'Aye, well, she can bloody well wait,' Logan said. 'We've got Olivia Maximuke in one of the interview rooms.'

'We're pretty sure she *was* dealing, sir, like Jonathan MacInally told us,' Hamza piped up. 'I interviewed him again at home, put a bit of pressure on, and he admitted to supplying to some kids in school on her behalf. We think the list from Borys' car—'

'Was a list of the other kids she had working for her. Aye, she's told us everything,' Logan said. 'But that's just minor details compared to the main event. So, let's get Mitchell phoned, then you can catch us up on anything we've missed before she gets here.'

The phone call was placed. Logan felt the chill of the Detective Superintendent's response from all the way along the corridor.

While they waited for her to arrive, Hamza ran through the latest developments. Thanks to them still having access to the shared inbox, there wasn't much they weren't already aware of.

The press conference had gone well. A little too well, actually, and there were dozens of reports flooding in every hour, mostly to report sightings of girls in school uniforms.

As of yet, though, there were no firm leads on Sinead, Shona, or Alexis Maximuke. No hits on Oleg, either.

The DS was running through Mrs Howden's post-mortem results when Logan cut him off. 'Conrad killed her.'

Hamza stopped, glanced across to Ben, then frowned. 'Sir?'

'Mercy killing. Or, I don't know, maybe he was just sick of looking after her,' Logan said. 'It's the only thing that fits. Well, I mean, we could speculate about other possibilities, but I'd start there. She was in pain, she was suffering, and she was ultimately facing a nasty, lingering death. I reckon either she preferred the thought of a pillow over the face, or Conrad did. Either way, I'd bet that's what happened.'

'Shite. Aye. That makes more sense than my ideas, boss,' Tyler admitted.

'Most things generally do, son.'

'So... what?' Ben asked. 'He went back to deal with the body, and got attacked then?'

'Works for me,' Logan said. 'We know they looked in his house, but didn't find him. Assuming they'd been watching him for a while, they would've known where else to check. Went to his mum's, there he was.'

'I still don't get the microchip thing,' Hamza said. 'Why lead us back to Conrad? Why like that?'

'Where's the dug, by the way?' Dave asked. 'Did you get rid of it?'

Ben's eyes widened. 'You didn't *get rid of it* get rid of it, did you?'

'Probably for the best,' Dave said. 'It's thick as mince.'

'He's a dug!' Logan said again. 'They're all thick as mince. And, no, I didn't get rid of him. He's in the interview room with Olivia. Keeping her company.'

'Sounds like the whole place is positively brimming with unwelcome guests,' said Detective Superintendent Mitchell, who had appeared once again just inside the door without anyone noticing.

'I swear to God, you must bloody teleport,' Logan grunted. He pointed to one of the office chairs. 'Sit down.'

Mitchell's eyebrows rose in disbelief. 'I beg your pardon?'

'You're going to want to take a seat for this, ma'am,' Logan insisted, then he begrudgingly threw in a 'please', to help hurry things along.

'This had better be good, Detective Chief Inspector,' Mitchell said. She lowered herself onto one of the swivel chairs like it might be booby-trapped. 'In fact, no, from your current starting point, it had better be spectacular.'

'It is,' Logan assured her. He took a moment to get everything straight in his head, then launched into it. 'We all remember the Iceman case. From before Christmas, I mean, as well as the larger investigation from previously.'

'We do,' Ben said.

'As we know, Olivia Maximuke was involved in the investigation, though only tangentially, as a witness. Or so we thought.'

'She knew the Iceman?' Hamza asked.

Logan shook his head. 'No. But she found one of his freezers. The last one we found, earlier this year.'

'With the body in it?' asked Hamza.

'The very one. But that's the thing. As far as Olivia knew, there were two bodies in there.'

Mitchell sat forward a little. 'Two?'

'Aye. See, Oleg Ivanov was in a relationship with her mother at the time, and he was getting Olivia to act as a courier for him, bringing drugs to guys he had working under him, and collecting cash,' Logan explained. 'She started to think he was going to kill her, so she lured him to that building, and tricked him into going inside the freezer.'

'Jesus. And she left him there?' Ben asked.

Logan nodded. 'Aye. Left him to die. Though she swears it was self-defence.'

There was silence for a few moments, as they all processed this.

'There was other DNA in the freezer that we couldn't identify. Besides the victim, I mean,' Logan reminded them. 'What's the bet it's a match for Oleg?'

'So she locked him in, but he clearly got out,' Mitchell said.

'Seems like it, aye. But Olivia insists the door was locked from the outside, and that he had no means of contacting anyone. The freezer was running. He should've died within hours.'

'So what are we saying?' Ben asked. 'That Oleg *isn't* responsible for what's happening?'

'We've literally just put out a press statement based on your intelligence,' Mitchell said, glowering at Logan. 'If you're now saying he isn't involved…'

'No, I'm saying he is,' Logan assured them. 'He wasn't there when we found the freezer. He couldn't have got out on his own, so someone else must've let him out. Someone who went to that building within hours of Olivia locking him in there, and let him out.'

'Couldn't have been a randomer,' Hamza said. 'Or they'd have reported it, surely? They wouldn't just have left the other body there.'

'But we had the Iceman by then,' Ben said.

'Aye, but we know there were more than one of him. *Them*. Whatever,' Logan said. 'What if we didn't get the top man? What if everyone we've come across has been just another one of his wee protégés? What if the real, main, original Iceman is still out there?'

'Why would Oleg wait until now to get back at Olivia?' Mitchell asked. 'If he was freed in December, why wait all these months to take his revenge?'

'I wondered the same thing myself,' Logan said. 'Tyler had an idea on that. Tyler?'

Behind him, DC Neish blinked in surprise. He shrunk a couple of inches as Mitchell turned her gaze on him, and babbled out his answer as quickly as he could.

'I just thought, like, recovery time,' he said. 'If he was in there a while, it would've had effects on him. Like… he'd be injured, or whatever. From the cold. Injuries like that, they'd take time to heal.'

'Works for me,' Logan said.

Mitchell clicked her tongue against the back of her teeth, then nodded. 'It's one possible explanation.'

'If you're in that much of a state, you don't just get better on your own,' Ben said. 'He'd have needed medical attention. Someone must've nursed him back to health. Someone with medical experience.'

'Presumably the same person who let him out,' Hamza added.

'The Iceman,' Logan concluded. 'Has to be. Or someone connected to that case, anyway. Too much of a coincidence, otherwise.'

'And he was a vigilante killer. Borys Wozniak was dealing to school kids,' Hamza said.

'That was the sort of target he went for, right enough,' Ben confirmed.

'And Conrad Howden was a conman who'd done time,' the DS continued.

'They're all connected to Olivia, though,' Logan said. 'One way or another. I mean, there's her mother, of course, but Shona, too.'

'What about Sinead, boss?'

'I think just… wrong place at the wrong time,' Logan said, all too aware of the fact that he was the one who sent her to that place at that time. 'They must've been watching the house, saw her go in, and grabbed her.'

Tyler nodded. 'Aye,' he croaked through his tightening throat. 'Must've been that, right enough.'

'So, who do we think is responsible for it all? The Iceman or this Oleg?' Mitchell asked.

'I don't know,' Logan admitted. 'Both, maybe? One guiding the other. Or using him. The Iceman, or Icemen, or whatever, always had a very specific M.O. that we're not seeing here.' He thought of Shona and Sinead, their whereabouts currently unknown. 'So far, anyway.'

'So, if it's the Iceman, then he's mixed it up a bit,' Hamza said. 'Ditched the freezers in favour of... what? Kicking the shite out of someone in their mum's house?'

'Like I say, I don't have all the answers,' Logan said. 'But I know someone who might.'

He took a swig from a mug on the table beside him, then grimaced when he realised it was stone cold, and not his. He set it down again with a clunk and the slightest suggestion of a retch.

'I'm going to head in and talk to Olivia. See if she has anything else to tell us.'

'No, you are not,' Mitchell said, getting to her feet.

Logan sighed. 'We're not still on this "off the case" shite, are we?'

'No. I mean, yes. But that's not the point.'

'What's the point, then?'

'She's a child,' Mitchell reminded him. 'There are rules we need to follow.'

'We've got three women whose lives are in danger,' Logan said. 'Olivia wants to talk. She wants to help us get them back.'

'That's irrelevant.'

Logan bristled. 'Which bit?'

'All of it,' Mitchell replied. 'Look, Jack, I share your concerns—'

'My *concerns*? Clearly, you don't. Clearly, you don't have the first fucking clue about my concerns, or you wouldn't be spouting any of this rubbish.'

'She's a minor, Detective Chief Inspector. What she wants—what we want—is irrelevant. She needs a solicitor present. By law. Otherwise, any information gained is going to be challenged in court, and potentially dismissed.'

'To be honest, I'm not thinking about any court case. I just want to get Sinead and Shona back.'

'We all do. But there are rules, Jack. The solicitor, for one. And, without a parent available for her, we'll have to bring in someone from Social Services. We'll have to surrender her to their care, in fact.'

'How long's all that going to take?' Tyler asked.

'Far too bloody long!' Logan spat.

'It'll take as long as it takes,' Mitchell said, standing her ground. 'As long as you're interviewing her here in this station, then there are rules that must be followed.' She glared up at the much larger DCI like she was trying to forcibly implant her point in his brain. 'Have I made myself clear, Jack? Or do I need to spell it out to you?'

Logan gave a little snort. 'I understand, ma'am.'

'Boss, we can't wait for all that!' Tyler protested.

'She's right, son. We shouldn't be on the case,' Logan said, and Mitchell nodded, satisfied.

'What?' Tyler cried. 'We can't just—'

'We all right letting Olivia walk the dog downstairs for a few minutes?' Logan asked the Detective Superintendent. 'While you're calling Social Services.'

'I'm sure that would help take her mind off things,' Mitchell said. 'Just make sure you don't lose her.'

'We'll do our best,' Logan said, pulling on his coat.

Tyler frowned. 'But what about…?' he began, then his whole face changed when the realisation hit. 'Oh!' he said. 'Right. Aye. Gotcha.'

'I don't expect to see either of you back here until this case is wrapped up,' Mitchell told them. 'Is that clear?'

'Aye. We understand, ma'am,' Logan said. 'We'll see ourselves out.'

With a curt nod at the other detectives, he turned and led the waddling Tyler out through the double swing doors and into the corridor beyond.

There was silence in the Incident Room for a few seconds, before Detective Superintendent Mitchell interrupted it.

'Detective Inspector?' she said, still watching the door.

'Yes, ma'am?'

'Kindly stop grinning.'

'Yes, ma'am.'

She turned then and met Ben's eye. 'Bring them home.'

'Yes, ma'am.' He nodded. 'We will.'

Chapter 35

Sinead's toes wiggled. Her fingers twitched. She was aware of a cool breeze across her bare legs, and a pain across her back and shoulders from lying in an awkward position for... however long she'd been lying there.

Her head was clearing, bit by bit, and as the numbness faded, the fear rushed in to fill the void it had left behind.

She couldn't lift her head yet, but she could turn it a little. Enough to see part of Jason Hall's body on the floor, the trousers of his uniform hooked around one ankle, his flaccid penis poking out from the slit on the front of his boxers.

She couldn't see his top half from where she lay. That was probably a blessing.

The other man—the man who had killed him, the man who had saved her—was gone. He'd left before she could see him. She'd lay there, perfectly still, eyes glassy, and listened to him fretting for a few moments before he'd gone running outside.

A car door had slammed. An engine had started. Tyres had gone skidding on gravel, and only then did Sinead let out the breath she'd been holding all that time.

Time had passed since then. Minutes had crawled by as she listened for the sound of the car returning. As she focused on her fingers and toes, and tried to force them to obey her commands.

And they had. Vaguely. Eventually.

She lifted an arm, just an inch, maybe two, before it fell back down again. With a grunt, she bent her right leg a little, bringing her heel up closer to the knee on the opposite side.

The muscles burned. She welcomed the pain. It sharpened her. Cut through the fuzz.

In a few minutes, she'd be able to move. She wouldn't be able to walk far, if at all, but Jason had a radio. She could call back to dispatch. She could get help.

Please, God, let her get help.

She lifted the arm again, a little higher this time, and twisted it across her body. Her hand slapped onto the opposite forearm, then crawled up to the crook of her elbow, until it found the source of the pinprick pain that had been niggling at her for the past few minutes.

Sinead winced as she pulled the soft plastic needle free. Her head spun, either from the lingering effects of the drugs, or the effort she was expending. Either way, she needed a moment to rest and recover.

She shut her eyes to stop the spinning. Breathed, to bring her quickening heart rate back under control.

Time passed, before the pain in her back, and her sides, and her shoulders all jerked her awake again.

She raised her head. It was heavier than she remembered. The texture of the light outside had changed, though she couldn't tell if it was the weather or the time of day that were different.

Jason Hall was still on the floor. The room was still otherwise empty.

Her limbs responded after only a slight delay. Pain formed as spit bubbles on her lips as she rolled onto her side, one hand clutching the edge of the bed, a foot stretching out, exploring for the ground.

Her balance betrayed her. There was nothing she could do but fall, nowhere she could go but down. Her shoulder hit the floor first, then her chin, then the rest of her. The arms, which had been responsive a moment ago, went back to ignoring her, as if chastising her over this latest indignity.

Down there, she was looking straight into the eyes of the dead constable. They were open wide and so bloodshot they

237

were almost demonic. His neck was a faint blur of black and purple, with a sharply defined red line running all the way across it. The wire that had been used to strangle him was still partly buried in his windpipe.

Gritting her teeth, she turned away, and forced her arms to move beneath her. They shook as they took her weight. Her legs were a long way from being strong enough to use. Even getting them to move was still a struggle. Standing was impossible, let alone walking or running. Those would take time. Time she couldn't afford to waste.

Arms trembling, she began to drag herself towards the body of PC Jason Hall, her feet kicking limply, socks sliding on the wooden floor.

She made it all the way over to him before she realised that his radio was not on his shoulder. Panic kicked in again as she scanned the ground around him, hoping that it had just been knocked off, that it would be lying somewhere nearby.

It hadn't. It wasn't.

Tears sprang to her eyes. Her heart leapt into her throat.

Outside, tyres crunched on loose gravel.

Chapter 36

Taggart sniffed suspiciously at the tyre of Logan's car, then squatted and peed on the tarmac beside it. That done, he trotted over to Tyler, barked twice, then tried to sit on one of Logan's feet, and appeared genuinely offended when the DCI shook him off.

Olivia hadn't said a word as they'd made their way down in the lift and across the car park. She sat in the front passenger seat of Logan's car now, with the door open and both detectives crowding her.

There wasn't much more she could tell them, she insisted. She'd already given them all the information she had. She knew nothing more about Oleg, where he might be, or what he might be planning.

'There must be something else, Olivia,' Logan insisted. 'Some place he mentioned. Some friend.'

'There's nothing. Nothing I can remember,' she replied. 'If I did, I'd tell you. I've told you everything else. I just... I want my mum back.'

'Then you need to think,' Logan told her. 'There's got to be something he said, or something you saw.'

'You're the police! You're meant to find him!' Olivia yelped. 'I thought you could trace phones and check banks and all that? You're meant to be good at this.'

'We can. We have, and there's nothing,' Logan told her. 'He hasn't used his bank account, you tell us you destroyed his phone...'

'I did. Then I threw it away,' Olivia admitted. 'But he might have another phone, now.'

'Aye, but since we don't know the number, that doesn't do us a whole lot of good,' Logan pointed out.

'He's related to you, isn't he?' Tyler said. 'Are there any other, like, cousins, or whatever he might have been in touch with?'

Olivia shook her head and shrugged simultaneously. Down on the ground, Taggart let out a little 'arf' just to remind everyone he was still there, should they fancy patting him or giving him some food.

'Where were you getting the drugs you were selling?' Logan asked. 'Those came from Oleg, right? So, where was he keeping them stashed?'

'I don't know. He gave me some to deliver. That's what we were selling,' Olivia told him. 'If there's more, I don't know where it is.'

Tyler tapped the DCI on the arm. 'Can I get a word, boss?'

Logan pointed to Olivia. 'You wait right there,' he told her, then he walked with Tyler far enough from the car that she wouldn't hear their conversation.

Taggart followed them, swiping and lunging at Logan's feet like this was all part of some game.

'This feels like a waste of time,' Tyler said when they were out of earshot. 'I don't think she knows anything else.'

Logan conceded the point with a sigh and a shake of his head. 'No. I think you're probably right.'

'But I've been thinking. It's her he wants, isn't it? Oleg. She's the one he's after.'

Logan blinked. 'What are you saying, Tyler?'

'I'm not saying we hand her over. I'm just saying that… if he thinks we might. If he thinks maybe we'd do a swap, it might lure him out.'

'Use her as bait, you mean? She's a child. I know we're desperate here, son, but—'

'Aye. Exactly. We're desperate, boss,' Tyler whispered. 'We've got no idea where Sinead and Shona are. Or Olivia's mum.

We're clueless. The only thing we've got going in our favour is her.'

They both looked over at Olivia sitting in the car. She pretended not to notice.

'No way he's going to believe we're just offering her up on a plate,' Logan said. 'He'd see through it right away.'

'Maybe he would, aye. Or maybe, if it's him and the Iceman working together, they'll think they're smarter than we are. They'll know it's a trap, but they'll think they can outsmart us and get her, anyway.'

Logan frowned. 'And how will that help?'

'Because we'll actually be smarter than them! We'll be two steps ahead,' Tyler said, and the slightly hysterical screech to his voice said it all. He was reaching. He was desperate.

Logan knew how he felt.

'I'll do it,' Olivia said from the car. She rolled her eyes when the detectives turned her way. 'You're not as quiet as you think you are. You want to use me as bait? Fine. I'll do it. I just… I want my mum back. I don't want anything to happen to her.'

'We can't do that, Olivia,' Logan said. 'We can't put you in danger.'

She shrugged, then hopped down from the car. 'Fine. I'll go do it myself.'

'What will you do, exactly?'

'I'll offer myself up as a swap.'

'How? I thought you didn't know where to find him?'

Olivia's eyes darted around as she ran through her options. 'I'll… go on the radio,' she announced. 'They'll let me on. I'll tell them everything. He'll hear it, and we can sort it out that way.'

'Sort what out? You can't hand yourself over to him,' Logan said.

'I can if I want!'

'No. You can't. And what bloody good would it do, anyway?'

'He might let them go!' Olivia cried, and her voice was even more of a screech than Tyler's. 'If he gets me, he might let them go.'

'And what will he do to you, do you think?' Logan asked.

'I don't... it doesn't matter. It's my fault, anyway. Everything. It's all my fault!' She tried, but failed, to fight back tears, and stood there between the detectives and the car, shivering in the cold. 'I just... I don't want to be scared anymore. And I just... I just want my mum back. I just want my mum.'

Logan put his arms around her, catching her before she could fall. 'I know you do. But that's not the way to go about it. That's not—'

A shout from over by the station door brought the sentence to a premature end. He and Tyler both looked to see Hamza racing towards them, his tie blowing backwards over his shoulder, his eyes wide and frantic.

'Tyler!'

Taggart barked excitedly and began turning in tight circles on the tarmac.

DC Neish shot a sideways look to Logan, then called back to the approaching Detective Sergeant. 'Ham? What's wrong? What's the matter?'

Hamza skidded to a stop a few feet away and held out a hand. 'Give me your phone, Tyler.'

'What? Why?'

'Just give me your phone.'

Something that was the shape of a smile raised the corners of Tyler's mouth. It wasn't a smile, though. Not even close.

'Hamza, what is it? What's going on?'

'That's an order,' Hamza said, taking a step closer. 'Just give me your phone, and don't look.'

Something electric tingled across Tyler skin. The hairs on his arm and the back of his neck came alive.

'Please, Tyler,' Hamza urged, and there was anguish and pain there on the Detective Sergeant's face. 'Just... just give me the phone, mate.'

Tyler shook his head and backed off, reaching into his pocket for his mobile. Hamza lunged for him, grabbing for the phone, but Tyler turned his back, blocking him.

'Tyler, don't!'

There was a notification on the screen. An email to the team's shared inbox, the sender name blank. The subject line hit Tyler like a stab to the heart.

'*This little piggy went wee-wee-wee-wee.*'

He staggered back against Logan's car as he read the words. They hadn't mentioned Sinead, but he knew. He just knew.

'What the fuck is this?' he asked.

Hamza looked imploringly to Logan. 'Sir. He can't.'

'Tyler,' Logan said.

But the DC had already tapped on the notification. Was already watching the screen. Had already felt the first few pangs of panic as he tapped on the icon for the attached video clip.

And like that, standing there in the car park at Burnett Road polis station, DC Tyler Neish's whole world fell apart.

Chapter 37

'How the hell did he know where to send it?' Logan hissed.

He, Ben, and Detective Superintendent Mitchell were in Logan's office, leaving Hamza out in the main Incident Room with Tyler. The lad was shaken, and barely holding it together. Nobody was blaming him for that, of course.

The footage had shown what was unmistakably Sinead lying on a bed in a dimly lit room, hooked up to some sort of intravenous drip. Her eyes were open. Staring. She'd looked dead at first, until a prod from the cameraman had elicited a low groan from somewhere deep within her.

She had wet herself while unconscious, or whatever it was that was happening to her. The croaky-voiced bastard behind the camera had taken great delight in pointing that out. He'd also pointed out that he could do anything he wanted to her, and there would be nothing she could do but lie there and take it. Conscious, but frozen. Aware, but unable to do a damn thing about it.

There had been no demands made in the video, nor in the body of the email. No requests for money, or hostage exchanges, or anything of the sort.

There had just been the video, and a single instruction to call a Russian phone number at the bottom of the email.

Tyler had been trying to dial the number when Logan had finally managed to get the phone off him. He'd fought back, pushed and punched at the DCI, tears streaming down his face while he shouted and screamed in the bigger man's face.

It was Ben who had finally calmed him down enough to come inside. He'd appeared a few minutes after Hamza, then stepped straight in and grabbed Tyler in a bear-hug, pinning his arms to his sides while the DC wriggled and squirmed and raged against him.

It had taken just a minute or so to burn itself out. Tyler's head had fallen against the older man's shoulder then, and they'd stood there together while his grief flooded out of him.

Logan had spotted the faces watching on from the upstairs windows of the station, peering down at them like this was all show meant for their entertainment. He and Hamza had positioned themselves to block their view of Tyler and Ben. Logan's crossed arms and furious glare sent all but the nosiest bastards scurrying back to work, and he paid very close attention to the faces of those who remained, memorising them for the weapons-grade bollocking that waited in all of their futures.

After a minute or two of this, Ben had suggested that they all go in and get a cup of tea inside them, and Tyler had mutely followed behind.

Now Olivia and Taggart were being given something to eat in the canteen, Hamza was doing his best to console Tyler, and Logan had called the crisis summit in his office, earning himself some fairly withering remarks from Mitchell, who had not counted on him disobeying her direct orders *quite* so quickly.

'Well?' Logan demanded. 'How did he find out the email address for the team's inbox? That's internal use only. Someone must've given it to him.'

'That ties in with your Iceman theory,' Ben said. 'He seemed to know everything about us when he first appeared on the scene. I think we can assume that's where Oleg got the details from.'

Olivia hadn't been sure if the voice on the video belonged to Oleg. It was far harsher and rougher than it had been when she'd last heard it. Some of the words seemed to hiss at the end, too, which wasn't something she'd heard him do before. And yet, there was something familiar about the accent that had stopped her from ruling it out as his. It might be him, she'd concluded, but it equally might not be.

Fat lot of bloody use that was.

For now, they were working on the assumption that it was. They were working on a lot of assumptions, in fact. That Oleg had been rescued by the Iceman, and now the two of them were paired up in some way, each helping the other on their own twisted missions of vengeance.

'What have we got on the number?' Logan asked.

'Russian area code. Moscow,' Ben said.

'Who the hell's in Russia? They've no' shipped Sinead over there.'

'It's one of them internet numbers,' explained Ben, stretching his technical knowledge to its very limits. 'Apparently, it could be pointing anywhere. No saying you'll actually be calling Russia.' He looked from the DCI to Mitchell. 'You, eh, you will be the one calling, aye?'

'Aye,' Logan confirmed, but Mitchell had some thoughts of her own on the matter.

'That's not your decision to make, Jack,' she said, then she held a hand up to silence him before he could say anything he would almost certainly regret. 'But fine. Yes. It's your case, so you make the call.'

Logan nodded. 'I'll take full responsibility for anything that—'

'No, you bloody well will not,' Mitchell bit back. 'I've put you back in charge. I'm the one breaking the rules. The buck stops with me. The responsibility is mine. So, do not mess this up, because if you think my predecessor was a sight to behold when he was angry, I can assure you that you've seen nothing yet.'

'Understood, ma'am,' Logan said, then he swung into action. 'Right, we're going to want this recorded. Get the tech bods in here, see if there's any way of tracing these internet numbers.

I want that video and email scrutinised, too. See what we can get off it.'

'Already in hand, Jack,' Ben assured him. 'Nothing from the email—apparently it's some free online address, and was bounced around some, I don't know, foreign servers or something. I don't know the jargon, but I know it's untraceable. The video, they're still working on, but they're not holding out much hope of getting anything useful from it.'

'Shite,' Logan spat. He sat back in his chair and rubbed his forehead, trying to fend off a headache that had been threatening to get much worse for a while now.

The sight of Sinead there on that bed had shaken him more than he'd care to admit. Not just for what was happening to her, or what *might* happen to her, but because if that's what they were doing to someone who'd been in the wrong place at the wrong time, then how were they treating Shona, given her connection to Olivia?

Why hadn't the bastard showed her in the video, or even mentioned her?

If he was keeping her hidden, then why? What did he have to gain by not showing her?

Or what might he lose, if he did?

There had been no word on Alexis Maximuke, either, for that matter.

Three women taken, only one being paraded on camera. Why? Why not strengthen your hand and give your message more clout by showing them all?

'He's keeping them in different places,' Logan muttered, drawing puzzled looks from Mitchell and Ben. 'Sinead, Shona, and Alexis, I mean. He's keeping them in different places.'

'What makes you say that?' Ben asked.

'Because he would've shown us all three of them if he could. But he didn't, so Shona and Alexis must be somewhere else,' Logan reasoned.

There was, of course, another potential explanation. An explanation that he dared not let himself linger on.

'Assuming you're right, how does that help us?' Mitchell asked.

'It doesn't,' Logan admitted. 'Not yet. It just makes it harder, in fact. Even if that video leads us to Sinead, it probably won't help us get Shona or Alexis back.'

'But it'd be a bloody good start,' Ben said.

'Aye, you can say that again,' Logan agreed. He checked his watch. 'Right, ten minutes, then we're calling this bastard. Let's get the tech stuff set up in here.'

He rose to his feet, prompting the others to do the same. Mitchell regarded him with suspicion as he unhooked his coat from the back of the door and pulled it on.

'You leaving us, Detective Chief Inspector?' she asked. 'Now would hardly seem the time to go gallivanting.'

'It's connected to the case,' Logan assured her. 'I just need to make a call.'

'You can use my office,' Mitchell told him.

Logan shook his head. 'Probably better if I don't, ma'am,' he said. 'I think it might be best if I do this one away from the ears of the easily offended...'

–

'What the fuck do *you* want?' demanded Bob Hoon, his voice a venomous crackle over the speaker system in Logan's car.

Night was closing in around the vehicle, another long day meandering towards its close. For other people, at least. For him, the day would simply continue, rolling over into the next in a few hours, and onwards towards the morning light.

'You've changed your tune,' Logan told him. 'A few days ago, you were all sweetness and light, asking for my help.'

'How are the new glasses treating you?' Hoon asked.

Logan frowned. 'What new glasses?'

'The fucking rose-tinted ones you must be wearing to have painted yourself such a vivid fantasy image of those conversations, Jack,' Hoon retorted. 'Because that's no' how I fucking remember them.'

Logan conceded that 'all sweetness and light' was possibly something of an exaggeration.

'How's it going down there?' he asked. 'You still in London?'

'Be here a while yet, aye,' Hoon said. 'No' that it's any of your business. What do you want?'

'I've got big problems here, Bob.'

'Is it the halitosis?' Hoon asked. 'High fucking time someone mentioned it. Packet of Polos'll sort you right out.'

'It's Sinead. Well, Sinead and Shona.'

'Shona? That the pathologist bird you're trying to fire into? You've got no chance there, by the way. Polos or no fucking Polos.'

'They've been taken.'

There was something close to silence then. Just the faint rumble of London traffic, and closer, the sound of lapping water.

'Taken? The fuck do you mean?' Hoon asked, although the length of the pause said he understood full well. 'Taken by who?'

'We think it's connected to the Iceman case,' Logan said.

He sat and listened to an outburst of creative swearing from the other end of the line. 'That boomeranging bramblewank? I thought he was fucking dead, or in the jail, or something? He's no' back again, is he? I swear to Christ, that prick's had more comebacks than Elvis.'

'We think this might be the original, we're not sure,' Logan said. 'Everyone else was just… henchmen, or I don't know… sidekicks, or whatever. Or maybe it's a new guy, I don't know.'

'You don't know very fucking much, by the sounds of it,' Hoon spat. 'That what you're phoning me for?'

'You dealt with him the first time around,' Logan said. 'I thought maybe you might have some insight.'

'I'm fucking full of insight, Jack. I've got so much insight it's pouring out of my arse. It's rapidly becoming *outsight*, in fact.'

Logan waited. When it was clear that nothing else was forthcoming, he offered up a prompt. 'Well?'

'Well, what?'

'Who do you think it is?'

Hoon's scowl was somehow audible over the phone. 'How the fuck should I know? I thought we had him.'

Logan sighed. 'You said you had insight.'

'I meant in general, no' about this specific thing,' Hoon said. 'You're the one dealing with it. I've got my own shite going on.'

'Right. Aye. Fair enough,' Logan grunted.

'What does he want?'

Logan hesitated. 'The Iceman?'

'Aye. He had a list of polis before, but why the pathologist?'

'We think she's connected to...' Logan shook his head. 'It's complicated.'

'Fine. I don't care,' Hoon said. 'He always seemed to fucking know what we were up to. Freaked us all out. Never figured out how he knew it all. We thought he might even be polis at one point, playing us from the inside, but the leads didn't take us that way, so we ditched it. Might be worth a wee dig around now, though.'

'Maybe, aye,' Logan said. 'It's a bit different this time, though. We think he's working with someone else. Someone new. We're not sure what's the Iceman and what's the new player.'

'Basic fucking maths,' Hoon said.

'Eh?'

'Jesus Christ, Jack. Have I got to explain everything? Did they no' give you a fucking "How To Be a Detective" booklet when you signed up? Basic maths. Take what you know about this new guy, deduct it from what you've got, whatever's left over is the Iceman. Or fucking vice versa. Take one away from the other. Sticking guys in freezers? Iceman column. Fucking...'

doing whatever this other prick's doing? Take that away. Basic maths.'

Logan ran a hand down his face. He wasn't sure what he'd expected from a conversation with Bob Hoon—he rarely knew what to expect from such an encounter, and when he did, he was usually wrong—but he'd been hoping for something more useful than this. Some nugget of information, maybe, that would point them towards their man, and start the chain reaction that would get Sinead, Shona, and Alexis Maximuke all home safe. The Iceman to Oleg, Oleg to the women. A happy ending, and two more sick bastards off the streets.

A lesson in 'basic fucking maths' was unlikely to help him knock down that first domino.

'Aye, well, thanks for that, Bob,' he said. 'I'd better get back to it.'

'Same here,' Hoon said. There was a momentary pause before he spoke again. 'How's Boy Band doing?'

Logan blew out his cheeks and exhaled. 'Tyler's... OK,' he concluded, although he wasn't sure that this was entirely accurate. 'He's scared. He's angry. But he's dealing.'

'Aye. Well, tell him...'

Logan waited while the other man considered his next remark.

'Tell him to man up,' Hoon said. 'No point fucking crying over spilt milk.'

'I'm sure he'll be touched by those kind words,' Logan said. 'I'll pass them on.'

'Good,' Hoon said, either missing or choosing to completely ignore the sarcasm. 'Good luck, Jack.'

'Cheers, Bob.'

'And don't forget the fucking Polos.'

Chapter 38

They made the call from Logan's office, on a phone that was routed through a laptop, the audio broadcasting through the speakers for everyone else in the room to hear.

Currently, that consisted of Logan, Ben, Detective Superintendent Mitchell, and one of the tech bods who sat hunched over the laptop with a finger poised above the keyboard. He was a young guy, built like a stick-insect, and the way he sat there made him look like a teenager getting ready to Alt-Tab away from a porn site should his parents walk in the room.

Olivia had been brought in, too, despite Mitchell's deeply held objections. Logan had argued that there was nobody else better qualified to tell them if the voice was Oleg's. Mitchell had suggested she could listen back to some edited highlights later, but Logan insisted her live input could be crucial to the negotiations, and the Detective Superintendent had eventually relented.

What he hadn't told her was the real reason he wanted Olivia there. He needed Oleg to be sure that they had her. He needed the bastard to know that they weren't bluffing.

Tyler and Hamza sat out in the Incident Room, listening in on a secondary audio feed. It was Logan who hadn't been keen on that idea—the lad was struggling enough, as it was—but Tyler had insisted he'd be fine. Insisted that he wanted to listen, that he *needed* to listen.

'Please, boss. Give me this,' he'd said. 'Just give me this.'

And so, against his better judgement, he'd agreed that Tyler could listen in. He wasn't going to be on the call—in his current state, he was too unpredictable for that—but he could listen in from a safe distance, and with Hamza there to shut the feed down if it all started to get too much.

Taggart, sluggish from his feed at the canteen, lay curled up under the desk, between the feet of both detectives. He snored contentedly like he didn't have a care in the world.

Logan snorted a little jet of air out through both nostrils. And to think people said, 'it's a dog's life' like it was a bad thing. Seemed like a right cushy bloody number from where he was standing.

'Right. We all ready?' he asked. He was whispering. He wasn't quite sure why, other than that speaking at full volume would seem disrespectful, somehow.

The others nodded, but didn't speak. Clearly, they felt the same sense of hushed solemnity as he had. Even the tech guy, who Logan had been able to tell at a glance was not blessed with any social skills whatsoever, simply gave a thumbs up. Logan met Olivia's eye, and she managed a fleeting smile that did little to hide her nerves.

He felt a twinge of sympathy for her. Regardless of what she'd done, she was a scared kid who had an absolute shit-storm ahead of her, no matter what happened next.

'OK. Here goes,' he announced, punching in the digits.

There were quite a lot of them, so this took him some time.

And then, the phone was ringing. The burr of the tone was different. Foreign-sounding.

The tech guys had already analysed the number and confirmed it was an internet-based VOIP number from a Russian provider, so getting the details of the person it was registered to was going to be difficult, short of government intervention.

There was a click from the other end of the line, followed by a long, drawn-out wheeze.

Eventually, a voice emerged from the Bluetooth speakers that had been hooked up to the laptop. It resonated around the office, and echoed a fraction of a second later out in the Incident Room.

'I was beginning to think you weren't going to call.'

Male, definitely. The faintest hint of a Russian or Eastern European accent, but trampled down and smoothed out by a Highland twang.

'This is DCI Jack Logan of—'

'I know who you are.'

'Then you've got the advantage,' Logan said.

There was a wheeze that became a cough. 'I have many advantages, *DCI Jack Logan*. You would do well not to under-estimate them.'

While he spoke, Logan looked across the room to where Olivia sat with Ben. She pulled a face that didn't quite commit to anything, then shrugged. Logan tapped his ear, indicating she should keep listening, then went back to the conversation.

'Maybe you could tell me your name,' he said. 'Much easier to have a conversation if I know who I'm talking to.'

'Don't insult me, DCI Jack Logan. You know my name. You already told the media about me,' the voice replied. 'So, say it for me.'

Logan glanced around at the others. Mitchell sat forward, her elbows on his desk, her fingers kneading her temples like she was trying to stop her head from exploding.

'You're Oleg Ivanov,' Logan said.

'I am,' Oleg replied. 'She told you about me, yes?'

'Actually, Bosco told us.'

'Aha, yes. But she confirmed it.' He wheezed out another breath. 'Is she there? Can she hear me?'

'No,' Logan said.

'You are a bad liar, DCI Jack Logan. I think she is there,' Oleg continued. 'Can you hear me, malyshka?'

Logan put a finger to his lips. Ben laid a hand on the girl's arm.

'She's not here,' Logan insisted.

The shouted reply made the speakers crackle. 'Do not fucking lie to me! Tell her to speak, or I fucking kill your women.'

'I'm here!' Olivia said. 'I'm here, just… don't hurt anyone. Please.'

'Ah, malyshka,' Oleg whispered. 'I knew you were there. I could sense you. Feel you.'

'This is not going to end well, Oleg,' Logan said. 'Your name and your face are out there in front of the whole world. We've got hundreds of officers looking for you. It's just a matter of time before we catch you. Make it easier on yourself, eh? Tell us where the hostages are. Turn yourself in.'

'My *face*,' Oleg spat. Despite his obvious anger, he ejected something like a chuckle. 'My face… all of me… is different now. After what she did to me.'

'What did she do to you?' Logan asked.

'It doesn't matter. All that matters is that I was reborn in the cold, and in the dark. I know nothing now but the pain. And the hatred.'

The wheezing returned, air clicking in and out as if being pushed by a pump.

'What do you want?' Logan asked.

'You know what I want, DCI Jack Logan. I want what I have dreamed of every night since my awakening. What I have longed for, through every long, agonising moment.'

Logan's eyes crept over to Olivia. 'I can't do that, Oleg.'

'Then your women will die. Slowly. On their knees. One at a time. We will carve their eyes from their heads and feed them to them. We will cut their tongues out so they cannot scream. We will defile them in ways that will make you wish you had not found their bodies, so you would not know the extent of their suffering.'

He was becoming more breathless now, either through the effort of speaking or his excitement about the words he was saying.

'And I will film it all. Every moment of their shame, and their agony, and their fear. I will send it to you, and to their families. I will share it online, to be spread, and copied, and disseminated forever, so that generations from now, people will still speak in hushed tones of their deaths, and of the coward who could have stopped it all with a single word.'

'And what word might that be?' Logan asked.

'Yes.'

Logan leaned in a little closer to the phone, then was directed towards the laptop's microphone by a point from the boffin.

'Yes? I don't understand.'

'Because I haven't asked the question yet,' Oleg said. 'Will you be my big, brave girl, malyshka? Will you give your life for theirs?'

Logan held a hand up to silence her before she could say anything. Judging by the stunned look on her face, he needn't have bothered. Speaking appeared to be beyond her capabilities for now.

'Before we even discuss this, I need proof of life,' Logan said.

'You do not get to dictate this conversation, DCI Jack Logan. As we have already established, I have the advantages.'

'Aye, but you've got to understand, Oleg, what you're asking is… it's huge.'

'It is two lives for one. It is a bargain.'

Logan looked across to Mitchell and Ben and saw that they'd both picked up on the same thing he had.

Two lives.

Two.

'But we need to know they're still alive,' Logan insisted. 'Without that, we don't know you've got them.'

'You saw the video of your little piggy friend,' Oleg said.

Logan looked out through a gap in the blinds to where Hamza and Tyler were sitting listening. 'That could've been hours ago. I need to know they're still alive *now*.'

There was some thumping down the line. Movement. For a moment, Logan thought Oleg was hanging up the phone, but then another voice came on, her Irish accent unmistakeable even through her tears.

'Jack!'

He almost choked on her name. 'Shona? Listen to me, you're all right. It's going to be OK. We're going to—'

'There. Proof of life,' Oleg said. In the background, Shona's sobs became muffled, then fell away into silence.

Something stirred in the pit of Logan's gut. Not the primal animal instincts he had battled with for so many years, but something older still. More savage.

He flexed his fingers, and they were claws now. Talons, designed for ripping through flesh. He clenched his jaw, grinding his teeth together while he swallowed back the urges that might blow this whole thing, and condemn Shona and Sinead to death.

He could feel Mitchell watching him. Staring. Praying she was wrong, but waiting to be proven right that this was a mistake, that he was too close, too involved in the case.

'That's one,' he said, his voice a flat, monotone thing. 'I want to hear from both.'

'Don't get greedy, DCI Jack Logan,' Oleg warned.

There was a commotion from out in the Incident Room. Logan and the others turned to look just as Tyler shrugged Hamza off and came barging into the room. Taggart trotted happily behind him, like this was all some game he didn't quite understand, but was fully committed to taking part in.

'Where is she?' Tyler bellowed. 'Let me hear her. Put her on!'

'Tyler!' Logan hissed, rising to his feet. He grabbed for the DC, but a surprising show of dexterity and a not inconsiderable amount of force allowed Tyler to slip past him.

'If you fucking touch a hair on her head, I'll kill you!' he hissed. 'I will find you, and I will fucking kill you!'

'DC Neish!' Mitchell was on her feet now, too, her face alive with rage even as Logan caught Tyler's arm and yanked him back.

The tech boffin tapped a button on the laptop. 'We're muted,' he announced. 'He can't hear us.'

'Get him out of here!' Logan roared, a one-handed push sending Tyler stumbling back into Hamza's arms. 'Take him home. Fucking sit on him if you have to!'

If Mitchell looked furious, then Tyler was positively demonic. 'You heard him, boss! You heard what that sick bastard said! What he's going to do!' The anger was already burning itself out, and the DC's eyes shone with tears. 'I just... I want to know she's OK. I want to know that he hasn't... that she's not...'

'Come on, son,' Ben urged, taking one of Tyler's arms, while Hamza clamped a hand around the other. 'Let's get you out of here. This isn't the best place for you to be right now. Come on we'll get some fresh air, and—'

'You must care about her very much.' Oleg's voice was a giggle from the speakers. 'Is she someone special to you, I wonder? A close friend? A sister, perhaps?' He wheezed. Clicked. Exhaled. 'A wife?'

Looks of concern were exchanged. Nobody made a sound, not even Taggart.

'You can save her, DC Tyler Neish. You can bring her home, safe and sound. You can be her hero. Her knight in shining armour,' Oleg continued. 'Just bring me the girl, and her suffering will end.'

'Get him out of here,' Logan growled, stepping between Tyler and Olivia. 'Take him home. Take him bloody anywhere but here. I want him out of my sight.'

Tyler tore his eyes from the laptop speaker and met Logan's gaze.

'You idiot! Do you have *any* idea what you might've done?' the DCI growled.

'Boss,' Tyler began, but whatever the rest of the sentence was going to be, it ended there.

He didn't resist as Hamza and Ben led him out of the office, and didn't say a word when the door was slammed and the blinds were drawn.

Logan turned back to the computer and gave the tech guy a nod. After a key press and a thumbs up, Logan inserted himself back into the conversation.

'Sorry about that, Oleg. As you can imagine, emotions are running high here.'

'I should think so. It's a stressful time for all of us, DCI Jack Logan,' Oleg replied. His breathing was becoming more laboured now, like the call was taking a lot out of him. 'You have until midnight—just under three hours—to consider my proposal. Olivia for the prisoners. A swap. A girl you hardly know, for the women you all so evidently care for. Two for one deal. Once in a lifetime offer. Don't miss out!'

He coughed. It was a rasping, hacking sort of cough that ripped at the back of the throat. It lasted for twenty seconds or more, and when Oleg next spoke his voice had a definite slur to it.

'Call me with your decision before midnight, or one of them dies,' he said.

And then, before Logan could respond, the call was terminated, and the sound from the speakers became a single, monotonous tone.

'Bollocks,' Logan grunted, then he rounded on the tech guy. 'Any way of tracing that call?'

'It's all on the net, but he'll have been using proxies, VPNs, IP spoofing—'

'I don't need a bloody computing science lesson, son. Yes or no?'

The boffin's head all-but retreated into his chest, like a tortoise tucking itself away from danger. 'No. I mean…' He shot an imploring look at Detective Superintendent Mitchell. 'No. Sorry.'

'Fuck. OK. OK,' Logan said. 'On you go, then. If you're no use to me, get out.'

The tech bod practically bowed as he retreated out of the room. 'I'll, eh, I'll come back for my kit tomorrow,' he said, then he was out the door before anyone could suggest that he stick around to unhook it all now.

'Olivia, could you wait outside for us?' Mitchell said once the tech guy was out of the room.

Olivia blinked. She was visibly exhausted, and for a moment it looked like her eyes might not open again. 'Outside?' she mumbled, shooting a look at the window. 'It's dark.'

'Not all the way outside. Just wait in the main office,' Mitchell explained. She hadn't taken her eyes off Logan yet, and the DCI was bracing himself for what came next. 'We'll be right out.'

'Oh. Right. Um, yeah,' Olivia said, though she waited until Logan had given a nod of confirmation before she got up out of her seat.

Mitchell held back until the girl had left, then clicked the door closed and turned to Logan. 'So—' she began, but Logan silenced her with a look.

'Don't,' he said. 'Please. Just… just don't. Tyler was… he's upset. He messed up, but he was upset. The last thing I need right now is an "I told you so".'

'It's the last thing you're going to get,' Mitchell said.

'Oh. Right,' Logan grunted. 'Well… good.'

'He has two prisoners. Two. Sinead and Dr Maguire.'

'So, where's Alexis Maximuke?' Logan asked, finishing her thought for her.

'Do we have any word on her phone or bank cards?' the Detective Superintendent asked.

Logan hadn't seen anything. Whether he wanted to admit it or not, finding Sinead and Shona had been his top priority, and he hadn't paid as much attention to everything else as he otherwise might have done.

'I'll get it pushed through,' Mitchell told him, heading for the door.

'Aren't you heading home, ma'am? It's late.'

Mitchell stopped to reply. 'No rest for the wicked, eh, Detective Chief Inspector?'

'No, ma'am. Suppose not.'

'We have less than three hours until midnight,' Mitchell said.

'Midnight.' Logan tutted. 'Got a flair for the bloody dramatic, it seems.'

'Yes. Yes, they often do, don't they?' Mitchell said. 'Theatrical timing or not, we need to have made some good progress by then. That's our deadline. If he's true to his word, the hostages are safe until then. After that, we don't know what might happen to them.'

'Don't suppose we can just do the swap?' Logan suggested. He nodded at the door through which Olivia had gone. 'From what I know of her, she can be a right pain in the arse.'

'Probably best keeping that one in the hip pocket for now,' Mitchell said, and she smiled. She actually smiled. Like a real human being.

'Aye. One for the back burner, maybe,' Logan said.

Mitchell nodded. 'Quite. Yes.' She started to leave, then stopped again. 'Oh, and if anyone's thinking of getting them in, Detective Chief Inspector, mine's a double espresso.'

Chapter 39

Tyler's waddle had evolved into a sort of forlorn trudge as he made his way across the foyer of Burnett Road station, with Hamza steering him by the arm. There were fifteen or more Uniforms cutting through the reception area in both directions, and a couple of CID boys standing by windows, talking furtively into phones. It was unusual for the place to be this busy in the middle of the day, much less at this time of night.

Well, maybe on a Friday.

'I'm fine, Ham. I just… I let it get to me,' Tyler protested, as they weaved through the throngs of passing polis. 'Which was a mistake, I know. I shouldn't have done that, but I'm fine now. Honest. I can help.'

'Come on, Tyler. You're exhausted. You're strung out. You need to get some rest,' Hamza said.

'How am I meant to rest?' Tyler asked. 'You think I'm going to be able to go home and sleep now? I'm going to be up all night, pacing the floor, worried sick. At least here, I can be useful.'

'I don't think the boss is going to go for that,' Hamza said. 'If he sees you again tonight, I think he might strangle you.'

'He won't. He just… I'll explain. He'll understand,' Tyler insisted. He stopped to turn back, but Hamza's grip tightened on his arm, and his momentum forced the DC onward. 'Jesus Christ, Ham, just… I need to stay.'

'I'm sorry, mate. I really am,' Hamza said. It was clear that he didn't like this any more than Tyler did, but orders were orders.

Especially when they were right.

Tyler's outburst had given Oleg more information about Sinead, about Tyler, and about their relationship. Knowledge was power in situations like these, and Tyler's interruption had only made Oleg stronger.

Another screw-up like that, and people might get hurt. Or worse.

They were almost at the front door when they heard a shout. In fact, they'd heard the shout—a bellowed 'Oi!'—a couple of times on the way across the foyer, but it was only now that they realised it was aimed at them.

'Bloody hell, are you pair deaf?' asked Dave Davidson, wheeling himself over to them in his chair.

'All right, Dave?' asked Hamza. 'Missed you upstairs. Where you been?'

'Been helping coordinate things, haven't I? Following up on reports from the public, and that,' Dave said. He sniffed, either to signify that he was quite proud of this fact, or to indicate that he really didn't care. 'I tell you what, they're arseholes the public, though. You forget until you have to deal with them, don't you? Then it all comes rushing back. Right bunch of whinging bastards I've been dealing with.'

'Eh, aye. They can be, right enough,' Hamza said. He looked very deliberately at the door beside them, but Dave either failed or chose not to pick up on it.

'I was about to call up to you, actually,' he said. 'Just saw something interesting.'

Tyler's ears practically pricked up. 'About the case? What is it?'

'Tyler,' Hamza said. He put a hand on the DC's arm again, but it was quickly shrugged away.

'What is it?' Tyler asked again.

Dave looked down at a notebook he had open in his lap. 'Constable went to check out a farmhouse earlier. He hasn't reported back. Should've called in ages ago, but the fact that he hadn't got missed in all the excitement. I just spotted it when

263

I took over. I'm due a break, so thought I'd give you a shout about it.'

'What, nobody's heard from him at all?' Hamza asked.

'Who is he, do we know?'

Dave checked his notes. 'Jason Hall. Younger guy. I don't really know him, but I've seen him around.'

Tyler's brow was lined with ridges. 'She's mentioned him before. Said he was a bit of a creep. I was going to say something to him, but she told me not to.'

'We've tried radioing him?' asked Hamza.

'Aye. Hee-haw back from him, though. I was going to get a unit to swing by and check it out.'

'We'll do it,' Tyler said, jumping on it.

Hamza shook his head. 'Eh, no, we won't.'

'Aye, we will,' Tyler insisted. 'Give us the address, Dave, we'll go scope it out.'

'Are you mental? I'm taking you home. I'm not driving you out to some bloody farmhouse.'

'Fine, I'll drive myself.'

'Your car's not here.'

'Jesus! Fine. Dave, you've got a car, haven't you? Can you drive me?'

Dave grinned, rubbed both hands together, then slapped them on his thighs. 'Do you know?' he said. 'I thought you'd never ask.'

–

A seven-year-old Peugeot 208 that had been specially adapted with fitted hand controls shot out of the Burnett Road car park with a screech, a sparking of metal on stone, and a shriek of 'fuck, fuck, fuck!' from the passenger seat.

Tyler sat braced, one hand clutching the handle of the door on his left, the other jammed against the dashboard in front of him. Both things vibrated violently in time with Iron Maiden's

'*Bring Your Daughter... to the Slaughter*' that came blasting out of the vastly overpowered speaker system.

Despite his anchor points, Tyler rolled so far in his seat that his belt tightened across his chest as the car raced up to the first roundabout, and hung a tyre-churning left onto Longman Road.

'Christ!' he ejected. 'Is this legal?'

'What bit?'

'Any of it! All of it!' Tyler cried, then he screwed his eyes shut as Dave powered the car directly up the arse of a Volvo estate, and felt his stomach lurch when the Peugeot switched lanes at the last possible second.

'Legal, yes,' Dave said. 'Safe? Well, that depends.'

'On what?'

'On whether the airbags go off. Because if they do, your arm's fucked.'

Tyler stared at his hand splayed on the dashboard, blinked several times as his brain tried to grasp the point the PC was making, then whipped the hand away like the dash had suddenly become blisteringly hot.

'Why would the airbags go off?' Tyler asked, gripping the seat now, his fingers digging deep into the fabric.

Dave shrugged, then pulled on one of the hand levers fixed to the side of his steering wheel. The car sped up so suddenly that Tyler's shoulders were driven back into the chair.

'Dunno. Faulty switch. Dodgy electrics,' Dave said. 'Head-on collision. Could be anything, really.'

He blasted the horn and flashed his lights, forcing a slower moving vehicle ahead to pull aside. Given the speed he was doing, 'slower moving' was a descriptor that applied to pretty much every other car on the road.

Tyler could only ignore the dirty looks from the other drivers as the Peugeot went powering past, its engine screaming in distress and its chassis rattling away underfoot, while Iron Maiden enthusiastically proclaimed the merits of bringing your offspring to scenes of evisceration and murder.

Another burst of acceleration let them beat the light change at the Longman roundabout. Tyler shrieked out another assortment of swear words as Dave swung into the left-hand lane, mid-turn, and slid past an old fella on a motorbike.

He was thrown left, then right, as the car powered out of the junction and onto the A9, and then was reintroduced to the springs of his seat when Dave put the pedal to the floor again—or whatever the hand-control equivalent was.

'How long?' he asked, swallowing back something that burned as it travelled in both directions through his throat.

Dave turned his head to look at him. 'How long's what?'

'Watch the road!' Tyler wheezed, stabbing a finger ahead. 'Until we get there. How long until we get there?'

'Oh. Seven or eight minutes. Not long. I can slow down, though, if you like? If I'm going too fast for you, I mean.'

Tyler didn't even consider his answer. Not for a second.

'No,' he said. 'Just get us there, quick as you can.'

Dave's whole face seemed to illuminate with his smile. If the car hadn't been an automatic, Tyler was sure the PC would've crunched down into second gear. 'Right, then,' he said with a wink. 'You asked for it.'

—

Ben returned to the Incident Room with two black coffees and a hot chocolate he'd grabbed from the vending machine downstairs. Logan advised polishing them off before Mitchell came back, and both men blew on their scalding coffees while Olivia sipped furtively at the hot chocolate.

She hadn't said a word since the call. She'd barely even looked at either of the detectives, in fact, aside from a momentary glance in Ben's direction when he'd passed her the hot drink.

Instead, she mostly focused her attention on Taggart. The dog was sitting bolt upright in front of her, his eyes fixed unblinkingly on the cup in her hand like it might contain treats.

On the other side of the room, Ben sat down opposite Logan and lowered his voice to a murmur. 'You called Social Services yet?'

Logan shook his head. 'Not yet.'

'Jesus, Jack. She can't kip here all night.'

Logan swilled his coffee around in his mouth before swallowing it down. It really was awful stuff.

'I know. Can you get someone to give them a ring?'

'Of course, aye,' Ben said.

He sipped at his coffee and grimaced at the taste of it. The stuff from the vending machine didn't taste like real coffee at all. It was like a computer's idea of coffee, based on written accounts from people who had tasted the real stuff once, years previously, and who, on balance, hadn't been all that keen.

'How you doing, Jack?' he asked.

'Better than I could be. Worse than I'd hoped,' Logan replied. He jammed a finger and thumb into his eyes and rubbed them, while fighting back a yawn. 'Bloody exhausted, too. If I could wake up, I reckon I could figure it out.'

'Which bit?'

'I don't know. All of it. Just… it would make more sense. I feel like there's a connection we're missing, or an angle we haven't explored. Something, anyway. Something that's just sitting there, waiting for us to find it.'

'Aye, well, here's hoping, eh?' Ben said. He took out his phone, tapped the button to wake it, then returned it to his pocket again.

'Expecting a call?'

DI Forde raised his bushy eyebrows. 'Hmm? Oh. No, not really,' he said. 'Just… I was meant to phone someone earlier. I promised I'd give them a ring.'

Logan studied the older man over the plastic rim of his cup. 'Who?'

'No one. Just a friend who's a bit lonely at the moment.'

'What friend? Since when did you have a friend?' Logan asked, then he groaned. 'It's not one of them holy moly bastards, is it? I'm telling you, Ben, that church is a bloody cult.'

'That? No. God, no, I don't go there anymore,' Ben said. 'That was… I don't know. That was a coping strategy. After… everything. It helped at the time. But I'm grand now. Or I'm getting there, anyway.'

'Glad to hear it,' Logan said. He took another sip of his terrible coffee. 'So, who's this friend, then?'

Ben smiled and patted the DCI on the arm. 'Never you bloody mind,' he said, then he knocked back what was left of his drink in one go, convulsed violently, and got to his feet. 'I'll go get Uniform to contact Social Services. See if we can get the lassie sorted out somewhere for the night.'

'Cheers, Ben,' Logan said.

Ben had barely turned to leave when a blast of what Ben might very generously describe as 'music' but more accurately as 'noise with a beat to it', rang out. It took a moment for the detectives to pinpoint where it was coming from.

Olivia.

She shifted her weight onto one hip, reached behind her, and pulled her mobile from her back pocket. As she did, the volume of the tuneless din increased.

She stared down at the screen for a moment, then her legs fired like pistons, springing her upright.

'What is it?' Logan asked. 'Who's calling?'

'It's… it's her,' Olivia whispered. She turned the phone so the detectives could see the screen. 'It's my mum.'

Chapter 40

There was a polis car parked out the front of the farmhouse, its edges picked out by the pale moonlight. That was the first thing Tyler noticed, once Dave had skidded to a stop at the far end of the long driveway, in a spray of gravel and stone chips.

The second thing he noticed was the lack of lights in the building. Every window was in darkness, and not a puff of smoke rose from the brick chimney that slouched atop the ageing tiled roof. This far out of town, there were no street lights, either, and had it not been for the moon, and the overspill from the headlights of Dave's car, the farmhouse would be practically invisible in the darkness.

The third and final thing Tyler noted was the house's front door, which stood ajar. It would probably have been impossible to tell this during the daytime, but the moonlight played across the glass as the door inched open on the whims of the breeze, then bounced back against the frame a moment later.

Even from this distance, nothing about the scene was good. Everything about it filled Tyler with a sense of dread, and a rising sensation of nausea.

Although, that last one might've been his balls talking. That, or Dave's driving.

Tyler unclipped his belt. 'Call it in,' he instructed, then he opened the car door and stepped directly into the path of another vehicle that was forced to pull an emergency stop to avoid smashing him headfirst through the windscreen.

'Careful! You nearly got yourself killed!' Hamza said, leaning out of the driver's window. 'You didn't even look!'

'I didn't know you were coming,' Tyler pointed out.

'Weren't the full beam headlights racing towards you a bit of a giveaway?'

Tyler scowled, then pointed to the polis car. 'Check that out.'

Hamza shut off the engine and joined Tyler on the driveway. 'That the fella who didn't report to base?'

'Presumably, aye,' Tyler said. 'Dave's calling it in.'

'The front door's open,' Hamza pointed out, after a bit of squinting. They were about eighty feet from the house, half-hidden by some overgrown trees.

'I know. No lights on, either. Doesn't feel right to me. Does it feel right to you?'

'None of this feels right to me,' Hamza said.

'Can we get a shifty on?' Dave called from the car. 'My break's only half an hour.'

'Right, come on,' Tyler said. He shuffled a few steps towards the house, then Hamza caught him and pulled him back.

'What are you doing?' the DS asked.

'Going to look.'

'No, you're not. Not until we've got backup. Anyone could be in there.'

'Exactly. Sinead might be there. Or we might have an officer down. We need to go and look.'

Hamza groaned and ran a hand through his hair. He had a pained expression on his face and was clearly wrestling with himself.

'Right. Fine. But you wait here. I'll go.'

'What? No way!' Tyler protested. 'I'm going in.'

'No. You're not. You're still hurpling,' Hamza said. He indicated the house at the far end of the long driveway. 'It'll take you twenty minutes just to get there. Wait here. Make sure backup's on the way. I'll go take a look.'

'Ham, you can't be—'

'Stay here, Tyler. Cover the door. I'm telling you as your sergeant, and I'm asking you as your friend. If you rush in there in your condition and there's someone in there, you're liable to get yourself hurt. Or get someone else hurt. Me. *Sinead*. It's too risky.'

'Aye, but—'

'Tyler. Just… trust me, mate, all right?' Hamza said, laying a hand on the DC's shoulder. 'I've got this. If she's in there, I won't let anything happen to her.'

Tyler's gaze went to the house. He chewed his bottom lip for a few moments, before finally relenting. 'Right. Aye. But shout, all right? If you need me, and I'll come… well, running's probably a stretch, but…' He smiled. Sort of. 'Be careful, all right?'

Hamza replied by patting his shoulder, then he went to the boot of his car and fetched the polis baton he kept there. He gave it a couple of experimental swishes to get a feel for it again, then shut the boot and set off towards the house, sticking close to the tree line.

Their arrival hadn't exactly been stealthy. If anyone was watching from inside, they'd already know he was coming. It felt safer lurking in the shadows, though. If there was a gunman guarding the place, then he was going to make the bastard work to get the shot.

He reached the front door without being riddled with bullets, which was always a big plus. There were grubby net curtains on the windows, and the darkness of the rooms beyond the glass made it impossible to see what lurked inside.

A few feet away, the door thunked against the frame, then bounced back again as a breeze tickled across his skin.

The polis car had been empty. He'd stolen a peek inside on his way past. There had been nothing to indicate where the officer was, or what had happened to him, so Hamza had to assume that he was in the house somewhere.

His hand adjusted its grip on the baton, fingers tightening. He clutched it low by his right side, ready to swing at a knee, or a wrist, or a head, depending on what the situation called for.

He could feel it already—the shudder of the impact reverberating through his hand and up his arm as baton met bone. The sickening crunch, the animal squeal. He hated using the bloody thing.

Of course, he hated most of the alternatives even more.

Besides, he had a history with creepy old farmhouses in the arse-end of nowhere. That one had almost ended his career. Not because of the injuries he'd sustained, but because Amira had forbidden him from ever returning to work.

She'd come around over the weeks that followed, but if it happened a second time, there'd be no way she'd back down.

Mind you, if it happened a second time, there was no saying either of them would get a say in his fate.

He took a breath at the door, his heart driving his blood through his veins so quickly his head thrummed with pain. The last time he had opened a door into a stranger's house, he'd found the young owner dead. He'd been too late to help her. Too late to do anything but grieve for a life thrown away.

Hamza couldn't bear another day of grieving. He couldn't tolerate another moment of heartbreak, or loss. Especially not here. Not now.

Not Sinead.

He looked back along the driveway. The car headlights were out, but he could just make out a suggestion of Tyler's outline in the moonlight.

Oh, God. Let her be OK.

He didn't announce himself before nudging open the door. The hallway he stepped into was dark—too dark to do anything but feel his way around. Hamza listened, but heard nothing. The house wasn't just quiet, it was empty of sound. Not a whisper. Not a creak.

Keeping his baton in his right hand, he took out his torch and pushed down the rubber switch. A distorted oval of light picked out a set of eyes in the darkness. Hamza almost swung at it, before he noticed the antlers, the fur, and the wooden wall plate the head was mounted on.

He turned with the torch, sweeping it across the faded wall-paper and mouldy coving. The light bounced back from dozens of eyes of all shapes and sizes—a menagerie of death, watching his every move.

It was, he reckoned, up there with the most disturbing things he'd ever seen. And, considering the things he had seen, this was saying a lot. Throw in a couple of porcelain dolls in Victorian dresses and a grinning ventriloquist's dummy, and it would fuel his nightmares for years to come.

Four doors ran off from the hallway of horror. They all stood at least partly open, but nothing appeared to be moving in any of them, so he went for the door on his left first for no reason beyond the fact that 'clockwise' was as good a strategy as any.

The room he found himself in took the phrase 'sparsely furnished' to an entirely new level. It contained two folding mesh garden chairs, an upturned cardboard box that was serving as a table, and a large glass ashtray overflowing with dog ends.

It had exposed floorboards, but not the nice, carefully sanded and polished kind. Bent and rusted nails stuck up at random intervals—either booby traps for the unwary, or sloppy work-manship by the careless. Either way, he wouldn't like to wander around in there in bare feet.

There was an old stone fireplace against one wall, and a grubby mirror mounted above it. A crack ran down the centre, separating his reflection into two versions of himself, each at a minutely different angle.

Beyond that, the room held nothing of note, so he turned around, moved onto the next door, and stepped inside.

That was where he found the body.

And that was when a floorboard went creak.

Chapter 41

Logan, Ben, Olivia, and—to a lesser extent—Taggart, who had jumped up onto Hamza's chair, all stared at the phone sitting on the desk. Logan looked to Ben for confirmation that he'd just heard what he thought he'd heard, but Ben's only response was a shrug of the shoulders and a shake of his head.

'Sorry,' Logan began, leaning a little closer to the mobile. 'Did you say you were at a *spa day*?'

'Yes.' The reply from Alexis Maximuke echoed tinnily from the phone's speaker. 'That's right. Well needed, too. I went yesterday and stayed over.'

'A fucking *spa day*?!' Logan said again, the pitch of his voice rising a full octave and a half. 'Your daughter was missing, and you were at a *spa day*?'

'What do you mean she was missing? How's she missing? Olivia, you're not missing, are you?'

Olivia looked from one detective to the other, then back to the phone. 'I mean, no. Not now.'

'Well, then!' Alexis said.

'She was gone all night!'

'Well, I didn't know that, did I? I'm not her keeper.'

'No, but you are her bloody mother!' Ben pointed out.

'I left a note! It was on the fridge.'

'Do you have *any* idea of the trouble Olivia's in? That *you're* in?' Logan barked. 'We've got officers hunting for you all over the bloody country. We put out a TV appeal!'

'Oh.' Alexis took a moment to process this. 'That'll be what all the messages are about. I had my phone switched off.'

Logan sat back, threw his arms up above his head, and turned to Ben. 'You hear that? She had her phone switched off! That's all right, then!'

'What do you mean *trouble*? What trouble am I in?' Alexis asked.

None of them sitting at the desk, with the possible exception of the dog, failed to note the use of 'am I in' rather than 'is Olivia in'. None of them mentioned it. None of them had to.

A spa day.

A bloody *spa day*!

Everything that had happened—all the worry, and stress—and Alexis Maximuke had been melting her tension away with a pedicure and a massage.

Not for the first time in his career, Logan wished he could reach down the telephone and strangle the person on the other end with his bare hands.

Ben, seeing the telltale little flecks of foam at the corners of Logan's mouth, intervened before the shouting could begin.

'We believe Oleg Ivanov is after you and Olivia,' he explained.

There was a momentary pause, then something like the first few notes of a laugh. 'Oleg? What do you mean? He hasn't been around in months. I don't know where he is.'

'Nor do we,' Ben admitted. He glanced across at Olivia. She noticed this, met his eye for a moment, then quickly looked away again. 'But we know where he's been for at least some of that time.'

'Where?'

'Probably best if we explain here at the station, Mrs Maximuke,' Ben said.

Logan leaned sharply forward. 'Wait. Where are you?'

'I'm just walking home. Why?'

'You're walking?'

Olivia piped up. 'She doesn't drive.'

275

'I don't drive,' Alexis confirmed. 'Bosco always got someone to do the driving. I keep meaning to start lessons, but—'

'How far away are you?' Logan asked, cutting her off.

'Just turned onto the street. Be home in, I don't know, less than a minute, probably.'

'Stop right where you are,' the DCI told her.

'What? But it's dark. I can't just stop outside someone's house. They'll think I'm casing the place.'

'Mum, just do what he says,' Olivia instructed. 'Please.'

Down the line, there was the faint scuff of a heeled shoe on hard pavement. 'Right, fine,' Alexis sighed. 'I've stopped. What now?'

'Can you see your house from there?' Logan asked.

'Yes. Sort of. It's at an angle, but I can see the door.'

'Is anyone there?'

'What, at my house? Why would there be—?'

'Mum!' Olivia said.

'No. There's nobody at the house,' Alexis said. 'It's cold out here, can I go in?'

'What about out front?' Logan said. 'Cars. Vans. Anything look out of place?'

'Not that I can see,' she replied. Then, 'Wait. There's someone in a car, I think. They just lit a fag.'

'What are they doing?' Logan asked.

'Well, smoking, presumably.'

'Are they watching your house?'

'How should I know?' Alexis asked.

Logan clenched his fists, but successfully resisted the urge to smash them down on the desk. 'Is it *possible* that they're watching your house?'

There was silence. Around the table, everyone but Taggart held their breath.

'Mum?' Olivia ventured, then she exhaled when the reply came.

'Sorry, I was just thinking. Yeah, maybe. They could be watching it, I suppose.'

'Can you see a number plate?'

'Of what?' Alexis asked.

'Of the fu—'

'You mean of the car?'

Logan sighed. 'Yes! The car. What else would I mean?'

'No, can't see a number plate. It's blocked by the car behind it.'

'Can you describe it?' Logan asked, then he clarified, to be on the safe side. 'The car with the person in it, I mean, no' the one behind it.'

'I don't know. Blue. Like… small and blue. But, like, quite a *blue* blue, not dark blue.'

Logan realised this was probably as good as he was going to get. He rose to his feet. 'Right, I want you to turn around, find a cafe, or bar, or some other public place, and go there. My colleague, DI Forde, is going to meet you. He'll have Olivia's phone, so you can keep talking to him.'

Ben stood, too. 'Be quicker to get Uniform over there.'

Logan shook his head and dropped his voice to a whisper. 'No. If the bastard's got someone inside, I don't want him getting wind of this. You go.'

Ben took the phone the DCI offered him. 'What are you going to do?'

Logan pulled on his coat. Taggart jumped down from Hamza's chair and ran in circles at his feet. 'I'm going to go and have words with whoever it is that's sitting outside Alexis Maximuke's house.'

–

This was not how things were done. You didn't go alone to face an unknown threat. You waited. You gathered data. You rushed in only when necessary, and ideally with a squad of

277

baton-waving bastards behind you, and the Armed Response Unit on standby.

What you did not do was park your car out of sight on a darkened street, wrap your fingers around your keys so the three largest and most lethal protruded from between them, and march into danger alone.

That was not what you did. Not if you wanted to keep your job. Not if you wanted to keep your life.

Logan was all-too-aware of these things, and yet tonight, he was happy to forget all of it.

There were thirty or more cars parked all along the street, lining the side nearest to the Maximukes' house. The streetlights burning overhead did little to illuminate the insides of any of the vehicles, though. If anything, they cast them deeper into shadow, making it almost impossible to see if anyone lurked inside until he was up close.

Not that he could stop to look, of course. Doing that would draw attention to himself, and he needed to maintain the element of surprise. Getting his hands on whoever was watching the house might be the key to everything. It might bring Shona and Sinead home.

He tried not to think about that, and to instead focus on the here and the now. One street. Thirty-odd cars. Most of them were facing away from him, but there was still every chance that he'd already been spotted.

Still, nobody had gone speeding off yet, so if they had seen him, then they hadn't recognised him. That, or they were waiting until he drew closer, then were going to jump him.

He hoped, more than anything, that it was the latter. Some tough guy jumping out of a car and taking a swing at him would genuinely be the best thing that had happened to him all day. He almost felt giddy at the thought of it.

Somewhere, not too far away, sirens rang out in the darkness. He'd passed half a dozen polis vehicles on the short drive over, following up leads, or just making their presence felt. The whole force was out hunting for Sinead and Shona. Officers from other areas had been drafted in to assist.

So, why did he feel like finding them rested on his shoulders alone? Was it some control freak tendency, or something more?

Could it be because he'd sent Sinead to this street, to that house? That he'd introduced Olivia Maximuke into Shona's life, all those months ago?

Could it be because whatever was happening to them now was all his fault?

Aye. That would go some way towards explaining it, right enough.

He'd passed eight or nine cars now. All empty. He was still a good way away from Alexis and Olivia's house, though, and there were plenty of vehicles still to go. If some bugger was lurking there, he'd find them.

Of course, maybe they weren't lurking there, at all. Maybe they'd already moved on. Maybe they'd spotted Alexis's about-turn and gone after her.

But, no. If she'd stopped talking to Ben, the DI would have been straight on the phone. Logan took his mobile out and checked his screen to make sure he hadn't missed any calls, then returned it to his pocket.

That was when he saw the movement in a car eight vehicles ahead. Volkswagen Golf. Electric blue. Big spoiler on the back.

Classy.

Someone was in the driver's seat. They turned, as if talking to another person sitting in the passenger seat beside them, then sat back with their head against the headrest, like they were going to sleep.

Logan fought the urge to pick up the pace. He sauntered along the street and fixed his gaze on the houses on his right, like he hadn't even noticed the cars, much less anyone sitting in them.

He clocked the vehicles from the corner of his eyes, counting them down as he passed.

White Nissan.

Red Ford.

Silver Vauxhall.

He tightened his grip on his keys as he passed the last few vehicles. A sideways glance confirmed he was closing on his target. The driver hadn't moved to pull away yet. If they were getting ready to jump him, they were in for a very nasty surprise.

As he drew closer, he realised he hadn't actually planned this far, and wasn't quite sure what he was going to do next.

The proximity of the car behind the target vehicle made it impossible to see the number plate. If he knocked on the window and asked for a chat, the driver was liable to either immediately speed off, or shoot him through the door, depending on what level of criminality the DCI was dealing with.

Element of surprise it was, then.

He swerved at the last moment, grabbed the handle of the driver's door, and pulled it open.

'Right, you bastards!' he boomed, drawing the hand that clutched the keys from his pocket.

Inside the car, someone gasped, and someone screamed. A female hand, which had been tucked down the front of a pair of male boxer shorts, withdrew so suddenly and so sharply that it drew a yelp of pain from the young man in the driver's seat.

'Argh! Shit, shit, sorry, sorry, we weren't doing anything!' the young man cried, frantically trying to pull up the jeans that had been slid down to his thighs.

Over on the other side of the car, his female companion was pressed right up against the passenger door, as if she was trying to phase through it like a ghost.

'Is he your dad?' the lad yelped, his head snapping back and forth between his lady friend and the furious giant who looked like he might rip his car door off at any moment. 'Are you... are you her dad?'

Logan felt a moment of nausea as his heart dropped into his stomach.

This was nothing. Two stupid teenagers having a late-night fumble away from their parents. No one who could tell him anything. No one who could help him bring Shona and Sinead back home.

Rage surged through him. He'd wasted time here. Time he couldn't afford to lose. And for what? A couple of horny teenagers.

Idiots! Stupid bloody *idiots*!

The lad had managed to get his jeans back on, and was now struggling with the button. Logan caught him by the front of his hoodie and tore him out of the car. The girl cried out a half-hearted 'leave him alone!' as her beau hit the pavement and rolled to a stop against Alexis Maximuke's garden fence.

He tucked his chin in against his chest, wrapped his arms over his head, and curled up into a ball. Clearly, he'd been on the receiving end of a kicking before, and had learned the best way to brace for it.

The sight of him cowering there brought Logan back to his senses. The rush of anger that had driven him to pull the lad from the car subsided enough for him to take a step back. He dropped his keys back into his pocket and produced his polis ID. The lad's eyes almost popped out of his head at the sight of it.

'How long have you two been here?' Logan demanded.

'Not long. N-not long!'

'I need more than that,' Logan told him. 'Minutes, hours? How long?'

The lad's mouth flapped up and down, but no sound came out. He looked imploringly into the car, and the young woman in there offered up the answer.

'About forty-five minutes,' she said, her voice trembling almost as much as her boyfriend. 'But we weren't doing anything for most of that. We were just... we were talking.'

Forty-five minutes. That fit.

'You smoke?' Logan asked the lad on the ground.

'Wh–what?'

Logan leaned down and spoke more slowly. 'Do. You. Smoke?'

'Eh… aye, aye,' the lad said, nodding like his head was on a spring. 'But… but I'm fine for now.'

'I wasn't bloody offering,' Logan said. He straightened, squeezed the bridge of his nose, and sighed.

That confirmed it, then. This randy little scrote must be who Alexis Maximuke had seen.

'Was there anyone else here?' Logan asked. 'Anyone in other cars?'

'What…' the lad looked over to his girlfriend. '…shagging?'

'No. Not… just sitting in their car. Did you see anyone else here, watching this house?'

The man on the ground shook his head. 'No. No, I didn't notice.'

Logan turned to the young woman. 'What about you? You see anyone?'

'I, eh, I wasn't really looking.'

'Aye. Suppose you had your hands full at the time,' Logan grunted. He gave a dismissive wave. 'Right, piss off, the pair of you, before I have you put on the sex offenders register.'

'We're not paedos, or anything! We're both eighteen!' the lad protested.

He pulled himself to his feet using Alexis Maximuke's fence. He was short, and barely came up to the middle of Logan's chest. If he suffered from the exaggerated cockiness of Small Man Syndrome, though, he was hiding it well.

'I don't care if you're eighteen or eighty, she was wanking you off on a public highway, son,' Logan said. 'So I suggest you shut your mouth and get lost, and spare yourself a future of missed job opportunities and angry mobs.'

For a moment, it looked like the lad might have something more to say, but then he launched himself across the pavement and practically flew, head first, into the car. Logan jammed the door with his hip, preventing it from being closed.

'Wait,' he instructed, then he leaned down and both teenagers stared back in shock as he took a photo of them on his phone. 'Right. Got you. And I'll get the reg, too, so I can always find you, if I need to.'

He looked at them both in turn, letting that sink in, then stepped back and slammed the door so hard the whole car rocked on its axle.

The engine spluttered to life. The car lurched, stalled, and died.

Logan heard a muffled scolding from the lassie, and then the Golf gave a roar, crept out onto the road, then pulled away at a speed Logan suspected would turn out to be marginally below the legal limit.

Then, and only then, did he let out the long, drawn-out, and bellowed 'fuck!' he'd been holding in for the past couple of minutes.

He took out his phone. A message from Ben Forde was there in his notifications.

'Got her.'

Logan pulled an about-turn and began the trudge back to his car.

And the clock ticked on down towards midnight.

Chapter 42

Hamza spun on the spot, braced to find some big scary bugger with an axe standing behind him. To his immense relief, he didn't, and he lowered his baton back to his side.

The house had shifted. That was all. Old houses like this did that all the time.

He turned back to the dead officer lying on the floor beside the empty bed. Checking for a pulse was largely unnecessary, but he did it, anyway.

Another victim. Another life lost.

Too late, once again.

Now that he'd seen his face, Hamza remembered PC Jason Hall. Bit of an arsehole, from what he could gather, although obviously that didn't make this any less tragic.

Well, maybe a *tiny* bit less tragic, but not really. Not much.

He spent a moment taking in the room—the soiled and crumpled sheet on the bed, the empty intravenous drip bag hanging from the stand, its transparent tube flapping loosely above a small sticky puddle on the bare wooden floor.

Then he backed out of the room in as few steps as possible, preserving the scene for Geoff Palmer and his crew.

Out in the hallway, he took out his phone and called Tyler.

'What's happening? Is she there?' the DC asked before Hamza could get out a word.

'Not so far. Still looking. But that PC is dead.'

'Dead?!' Tyler spluttered. 'Fuck.'

Hamza heard Dave in the background. 'Aw, shite. Aw, Tyler, I'm so sorry, man.'

Tyler's voice became quieter as he removed the phone from his ear. 'No, not Sinead. The PC.'

'Oh. Jason?'

'Aye.'

'Right,' Hamza heard Dave say. 'That's a relief. I mean… no offence to the guy.'

'Call it in,' Hamza instructed.

'Backup's already on the way,' said Tyler.

'Still, best to let them know what we're dealing with. We'll need…' He almost said 'Shona', before he remembered. '…a pathologist to come do their bit.'

From one of the other rooms there came a creak. Not the house this time. Something more. Hamza lost an inch or two in height as he dropped into something like a crouch and whispered a breathless, 'Shit.'

'What's the matter?' Tyler asked.

'There's someone else here.'

'Sinead?'

'I don't know,' Hamza whispered. 'Call in the body. I'll go check.'

'Whoa, whoa,' Tyler said. 'Hold on. I'm coming in.'

'No, you're not.'

The sound down the line changed as Tyler opened his door and struggled out of the car. 'Aye, I am. You shouldn't be in there yourself.'

'We discussed this,' Hamza reminded him.

'Aye, that was before you found a dead bloke.'

'Stay where you are, Tyler. That's an order,' Hamza told him.

He angled the torch into the room where he thought the sound had come from. It was an old farmhouse kitchen, with dated cabinets that barely clung to the walls and an old Aga range that was thick with grease and soot. A tap dripped, the sound of it hitting the metal sink becoming deafening in the silence.

'At least wait for backup to arrive,' Tyler protested.

'It might be Sinead,' Hamza whispered.

'Aye. I know,' Tyler replied, and his voice spoke of his torment. 'But it might not be.'

Hamza didn't respond to that. Tyler was right, of course. If there was someone in the kitchen—and he hadn't heard anything else to confirm that, either way—then it could be the killer. It could be multiple killers, in fact—a whole gaggle of the bastards waiting behind the door to jump him.

But it could be Sinead. She could be hurt. He could be her only chance.

And nobody else was dying today, least of all her.

The lack of response told Tyler all he needed to know about the DS's next move.

'Right, keep me on the phone, at least,' he said. 'Dave's calling in the body. Put the phone in your pocket so I can listen.'

'Aye. OK.'

Hamza slipped the phone into the front zip pocket of his jacket. Steeling himself, he took a couple of steps closer to the kitchen door, allowing himself a better angle of the room.

There was a small dining table down at one end. Condiments and half-empty sauce bottles were arranged on the top like ancient standing stones. Hamza might have assumed the scene had been this way for decades, had it not been for the ridged cardboard Costa cups interspersed between them.

He stepped into the room, the torch sweeping into the corners, but finding nothing there but dirt, and dust, and pock-marked, half-eaten lino.

Something went click on his right. He jumped, spinning with the torch, and a sickening realisation hit him as he brought up his other arm.

The baton. He'd left the baton next to the body when he'd checked for a pulse. He was unarmed.

The torchlight settled on an ancient-looking fridge. It clicked again, then shuddered, then settled into a low, vaguely ominous sort of hum.

Hamza breathed out. So there was power, after all.

He backtracked to the kitchen door and threw the switch. A dusty fluorescent tube on the ceiling dimly illuminated at both ends, then blinked and flickered erratically.

Hamza gave it a moment to settle down. When it didn't, he reached for the switch to turn it off again, just as a pantry door was thrown open behind him.

He heard the footsteps. Turned. Saw the knife, the light strobing off its sizeable blade. He made a noise he wasn't proud of, and threw himself in the opposite direction to his attacker, putting some space between them.

There was a clatter in the darkness as he collided with a chair. Pain ignited as his hip was introduced to the solid oak tabletop. He sprawled onto his back, bringing a leg up to his chest so he could fire a foot at whoever was trying to stab him, but they were already too close, moving too quickly.

The lights blinked on again just as the knife came down. He threw himself sideways and heard the thunk of the blade burying in the wood.

'Stop, stop, stop!' he yelped, scrabbling to his feet. He lunged for his assailant, wrapped his arms around her, and pinned hers to her side. 'Sinead. It's me! It's just me!'

She didn't say his name. She didn't say anything, in fact. She just closed her eyes and buried her head against his shoulder, as her legs gave way beneath her.

'Tyler,' Hamza said, though with Sinead pressed against the pocket with the phone in, he had no idea if the DC could hear him. 'I've got her, mate. She's all right. I've got her.'

Chapter 43

Ben was on his feet when Logan returned to the station, alone but for Taggart bounding excitedly around in circles as he chased his tail.

'Jack,' Ben said, practically flying across the Incident Room to meet him. 'We've got her.'

'What? What do you mean?' Logan demanded, not daring to hope. Not yet. He knew, from experience, where hope got you.

'Sinead,' Ben said, and his big, beaming smile faded a little. 'Just… *just* Sinead.'

If Logan was disappointed, he concealed it. 'Jesus! What? How? When? Where was she?'

'Old farmhouse out by Newton of Leys. Hamza and Tyler have her, they're headed to the hospital.'

'Hospital? Why? Is she—?'

'She's not hurt, they don't think. But it looks like she's been drugged. Sedated, or something,' Ben said. 'There was an officer there. Uniform. Dead. We don't know yet what happened. We've blocked the road and shut the place down while we wait for Scene of Crime and…'

'Pathology,' Logan finished for him. 'It's fine, Ben, you can say it.'

He flopped down into his chair, buried his face in his hands for a moment, then ran them back through his hair and breathed out the tension that had been constricting his chest for the past two days.

Or half of it, anyway.

'Thank God,' he whispered, and he didn't even complain when Taggart leapt up into his lap and licked him on the chin. Instead, he put a hand on the dog's back and smoothed down its wayward fur. 'You told Mitchell yet?'

'No, not yet. Tyler just called. Poor bugger's in floods of tears. Nearly had me going at one point.'

'Do I want to know why he was out there, and not following orders?'

Ben shook his head. 'Probably not, no.'

'Who found her?' Logan asked.

'Hamza.'

Logan nodded. That was just what he'd been hoping to hear. 'Good on him,' the DCI said. 'He needed a win.'

'It's about the only win we've got,' Ben told him. 'Hospital called. Conrad Howden passed away within the last hour. Brain injuries were too severe.'

Logan looked up at the ceiling, possibly taking back the 'thank God' from earlier.

'Shite.' He closed his eyes for a moment, building up to asking the question he really didn't want to ask. 'What time are we on?'

Ben also hesitated, bracing himself to deliver the answer he didn't want to give. 'Twenty to eleven.'

Eighty minutes. That was all they had. All *Shona* had. Eighty minutes, then all bets were off.

'Is Alexis Maximuke in an interview room?'

'She is. Her and Olivia,' Ben confirmed. 'But, cards on the table? I don't think she's going to be able to tell us much. She's refusing to believe Conrad wasn't an actual priest, despite the fact that she never saw him in church, he lived in a council house, and he filmed himself shagging a *lot* of different women, of which she was just one. She says we're lying.'

'I don't give a shite what she says. Or about her relationship with Conrad Howden. I want to know everything she can tell us about Oleg. Get everything you can that can help us find him.'

Ben frowned. 'You're not coming in with me?'

Logan shook his head. It felt heavy, like his skull was full of lead.

'No. I'd better go check out this farmhouse.'

'Jesus, Jack, when did you last sleep?' Ben asked.

In all honesty, Logan had no idea. Longer ago than he cared to dwell on, though.

'I'm fine,' he said. He stood up, forcing Taggart to perform a clumsy backflip that culminated in a messy landing and a yelp of surprise. 'What's Hamza doing, once he's got Sinead to hospital?'

'Don't know,' Ben admitted. 'Want me to get him back in?'

'No. Tell him to wait with her and get a statement as soon as she's able. Tyler's going to be about as much use as a chocolate teapot.'

'Same goes for you, if you don't get some rest,' Ben replied, but Logan waved his concern away. 'Just… give Mitchell a knock on the way to the interview room, will you? Let her know what's happening.'

'You sure you're all right, Jack?' Ben asked.

'I will be, if you do as you're bloody told for once,' Logan retorted, but there was no venom to it. He managed something that could, under very specific lighting conditions, be classified as a smile. 'I mean it, I'll be fine. I just need a minute.'

Ben considered his response carefully. Logan was a stubborn bugger, and pushing him too hard in any direction would only make him shove back. And he could shove a lot harder than Ben could.

'Right. Well, you know where I am.'

Logan nodded, then deliberately turned his back on the DI and regarded the Big Board.

Down on the floor, Taggart watched Ben leaving, started to follow, then decided against it and returned to the other man's side. He sat upright, tongue lolling, ears pricked up, and fixed his gaze on the two side-by-side boards, just as Logan was doing.

When the door swung closed, Logan let out a long, drawn-out sigh. He was delighted that Sinead was safe. The sense of relief when he'd heard the news would have made other men burst into tears, jump for joy, or surrender to some other grand display of emotion.

That wasn't him, though. The feeling was the same, yes, but there was no need to make a bloody song and dance about it.

Especially not when Shona was still unaccounted for.

He went over what was on the board, mentally updating it with the new information they had.

The farmhouse.

The sedation.

Alexis Maximuke being found safe.

Conrad Howden's passing.

None of the new information helped him right now. Sinead might know something, of course, or Alexis might spill a secret or two, but right now—right at this moment—he was no closer to finding Shona than he had been an hour ago.

An hour from now, and time would almost be up.

He put his hands in his pockets and paced along the boards, only half-reading the notes written there.

Hopefully, there would be clues of some kind found at the farmhouse. Something that would point them to where Oleg was hiding, or at least where he was keeping Shona.

'They weren't kept together,' he muttered, which drew a quizzical whuff from the dog. 'Shona and Sinead. Why weren't the two of them kept together?'

He reached the end of the second board, turned on his heels, and paced in the opposite direction. There was, he thought, no way of knowing yet why the women hadn't both been kept in the same place.

But what did it tell him?

Oleg had more than one hideout. At least two, possibly more.

Oleg's or the Iceman's? Did that matter?

They already knew the Iceman had access to multiple properties. All the past locations connected to him had already been checked out by Uniform earlier that day. Nothing had been found, but that didn't mean he didn't have other properties they weren't aware of. He could own or rent dozens of other buildings all over the city.

Wealth and resources.

A working knowledge of Logan's team.

He stopped pacing and stared. And thought. And calculated.
Basic bloody maths.

No. Surely not?

The door opened behind him.

'I just heard the news,' Detective Superintendent Mitchell announced.

Logan didn't turn. His gaze darted across the boards. 'Which news is that?'

'All of it, I'd imagine. DC… is she going by Bell or Neish?'

'Bell,' Logan muttered, still not tearing his eyes from the boards. 'Saves confusion.'

Mitchell appeared beside him. The dog sniffed at her leg until she nudged it away with the side of her foot. 'Makes sense. I also heard about the murdered officer. Obviously, that's less happy news.'

'Obviously,' Logan agreed. 'Scene of Crime is en route. I'm just about to head there myself.'

Mitchell exhaled slowly through her nose, like she was trying to clear away a bad smell that was lingering in her nostril hairs.

'The Assistant Chief Constable called,' she said. 'He's very much not happy with you still being on this case.'

'I can imagine,' Logan murmured, eyes still darting from note to note, brain making deductive leaps that he wasn't quite sure he could believe.

'He ordered me to take you off it,' Mitchell continued.

'And?' Logan asked. He still hadn't glanced away from the case notes laid out before him.

'I told him I'd take his concerns on board,' Mitchell replied. 'But that I considered you the best man for the job.'

Logan shot her a sideways look at that, his eyes widening just a fraction in surprise.

'He suggested I might want to start surrounding myself with better men,' Mitchell said. 'I get the impression he doesn't like you much.'

'The feeling's mutual,' Logan said, turning his attention back to the board.

'DI Forde also tells me I should send you home to get some rest,' Mitchell told him.

'Did he, indeed?'

'Is he right? Should I send you home?'

'By all means, you can try, ma'am.'

Mitchell nodded. 'Yes. That's what I thought,' she said. 'I was almost tempted to do it, just to see what you'd say. Thought best to save us both the disciplinary proceedings, though.'

'I appreciate that,' Logan told her. He finally turned away from the board. 'I better get going.'

'The farmhouse?'

'Aye. Better no' keep anyone waiting. But before I do...' He scribbled a note on a piece of paper and handed it to her. 'Can you have CID look into this as a matter of urgency? Have them text me an update as soon as they have one.'

Mitchell regarded the page, her eyebrows creeping closer together as she deciphered the scribbled handwriting. 'Really? You don't think...'

'I do, ma'am,' Logan said. 'It's the only thing that makes sense. This should help confirm it.'

Mitchell folded the paper in half. 'I'll get them right on it.'

'Thank you,' Logan said.

He headed for the door, then stopped, an idea occurring to him. He whistled through his teeth, beckoning the dog. It would've been far more impressive had Taggart understood, but he just stared with his head tilted to one side until Logan sighed, tapped his thigh, and said, 'Well, don't just sit there looking stupid. You coming, or what?'

The message got through that time, and Taggart went bounding across the Incident Room, all-but tripping over his own tongue in his hurry to catch up.

'You're taking the dog?' Mitchell asked.

'I am.'

'To an active crime scene? To the scene of an officer's murder?'

'Aye, well, it'll do him good to stretch his legs,' Logan said. 'Besides, I've got a feeling that he might be able to help me with something.'

Chapter 44

For all his easy-going charm and friendly demeanour, DI Forde was getting nowhere with Alexis Maximuke. Either she had watched too many crime dramas, or all those years living with Bosco had rubbed off on her, because she had offered 'no comment' to all his questions so far.

Even the one about a cup of tea and a biscuit.

She had declined a solicitor, which was often good news. Right now, though, Ben would have killed for an impatient brief to come along and cajole her into answering his questions. None of them were exactly incriminating—he'd made it clear that Alexis wasn't suspected of anything, and that answering was in her own best interests—but she was having none of it.

'I just need to know if you have any idea where he might be,' Ben said, for the fifth time since sitting down with Alexis.

'No comment,' came her reply, also for the fifth time.

Ben had called Uniform in and had them take Olivia to one of the family waiting rooms, where she could get a bit of kip on a couch. God knew the girl must be exhausted. Everyone else certainly was.

Everyone who hadn't spent the day being pampered in a bloody spa, at least.

'Look, Alexis. Can I call you Alexis?'

'No comment.'

Ben sighed. 'Look, Alexis. You're not a suspect here. Nobody's pointing a finger at you. We just... a woman is missing, Alexis. We think Oleg has her. We're worried he's going to hurt her. Or worse. So if there's anything you can tell us—anything at all, it might just save her life.'

Alexis rolled her tongue around inside her mouth, like she was adjusting a set of false teeth. Ben leaned forward and nodded encouragingly, his warmest smile playing across a face that was wide open with well-practised honesty.

'No comment.'

Ben let his head drop until he was looking directly down at the tabletop. They'd been at this for twenty minutes now, and he was getting nowhere.

Time was running out.

'Look, I know your family doesn't have the best history with the polis, but this isn't about that, Alexis. This isn't about you versus us. It's not about you trying to get one over on us, or trying to prove a point to Bosco, or whatever it is you think is going on here. It's about a young woman's life. A young woman who has done nothing wrong but be a friend to your daughter. That's her crime. That's why they took her. And that's why, unless you help us, they're going to kill her.'

Alexis leaned back in her chair. She blinked slowly, and looked across to the mirror that took up most of the wall on her left. She examined her reflection for a while, patted her hair, then turned back.

'No comment.'

Ben's open hand rose all on its own and came down as a fist on the table. The boom of it made Alexis jump in her seat.

'Jesus Christ, what's wrong with you?' he demanded, in a voice that made Alexis shrink back in her chair. 'Have you listened to a bloody word I said? Do you know what's at stake here, you shallow, selfish cow?'

There was a buzz from the interview room door. Detective Superintendent Mitchell entered with all the presence of a hurricane. She was at Ben's side in three big paces, and for a moment it looked like she might drag him out of his chair by his collar.

Instead, she offered a clipped, 'I think that's quite enough, Detective Inspector.'

Ben held up his hands in apology. 'I'm sorry, ma'am. I just... I'll keep the heid.'

'You'll leave the room,' Mitchell told him.

'What? But, ma'am—'

'That's an order, Detective Inspector,' the Detective Superintendent said. Her voice was a cold, frigid thing that did not invite further discussion on the matter. She was not a tall woman, but her presence suggested that nobody had thought to tell *her* that. 'Go check in with DS Khaled. I'm sure we'd all like an update on DC Bell.'

Ben stood slowly. He didn't turn to see for himself—he daren't—but he could *feel* the smug look on Alexis Maximuke's face as he conceded to Mitchell and started to gather up his notes.

'Leave those,' the Det Supt instructed. She leaned over the table, and addressed the microphone built into it. 'Detective Inspector Forde leaving room at the request of Detective Superintendent Mitchell. Interview paused.'

She jabbed the button that stopped the recording, then waited for Ben to leave the room.

He hesitated at the door and very deliberately looked up at the clock.

11:08 PM.

Mitchell caught the look, nodded, then ushered him out.

'I'm sorry about that, Mrs Maximuke,' Mitchell said, once the DI had left. Her shirt was so white against her dark skin that it seemed to glow in the glare of the overhead lights.

'I should bloody think so, too. He's not allowed to shout at me like that. I could sue.'

'You'll understand that it's a stressful time for all of us,' Mitchell continued. As she spoke, she pulled the chair that Ben had been sitting on over to the corner where a camera watched over the room.

'What are you doing?' Alexis asked, as Mitchell climbed up onto the chair and, with a bit of jiggery-pokery, angled the camera towards the ceiling.

She looked back over her shoulder at the woman on the other side of the table. 'Hmm?'

'What are you doing?'

'No comment,' Mitchell replied, then she stepped down from the chair. 'Like I say, Mrs Maximuke, we're all up to high doh at the moment. The woman who is missing is a very good friend and colleague of us here at the station.'

Alexis was trying to keep watching Mitchell, but her eyes crept back to the camera.

'But that is no excuse for DI Forde losing his temper. That was unprofessional.' She sat in Ben's chair and clasped her hands. 'Rest assured, I do not lose my temper. I do not act out of anger or frustration. I am told that I am not an "emotionally giving" person. I'm also told that this is a bad thing, though I tend to disagree.'

'What are you on about?' Alexis asked. 'Why are you telling me this?'

She was wary now, inching all the way back in her chair as some primal survival instinct flashed the word 'DANGER' in big red letters inside her head.

'I'm telling you this because I want to make it clear that nothing I'm about to do is done on a whim. Everything has been thought through. Carefully considered. I've looked at the pros, and I've listed the cons, and I'm comfortable with how they stack up.'

'I don't—'

'What this means for you, Mrs Maximuke,' Mitchell continued, shutting the other woman down. 'Is that no amount of begging, or pleading, or reasoning will change my mind. Anything you might suggest—any reasons you might offer to try to make me alter my course of action—I have already thought of, and disregarded. My mind is made up. Nobody, least of all you, will change that.'

There was no sound then in the room, but the faint gulp of Alexis swallowing. 'What are you going to do?'

'I'm going to send you home. You and Olivia. Together,' Mitchell said. 'I'm going to pull away all my officers. I'm going to leave you entirely unprotected. And then I'm going to phone the number Oleg Ivanov gave us, and I'm going to tell him where you are.'

Alexis snorted. 'Nice try. You can't do that.'

'I assure you, I can,' Mitchell countered. 'I'm going to tell you something we in the police don't want people to know. The secret we don't want getting out.' She leaned closer, lowering her voice. 'The truth of it is, Mrs Maximuke, most of us can do whatever we like at any point. The limiting factor in the decisions we make is rarely what we *can* do, but what we will and won't do. What we are prepared to do. What consequences we are willing to face. I *can* set fire to this building right now, but I won't. I can step outside and kill the first person I see, but—of course—I would not.'

'Well, I mean, yeah, but—'

'I *can* ensure that videos of you having sex with another man are given to your husband and made available online. I *can* send you and your daughter home, unprotected, and tell the man who wants to kill you both where you are.' She held Alexis's eye until she was sure the message was getting through. 'And I will do both of those things, unless you start answering our questions. Do we understand each other, Mrs Maximuke?'

Alexis narrowed her eyes. 'You're a nasty bitch.'

'Yes. So I've been told,' Mitchell replied. She flipped open the folder in front of her. 'Now, shall we begin?'

Chapter 45

Logan stood in a pool of light on the driveway, watching the car that came rumbling through the dark towards the farmhouse. He watched a uniformed constable directing the beat-up old Volkswagen to pull in behind Logan's BMW, and caught snatches of the conversation that took place through the driver's window.

Midges flocked around the two high-powered lamps that Uniform had set up to shed some light on the exterior of the house. They swarmed in their millions towards the searing beams, their dancing shadows making the light shimmer as if everything was underwater.

Logan could hear their bodies sizzling, and smell the burning from here.

He wished he still smoked. His fingers were crying out for something to do. Something that didn't involve him pulling back his sleeve to check his watch for the fourth time that minute.

Eleven fifteen.

Forty-five minutes.

Dear God, what was keeping the bastard?

'Right, just let him through,' Logan called over to the Uniform. 'We've no' got all bloody night.'

The constable stepped back smartly, reached for the driver's door handle like he was running a valet parking service, then shuffled aside when it was opened from inside.

Ricketts unfolded himself, like some sort of insect emerging from its pupal stage. He stepped out of the car, closed and locked it—because the presence of a dozen uniformed polis officers wasn't enough of a security precaution, apparently—then set off on a series of long, lumbering strides in Logan's direction, with his leather medical bag swinging at his side.

Logan intercepted him at the BMW. 'Albert.'

'Detective Chief Inspector.'

Ricketts' greeting was partly drowned out by the sound of barking from Logan's car. Taggart was on the back seats, front paws spread wide, weight mostly on his back legs, his collar standing up as he loudly made his presence felt.

'All right, all right, shut up,' Logan said, rapping a knuckle on the glass. He took Ricketts by the arm and guided him past the car. 'Sorry about that. He's still a bit skittish around strangers or, you know, people he doesn't like.'

The pathologist glanced back at the car. Taggart had made his way through to the front, and had two paws on the dashboard, his breath fogging the glass as he panted.

'We're in here,' Logan said, gesturing towards the house. He waited for Ricketts to take the lead, then fell into step beside him. The pathologist barely glanced up at the place as they approached. 'No' what you need, getting called out at this time of night.'

'Not really, no. But needs must,' Ricketts replied. 'Any word yet on Shona?'

Logan bristled. His top teeth scraped across his bottom lip. 'No. Nothing yet.'

'I'm very sorry to hear that,' the older man said, stopping to wipe his feet on the mat on the outside doorstep. 'I know you two are… well. Whatever you are.'

'Thanks for those kind words, Albert. That really means a lot,' Logan said. He hung back a little, cleaned his own shoes on the mat, then followed Ricketts through into the room that was second on the left.

'Ah. Yes. Oh, dear. Here we are,' the pathologist said. He peered down at the body on the floor. 'Strangled, by the looks of it. Within the last few hours.'

'That's pretty much the conclusion I'd come to,' Logan said.

'Clearly dead, but for the purposes of completeness…' His knees went 'crack' as he squatted down beside Jason Hall's corpse, and pressed two fingers against his ravaged throat. 'No pulse. As expected.'

'Aye. No' exactly a surprise,' Logan agreed. 'But important we do things right, I suppose. Play by the rules.'

Ricketts regarded him curiously for a moment, then shrugged. 'Whatever you say, Detective Chief Inspector. I'll do some quick tests and get the paperwork done, then can come back to it fresh tomorrow.'

'Sounds like a plan,' Logan said. His voice was light. Uncharacteristically so. 'But before you get started, mind if I ask you a quick question?'

'By all means.'

'How did you know where to find him?' Logan asked.

Ricketts blinked. Once. Twice. He smiled and frowned at the same time, each more or less cancelling the other out. 'Well, I got a phone call. Got me out of bed, as it happens. I mean, it's all part of the job, so I don't complain, but—'

'Not the house. The room,' Logan said. 'How did you know what room he was in?'

Ricketts looked down at the body, then past Logan to the hallway beyond the door. 'Well, I mean, I saw him when I came in the front door.'

'No, you didn't,' Logan said. 'See, I made sure that wasn't possible. I checked every angle, positioned the door to this room just right. From out there, there was no way of knowing that the body was here. And yet you went straight to it. Why was that, do you think?'

Ricketts took a backwards step, carefully placing his feet so as to avoid trampling on the corpse. 'Well, I mean… it was probably the smell.'

'The smell?'

'Dead bodies smell, Detective Chief Inspector.'

'This whole house smells, Albert. And our man there's only been dead a few hours, you said so yourself, so he's no' exactly ripe.' He gave a nod of encouragement, inviting the pathologist to try again. 'So, let's try again. What was it? A lucky guess? Women's intuition?'

Ricketts sighed, making a show of his impatience. 'I suppose it must've been something like that, yes. Now, do you mind? I'd like to get this wrapped up soon.'

'Funny the dog didn't like you, eh, Albert?' Logan said, taking a sudden conversational left-turn. 'What I said about him being aggressive towards strangers, that's no' true. He's a biddable wee thing. I mean, aye, he was a bit unsure of DC Neish to start with, but then weren't we all? You, though? I've never seen him react like that to anyone before. Why do you think that was? What made him take such an instant dislike to you?'

The bag of bones that made up Ricketts' shoulders shrugged. 'I've always been more of a cat person.'

Logan stepped further into the room. The pathologist retreated another foot or so, until he found himself trapped beside the bed, with its thin mattress and stained sheet.

'You know what some bastard did to him?' Logan said. 'Cut the microchip out of him with a scalpel. Right out of his back.' He sucked in air and shook his head. 'What sort of person does that?'

'I don't know.'

'I'll tell you what sort of bastard, will I, Albert?' Logan asked. He pointed to the body on the floor. 'Same sort of bastard who does this.'

He had advanced further now, narrowing the gap between him and the other man. Ricketts lifted his medical bag up to stomach height, and held it between them, like it might prevent the detective from coming any closer.

It did not.

'Where is she, Albert? Where's Shona?'

And there it was. That look, there one moment, gone the next. The look that told Logan everything he needed to know. That told him he was right, and that anything this wizened old fucker might say to the contrary was a lie.

'I'm sorry?'

'You heard me. Shona. Where is she?'

Ricketts looked perplexed. Or tried to, anyway. But it was too late for that.

'How should I know?' he asked.

Logan's hands were on the bastard before he could stop them. Not that stopping them was high on his list of priorities. His grip tightened on the old man's jacket, and a jerk of his arms hoisted Ricketts clean off the ground.

'Do not fucking try me, Albert!' Logan hissed, his breath like dragon fire in the pathologist's face.

'Help!' Ricketts cried. 'He's gone crazy! Help me, please!'

Logan dropped him to the floor, then immediately caught him by the back of the neck with one hand. Ricketts almost tripped on the body as he was dragged out of the room and into the hall.

'Help me! Police, help me!'

Logan threw him out the front door and into the rippling puddle of light on the driveway. Ricketts landed heavily and whimpered as he slid across the rough gravel.

'Take a look around, Albert,' Logan said, gesturing into the darkness. Aside from the car of the dead officer, there were no other polis to be seen. 'I asked them to give us a few minutes alone. So shout all you like, nobody's coming. It's just you and me.'

'Why are you doing this?' Ricketts sobbed. 'Please, Detective Chief Inspector—Jack! Please, don't—'

Logan closed the gap between them in a few furious bounds. He caught the pathologist by the jacket again and started hauling him to his feet, then the flash of a scalpel blade made him release his grip and jump back.

Albert stumbled, but managed to stay upright. He held the scalpel before him at arm's length, aiming it at Logan's face like it was some sort of projectile.

'There he is,' Logan said. 'Let him out, Albert. Let me talk to him. Let me talk to the real you.'

He became aware of something tickling along his arm, and glanced down to see a trickle of blood falling from his pinkie finger onto the gravel. The bastard had cut him through his coat. Whether through his surging adrenaline, or the sharpness of the blade, though, he couldn't yet feel it.

'I don't know what you think you're doing,' Ricketts said. The blade was rock-solid, his hands not shaking one iota. 'But I won't have it. You stay where you are. You hear me? You're clearly experiencing some sort of breakdown.'

'Cut the shite, Albert,' Logan roared, and the hand with the knife did flinch then, but only once, and only for a moment. 'It's you. I know it's you. You're the Iceman. The original and best.'

'That's preposterous! You've lost your mind.'

'No. Not yet. But I'm dangerously fucking close,' Logan warned. 'But not about this. This, I'm right on.'

He could hear the blood pit-patting onto the ground now, but ignored it. There was still no pain. That was good.

'It was something Shona said that got me thinking. Said you owned properties all over town. But, see, I looked into that, Albert. Well, technically I had CID looking into it tonight, but I asked them to. Because I'm a nosy bastard like that. And it turns out, you don't own properties all over town, do you, Albert?'

'I never said I did.'

'But you do own shares in an offshore company. And that company owns shares in other companies. And those companies own properties. Several properties, in fact.' He indicated the building behind them with a thumb. 'Including this one.'

Ricketts didn't reply to that. His gaze remained fixed on the DCI, but his hand was a little less steady than it had been a moment before.

'Oh, it's not as simple as that, of course. You've made it much harder than that to follow the trail, but it's amazing what you can find out with the full might of Police Scotland CID behind you,' Logan continued. 'They made connections to one of the properties used by the Iceman. One of them with the big freezers. The one where Olivia Maximuke shoved Oleg Ivanov. The one you rescued him from.'

'I don't know what you're talking about,' Ricketts insisted, though with less conviction than he'd shown until now.

'It was obvious once we went through it all. Oleg being nursed back to health. The stitches on Borys Wozniak's arm. The surgical way the chip was taken out of Taggart here. Someone with medical expertise had done all that. And it had to be someone with knowledge of my team. Someone who'd sent stuff to our email inbox before. Someone who knew us. Someone who'd known us for a long time.'

'I don't… this is nonsense. This is…' Albert's protests started well, but then fell away into a sullen sort of silence. When he spoke again, his tone had changed. The pleading was gone. The whining had been replaced by something solemn and grim. 'What choice did I have?'

'I'm sorry?'

'Do you have any idea what it's like?' Ricketts asked. 'Seeing those victims coming in, week-in, week-out? For years. *Decades*. Women. Children. Babies, sometimes. The things that were done to them. The ways they'd been hurt. Degraded. Defiled.'

Logan knew better than to say anything, much as he wanted to. Let the bastard get the truth out. Give him a minute, just one, for that, and everything that came after would be easier.

'She was a toddler. The one who finally did it,' Ricketts said. His voice was even more of a dull monotone than usual, but

Logan sensed that he was having to fight back a lot of emotion to keep it that way. 'Two years old. Well, twenty-three months. Karen Elizabeth Wilson. Wee thing for her age. Malnourished, it turned out. Blonde curls. Where it hadn't been pulled out, at least.'

He exhaled, and his breath clouded in the cooling night air.

Logan felt an ache in his arm. There was a concerning amount of blood on the ground by his feet now.

He chose not to dwell on either of those facts.

'They'd stubbed cigarettes out on her. For months. A year, maybe. Her hands and feet were blistered where they'd poured boiling water on them,' Ricketts said, and the monotone gave way to a crack of despair. The searing spotlights picked out the tears that swelled in his eyes. 'Her wee hands. They were tiny, just these tiny wee things. Like a doll. And they were… they were twisted. The water had scalded her, burned her right down to the muscle. Down to the *bone*.' He sniffed. Swallowed. 'They did worse to her, too. Far worse. Her own parents. Her own mother and father.'

Some dark fury contorted his features and tightened his grip on the scalpel. He shook his head like he was trying to drive something out of it.

'Have you ever seen what happens to the insides of an infant after it has been repeatedly penetrated by a grown man's erect penis, Detective Chief Inspector?' he hissed through gritted teeth. 'I have. *I have*. Eleven times. I can give you all their names. And that's what they did to Karen. That's what they did to their own daughter. That's what *he* did.'

The knife was trembling in his hand now. He ran the arm across his eyes, wiping away the tears, then let it drop to his side. His voice took on the same controlled monotone as earlier.

'They got off with it. "Not Proven". They walked free. Both of them. The Procurator Fiscal and your lot "mismanaged the investigation". So the official probe concluded.'

'I don't remember the case,' Logan admitted.

'Before your time. But I do. I remember. Every night. I remember all of them. All of them,' Ricketts whispered. 'But that wee girl—Karen Elizabeth Wilson—that was the start of it.' He took a deep breath, held it for a moment, then breathed out his confession. 'I killed her parents. Slowly. I sat them across from one another, and I... *dismantled* them. Bit by bit. Did it in turns, so they'd each have to watch. So they'd know what was coming.'

Logan felt some long-buried memory stir, but there was a fuzzy edge to his thoughts that made it harder than usual to focus.

On the ground beside him, another droplet of blood plinked into the puddle.

'This was way back, wasn't it?' he asked.

'Nineteen-seventy-two,' Ricketts said. 'That was the first.'

'How many?' Logan asked.

The reply came without a moment of hesitation. 'Forty-seven. All child killers at first. People the police didn't have enough evidence to prosecute, mostly. People who thought they had gotten away with it.'

'But then you thought, "why stop there?"'

'It's a cancer. Crime. It starts small. Some petty theft. A bit of drug dealing. A couple of slaps to a girlfriend who won't stop nagging. And it snowballs from there. You know that,' Albert said. 'You know that, and yet you do nothing about it.'

'We do everything we can,' Logan countered. 'We do what the law allows.'

'It's not enough!' Albert snapped. 'Besides, how can we even trust you to do the right thing? That one in there— the constable—he was going to rape her, you know? Your colleague. I stopped him. I did that. Not you. Not "the law". Me.'

'You're lying,' Logan said.

'Ask her yourself. I'm assuming she's safe now?' Ricketts continued. 'I didn't put her there, by the way. I only found out she was there earlier today. That one's not on me.'

'You'll forgive me if I have some difficulty believing that.'

'I don't care. I've never cared about what any of you did. You all act like you're the be-all and end-all, but nothing you did was ever important. Even if you did put people away, they'd get back out,' Ricketts said, flecks of foam forming at the corners of his mouth. 'Oh, they'd claim they were reformed. That they'd learned their lessons, done their time. But they'd be back at it in no time. Dealing. Abusing. Killing. And I'd listen to their solicitors defending them. Giving excuses. Explaining *the circumstances*. Haggling their sentences down, whittling away at the years.

'And I'd had enough. I'd just… I'd had enough. If you lot weren't going to do something about it, then I was. And I did. Over and over and over again, I did what you would not. What you could only *dream* of doing.'

Ricketts gazed across the gap at the detective. There was something taunting in the look.

'Because you do, don't you, Jack? A man like you, the things these people do, you wish you could do what I've done. You wish you could've looked into their eyes at the end, like I did. I think we have that in common.'

'Why the freezers?' Logan asked, brushing off the question. 'Why start that?'

A smile tugged at the corners of the pathologist's mouth. The lack of denial had been answer enough.

'Old age doesn't come alone, Detective Chief Inspector,' he said. 'And torture is a young man's game. But the cold? The cold is one of the cruellest tortures of them all. And so easy. So effortless.'

'Why not freeze Borys Wozniak, then? What was with the hand? Why leave him somewhere so public?'

For the first time since he'd started ranting, uncertainty crept into the pathologist's voice. 'To send a message. People… people needed to know who he was, and what he'd been doing. That's why we left his drugs there. So everyone would know.'

Logan wanted to push him further, to get all the information from him now. He had so many questions, like when and why he'd started 'franchising' the Iceman name to others. How he'd recruited them.

How many of them were still out there?

But time was running short. There was barely half an hour left until Oleg's deadline. Shona's life was hanging in the balance.

And that, he hoped, was his ace in the hole.

'And what about Shona, Albert?' Logan asked. 'What's her crime? What's she ever done?'

Ricketts' smirk evaporated. He shook his head. 'Nothing. That wasn't me. That was… he doesn't listen to me. He's not like the others. I tried to explain how we do things. I tried to tell him, but he had his own ideas.'

'Oleg.'

Ricketts practically flinched at the name, then nodded.

'You found him in the freezer. You nursed him back to health.'

'He wasn't supposed to be there. I didn't know who he was. As far as I knew he was innocent.'

Logan let out a sharp, mirthless laugh at that. 'Innocent?' Anger gripped him then and he took a sudden step forward. Ricketts brought the blade back up and waved it threateningly in his face. 'Shona's innocent, Albert.'

'But… the girl. He said he was just going to get back at the girl.'

'By killing Shona!'

'N–no. I spoke to him. He's not… he won't kill her. I don't… I don't think he'll kill her.'

'Oh, you don't *think* he'll kill her? Well, that's not what he's told us. She's got…' He checked his watch. '…twenty-five minutes. Twenty-five minutes, and she dies.'

'He just wants the girl.'

'The girl? The thirteen-year-old? And what's he going to do to her, do you think?' Logan demanded. 'What are her injuries going to look like when she's lying on that slab, Albert? What condition is her body going to be in?'

'She's… she tried to kill him. And she was dealing drugs. To children!'

'*His* drugs! She was dealing his drugs, Albert. He's no' another of your wee fucking disciples, he's everything you claim to hate. Everything you say you've spent the last fifty years fighting against!'

'No, that's… you're not…'

'You didn't leave a big bag of drugs on the dashboard of Borys' car, Albert. It was sherbet,' Logan said. 'What do you think happened to the real drugs, eh? Who do you think took those?'

'No. You're lying.'

'He's going to kill Shona, Albert. Even if he gets Olivia— which he won't—he'll still kill her. And I don't think you want that. I know I don't. That's what we've got in common, Albert. Me and you. We care about her. And we're not about to stand by while some third-rate Russian drugs baron hurts her, are we? You and I, we won't stand for that, will we?'

Ricketts was vibrating now, the knife hand swaying drunkenly in the air between them. He looked older than he'd ever looked, Logan thought. That officious air that he'd always held himself with was gone, replaced by something grubby and desperate.

'Take me to her, Albert. Let me stop this. Let me bring her home.'

The pathologist studied the detective's face, then looked past him to the house. He stared at it for several seconds, like he was reading something there. The writing on the wall, perhaps. It was over. Five decades after it had begun, it was finally over.

His hand trembled as he brought the knife closer to his own throat. 'I am the Iceman,' he announced, drawing himself up to his full, spindly height. 'I have always been the Iceman.'

The words were chillingly familiar. Logan had heard and seen them written before, and knew precisely what came next.

But not now. Not here. Not tonight.

He closed the gap between them in one big lunge. His fist smashed into the centre of the bastard's face, making him choke on what was left of his big moment. Logan caught the knife arm, twisted, and a shriek of pain was followed by the sound of the scalpel hitting the gravel.

Ricketts recoiled, choking back blood, and snot, and tears, his eyes spherical with shock.

'You're not getting out of it that easily,' Logan hissed. 'You want to slit your throat, Albert? Fire on. I'll hand you the bloody knife myself. But first, you're helping me get Shona back. You owe her that much.'

The pathologist sobbed, but a shake from Logan eventually forced a response out of him.

'OK, OK! I can… I can try. I can try,' he whimpered. 'But… there are conditions.'

'Conditions?' Logan shook him again. Pain radiated up his injured arm and the world lurched unsettlingly beneath his feet.

'We'll have to take my car. Oleg knows it. He'll know it's me.'

'Fine,' Logan said, dragging Ricketts by the scruff of his neck over towards the Volkswagen.

As they passed the BMW, Taggart erupted into panicky barking. Logan raised a hand to calm him, and felt his stomach lurch at the sight of his coat sleeve. Blood had seeped through the material all along the length of his arm, from just above the elbow. A *lot* of blood.

'And leave your phone,' Ricketts said.

'No.'

'You want me to take you to Oleg, leave your phone,' the pathologist said again.

Logan's eyes narrowed, his grip tightening on the other man's collar. Ricketts had rediscovered his backbone, though, and dug his heels into the gravel.

'Shona doesn't have much time. Nor do you, by the looks of you,' he said. 'If you want me to take you to her, leave the phone.'

Logan didn't bother to argue. He fished the mobile from his pocket and dropped it on the ground beside his car. 'Right. Go.'

A shove sent Ricketts stumbling towards his car. Logan waited for him to climb in, then squeezed into the rear passenger seat directly behind him.

'Drive,' he instructed, leaning forward to speak directly into the older man's ear. 'And I'm warning you, Albert, if you try any funny stuff, I'll open your eyes to tortures you've never bloody imagined.'

'I don't care about your threats, Detective Chief Inspector,' the older man said. The car's engine coughed awake. 'I'm not doing this for you, or for me. I'm doing it for Shona.'

Logan blinked. It seemed to take longer than usual, and when he opened his eyes there was a first aid kit on the seat beside him.

'You're going to want to put pressure on that wound,' Ricketts said. Gravel crunched beneath the car's tyres. 'Or you're going to be no use to her by the time we get there.'

'We don't have much time, Albert,' Logan said, shuffling his arms out of his coat. 'So shut up and drive.'

Chapter 46

The Scene of Crime officer who had drawn the short straw sat in the front passenger seat, a fixed smile on her face as Geoff Palmer spoke at her from behind the steering wheel.

He'd been speaking at her for quite a while now. She had listened intently for the first few minutes then, when she'd realised that he wasn't expecting any input from her whatsoever, her attention had drifted off, leaving only the slightly vacant smile behind.

The main roads through Inverness were not in the best condition, but they were silky smooth compared to the back roads out here beyond the city limits. Mind you, the surface of the moon was probably smoother than the one they were on right now. The van rolled and rumbled over the crater-like potholes as it pushed on through the darkness.

Geoff was still talking. She tuned herself back in for a few seconds, caught a fraction of a lecture on how to effectively deal with hecklers at a comedy gig, then let her mind wander again.

Christ, he was incessant.

She looked down at her hands, just for some other external stimulus. Some input that wasn't Geoff's droning voice.

They were all right, as hands went, she thought. Bit bony, maybe, but decent enough. The nails needed a bit of work, and she'd picked at the skin around the base of the one on her left thumb, but these were relatively minor flaws.

She sighed. Was this what it had come to? Critiquing her own cuticles to avoid listening to her boss talking about... well, anything, really. Was this what her career had in store for her?

She stole a glance back at the rest of the team sitting in rows behind her. They were chatting quietly, conversation flowing freely in multiple directions, not just one.

Lucky bastards.

She looked up from her hands and realised that Geoff was staring at her expectantly. *Shit*. He must've asked her a question, but she didn't have the faintest idea what it was.

'Yes,' she said, taking a wild stab in the dark. She could tell from the smile and the way his body language perked right up that she'd made a grave mistake.

'Really? Well… great!' he exclaimed. 'What do you fancy? Indian? Chinese?'

Bollocks. That'd teach her.

She delayed having to answer by facing front, then let out a sudden shout of panic and jabbed a finger ahead. 'Geoff!'

Palmer turned his attention back to the road. He screamed—actually screamed—and slammed a foot all the way down to the floor as he threw the car into a lurching left turn that drew cries of fright from the passengers who suddenly found themselves tossed around in the back.

The front of the van hit a verge and all its forward momentum was transferred to the occupants sitting inside it. They were all thrown forwards until their seatbelts tightened and slammed them back again.

'Fuck!' Palmer ejected.

Outside, the old Volkswagen that had caused him to swerve off the road swept past, its tail lights staring back at them like demon's eyes in the darkness.

'Watch where you're going, you daft bastard!' Palmer cried, shaking a fist at the rearview mirror. He turned to the woman beside him, shook his head, and rolled his eyes. 'I dunno,' he muttered. 'Some people just shouldn't be on the bloody road.'

–

Tyler and Hamza sat in a waiting room at Raigmore Hospital, their heads back, eyes staring blankly at the ceiling. Tyler's left leg bounced impatiently. It shook Hamza's chair, but he'd given up asking the DC to cut it out, only for it to start again a few seconds later.

'What's keeping them?' Tyler sighed. 'Why can't we see her?'

'They're doing tests,' Hamza explained. Tyler knew this, of course—they'd both been there when the doctor had explained the next steps—but the occasional reminder seemed to calm his nerves for a while. 'And she's going to need to rest.'

They had been told to go home and come back in the morning, but Tyler was having none of that. Hamza had called into base, but Ben had been tied up in an interview with Alexis Maximuke, and Logan wasn't answering his phone, so he'd decided it best to keep Tyler company.

'I need to know what happened to her,' Tyler said. 'I need to know if she's OK.'

'He said she was OK.'

'He said she was "stable",' Tyler said. He turned to the DS, his eyes ringed with red. 'What does that even mean. *Stable*? It just means she's not getting any worse. It doesn't mean she's not in a bad way.'

'She was fit enough to try and kill me,' Hamza said. He bumped a fist against the other man's leg. 'So, I reckon she's going to be fine, mate.'

'She was barely conscious when we brought her in.'

'I know. I know. But this is Sinead we're talking about. She's made of tough stuff.'

'I don't know. I've just...' Tyler swallowed, his voice cracking. 'She was nearly naked. Why was she nearly naked?'

Hamza had no answer for that beyond a supportive smile and a pat on Tyler's leg. The leg started bouncing too hard to contain, and Tyler sprang to his feet, only for a sharp pain in his groin to make him regret it.

He grimaced, then did a hobbled lap of the compact waiting room, trying to burn off his anxiety. 'I just wish I could see her. Talk to her. I'm climbing the bloody walls here.'

'It could be hours. You should try to get some sleep.'

'Sleep?! How am I meant to sleep?' Tyler practically shrieked.

Hamza had to admit that sleep did feel like a distant, far-off prospect at the moment. Something it wasn't even worth thinking about.

The buzzing of his phone in his pocket derailed his train of thought. 'This might be news,' he said, unzipping the pocket and fishing for the mobile.

He'd expected to see a number he recognised on the screen, but instead found a mobile number waiting for him that he couldn't identify.

'Hello?' he said, answering the call. 'Detective Sergea—aye. It is. But slow down. I can't…' He looked across to Tyler, who had stopped pacing when the call had started. 'When was this?' Hamza checked his watch. 'Right. And you're *where* now?'

Chapter 47

Logan knew what was coming. It was inevitable.

Faces appeared at the side windows of the car, shining torches at him, peering in through the glass. He wasn't sure if it was the reflection from their lights, or the loss of blood, but there was something nightmarish about them. Something not quite real.

The hand that opened his door and pulled him out was real enough. He didn't fight back. Fighting back would only slow things down.

Besides, Ricketts was going to do the talking. Logan didn't trust the bastard—not by a long shot—but he was all out of other options. He had to believe Albert wanted to get Shona out of there. Anything else that happened after that was irrelevant. Getting Shona to safety was the only thing that mattered now.

'He's expecting us,' Ricketts said to one of the men. 'I phoned ahead.'

He had. Logan remembered him making the call, although the fact he couldn't remember much about its content was worrying.

He'd managed to patch his arm up a bit, but the cut was longer and deeper than he could deal with properly. He'd need stitches. Possibly a couple of pints of O Negative. Definitely some paracetamol.

That could all be sorted later.

Assuming there was a later.

His left foot squelched as he fell into step behind Ricketts, his boot, which had been slowly filling with the blood running down his body, leaving dark red prints on the stone floor of the garage the pathologist had pulled the car into. It was a big space, meant for several cars. Besides the Volkswagen, there was just one other car there—a silver something-or-other he couldn't identify. One of those generic saloons that all manufacturers made from the same basic template, with a couple of tweaks here and there to convey some illusion of originality.

He wasn't sure what sort of place he'd been expecting Ricketts to bring him to. Some sort of secret underground headquarters, maybe. Or a lair built below a volcano. Or, given his Iceman persona, perhaps some hidden base in the Polar Bear enclosure at the Highland Wildlife Park outside Aviemore.

It was, of course, none of those things. Ricketts wasn't some *Batman* or *James Bond* villain, he was just a killer with a list of excuses. Just like all the rest of them.

They'd driven north to Nairn, arriving at a low, squat building tucked away at the back of an industrial estate with just a couple of minutes to spare before midnight. The three heavy-set, torch-wielding men had let them into the garage, then one of them had rolled the door down behind the car, trapping them all inside together.

Logan had no complaints on that front. He had no intentions of going anywhere, and the locked door would only make it more difficult for every other bastard to run.

They were led through something that looked like a workshop. A large, walk-in freezer stood at the back of the room, a small porthole window in the door showing only darkness within.

'She's not in there,' Ricketts said, reading the detective's mind. 'It's off.'

'Enough talk,' one of the men leading them said. He was one of Bosco's old henchmen, Logan thought. Although, to be fair, a lot of these Eastern European skinheads looked the same after a while, especially after quite a substantial amount of blood loss.

Ricketts frowned and looked the other man up and down. 'I beg your pardon?'

'You heard.'

'Yes. Yes, I did hear. Don't forget who you're talking to,' the pathologist spat.

'Albert,' Logan grunted.

'Remember, I'm the one in charge here,' Ricketts insisted, ignoring the detective.

The skinheads stopped.

The skinheads glared.

'You're not,' Logan said.

Ricketts's gaze swept slowly across the faces of the henchmen, then settled on Logan. 'What?'

'You're not in charge. Not anymore,' the DCI said. The words felt awkward in his mouth, like the shapes were all wrong. 'He is.'

'Move,' the lead skinhead instructed.

Something prodded Logan in the back, and he resumed his squelching plod through the workshop, headed for a set of double swing doors.

The dimly lit room beyond the doors had been an open-plan office once. Dust-covered desks and dividers were still set out, turning the long, narrow space into a maze of alleyways and workspaces.

And there, sitting at the far end, was something that had once been a man.

Once again, Logan wondered if his mind was playing tricks on him. The face of the figure in the chair seemed to shift beneath his gaze, like the flesh itself was alive. He had a plastic mask pressed to his mouth, the clear vinyl fogging as he inhaled an oxygen mix from a cylinder beside him, and exhaled the used air from his ravaged, rattling lungs.

'Jesus,' Logan whispered. 'Is that him?'

Ricketts nodded. 'The cold,' he said. It was the only explanation necessary. Logan had seen what the Iceman's freezers had done to the dead. What they did to the living, it seemed, was even worse.

Logan looked down at his filthy, untucked shirt and bloodied arm.

'Fuck me, and I thought I looked a state.'

'Detective Chief Inspector Jack Logan,' Oleg said. His voice echoed inside the mask, but Logan recognised it from the earlier call. Oleg beckoned with a hand, and even from that distance, Logan could practically hear the creaking of his muscles and the stretching of his skin. 'Come. Let me see you, face to face.'

A hand shoved Logan forward. Usually, it would take a damn sight more than that to shift him, but his legs lacked their usual strength, and his balance was not what it normally was. He found himself shuffling through the labyrinth of desks and cubicle dividers. He wasn't sure if Ricketts or the other men were following. He just knew that the bastard who had taken Shona was sitting up there, and that every warm, squelching step brought him closer.

The carpet tiles around the desks were faded and scuffed by the castors of chairs that were no longer there. The desks themselves were solid-looking, though their white laminate surfaces were scratched and pitted from years of use by employees who knew they weren't going to be held liable for any damages.

By the time he was within a few feet of Oleg, Logan had mapped out most of the room. He'd identified the exits, figured out the quickest route to the closest one, and taken note of anything he might be able to use as a weapon should the need arise.

Unfortunately, with the blood loss clouding his brain, hanging onto this information had proven difficult, and he found himself second-guessing all of it as he stumbled to a stop before the monster in the chair.

And he was a monster. From a distance, he'd looked bad enough, but up close he was terrifying. Most of his eyelids were gone, replaced by slivers of scar tissue that twitched every few seconds, as the dying spasms of muscle memory tried desperately to blink.

The end of his nose was gone, turning his nostrils into two elongated dark holes that led deep inside his head. His lips, too, were missing, the skin shiny and smooth where the flaps of mouth flesh used to be joined on. With the nose and the exposed teeth, he had the look of a skeleton about him.

Although, *zombie* would probably be more accurate, Logan thought. He had more or less come back from the dead, after all.

Parts of him, anyway. The hand pressing the mask to his face was missing a couple of fingers, and the three that remained were not as long as they should have been. He didn't look like something that the cat had dragged in, exactly—more like something it had struggled to shit out.

'You're looking rough, pal,' Logan told him. The DCI frowned then, like the words had surprised him. All those watching saw his drunken sway, and the blood that dribbled down his arm and onto the carpet tiles.

He'd removed his jacket in the car, and managed to tear off one sodden shirt sleeve so he could get at his wound. His attempts to stem the flow of blood had been made all the more clumsy by only having one hand to do it with.

The arm was a rainbow of reds now, from the darker merlot of the dried blood, to the cheeky ruby of the fresher stuff.

He couldn't feel the injury, which was good.

He couldn't feel the arm, either, which was less positive.

Just like with Ricketts, Logan had a list of questions. And, just like with Ricketts, he had no intention of asking them. Not yet, anyway. Not until he knew Shona was far away from here and safe.

'Where is Olivia?' Oleg asked, and Logan blinked suddenly, like he'd been in the process of nodding off.

'Where's Shona?' he retorted.

Oleg smiled. At least, the exposed muscle fibres of his face tightened in such a way as to imply that's what was happening. 'I asked you first.'

'Aye, well...' Logan tried to think of a suitably clever response, but fell short. '...you're an arsehole.'

Oleg neither took offence, nor saw the funny side. Instead, he just drew another few wheezed breaths through his mask, and manually adjusted the position of one of his legs with a claw-like hand.

'Do you have any idea what she did to me?' he asked.

Logan gestured vaguely in the other man's direction, indicating the horror of him. '*That*, I'm guessing.'

'She killed me. That's how I've come to look at it. How I have found some peace with it,' he said. His voice was equal parts dry rasp and phlegmy rattle. It was a whisper that scurried up the walls around them. An itch in Logan's brain that he knew he could never scratch. 'She killed me. She killed me, and I was reborn in fire and pain.'

'I don't care,' Logan said. 'Bring me Shona. Now.'

Oleg's unblinking gaze lingered on him for a moment, then went to Ricketts, who had been ushered into position beside the detective.

'You told him where to find me. You brought him here.'

'He knew,' the pathologist said. 'He worked it out. They found the policewoman that you'd...' He pinched the bridge of his nose and shook his head. 'What were you thinking? We were supposed to stay low profile. Not... not kidnap police officers. And he says you're a drug dealer. He says you gave the girl the drugs. Is that true?'

Even in his misty-minded state, Logan could read the expression on what was left of Oleg's face. The eyes said it all. He didn't need all the missing parts.

'Well?' Ricketts demanded. 'Is that what you are? A dealer? One of *them*?'

'Albert, shut the fuck up,' Logan urged.

'Don't you talk to me like that, *Jack*,' Ricketts said, spitting the name out. 'You're not in charge here. You're not the big man, anymore. You're bleeding to death. Nobody knows where you are. You'll keep your mouth shut until I tell you otherwise.'

Logan slapped him. It wasn't particularly hard. And, if he was honest, the DCI was probably even more surprised by it than Ricketts.

'Sorry,' he grunted. 'You were getting on my tits. And also, he was about to kill you.'

He indicated Oleg, who flicked his bloodshot gaze in Albert's direction. 'He's right. I was.'

Ricketts tried to step back, but a hand caught him by the shoulder from behind and manhandled him back into place. 'What? But… no. I'm the Iceman. I'm in charge. I make the rules. I decide what we do, and when we do it. Me.' He looked back at the men behind him. 'I saved you. You work for me. You hear me? You work for—'

This time, it wasn't a slap Logan gave him, but a jab straight to the middle of his face. The pathologist's hawk-like nose, already bloodied from the earlier punch, gave way with a crunch, and he landed on his arse on the floor. His eyes rolled, like he was seeing wee tweety birds flying in circles around his head, then he flopped sideways against Logan's leg, before falling all the way backwards, out for the count.

'Sorry, he was doing my head in,' Logan said.

'Don't apologise. You just saved his life for a second time,' Oleg replied. He shifted his weight, his face contorting with the pain it brought. 'Now, let's see if we can save yours. Where is my *malyshka*? Where is Olivia?'

Logan patted his pockets. 'Shite. I forgot to bring her,' he said. 'Guess the memory's no' what it used to be. But I tell you what, you let Shona go, and I'll take you straight to her. You're welcome to her. Her mother, too. Pain in the arse, the pair of them.'

Oleg waved one of his stunted fingers and made a sound like a ticking clock with what was left of his mouth. The plastic of the mask distorted the sound, so no two ticks or tocks were the same.

'Do not try me, Detective Chief Inspector Jack Logan. I was not a patient man before. Now… like this? Even less so.'

'It's a bit creepy, this obsession with a thirteen-year-old,' Logan said. 'I mean, killing Borys and leaving him at the school was bad enough, but then linking that to her mum's boyfriend? You really wanted to scare her, didn't you?'

'I wanted her to suffer. And I wanted her here. Now. You were meant to bring her to me. That was the arrangement. That was the deal. And you broke it.' Something creaked as he leaned forward. Logan couldn't tell if it was the chair or the tight, leather-like skin of the man sitting in it. 'And because of that—because of your choices—your friend dies.'

Logan's hand reached under his untucked shirt to the waistband of his trousers, and the heavy hunk of metal that he'd tucked there. He lumbered sideways, bringing the gun up, trying to remember how many men there had been behind him when he'd come in. Three? Four? No more than that, surely.

The condensation in Oleg's mask faded as he held his breath. His bulbous, bloodshot eyes went to the muzzle of the pistol and stayed there.

'This is Bosco Maximuke's gun,' Logan said, side-eyeing the henchmen and giving them his best *don't even fucking think about it* look. 'Olivia tried to shoot me with it today. Raging I was. But, I mean, I can't blame her really, can I? She thought I was you. And, frankly, Oleg, if I saw a face like yours leaping out at me from the shadows, I'd cave the fucking thing in with a spade.'

He adjusted his grip on the weapon, his blood-slicked fingers making it difficult to hold on to it properly.

'So even though she was shooting at me, she wasn't *actually* shooting at me. Not really. She was really shooting at you.'

A floorboard groaned on his left as one of the other men shifted their weight. Logan turned the gun on him. 'Normally,

I wouldn't even think about shooting a no-mark like you,' the detective said. His speech was a little slurred, the gun swaying in a figure-of-eight in front of the henchman's utterly impassive face. 'But I'm no' exactly thinking straight. For a variety of reasons. And I'm liable to blow your brains all over your wee skinhead pals there.'

One of the other men—one who didn't currently have the pistol pointed at his face—piped up. 'That is not a real gun.'

The thunder of the gunshot shook dust from the ceiling tiles. The henchman who had just moments before been directly in Logan's sights stood frozen in terror, his mouth hanging open and his eyes wide, like he was preparing himself for the terrible moment when he realised he was, in fact, dead.

The other men all covered their ears, except for Logan, who had braced himself for the shot only he knew was coming, and Oleg, who seemed remarkably calm about the whole situation. Also, Logan noted for the first time, most of the peripheral parts of ears were gone, leaving only a stubby core, around which his mask had been hooked.

Down on the floor, Ricketts jumped awake at the sound. His eyes swam around in panic for a few moments, then he curled himself into a ball and did his best not to draw any further attention to himself.

'It shoots like a real gun,' Logan said, indicating the hole in one of the padded cubicle divider boards. Nobody turned to look, the sound and flash of fire from the muzzle apparently having been evidence enough of the weapon's legitimacy.

He swung it back in Oleg's direction. The monster in the chair remained statue still.

'Where is she?' Logan demanded.

Oleg still did not look away, not even when Logan took a step closer so the end of the gun was pressed against the other man's cold-ravaged forehead.

'Where. Is. She?'

Another coating of condensation formed on the inside of Oleg's mask as he sighed. With a twitch of a hand and a sideways glance, he indicated a door with 'Office' marked on it.

Logan gave Ricketts a dunt with the side of his bloodied boot. 'Albert. Go get her.'

Ricketts continued to pretend he was dead, until Logan kicked him again.

'Move!'

There was a whimper. Some creaking. Albert rose off the floor into a sort of bent over scurrying position. He avoided all eye contact as he weaved his way through the knot of men and hurried to the door.

'It won't do you any good,' Oleg told Logan.

'Shut up,' Logan retorted. Once again, it wasn't the zinger of a response he'd been reaching for, but his head was aching now, each painful throb pushing down on him, trying to force him to his knees.

He was also acutely aware of his breathing. It was faster than usual, yet he didn't seem to be getting as much air as he needed. Not by a long shot.

The gun was heavy. The arm holding it, even more so. The muscles burned under the strain.

'Ricketts, hurry up!' he bellowed, and he thought he heard a snigger from one of the men on his left.

'Like I already told you, this won't do you any good,' Oleg said.

Logan's only response was a tightening of his hand on the pistol's grip.

Albert was taking a long time. Too long.

'Albert? What's happening?'

No response. Oleg's ruined face was smiling at him. Leering. Logan blinked, and it took a full second for the darkness to clear.

'Albert?' Logan called again, and he heard the fear in his own voice. The dread.

He stole a glance at the office door and saw the pathologist shuffling out. He stood rigid, his face telling a story of shock, and of shame, and of horror.

'No,' Logan muttered. He shook his head. 'No. No.'

What had they done?

What had they done to her?

And then, Ricketts took a lurching step forward, like he'd been pushed from behind, and Logan saw the glint of the scalpel blade pressed against his throat.

A dirty, half-dressed Shona sidled into the room behind him, stared wide-eyed at the men gathered together by the window, then her face crumpled, and her eyes filled with tears when she spotted Logan standing there, the gun shaking in his hand.

'Jack!'

'Shona! You're all right! It's OK. I'm here.'

'Albert's with them,' Shona said, sniffing away the tears and forcing herself back together. 'I've heard them talking.'

'Aye. I know,' Logan confirmed. 'I always said he was an arsehole, but would you bloody listen?'

Oleg's sigh echoed inside his mask. 'This is pointless. It won't do you any good,' he said.

'Going pretty well so far,' Logan countered.

'Is it? And what are you going to do now?'

'We're going to walk out of here. Me, her, and the Iceman there.'

'No, you aren't.'

Logan waggled the gun. It was such a sudden movement that he saw the henchmen duck beside him.

'You forgetting this?' he asked.

Oleg shrugged. There was something stomach-churning about the way it made the skin on his neck pucker up. 'The gun doesn't put you in charge.'

'You're right. I've been in charge since I walked into this room,' Logan countered. 'Being me puts me in charge. Being in charge is my default state, son.' He turned his head a fraction towards his shoulder. 'Shona, you OK taking Albert to the car? He knows the way.'

'What about you?' Shona asked.

'I'll be fine. Get him to drive you out of here, then call it in. Tell them where we are.'

'I'm not… I can't just leave you,' Shona said.

'Just bloody listen to me, will you? For once,' Logan said, and the urgency lent a harshness to it. 'You need to get out of here.'

'Jack…'

'Please. Just go.'

'No, I mean… Jack,' Shona said. She indicated the back door of the open-plan office space. Logan risked a glance at it and saw four more men entering, all sporting the same hairstyle as the other squad of bastards currently flanking him.

'Like I say, Detective Chief Inspector Jack Logan. Your theatrics won't do you any good. Kill me if you want, but how many can you shoot before we get you? Both of you. How long can you hold that gun before your arm gives out? Before your legs give way? Before your heart has no more blood to pump around your body?'

'Jack?' Shona's voice was filled with such concern he almost dropped the gun and ran to her. He wanted to put his arms around her, pull her in close, whisper in her ear that it was going to be OK. He wanted to tell her it was all going to be all right, and he had some great plan to get them out of this.

He wanted to lie to her.

Oleg stood up. It was a laborious process that seemed to take forever.

But then he was on his feet, leaning on a walking stick. Logan kept the gun trained on him as best he could, but the arm was vibrating now, and Oleg's movements—slow as they were—left a blur in their wake, like the smear of a dead insect on a car windscreen.

He pulled the mask over his head and let it fall to the floor, revealing his face in all its full glory and horror. His breath carried the odour of rot, and decay, and of things long dead. The laughter came out of him like the hiss of a snake.

'You are not going to bring me Olivia, are you?' he asked.

Logan shook his head. It was a big, sleepy sort of movement, and the room took a long time to catch up.

'That is unfortunate,' Oleg said. His voice was a whisper now that seemed to come from every direction at once. 'But not unexpected. Not to worry. I have time. Unlike you.'

Oleg was standing right in front of him now, and Logan realised the gun arm was hanging by his side. He brought it back up and jammed the muzzle against the underside of Oleg's misshapen jaw.

'Let Shona go.'

'No,' Oleg replied. 'But go ahead. Pull the trigger. See what these strapping young men do to her without my steadying influence keeping them in check. They wanted to, you know? Take her. They were going to do it in turns.'

'Shut up,' Logan hissed.

'I protected her. Me. Not you. Not the great Detective Chief Inspector Jack Logan. Me. I told them no,' Oleg said in that brain-itching whisper. 'I want you to remember that. How you couldn't protect her. For all your strength. For all your bluster. You couldn't save her. I kept her safe, not you.'

Logan was dimly aware of bodies closing around him. A forest of skinheads, too many to count. They were less wary now, he thought. Louder, anyway. Emboldened by their increased numbers, maybe, or by the fact that he was clearly incapable of putting up a fight.

'So shoot me,' Oleg said. 'You won't live long enough to see what happens next. But she will.' What was left of his lips drew back, revealing that skull smile. 'Oh, *she* will.'

Logan only processed half of what the thing standing in front of him had said. The floor beneath him was quicksand, sucking him down, so he couldn't move his feet, even if he'd wanted to.

He heard Shona shout his name, and mumbled some words he wasn't even sure meant anything. She sounded closer. He felt a hand on his arm but shrugged it off before realising that it might have been hers.

He turned, and there she was, standing beside him. She was glowing. Literally glowing, a halo of brilliant light surrounding her like an angel's aura.

'It's OK,' he told her. Or perhaps he only thought it. 'It's going to be OK.'

He heard laughter. Voices speaking in a language he didn't know. All of it distant and far away. All of it irrelevant, apart from her. Standing there. In the light.

And then he heard something else. Something he did understand. Something that cut through the chatter and the haze.

Something that triggered some instinctive sense of irritation deep down in his gut.

'All right, boss?'

And with that, the world descended into chaos.

Chapter 48

There were Uniforms. Dozens of them. Filling the room from all sides. Logan couldn't hear the skinheads laughing. Then again, he couldn't hear much over the raised voices and the crack of extendable metal batons striking flesh.

They swarmed the place, an explosion of movement and noise, a coordinated rush of shock and awe.

Logan felt fingers on his hand, on the gun, trying to wrestle it from him. He lashed out with it, felt a crunch, and heard the strangled gasp from Oleg. His focus returned enough for him to watch the monster falling backwards onto the floor, and to hear the howl of pain that burst from that ghoulish hole of a mouth.

The gun raised on instinct. Oleg lay squirming, blood oozing from a split in his parchment skin, which had been stretched beyond breaking point by the fall.

There was a roaring in Logan's head like crashing water. Right then, it was the only thing he could hear. The only thing that existed beyond him, the gun, and the monster on the floor.

He could do anything here, in this bubble. Nothing mattered in here. Nothing had a consequence. He could end this. One squeeze of the trigger, and he could put this bastard down.

And then, the bubble was burst by—appropriately enough—a wee prick.

'What you up to, boss?'

Tyler was beside him. Right beside him. A step away.

Christ, that was all he needed.

'Go home, son,' Logan grunted.

'Seems like everyone's telling me that tonight,' Tyler said.

Logan didn't understand the comment, and his narrowing mental bandwidth meant he didn't even bother trying.

'How about you give me the gun, sir?'

That was Hamza.

Jesus, he was here, too? Who else? Ben? Hoon? Caitlyn?

He shook his head. 'N-no.'

Not her. Not Caitlyn.

'Believe me, boss, I know how you feel.' Tyler was talking again. 'I get it. You're angry. So am I. But remember that time on the staircase? Me and Bosco? You remember what you said to me?'

Logan didn't. Then again, right now he remembered very little before the last few minutes.

'You said, "He's an arsehole, but you're not." You told me I wasn't a killer. You told me I was a good copper. I mean, you sort of took that bit back, but... you told me I should do my job. So how about you do yours, boss? In fact, we'll do it for you, if you like. Just put down the gun. Let us bring him in.'

Logan could sense the perfect response floating just beyond his reach. Something about doing what he said, not what he did, but he was too tired to reach for it.

'Jack? Jack, it's OK.'

He felt a warmth on his chest. A hand on his heart.

Shona. Alive. Safe.

'We need to get you help,' she said, and her face swam in and out of focus. Out of existence. 'Put the gun down, eh? Let me look at you.'

'*No*. Don't! Please. Kill me.'

Logan wasn't sure Oleg had said the words, but his eyes certainly had. Those bulging, bloodshot, unblinking eyes. They were pleading for it. Begging for an end. For the mercy of a swift death.

And the bastard deserved it. He did. The death part, anyway.

But not the swiftness. He hadn't earned that.

The gun fell to the floor. Logan's knees buckled.

The roaring in his ears rose to drown out everything else. He watched darkness slither across the ceiling, tentatively at first, then faster and faster.

And, as death came to claim him, DCI Jack Logan allowed himself the momentary satisfaction of a job well done.

Chapter 49

The first thing he saw when he opened his eyes was the baw-chopped face of Geoff Palmer. He reclined in a chair just a couple of feet away, helping himself to a bunch of grapes.

'All right, sunshine?' Palmer chirped.

'Christ,' Logan growled, his voice like the rasp of a hacksaw through metal. 'Is this Hell?'

'No, no, you're quite alive,' Palmer told him. 'All thanks to me.'

Even half-dazed, Logan could tell Palmer was fishing for something with that remark, so he left him hanging and took in his surroundings.

Hospital. Private room. Enough tubes and cables to make him think things had been touch and go.

'It was me who told them where to find you,' Palmer said, tiring of waiting to be asked. 'You nearly ran us off the road. And then when we went to the scene and saw the car there, and found your phone, I thought, "Oh-ho!" I thought. "Oh-ho, something's up here." So, we turned the van around, and we followed you. Easy enough to catch up on that single track road, then we stuck with you until—'

'Geoff?'

'Aye?'

'Gonnae shut up?'

Palmer tutted. 'Well, there's gratitude, for you! If it wasn't for me, you'd be dead. I'm the hero of this bloody story, I'll have you know! Me. Geoffrey Montague Palmer.'

Logan let his head sink back into the pillow. Maybe his initial reaction had been right. Maybe this *was* Hell.

'Who's the malingering bastard now, boss?'

Yep. That confirmed it.

He lifted his head enough to see the room filling up. The whole team was there, but it was Sinead that Logan fixed on first. She was bruised, but walking. Smiling. But only sort of, and only on the outside.

He wondered if the others had noticed.

'I was just telling him how I saved the day,' Palmer said, getting to his feet.

'Aye, and ate half his bloody grapes, by the looks of it,' Ben remarked. 'I'd call that even.'

Palmer frowned. 'What? No way. How's that even! He'd be dead!' He looked down at the half-empty plastic container and the nest of stems at the bottom. 'They're not even very nice grapes!'

'Geoff was just leaving,' Logan said.

There was a sudden flurry of movement that drew his eye. Taggart wriggled free of Tyler's grasp, landed on the bed, and Logan's field of view was suddenly nothing but tongue.

'Fuck's sake!' he grunted, struggling to fend off the excited pup. 'Are you allowed to bring dugs in here?'

'We snuck him in,' Ben said. 'He wouldn't stop whining.'

Logan hissed in pain as the wriggling animal ripped the plastic drip tube from his arm. Something he was connected to started to bleep.

A nurse appeared. She was an older woman, and formidable. She was not happy with the number of people in the room, and downright livid at the number of animals.

'We'll, eh, we'll maybe take him outside, sir,' Hamza said, catching the wriggling pup around the ribcage and lifting him off the DCI.

'Take Geoff, too, will you?' Logan suggested. 'Maybe walk them round the block a couple of times. See if it tires them out.'

Tyler and Hamza led both the dog and the Scene of Crime man away. Palmer said something, but Taggart's barking and the nurse's nagging drowned it out. Logan reckoned it was probably better that way.

Sinead hung back in the doorway for a moment. 'Good to see you awake, sir.'

'Good to see you, full stop, Detective Constable,' he replied. 'We'll talk later on, eh?'

She nodded. 'Aye. Let's do that.'

And then she was gone, leaving only Logan and DI Forde there in the room. Ben poked around in the plastic tray until he found one of the few half-decent grapes Palmer had left, then popped it in his mouth.

'You had us worried for a while there, Jack,' he said, perching himself on the end of the bed. 'You lost a lot of blood. We didn't think you were going to make it.'

'How long was I out for?'

'Six weeks.'

Logan choked. Ben grinned.

'Three days,' he said. 'Sorry, couldn't resist.'

'You're a bastard,' Logan grunted. Still, three days was bad enough. He climbed up the bed a little on his elbows, so he was propped in something more like a sitting position. 'What happened?'

'What do you remember?'

It was patchy, Logan explained. He told Ben what he recalled, and some of it only came back as he went over it all.

He remembered Ricketts. Oleg. The gun.

He remembered Shona, and the knife in her hand.

After that, it all got a bit vague.

Ben talked him through it. The call from Palmer, the rush to the scene, the observation through the window, then the mass onslaught of Uniforms when it looked like things were about to go south.

They had Oleg in custody. He was somewhere else in the hospital, in fact, well-guarded, and on suicide watch. Ricketts was in a holding cell. He'd spoken quite freely about what he'd done over the years. Proudly, even. He'd taken credit for dozens of cases stretching back decades. It was quite a collar.

'Mitchell managed to get some info on Oleg from Alexis Maximuke, too,' Ben said. 'Not that we need any of it to put the bastard away now, of course. She's given us some names, though. Folk higher up the chain. CID is going to take a nosy.'

'Good,' Logan said. He hadn't asked the question yet. He was too afraid to. Instead, he asked something else. 'What about the dog?'

Ben frowned. 'What about it?'

'What's happening with it?'

'Are you no' keeping it?'

Logan shook his head. 'No! Of course, I'm no' bloody keeping it. What would I do with a dog?'

'Well, I mean… it's company, isn't it?'

'I don't need company. I've got company. You need company, if anyone. You take it.'

'I'm no' taking it,' Ben said. 'Anyway, you're his favourite. He should go with you.'

'I'm no' dealing with a bloody dug,' Logan insisted. 'There must be someone else who can take it.'

Ben opened his mouth to offer a counterargument, then stopped.

Maybe Logan was right. Maybe he didn't need the company.

But Ben knew someone who might.

He got to his feet, already reaching for his phone. 'Leave it with me,' he said. 'Let me go make a quick call. I think I might know just the person.'

Logan watched him head for the door. The question got stuck in his throat, and only came out once Ben had disappeared out into the corridor.

'What about Shona?'

338

There was no answer. Not at first.

Then…

'What about me?'

And there she was. Right there. Right in the doorway. Alive. Smiling. Safe.

And then she was beside him. Sitting on the bed. Lying with him. Her hands on his face, on his chest. On his heart.

He put an arm around her, pulling her in close, ignoring the ache in his muscles, and the sting from where the drip had been torn out.

She was warm against him. Solid. Real.

His.

'Christ, you need a shower,' she told him, recoiling from his armpit.

Logan chuckled.

'Aye. Probably.' He turned to look at her, his face right next to hers. 'You could always give me a bed bath.'

'Smelling like that? No chance,' Shona said. 'It's a hose you need, not a damp sponge.'

She kissed him. Despite the smell, she kissed him.

It lasted until Ben cleared his throat in the doorway, and they both raised their heads to look at him.

'Sorry to interrupt,' Ben said. 'Just to let you know, I made the call about the dog. I spoke to… the person I thought might benefit from it.'

Logan raised an eyebrow. 'And?'

'And she said you can shove it up your arse,' Ben said, then he shrugged. 'So… aye. Sorry. But I'll leave you to it.'

With a nod to Shona, he left the room.

Logan's head fell back against the raised head of the bed. Shona propped herself up on her elbow and looked down at him, a finger idly wandering across the chest of his impossibly stylish hospital gown.

'You OK?'

Logan met her eye and nodded. He was. Despite everything. Against all the odds. Here, now, everything was better than OK, in fact. It was perfect.

Well, no. Not *quite*.

Not yet.

'I want to ask you something,' he said.

'Right...'

'Don't feel pressured, or anything,' Logan said. 'It's not... I'm not even sure it's the best idea. I mean, it's really soon. And it's probably the blood loss talking...'

'Jack,' Shona said. 'What do you want to ask?'

Logan drew in a breath. Held her eye. Took her hand.

'Shona Maguire,' he began, searching her face. 'I don't suppose you want a dug, do you?'

For a moment, she stared, and then she fell against him, and they lay there together and laughed, until the angry nurse came marching back in and told them both to shut the fuck up.

Do you love crime fiction and are always on the lookout for brilliant authors?

Canelo Crime is home to some of the most exciting novels around. Thousands of readers are already enjoying our compulsive stories. Are you ready to find your new favourite writer?

Find out more and sign up to our newsletter at canelocrime.com